In the crossfire of history...

International cable TV journalist Charlotte Ansari and her Asperger's son are caught literally in the crossfire of history when terrorists, the CIA, Mossad (Israeli intelligence) and the Vatican all converge in a pulse-pounding search for two relics that could eviscerate Christianity and forever change the balance of power in the world. In The Shekinah Legacy, author Gary Lindberg uses the form of the thriller to explore the limits and perils of belief.

IMPOSSIBLE TO PUT DOWN... UNTIL THE LAST PAGE

"Charlotte Ansari has hunted the big stories around the globe. Then in one week she becomes the hunted. Or are the secret societies that are chasing her throughout India really after someone else?

Gary Lindberg's thriller, *The Shekinah Legacy*, will delight fans of Dan Brown and James Rollins. Fascinating subplots bring together an unusual cast of characters, all searching for the same ancient objects with startlingly different reasons. This is a book that is almost impossible to put down until you've read the last page."

— Cynthia Kraack, author of *Minnesota Cold* and the *Ashwood Trilogy*

THE
SHEKINAH
LEGACY

**CALUMET
EDITIONS**
Minneapolis

Second Edition March 2023
The Shekinah Legacy. Copyright © 2023 by Gary Lindberg
All rights reserved

10 9 8 7 6 5 4 3 2
ISBN: 978-1-960250-23-0

Cover and book design by Gary Lindberg

THE
SHEKINAH
LEGACY

A Charlotte Ansari Thriller

GARY LINDBERG

**CALUMET
EDITIONS**
Minneapolis

Also by Gary Lindberg

FICTION

Sons of Zadok

The Unspoken

The Mount

John Ross

Deeper and Deeper

Ollie's Cloud

NONFICTION

Letters from Elvis

Brando On Elvis

The Roots of Elvis

The New Buffalo

The Soul of Humanity

Humanity Coming of Age

Seeing God In Many Mirrors

The Power of Positive Hamdwriting

An Improbable Series of Risky Events

The currents of history and prophecy
converge so that this story could have
only occurred in the year

2007

Chapter 1

From Charlotte Ansari's Notebook, 2007

Some day you will read this, my Dear, and see more clearly how things came to be. I pray to God that you will forgive me for not having had the wisdom or foresight to prevent the tragedies that befell our little family, though the great sweep of history was against us, as you know.

You may remember that I have always been a compulsive note taker; perhaps that's why I was drawn to broadcast journalism where my notepad and digital voice recorder were my most faithful companions. My notes are serving me well now.

I have never had trouble finding the start of a story except for this one. The real story, I'm sure, began thousands of years ago, but it seems now that the best lead-in to our story was in Iraq, so I will begin there. Every good news story starts with a teaser to grab the audience, and this one certainly got my attention.

I remember that it was impossibly hot and dry on that Tuesday morning in Baghdad. The wind had stirred up a dust storm so thick that you could stare directly at the sun without hurting your eyes. Everything around us was eerily tinted orange. It was like being stuck in a block of amber looking out. I turned to my cameraman, Curt.

"Oh yeah," he said, "been in worse dustups than this." He wrapped the small video camera in a big baggie he got somewhere in the Green Zone. "To keep the grit out," he explained. "The camera can see fine, but we gotta keep the dust out of its innards." That's about as technical as he ever got with me. His job was camera and sound, mine was telling a story.

We had worked on many dangerous assignments together, Curt and I, and we knew how to communicate without words. Sometimes, while we were prepping for an interview, the subject would be more candid than during the shoot. That's when Curt would start his camera. He was quite adept at aiming the lens while the camera was in a lowered hand. With my hot lavaliere mic picking up every word, we got many remarkable sound bites without the subject ever suspecting.

I smiled when I looked at the tiny patch of gaffer tape Curt used to cover up the telltale red light on the camera that lit up when he was shooting. Without ever mentioning it, I know we both hoped for an unguarded comment from this day's interviewee Siyyid Muqtada al-Sadr, the influential Shi'ite cleric who controlled the powerful Mahdi Army.

I had worked for two months to get this interview, manipulating every contact I had. Today was the appointed day. Perhaps my celebrity helped gain this opportunity. Who knows? On that morning I believed I was on the brink of another big ratings coup for CCN. Who else could have engineered an interview with the secretive Siyyid during a time of brutal sectarian conflict between the Mahdi militants, Sunní insurrectionists, Iraqi army and police, and the Americans?

Looking back on it, I am embarrassed by my arrogance and ambition. My career seems so insignificant now. I would give it all up—would give anything at all, even my life—to make things right again. As a journalist I was known for maintaining perspective in my stories, but I lacked that very quality in my personal life. I feel now that I was a fraud as a mother, mostly absent from your life as my mother was from mine. How could I have repeated that sad pattern after feeling the child's pain myself?

Nevertheless, on that day in Baghdad I could only think about the interview and how it would burnish my crown as the queen of international broadcast journalism. Was I afraid as our military convoy left the Green Zone? I suppose, a little. But mostly I feared the IEDs and their indiscriminate violence. My conceit was so engorged by past successes that I couldn't imagine enemy combatants not wanting my help to tell their stories. Why would they harm me when I could deliver their points-of-view to millions of viewers worldwide? I felt more protected by my celebrity and my audience than by my flak jacket or the dozen American soldiers who guarded me on the first leg of this journey.

And so we headed out, not knowing how much we didn't know.

Chapter 2

The convoy of four military vehicles grumbles out of the Green Zone with Charlotte and Curt in the third vehicle, an up-armored Humvee. Charlotte Ansari peers out of the rectangular side window as the sepia sandstorm chokes the groaning engines and grinds off the desert camo. It is already over 100 degrees Fahrenheit and sweat bubbles up on Charlotte's face and neck. Inside the Humvee it's closer to 120 degrees. She glances at Curt, who is busy shooting dim footage of a ten-year-old with one leg. The boy is steering a wobbly bicycle alongside the convoy into the teeth of the gritty storm.

Human interest stuff.

Bud, the Marine driver, and Chopper (who is "riding shotgun," according to Curt) are rudely silent. Charlotte knows they blame her for this dangerous foray into the nightmare gauntlet of Baghdad streets, a mission that puts a dozen soldiers at risk for no military purpose.

Instinctively Charlotte pulls her loose black veil protectively around her eyes though the driving sand can't penetrate the thick glass of the window. She starts to rehearse her questions for the Siyyid. "Is there any hope in your mind for peace with the Sunnís?" and "Is it inevitable that Iraq will be divided into Shi'ite, Sunní and Kurdish partitions?"

Curt is zooming in on the face of the youngster on the bicycle who has managed to keep up with the convoy while pumping the pedals with one leg. In close-up, Curt watches the boy pluck a cell phone from his pocket. Instead of punching buttons or putting the phone to his ear, the boy simply holds the device in his hand. And then stops.

Something is wrong here. Curt knows it. And then it dawns on him…

"Stop the truck!" he screams.

His voice is so loud that Bud squashes the brake pedal with his foot and the vehicle skids to a stop.

"Stop them all!" Curt yells.

Chopper turns angrily to Curt, snarling. "What the hell—"

3

"That boy…" Curt begins to say.

And then an IED explodes in a flaming ball of scrap metal and human flesh. The first two vehicles are torn apart. A Marine's dismembered body slams into Bud's windshield, cracking the blood-spattered glass. An axle from the second vehicle spears the radiator. Charlotte is thrown into Curt's lap, slicing her head on the door.

Chopper holds a hand to a bloody eye and desperately radios for help.

Within seconds three Toyota pickups surround them. Bearded men in plaid shirts pour out of the vehicles waving machine guns. Bud pulls a pistol and starts to fire, but then Charlotte hears a rattle of machine gun fire. When she turns, Bud's body is jerking with the impact of the bullets. Blood spurts onto her face. Hands wrench open Chopper's door and Charlotte sees the flash of a knife, then the Marine's neck begins to gush red.

She screams.

The back doors are torn open. She and Curt are dragged into the street. All she can hear now is laughter and Arabic cursing. She is kicked hard and her veil is stripped off. She can see Curt lying on the street, three rifles pointed at his head.

One of the men, a stout Iraqi with crooked teeth and a slashing scar across his cheek, kneels down to look at her face. "And who are you, riding in the American Humvee?" he asks in a thick accent.

The wind whips his dark hair as another man hands him the camera.

"Journalists!" he says. "Welcome to my country. Want an interview?" And then he laughs.

The one-legged boy steers his bicycle up to the stout Iraqi and hands him the cell phone. The man ruffles the boy's hair and pats him on the back. He looks back at Charlotte, staring, then takes the woman's chin in his sweaty hand to get a better look at her face.

"I know you," the stout man says. "From the television!"

Charlotte glances away. Her celebrity seems little protection right now.

"You are lady from CCN—am I right? Charlotte something. I am great admirer of your work."

The man says something to the others in Arabic and they all laugh.

The man turns back to Charlotte. "You are famous. And now I will be famous, too—the man who captured Charlotte something from CCN. They will pay a lot of money to get you back, Famous Woman."

Charlotte is lifted to her feet. A quick glance reveals that all the soldiers in the fourth vehicle are dead. She and Curt are thrown into the back of a pick-up, hogtied, and blindfolded. With mad yelps and shots fired into the air, the insurgents clamber into their trucks and bolt the bloody scene.

The pick-up rumbles down rutted streets, bouncing over debris and bashing the bound bodies of Charlotte and Curt. After half-an-hour the journey is over. Bruised and bloodied from the turbulence of the ride, Charlotte and Curt are pulled from the truck bed and their feet are untied. Prodded by the sharp barrels of guns, they stagger sightlessly down a rocky walkway, careen through a door, and climb a tall stairway. Hands shove them into a room. They crash into a stone wall and slide to the floor, scraping their foreheads and shoulders.

Charlotte is dizzy with fear and pain. She can hear the sounds of punching and kicking, and she knows the men are working over her partner. Curt grunts with each blow and Charlotte can hear him vomit. The sharp, sour smell assaults her nostrils.

Suddenly her hair is yanked upward. Are they going to torture her, too?

A voice barks, "Famous Woman, I am going to watch CCN now. Maybe they will tell that you are now hostage. You see, I make you even more famous!" It's the voice of the stout Iraqi, who laughs at his own joke.

But then he stops. In a bored tone he says, "But first, my men wish to welcome you to their home."

Rough fingers begin to tear open her long-sleeved blouse and pull down her skirt. She starts to kick, striking one man in the face. The man screams painfully but the others laugh, apparently believing that pain inflicted by a woman is hilarious.

Strong hands restrain her legs and push up her bra to expose her breasts. Charlotte can feel the humid heat of someone's breath on her skin, the prickly brush of a beard or moustache.

An Arabic phrase pops into her mind, an Iraqi tribal saying that had been taught her by a translator on a previous visit to Baghdad. At that time the phrase had made her laugh, it was so ridiculous. But the translator had urged her to remember it because, he said, in Iraq there would always be a time when all options were exhausted and it would be necessary to plead for protection.

"Ana bisharbic," Charlotte says. "Ana bisharbi*c.*" *I am in your moustache.* So silly! What a thing to say when you are about to be gang-raped by terrorists.

The room becomes quiet and still. She hears a slap, and then her legs are released. *I am in your moustache*, she thinks. *Protect me.* In Iraqi tribal tradition, if someone asks for your protection, it is shameful to refuse it.

She hears many footsteps and a door closing. She senses that the men have left. Her hands are still tied behind her back, but her feet are free. She twists her body to face the cool stone wall and presses her blindfold against it. The coarseness of the stone catches the cloth and she is able to lower her face, pulling the blindfold above her eyes. She turns so that her back is against the wall. At last she can see the room.

All their captors have left. There are three shuttered windows on the wall. Sunlight beams in from the edges. Curt lies unconscious on the floor. His face is bruised and puffy. Blood flows from his mouth, but he is breathing.

Sitting with her back against the wall, Charlotte lifts her butt off the floor and starts to wriggle her bound hands beneath her rump, but her arms are too short. She looks around the room. It is bare. Using her legs to push herself up the wall, she reaches a standing position. It feels good to stand. She feels more confident standing than sitting. She walks to the window. The shutters are on the outside, but the windows have glass. The room doesn't seem to have been prepared for a kidnapping victim. But then again, these men probably hadn't planned an abduction. They had just gotten lucky.

An idea occurs to her. She presses her buttocks against the glass of the nearest window. Hard. She hopes to break the glass but doesn't want the sound to alert her captors. She pushes harder and hears a crackling sound. The glass has broken. Slowly, she starts to lower her body, hoping to ease the shards soundlessly to the floor. Inch by inch she slides downward. One of the shards digs painfully into her flesh.

One piece of glass slips out and clanks brightly on the hard floor. Charlotte anxiously looks toward the door, trying to hear any approaching voices or footsteps.

Nothing.

She moves away from the window and turns to see a large broken splinter of glass still firmly lodged in the window. Perfect!

She stands again, her back to the window, and maneuvers her hands so that the edge of the shard is between her wrists. She starts to gently saw the cords that bind her wrists. It takes ten minutes, but finally her hands are free.

She pulls her bra down—amazing how this simple act helps to restore her composure—and rushes over to Curt. As she cradles his head, he begins to stir. Sighing, then groaning, he opens his swollen eyes.

"Are you all right, Luv?" he asks. "They did a number on me."

"I'm okay," she replies. "Do you think anything's broken?"

He begins to move his body. Everything hurts, but as he tests his limbs and joints he decides that no bones are broken.

"Help me sit up, Luv, will ya? There, that's better."

"I think we can escape through that window," Charlotte says. "If you can get that old body moving."

Curt grimaces in pain. "I think you should do it yourself. There might be something busted inside of me that isn't made of bone. I don't feel so good."

"Then we'll just wait a bit."

"No, you go. Get help."

"In this neighborhood? I'm not leaving without you."

Charlotte takes his hand. He is cold and shocky.

"Give me just a minute to think," she says. "Wait here, okay?"

"Not goin' anywhere right now, Luv. Let me know what you come up with. You're the brains of the outfit."

Charlotte stands and walks to the window. It's a good twenty foot drop to the street below. Yelling for help certainly wouldn't help—most of the people in this neighborhood are probably insurrectionists.

As she stares at the street, four men approach the wall and stand directly below the window. They are dressed in untucked plaid shirts that seem to be the official uniform of Iraqis. One of the men is pushing a cart covered by a rug. The men are whispering to each other.

Charlotte wonders if these are her captors, or perhaps more accomplices.

As she studies the men from above, she sees one of them whisk away the rug to reveal a cart filled with automatic weapons. In moves that seem well

Gary Lindberg

rehearsed, two of the men reach for the weapons and begin to move down the street.

Charlotte's heart is pounding. *What is going on?*

A loud crashing sound, like a door being knocked down, makes her jump. Suddenly there are shouts and curses, but no shots. Then the sound of footsteps charging up the stairs.

Charlotte crouches against the wall. *What is happening?* She closes her eyes and whispers the one word that might give her comfort—her son's name: *Greg!*

In the room below, the door crashes down and four bearded men enter. Two of them point machine guns around the room. One of the men, obviously the leader, points with a knife toward Curt. Two men race to the photographer's side, lifting him up. The leader walks to Charlotte and kneels down. Charlotte's eyes are still closed. She is shaking violently. A gentle hand strokes her cheek. She hears the words, "It's all right, but we have to hurry now."

Charlotte and Curt are rushed down the stairs. The stout Iraqi and seven others lie dead in the lower room. They seem to have been killed by knife wounds, not bullets. A nearly silent massacre.

A car pulls up at the doorway. Curt spies his video camera on the floor and grabs it before he and Charlotte are shoved into the back seat of the car. The leader of the team jumps into the front seat and the car roars away. The other three men simply begin walking down the street, casually blending into the city as if nothing had happened.

The team's leader turns to look at Charlotte. "That was close," he says. The man could be an Iraqi, but he has an American accent. "The time of kidnapping for ransom is past. They would have been instructed by higher-ups to kill you by evening."

"Who are you?" Charlotte asks. "Special Ops? CIA?"

The man turns to stare straight ahead.

"How did you find us?"

The man will say no more. Forty minutes later, Charlotte and Curt are dropped off outside the Green Zone. Their rescuers vanish into the disappearing light. Four marines rush to their side and escort them into the compound.

"Charlotte Ansari, right?" asks one of the Marines.

8

Charlotte nods.

"Damn lucky. Did they drop you off?"

"Who?"

"The bastards that killed your escort and took you?"

"You don't know who rescued us?"

The Marine looks confused. He stares at Charlotte, speechless. Then he turns to Curt and sees the video camera in Curt's hand. It is still wrapped in the baggie. "I'm afraid I'll have to take this, sir. You'll get it back."

Curt shrugs. He removes the baggie and surrenders the camera. Then suddenly he clutches his abdomen. "Don't feel so good," he says. "I need a latrine. Now."

The Marine points to a door about twenty feet away and Curt races to it. Inside he enters a stall and closes the door. He reaches into his pocket and removes a small cassette that he had removed from the camera on the way back to the Green Zone. He wraps the cassette in the baggie, tying it tightly, then drops the bagged cassette into the toilet tank. Curt had known the camera would be confiscated and the tape seized. The camera will be returned to him; of that he's sure. But the tape, if he gave it up, would certainly disappear into the U.S. intelligence bureaucracy.

Curt emerges from the latrine. "Feel better now," he says.

"We'll be escorting both of you to the dispensary," the Marine explains. "Follow me."

Curt knows this routine, too. They'll undress, put on hospital gowns, and during the physical examination their clothes will be thoroughly searched. If the video cassette were in his pocket, it would be lost forever.

Not this time, though.

The pudgy military doctor examining Charlotte is friendly but army-blunt. Looking at x-rays, he points to a blocky shape in Charlotte's upper left chest area and asks, "What the hell is this? You're too young for a pacemaker."

"For chronic high blood pressure," Charlotte says. "Drugs didn't help."

"My goddamn blood pressure's been through the roof since I got to this hell hole. Wonder why. So what'd they stick into you?"

"Pulse generator. Electrically activates my baroreceptors to help control the blood pressure."

"Really." The doctor is impressed. "Does it work?"

"You took my blood pressure. You tell me."

"Normal. Even after that scary shit you been through. Man, I've been in this hotbox too fuckin' long. Medical technology's passin' me by while I saw off legs and stuff guts back into my boys. By the time I get back to the States I won't be qualified to dump bed pans. Tough to get through airport security with that thing?"

"Got papers from my doctor. So how am I, doc?"

"Famous. All over the news. When one of CCN's people gets plucked you can't get away from the news. But I suppose you mean physically. You'll live."

"Thanks. Then I'd like to go home."

"Okay then. Just one more stop."

"Debriefing?"

"You could call it that."

Chapter 3

It is difficult to recollect the past, even the recent past. And yet I know that the order of events is important so I will do my best to stitch together this crazy quilt of memories.

During our interrogation in Baghdad, I was grilled. Both sides. Five hours, maybe more. I was treated like I was the kidnapper. I'm not really sure why they were so rude, but at one point I actually thought they were going to waterboard me. I'm sure they wanted to.

If they treated me this way, how do they treat the bad guys? (Curt said they treated him the same way—like a terrorist.)

They kept asking me where the tape was. The tape? Oh, the tape that was in the camera. The bad guys must have taken it, I said. No one bought that theory, but it was the only explanation I could come up with. Why was I withholding evidence, they wanted to know. Maybe there was something on the tape that would help them track down our abductors.

They must have thought we faked the kidnapping or something, maybe set it up to make news, because they kept asking me how come we were let go. And why so soon? Because I'm famous, I suggested, but this tart remark didn't go over very well.

They kept asking who rescued us. I thought you did, I said, but that just made them angrier. I honestly think they had no idea who saved us.

We were allowed to go only when Bill Riggins, our Baghdad Bureau Chief, found out what was going on and "stormed the fortress," as he put it. Cambridge Cable News flew us back by charter. Neither Curt nor I had any idea at that time how much international publicity our kidnapping and miraculous rescue had received. Probably our high profile abduction had embarrassed the military, and nothing pisses off the three-stars in Baghdad like public humiliation. Can't even protect a journalist with a whole U.S. convoy? You guys must be losing the war big time.

It wasn't until I stepped off the plane in Minneapolis and saw you and your father on the tarmac that I realized how terribly shaken I was. I could barely walk across the pavement, my legs were trembling so. I was more frightened in those few minutes than at any time since my rescue. Some sort of delayed stress syndrome? I don't know. But I do know that even though you could not hug me, your presence calmed me down. Somewhere inside you, beneath that impassive gaze, is a storehouse of love. I have always felt it—a mother's insight. We are more alike than you know.

The next couple of days are kind of blurry, but somewhere in there an event occurred which foreshadowed so many devilish things to come. We never could have guessed how it could have involved us.

Chapter 4

The expensive silent alarm system is ridiculously easy to bypass. An American scam. All the costly noise and motion sensors lead to one output, an analog phone line to the security firm. Jumping the line effectively mutes the entire system and evades a broken-line warning to the bored, glowing monitors downtown. The swindlers who set up this system hadn't even bothered to install a wireless backup. Chalk up an extra hundred bucks in profit.

Three intruders silently enter the house. They will need only a few minutes to find what they are looking for. A secret room in the basement houses a fabulous collection of religious relics collected from black market sources around the world. An eyewitness had described the exact location of the prize they seek.

How unfortunate that the drunken collector's need to impress an appreciative audience had undermined his judgment in people. That is how the informant happened to witness a special showing of the magnificent collection. One relic in particular had piqued the informant's curiosity. Was it not just two weeks ago—three at the most—that an inquiry had come to the informant about this relic?

This particular object, though, was not for sale by the collector. The word *priceless* would seriously understate the value of it. The collector had acquired it from a truly desperate person who had passed it along most willingly to save himself from its curse. But the collector had not believed in curses, nor had he fully appreciated the unbroken string of four deaths that had connected the relic's previous holders, a number that would soon increase to five.

Many of the relics are displayed in gleaming glass cases that are suddenly illuminated by amber light as one of the intruders flicks a switch. The room glows eerily, but the three men remain almost invisible in their black garments and ski masks. Two of them hold 9mm pistols with attached silencers. They stare nervously at the doorway while the third man, the tallest one, snorts in frustration, confused by the vast array of objects.

In Arabic, the shorter of the men curses and then hoarsely whispers a reminder to the confused one: "A small door under a bottom shelf."

This relieves the tall man's perplexity and he begins to search, finding a pair of doors beneath a shelf on the far side of the room. He grabs a brass knob and tugs, but the door won't open. He tries again, but the door is obviously locked. The tall man looks at his associates and grunts, giving the universal palms-up sign of frustration.

Clearly angry, the short man stuffs his pistol into his belt and marches across the room, grabbing the door knob and pulling it mightily. Once. Twice. Then repeatedly. The objects on the shelves above shake with the man's rage. Rebuffed, the short man pushes the tall one aside and pulls out his pistol, aiming at the door knob.

"No, no!" the tall man shouts. "You might destroy the relic!"

"It's not a bomb, you idiot. It's just a bullet."

Before the tall man can respond, the short one fires at the door and the wood splinters. The sound is much louder than he had anticipated. All three intruders freeze, as if by remaining motionless they can undo the disturbance. And then they all glance upward, toward the ceiling, their eyes drawn by the faint squeak of floorboards above.

The collector is home, and he is now awake.

The short man wilts beneath the whispered curses of his associates. The tall man motions for them all to press against the wall containing the open entrance and then flicks off the shelf lights. In the silence of the room they can hear their own breathing.

It seems like an hour, but it is only a minute or two before a faint swishing sound—slippers, or trouser legs—can be heard through the doorway. The swishing grows louder. And then the barrel of a rifle slowly enters the room.

The short man swiftly grabs the rifle and plunges a hard fist into the surprisingly soft body behind it. A man crumples to the floor with a loud yelp. The tall man flicks on the shelf lights and the amber glow reveals the short, squat, balding collector in a heap on the floor.

Seeing the men in black, the collector gasps and tries to scramble to his feet. But the short man whips the barrel of his 9mm across the collector's face, leaving a bloody slash.

"You will stay shut up!" the short man shouts. "Where is the relic?"

"Wha—what relic?" the collector replies. His eyes are watering and his hand is pressed against the bloody wound on his cheek, but then his eyes drift involuntarily to the small splintered door at the far side of the room.

The tall man sees this telltale glance and races to the door, swinging it open. Inside is a silver metal box. He removes it, but it is securely locked. Never mind—they can open it later.

"Take it!" the collector says. "Take anything you want."

"Is all we want," the short man says before removing his black hood.

"Don't hurt me," the collector whimpers. "I have money here. Let me get it for you." He is desperate, buying time.

The short man points the pistol at the man's face, touches the tip of the silencer to the collector's forehead. "You don't listen up very good," he says, grinning now. "I think you will listen more in hell."

"No, please—please."

The short man begins to pull the trigger.

The collector clamps his eyes shut, clenches his fists. All he can think of to say is, "You are the curse."

The short man doesn't know what this means, but he likes the sound of it.

"Yes," he says. "I am curse."

The gunshot, perhaps muffled by the man's skull, is not nearly as loud as the first shot.

Propelled by adrenaline, the intruders race from the room and fly up the basement steps. The tall man confidently grasps the silver box in his hands. Mission accomplished. And all the better that this was not a suicide mission, for the tall man's mind is dizzy with the promised earthly rewards.

Like a smudge on black paper, the dark men momentarily gather in the shadows outside the mansion's back door to take off their ski masks and congratulate themselves.

"I am curse!" the short man declares with a torrent of laughter. "I am curse!" He points his pistol at a window and fakes pulling the trigger. "Phhhht!" He makes the sound of the silenced gunshot then laughs again.

The tall man somberly grabs the box and sets it on the walkway. With the butt of his pistol, he tries to break the lock.

Another *Phhhht!* sings out. The short man jerks, then looks quizzically at his pistol before crumpling to the ground. The tall man's eyes widen, catching the moonlight as he looks down at his fallen friend.

Phhhht! Phhhht! The jaw of the other man disintegrates and he flies backward, dead.

The tall man now understands what is happening. He drops the silver box and plunges both hands into the air, hoping his surrender can be seen.

Two other men emerge from a hedge that surrounds the mansion. One of them shouts, "*Allahu Akhbar!*"

The tall man is confused. If these two men are Arabs, why have they killed two of their own? The tall man says, "*Assalamu alaikum,*" peace be unto you. The two men laugh as they approach. Both are pointing pistols at the tall man.

"*Shalom,*" the first one says. Peace.

The Arab shivers at the word. Hebrew! These men are Israelis. Probably a Mossad assassination team. He is doomed. "I give you silver box," he says in broken English, then quickly stoops to retrieve it from the ground. But a black boot stomps on it.

"No, we take it," the Mossad agent explains.

"Of course. My mistaken," the Arab says, still kneeling. And then he looks up to see the blunt end of the agent's Beretta.

"Your seventy-two virgins await," the agent says, "and they are impatient. *Elokim yerachem!*" God will have mercy!

Phhhht!

The Arab topples over, a neat black hole in the center of his forehead.

The second agent plucks the silver box from the ground. "They send idiots to do their work," he says. "Expendables."

"Yusuf, don't ever forget—we're expendable too."

"But we're not idiots."

"I beg to differ." A third voice has joined the conversation, and it comes from directly behind the first agent, who nervously begins to turn. "Uh-uh," the voice warns, "only an idiot would move right now."

The two agents stand motionless. "There are more of us here," the first agent says calmly.

"Actually, there aren't," the voice responds. "Just the two of you."

The first agent again starts to turn, but then yelps sharply.

"I mean, just the *one* of you," the voice says. "Don't even blink."

The first agent slowly drops to his knees and slouches over. The voice has an arm that withdraws a short dagger from the agent's back and pushes him forward. The agent lands on his face like a bag of sand.

The second agent has not moved, but he bravely mouths the words, "You want the box?"

"Yes I do," the voice says. "But first I want you to open it."

The agent tries to open the box, but it is locked. "Can't open it," he says.

"Too bad. I dislike failure."

"You are CIA," the Mossad agent says, his voice brightening. "We are on the same side! You must have mistaken us for Arabs."

"No mistake. And no CIA."

The agent is confused now. "But then—if you are not al Qaeda, and not CIA…"

"And definitely not Mossad…"

"Then—" The agent's voice quivers suddenly. "Then who are you?"

The voice is now directly behind him. "The angel of death."

And then a sharp, cold, finger of pain penetrates the agent's back. He sucks in his breath. It feels like an icicle! Long and jagged and freezing. In his lung now. Twisting. He wants to scream, but the air is gone out of him. No voice, no strength. Slowly, he sinks to his knees while the voice behind him whispers…

"*Allahu Akhbar. Elokim yerachem.* And may His countenance shine down upon you and give you peace. Amen."

Chapter 5

Home is not the comfort that Charlotte longs for. Her husband Mihad, who everyone in America calls "Mike," is loving and gracious before the hometown cameras at Minneapolis-St. Paul International Airport, but inside the chartered limousine he seems dispassionate and businesslike as he inquires about his wife's ordeal.

Charlotte detects in his flat tone the polite voice of a business partner, not a lover. And in the limo, away from prying eyes, there is no rapturous personal embrace in the back seat, only a protective arm around her shoulders. Kidnapped and tortured, she has returned to a husband who welcomes her home with less emotion than he showed Missy, their lost golden retriever, when that fawning mutt had been found and brought back to them.

After an awkward pause, Charlotte asks, "How is the restaurant?"

"Holding up. The new Applebee's hasn't hurt us as much as we feared. Massoud thinks our moderate-priced ethnic niche may have the combined advantage of novelty and quality."

"That's wonderful."

The new topic seems to stoke Mike's interest and he builds up some steam in talking about his latest business venture. Charlotte sighs quietly. What did she expect? After three successive business failures, her entrepreneur husband's wounded pride needs a dose of rehabilitation.

"Last month was very encouraging," he says. Receipts up 25 percent, not bad for a fledgling restaurant facing chain competition, huh?"

"I think you've done it this time, Mike." She is trying to encourage him, but the tepid delivery undermines her attempt.

"Maybe so, maybe so. Still early though."

Charlotte turns to Greg, her nearly thirteen-year-old son, who sits to her left. She seizes Greg's hand and grips it hard. He does not, *can not* respond, but continues to gaze out the window, reading the signs that pass by, perhaps memorizing them, as if each one contains a secret message that only he can decipher.

Mike's unceasing business chatter provides the soundtrack for the rest of the ride home. He so badly wants to prove himself to Charlotte and to talk away his own fear of failure that he can't stop babbling. The more passionate he becomes about the restaurant, the more Charlotte resents his lack of passion for her.

The Ansari home is a ten-thousand square foot mini-mansion on Lake Minnetonka, the largest lake in the Twin Cities. The house is ringed by tall spruce and guarded by an imposing locked gate that swings open as Mike presses a button on the remote in his pocket.

The fifteen-foot tall living room frames an enormous window that presents a spectacular view of Maxwell Bay. Late afternoon sun glistens off water skiers who skim across the surface of the lake. Charlotte slumps into a soft white sofa and closes her eyes.

"A drink?" Mike asks.

"Swore off booze. A trade for my life."

"Glass of wine then? Jesus turned water into it."

"Help yourself."

Mike walks to a small bar and opens a bottle of brandy. His cell phone rings and he picks up. "Mike here… uh-huh. Okay, wait, give me a minute."

Mike pours himself a shot of brandy and starts to walk toward a littered office that fronts the living room. "Sweetheart, it's Massoud. Gotta take this call."

He closes the office door behind him. Charlotte feels suddenly very alone. She staggers to her feet—her legs are shaky—and walks up a spiral staircase to Greg's room. The door is closed, so she knocks. Greg never answers a knock, but somehow she knows that he prefers an announced entry.

Greg sits at a desk in front of a 21-inch computer monitor listening to a Gregorian chant. The walls of his room are covered by family photographs.

"Hiya… mind if I come in?" Charlotte asks but gets no response. She enters and starts to study the family photos. "What have we got here?" she asks. A rhetorical question. Greg's room has become a historical mural of Charlotte's and Greg's lives. The boy has found the snapshots and negatives from their past and created a giant collage.

"Wow!" Charlotte says. "Had no idea we had so many pictures. Where'd you find them all?" She knows that she will not get an answer to her question. Instead, Greg will enter the conversation several exchanges from where it stands now. He is like a chess player thinking several moves ahead but unable or unwilling to pull himself back to the present tense to play out the intervening moves. He is brilliant. Also obsessive, dispassionate, perceptive, and often annoyingly aloof.

"Father cried when he heard you were kidnapped," Greg says.

"Did he, now?" Charlotte says, a bit startled. It always takes her a few minutes to get used to conversing with her son. Greg has skipped the small talk and gone directly to the point that she was inching toward.

"That's what you wanted to know," Greg explains. He turns but does not look into his mother's eyes, extending the distance between them. "He cried, but then he repressed his feelings. His obsession with the restaurant is a confused attempt to regain his place in the family. He feels emasculated by your fame."

Greg is also tactless. Painfully blunt, rather. The same genetic anomaly that stripped him of the ability to express emotion has also stolen any instincts for social grace. He does not mean to hurt anyone, simply to communicate the facts.

Charlotte approaches Greg and puts her arms around him. He sits motionless, frozen, knowing that the physical contact is important to her but unable to respond. She kisses his neck and his forehead, strokes his hair.

"I know you love me, son, even if you can't say it."

A voice startles her.

"Char, you know he doesn't like that." Mike is standing in the doorway.

"No, I don't know that." Charlotte takes a step away from Greg. She's not sure, actually, what Greg likes or doesn't like. "I think after what I've gone through I have the right as his mother to give him a hug, don't you?"

Mike looks at Greg, who is staring at the family pictures on the wall. "My God, Char—you've been gone for five weeks. You're gone so much the boy hardly knows you any more. He's changing, growing up. Greg? Would you like to be left alone?"

Charlotte stares at her son. He is brilliant in many ways, and is able to find connections between things that others never see, yet he is so oddly detached from reality and emotions. She stands there amazed at his brain and wondering why he was both blessed and cursed with Asperger's Syndrome.

The phone rings, filling the silence. Mike grabs the land line in Greg's room. "Char, it's for you. Why don't you take it downstairs?"

Charlotte turns to leave Greg's room.

"Pizza," Greg says.

Char looks at her son and says, "What?"

"You were going to ask me what I wanted to have for supper."

She was? Of course.

"Oh... Should we go out?" she asks. But Greg has left the conversation.

Chapter 6

From Charlotte Ansari's Notebook

I remember that you wanted pizza that night, but of course the phone call changed that, and everything else. Did I even explain that call to you? Probably not. A mother's protective instincts. It never occurred to me that this business call would involve you as much as me.

It was Robert "Bud" Schiebel, news director of Cambridge Cable News, on the phone. My first thoughts were not kind. Can't you give me one damn night at home with my family after I was almost beheaded for your frigging organization? But of course I didn't say that. I listened like a good little girl as he explained a breaking news story. Just across the Lake from us, a big-time business leader had been murdered in his home.

Creepy, sure, so close to home. But what did it have to do with me? He wanted me to look into it. I think that's when I actually became insubordinate and told him to go perform an unnatural act on himself. Don't know what got into me. But I'm the international correspondent, I said. I haven't covered local crime stories since I left Channel 12 in St. Paul years ago.

Turns out the guy who got killed was really big-time, the CEO of a huge healthcare conglomerate with tentacles all over the country. And there was something else, something a contact leaked to CCN that even the local media didn't know. The killers were found dead at this guy's mansion. Possible international implications... Was I listening now?

I do remember calling Marcus Elliot, an old friend of mine at the FBI. I did him a couple of favors when I was local—holding stories, things like that. He's the Minneapolis Bureau Chief now. He wouldn't talk to me about the murder on the phone but said he'd meet me at a local restaurant. So I went there, and Marcus showed up about fifteen minutes later. Real nervous. He said everything was under extra tight wraps, shouldn't talk to me.

Well, I've learned a trick or two in dealing with these guys—military, CIA, local cops—and I finally got a few juicy tidbits out of him, strictly off the record. We agreed it settled our account. Their theory was that one group broke into the CEO's house to steal a religious relic the guy had bought on the black market and ended up killing the owner. Then another group showed up and everyone ended up dead. Three Arabs and two Israelis. The five dead bodies were posed side by side with arms stretched straight out mimicking Jesus on the cross.

Obviously, *everyone* didn't end up dead. Someone killed the other five.

There was one other weird fact that Marcus let slip. The collector was found in a secret relic room with a bullet in his brain and a book in his hands. The book was "The World's Great Wisdom Traditions" by Thompson Walker.

Yes, *that* Thompson Walker. Your grandfather. My father.

But then I guess you knew about him, didn't you?

Chapter 7

Charlotte parks her Land Rover in the garage and bursts into the kitchen like a grenade with the pin pulled. A multiple murder across the Lake, a victim holding her father's book… Her whole family could be in jeopardy. They need to lock up, figure out what's going on.

"Mike!" she yells. "Mike, where are you?" Frantically she races into the living room, sees illumination in Mike's office and shouts, "Mike, I need you now!"

Mike opens the office door and looks out, obviously annoyed at the yelling. He holds a cell phone to his ear and points to it, mouthing the words, "On the phone."

Exasperated and frantic, Charlotte runs to the front closet and finds the security alarm panel. The system is unarmed. She tries to arm it but the system seems dead. More frightened now, she takes the stairs two at a time up to Greg's room. Without knocking, she opens the door. Greg is staring at his computer monitor. The screen is filled with text.

"Greg, are you all right?"

The boy does not answer.

"I—I'm sorry for barging in."

"It's an e-mail," Greg says without turning.

The non sequitur stuns her. *Who's talking about e-mail?*

Still worried, she tries to act calm. "That's good, dear. From a friend?" Greg has few friends his age. He doesn't make friends easily, so the possibility that he is communicating with someone—*anyone*—is encouraging.

"Kind of," Greg says.

"Don't mean to be nosy, but who's your friend? Perhaps we could have him over some time." It occurs to her that Greg is talking in real-time now. Twice in one day. The phenomenon calms her down.

"Not a him," Greg says.

Not a him? The boy is twelve. He's an Asperger child. How could he have developed a relationship with a girl? Maybe he's on Facebook.

"It's from Grandma Walker," Greg explains.

She couldn't have heard Greg correctly. Charlotte's mother, Miriam Walker, has been missing for over thirty years. One day, when Charlotte was seven, Miriam had simply vanished. Not a word since. Only a few photographs remain. It's almost as if she had never existed.

Charlotte glances at Greg's family history wall and sees a picture of her mother holding an infant Charlotte. The woman, pretty with long dark lashes, smiles tenderly as she looks down at her child.

"You know that's not possible, right?" Charlotte asks Greg.

"It's my fifth e-mail from her. She's trying to send me a picture, but I can't open it. I keep telling her that."

Charlotte apprehensively walks up behind her son. She stares at the monitor. Clearly, the message has been sent by someone named Miriam Walker. And the message begins, "My Dearest Grandson..."

"What the hell was all that shouting about?" Mike's voice flings up the stairway. "I'm off now. What's so damn important?"

"I'll be right down!" Charlotte replies and then quietly asks Greg, "Did you say you've gotten *five* messages from this person?"

"I don't know what's wrong with the picture."

Shaken, Charlotte rests her palms on Greg's shoulders for a moment, but her hands are trembling and she doesn't want him to notice. She turns and walks out of the room.

What's the matter with her? She's usually the cool one. But she's staggering now, feeling dizzy. She stubs her toe on the doorframe and holds onto the rail as she descends the stairs toward a glowering Mike.

"I was on the phone with Massoud. We've got some problems at the restaurant and..."

"Shut up, Mike," Charlotte says. "That goddam restaurant, it's all you think about." Her face is ashen. Her foot misses a stair and she winds up sitting on a carpeted tread.

Mike rushes up to her. "What is it, Char?" He sits down next to her.

She starts to tell him about the murders across the Lake, but her speech is jumbled. She shakes her head, as if that will sort her words. "The person who was murdered," she says, speaking slowly now, "Jack Curtis."

"My God! We were at a Christmas party at his place in December. He seemed kind of surprised that an Iranian would celebrate Christmas."

"Shot in the head."

"Holy shit!"

"Five of them, three Arabs and two Israelis," Charlotte says.

"You mean the killers?"

"They don't know, but they're all dead. Laid out neatly on the ground like little crucifixes."

"This is scary. Too close to home."

"When I think Arabs and murder, I think terrorists. But you don't know the half of it."

"I'm gonna lock up the house." Mike starts to rise.

Charlotte stops him by saying, "Hear me out first." Mike sits down by her, closer than before. "They found Jack in a secret room in his basement."

"A secret room? Don't tell me he was into some kinky…"

"Relics, Mike. Religious relics. He was buying them on the black market. They found Jack's body in the relic room."

"Guy was an asshole, but no one deserves…"

"Listen to me, Mike. They found Jack clutching my father's first book."

"What?"

"You heard me. He was holding a copy of 'The World's Great Wisdom Traditions' by the famous Thompson Walker."

Mike blows air through his lips as he thinks this over. "Okay, that's a pretty weird connection to the family, but maybe it's just a coincidence. Doing research or something. If Jack was into religious relics, there might have been some information in the book he needed."

"Mike, he was lying on the floor with his back against the wall and his brains scattered all over it. I hardly think he was reading a book while terrorists were ransacking his secret room. Someone put it there after he was killed."

"You don't know that for sure."

"I don't know anything for sure. Including whether we're paid up for our security service."

"I— I think so."

"You *think* so? Jesus, Mike, you took the responsibility to pay the bills! And now the system's dead."

Mike is embarrassed. He studies his knees. "The restaurant—it's been a lot happening here. It hasn't been easy with you gone and Greg needing…"

"Sure, blame us. Anyone but yourself. I've only been kidnapped by Arab terrorists and practically accused of treason by our own government. That fucking restaurant is going to be the death of us, Mike! I just hope not literally."

Mike stands up, feigning indignation. "You're making too much of this!"

"Sit down, Mike," she says sternly. He does. "There's one more thing you should know. Greg just got an e-mail from my mother."

Mike swivels his head to look at Char. "Impossible!"

"This is her fifth message," she says. "Know anything about the others?"

"Nothing. Swear to God."

"Ever talk to the boy when I'm gone, Mike?"

"Look, if you're trying to make me out to be the bad guy here…"

Charlotte rubs her face with her hands. She's got to focus on the issue at hand, not keep picking away at her husband. "Sorry, forget it. Odd timing, though, wouldn't you say, for a message from my mother?"

"You're saying the old gal's still alive?"

"I'm not saying anything. With you whining like a wounded puppy down here I haven't had a chance to read the messages."

Charlotte takes a deep breath and stands, looking around the house. Everywhere there are shadows. "I'm as afraid in my own house right now as I was in Iraq and I'm not even sure why. No one's directly threatened us. Have they?"

She looks straight into Mike's eyes.

"No," he says. "Not directly."

Chapter 8

The man in black whistles and taps his hand on the dashboard of his Mazda CX-9. The country music on the radio is sappy but sweet to the ear. It's been a good evening so far, but it's not over. Now that those arrogant Arabs have been put into the arms of Allah and the mighty Mossad agents have been dispatched to Yahweh, the man has just one more assignment. An easy one.

He lifts the silver metal box from the passenger seat then unlatches the lid and looks inside.

Still empty. Same as when he first broke into it.

He smiles and chomps a fat wad of gum, making it crack. Of course the relic is missing. Jack Curtis did not become CEO of a multi-billion dollar corporation by being stupid. He already would have sold the relic to another billionaire collector, or hidden it in some even more secret location with a counterfeit on display. This box is a fake—the man is sure of it—and the lack of contents means that Jack Curtis may still be waiting for a forged relic to place into it. Or not.

So many mysteries.

The man is at peace with his murderous work. Just as Jack Curtis was a relic collector, the man in the Mazda is a garbage collector. He helps rid the world of human trash, much of it toxic. His organization is global and its pedigree centuries-old, yet only a few of the most powerful men know of its existence. That secrecy is its power. That, plus a highly trained group of professional assassins.

The man removes a small knife from his belt. Made of carbonized plastic, it is lethal in his hands and transparent to airport scanners. When slipped between two particular ribs in a victim's back and expertly maneuvered, it produces a clean but mortal wound. Bleeding is almost entirely internal. At first the victim feels a sharp pain in the lung, like an attack of pleurisy—not enough to cry out, but enough to gasp sharply. Usually the victim places a hand on the chest, because the locus of pain is indistinct. Onlookers often suspect a heart attack; the imperceptible wound and the scarcity of blood encourage such mistakes and often allow the killer to slip away before the murder is even discovered.

Compared with the indiscriminate butchery of bombs, the technique is elegant—artistic, even—and produces no "collateral damage."

The man and his brethren pride themselves in the quiet, clinical precision of their knifecraft, though circumstances sometimes call for back-up weapons such as a 9mm Glock or a PSG-1 sniper rifle. To shoot an assigned victim, however, is to smudge one's reputation ever so slightly.

Parked just outside the gate to Charlotte's home, the man fondles the silver box and then spits his gum into it, closing the lid. Six men dead for an empty box.

The man removes a handheld device from the glove compartment and switches it on. A screen flickers to life, painting his shadowy face with a green glow. On the screen a small dot pulsates along the edge of a large, dark shape he knows is the Lake. Spidery lines define the road on which the man is parked. Yes, the target is at home.

The exhilaration of killing the Israeli agents has dissipated and fatigue is settling like ground fog in his bones. He sighs. By sunrise, his mission will be done and he can sleep.

The man steps out of the car and walks slowly toward the locked gate that is meant to keep out cars, not people. He walks around the east side of the gate and stalks the house, staying concealed in the moonshadow. As he approaches from the rear, he stops to study an illuminated second floor window. That would be the room of Greg Ansari, a boy of rare but unappreciated gifts whose mother stands in the crossfire of history.

He screws a silencer onto the barrel of his Glock and straps on night vision goggles. He will not fail to complete his mission.

Chapter 9

Greg scrolls through the e-mail from his grandmother. He knows almost nothing about this woman except her name and what she looked like as a younger woman. A few images of her are posted on his wall. Charlotte never talks about her mother except to say that she disappeared one day and was never heard from again.

The boy also knows little about his grandfather. Thompson Walker seems to have been erased from the family's history when Miriam Walker vanished, although Greg knows that Grandpa Walker occasionally sends letters to Charlotte. Greg has seen them unopened in the recycling bin.

The emails from Grandma Walker started to appear in Greg's Inbox just hours ago, whetting his insatiable appetite for unsolved mysteries. Where has his grandmother been all these years? Why has she not contacted the family until now? What picture is she trying to send to the grandson she has never met?

Greg knows that this mystery is dominating his thinking. No matter how often his parents explain that Asperger's is a gift and needs no cure, he still curses his brain for its extremes. When do extraordinary powers of concentration cross over into obsession? And when does an ability to find order in chaos become merely a freak show?

Greg's mind is whirring now. He prints off the e-mail and focuses on the cryptic header information:

```
Subject:
Hello
From:
miriam.walker@globexl.com
Date:
23 Jun 2007 20:16:41 CDT
To:
greg@ansari.us
X-Account-Key:
```

```
account2
X-UIDL:
446662569
X-Mozilla-Status:
0001
X-Mozilla-Status2:
10000000
```

The header information goes on for many more lines. Nothing seems unusual about it except that Greg can find no website for globexl.com and the WHOIS data about the owners simply lists John Smith (jsmith@globexl.com) at a post office box in Los Angeles as both administrative and technical contacts. Obviously, a bogus listing.

The message itself is friendly but terse, not what you'd expect from a grandmother who has suddenly appeared after three decades of absence.

```
Dear Greg:
I'd like to introduce myself. I'm your Grandma
Walker. Sorry I've been unavailable until now.
I hope you are doing well and that you like the
attached photo. Will write again soon.
```

The message is so simple and matter-of-fact that it's spooky!

Below the message is a block of gibberish. The string of characters looks like a photo that was improperly embedded into the e-mail. Greg has seen this before. Instead of the picture displaying, the page coughs up the ASCII characters that define the picture. Greg studies the undeciphered block of code.

```
!@# $ %^=QWE R TY QGDE #RTY*UI=ABCD EFGHIJK

Dyq4o9553k 697 j7w5 yqf3 29he343e 2y6 *
e8wq003q43e w9 jqh6 63q4w qt9. * dqh[5 3s0oq8h
h92 g3q7w3 * qj g38ht 2q5dy3e do9w3o6. * qj 8h
t43q5 eqht34. J6 9ho6 y903 8w 5yq5 697 28oo
e3d80y34 5y8w j3wwqt3 qhe e9 2yq5 8w h3d3wwq46
59 wqf3 j3l %y343 8w 9ho6 9h3 2q6l ^97 j7w5 r8he
5y3 43o8d g3r943 5y3 95y34w e9k qhe 5y3h o9dq53
5y3 wqf8941 W33i qhe 63 wyqoo r8hel * dqh wq6
```

```
h9 j9431 @y3h 697 yqf3 5y3 0499r, 43o6 59 5y8w
j3wwqt3l Q4j3e 285y 5y3 5475y * 28oo g3 wqf3el
G75 g3 dq43r7ol %y343 q43 jqh6 2y9 28oo i8oo 59
9g5q8h 2yq5 697 w33il * yqf3 h3f34 w59003e o9f8ht
```

It seems too short to be a picture; even a small picture would have many more lines and a lot of accented and other odd-looking symbols from the extended ASCII character set—the ones not found on the keyboard—such as:

```
#3RðbrÑ $4á%ñ&' ()* 56789:CDEFGHIJSTUVWXYZ
cdefghijstuvwxyz,ƒ„…kM²èíâ4wñ 2 ¦CQ
àêÖÄasû*"j°RiNtÓM$Ý_gG™»%.Wªî&jdåG%Í 4wñ
_/U¢ÜSå„œ£ ÍÍÁÍ¹µó{·m;Zèâáø Iãéô ¨õh´kM²èíâ
4wñ™½=,©ctšKN/šZ@ëSó)óW©W^ š‰aªT~ì"%.I°q"
²å•EN2» I$$ÔŸ+´´ 8pùN?nŒupNQRšI»Â-©O HÊÜ©ÞÎ× i
##x%Å:f±«ê×løjÎËáý÷Ä.'°ÒîuFÖÖ6xÞ]9ïb½tÖm›RäA
"ñ#6ê6sž,Áås&ö"õÔèËI¨ÆSi5í9SçŠwtÜ¢ì»›RV}™6A
áùÏ›UDà°ÔëFµzíªt£wk]ÎW 8«õr¼ÚëN#Kj&h>±¹ðÏŠ¼S-
KwŸ£Å"¢Çjéê°½Ë YelÅ\M&p'¦TÊ¬n2^…IÎ£mßh
```

Grandma's code seems very different. Greg decides this is not a corrupted picture at all, but a cipher concealed in some kind of code. And if Grandma Walker sent this cipher to Greg, she must have expected that he could break the code. That would mean the key is somewhere in the message, perhaps in the code itself.

Greg stares at the code, begins to lose himself in the alien landscape of characters. The room ceases to exist. Only the glowing screen with its precisely ordered letterforms remains. Each character, he knows, is an actor in disguise. The assemblage is a masquerade ball at which every guest has chosen a costume according to some secret rule. Discover the rule and the true identity of each guest is suddenly revealed. Somewhere in this cast of characters is a key that unlocks the secret rule. Probably a pairing of characters or groups of characters.

Greg leans closer to the monitor, so close he can see the tiny pixels that make up each character. He is certain that the key is hidden in plain sight, because nothing is invisible.

And it will be obvious, because Grandma wants Greg to receive the message.

Greg's mouth is dry with anticipation. He can hear his heart beating and he feels as though he has left his body, become pure intellectual energy, begun to float in front of the screen, become one with the code, moving inside it.

And then he sees it.

The key.

Just as he suspected, it is practically undisguised, wearing only half a mask instead of a full costume. Simple but elegant. And the key identifies a device for encrypting and decrypting this code. Astonishingly, the device is the keyboard that rests like a dumb animal beneath Greg's caressing hands.

Following the instructions provided by the key, Greg's fingers begin to tap the keys. Like an alchemist, the boy translates the leaden code into golden text. He does not look up at the monitor until he is done, and then he lifts his eyes, mouthing the words as he reads.

He squints and shakes his head. It can't be!

He reads the message again.

It has been a long time since he has felt fear, but he feels it now. His heart is thumping. Even the Asperger's Syndrome—that superb emotional anesthetic which unleashes the bliss of objectivity—does not protect him from the terror provoked by this message.

A hand touches his shoulder and he jumps!

"Greg, you're trembling. What's going on?"

His mother and father are standing behind him. What *is* going on?

"I broke the code."

There he goes again, leaping forward, leaving everyone in the dust.

"The what?" Charlotte isn't following him this time.

"There's another message from Grandma Walker—her real message."

"What are you talking about, son?" Mike begins to pace the room. "These e-mails from her have got to be a scam."

"Why would someone do that?" Charlotte asks Mike. "Who would know...?"

"I'll print out the cipher," Greg says. He taps the keyboard several times and the printer comes to life, spitting out a sheet of paper.

Charlotte stares at the printer. "This is her real message, you say? Then the uncoded message must have just been a cover."

"Jesus, you guys! This is nuts," Mike complains.

"So is Jack Curtis being killed and five dead bodies in his yard."

Charlotte watches her son turn pale at this news. "My God—I'm sorry. Didn't mean to just blurt it out like that." So odd, Greg showing *emotions* again.

"Nice move there, sweetheart," Mike says.

It has taken this long for Charlotte to understand the significance of Greg's response. "You're frightened—Greg, you're afraid, aren't you?" She can't remember the last time that Greg exhibited fear.

Greg just stares at her.

"That's not like you," Charlotte says. "Emotion, I mean. Is there something else?"

Greg turns and stares at the printer.

"Something in the message, right? Let me see it, Honey."

Greg reaches for the printer. But before his hand can remove the page, three muffled gunshots break the silence.

And then another shot. Suddenly the bedroom window shatters. Glass flies in all directions. Greg and Charlotte scream.

Ducking, Mike runs to them and pulls them onto the floor, covering them with his body.

Two more gunshots and a scream. And then quiet.

Charlotte is sobbing. "They've followed me home!" she screams. "Why won't they leave me alone?"

"Who?" Mike demands.

"The goddam terrorists, who do you think? They won't stop 'til they have my head." She is shaking violently. "They're coming, I can feel it!"

Greg is crying now. He hasn't cried in years, has had no reason to.

Mike reaches into his pocket and finds his cell phone. He dials 911. "We're being attacked at home. Men with guns!" he screams at the dispatcher and then gives his address. "Mihad Ansari—just get some police here right now." After a short pause, he says, "Jesus, okay—M-I-H-A-D A-N-S-A-R-I. That's important for the obits, right? 'Cause we'll be dead if you don't get some cops here!"

Chapter 10

The man in black starts his car and slowly pulls into the roadway. His headlights punch long beams of blue-white light through a gathering fog. As he drives along the winding road, which mostly follows the shore of the lake, two speeding squad cars with flashing lights and screaming sirens meet him head-on. The man knows what the police will find when they get to the Ansari residence.

He grunts in frustration. The night had not gone very well. The reports will show he had not anticipated that his adversaries would approach the house by boat. Obviously, he had not been in full command of the property. There had been minor collateral damage, but damage nevertheless. Even worse, the target had been tipped off to a threat and would now be wary. Everything would become more difficult.

The man slams his palms against the steering wheel. He has been too highly trained for such rookie mistakes. His entire life—every move, every waking moment—is focused on his mission. There is nothing else, because everything depends on his survival and performance.

With an almost religious zeal he is loyal to the organization, which has given him a sense of purpose and deep fulfillment. The organization is his only family, his sole means of support. He does not have other personal relationships except to further his mission. He does not eat breakfast in a restaurant without studying each employee and customer, then checking for escape routes. He never uses a credit card—too traceable. Always uses a cheap, pre-paid cell phone—untraceable. Never stays in the same place twice. When presented with a choice—which alternative flight to take, which door to use, which cab to hire—he uses a small random number generator to make the decision. Odd number, that cab; even, the other one. The pure randomness prevents his decisions from betraying preferences or a pattern discoverable by his adversaries. His job is to be a ghost, appearing and disappearing at will, blending into the terrain, haunting the enemy, always hiding in plain sight.

He has learned to be friendly, even to strangers—but not too friendly. He's been trained to remain generic in appearance—no beards, unless beards are the norm; undistinguished clothing that would match half the men in the neighborhood; no dark glasses or hooded jackets to arouse suspicion; no tattoos (he has had one removed) or other distinguishing marks that would make identification easier. He never speeds or violates traffic laws unless absolutely necessary. He does not swear or spit or provoke a fight. If provoked, he will negotiate his way out, or flee, rather than call attention to himself by fighting. Unless it involves his mission.

In short, like all his brethren around the world, he appears to be the average man within the cultural norm, which means practically invisible. Unexceptional in every way. Totally forgettable. And indescribable by an eyewitness.

He remembers his first contact with the organization. He was a disgruntled special forces soldier recently demoted because he would not perform a clandestine mission that he considered immoral—blowing up an Iraqi house that was thought to shelter one of Saddam Hussein's sons. There were many women and young children in the residence. Though he was trained to follow orders unquestioningly, he could not think of the children as collateral damage in the service of a greater good.

This was long before the "shock and awe" campaign that led his country into quicksand.

Three months after being reassigned to a desk job in Kuwait, the man—whose code name is Gideon—was offered a choice: dishonorable discharge or a court martial. He left the service. Though he was trained to the highest standards of combat and special operations, he suddenly found himself working as an elementary school janitor. At least, he told himself, he was helping to create a positive environment for children instead of blowing up kids for peace.

Since he had no work to take home with him, Gideon filled his evenings and weekends with physical training. He had enjoyed the physical part of special forces—even the pain that went with it. Now he could attempt to exorcise his demons by pushing his body to the limit. He started filling in as an assistant karate instructor and investing his meager left-over pay to buy guns and sharpen his marksman skills.

If the terrorists were trying to destroy his country, he'd be ready to fight. No qualms about killing bad guys. That's what he was trained to do.

After work one evening, as he was climbing into his car—a beat-up 1989 Dodge Charger—he was approached by a 40-ish man in a checked sport coat and open collared blue shirt. Could have been a teacher or an administrator, though Gideon didn't recognize him.

The man identified himself as Tom Grange and asked Gideon to confirm his own name, and then started going on about how unjust it was that Gideon had received a dishonorable discharge.

At first Gideon was embarrassed that anyone knew about that stain. But Tom smiled kindly and offered to buy Gideon a cup of coffee so he could "make an offer."

"What kind of offer?" Gideon asked. "I'm a Christian man, if you know what I mean."

"Strictly business," Tom replied with a sincere squint.

Gideon smiles as he remembers that day when he knew nothing about the organization, and how he would be drawn into a cause that he was born to serve. And my, how his life had changed since then.

Gideon's cell phone rings and he picks up. Only a few people have the number for this pre-paid phone. He is sure it's his superior, code named *Eve*.

"They're becoming more creative—and desperate," he says. "But I handled it. With just one little glitch."

Chapter 11

When Mike Ansari hears the sirens, he remotely opens the gate to let the squad cars through. Two officers march up to the front door, hands on their unbuckled pistols, and two more begin inspecting the grounds. The humid night air almost muffles the furious barking of neighborhood dogs.

Officer Davis bangs on the front door and yells, "Mr. Ansari, open up. It's the police. Are you all right?"

Within seconds Mike opens the door. "My God, am I glad to see you."

"Tell me what happened here."

"I don't—don't really know. A gunshot through the upstairs window and…"

Another officer shouts, "Over here. You've gotta see this."

The officers at the door rush to the home's lakeshore followed by Mike Ansari. All four officers are crouched over two bodies illuminated by flashlights. Each of the bodies has a number scrawled in marker on its forehead.

"Like those murders across the Lake," Officer Davis says.

A pudgy officer nudges one of the bodies with a foot and says, "Looks like an Arab. Were they Arabs got killed over in Orono?"

"They haven't said," Officer Davis replies. "Jimmy, call this in. And have them contact the FBI. Nothing over the radio about terrorists, right?"

"Terrorists? You think?"

"Jimmy, I'm not thinking anything. Just call it in so someone else can sort this out. Matt, Terry, check out the rest of the grounds and be careful."

The three officers disperse.

"If these guys attacked *us*…" Mike says, who killed *them*?"

Officer Davis looks up. "That's why I said be careful." He looks down again at the bodies. "Someone sure doesn't like Ay-rabs."

A blue-white flash startles the Officer, who turns to see Charlotte and Greg looking at the bodies. Greg is holding a camera. The Officer turns off his flashlights and prevents them from coming closer.

"Are those the bad guys?" Greg asks.

"Looks like it," Officer Davis replies. "I'd like you all to go back into the house now. Got a lot of questions to ask, as you might imagine."

Mike looks at Charlotte, who is still trembling. He walks over and puts his arms around her. "It's all right now, everything's fine."

"They want me, Mike. They came to get me."

"Shhhhh… it's okay. We don't know what they want, but we'll figure it out, so don't worry."

"They want me, Mike."

An hour later, the grounds are lit up like a night shoot on a movie set. Police guards and crime scene investigators scurry about like fleas on a dog. Local news teams have already set up camera trucks outside the police tape, but the only official comment so far is that two intruders were killed on the grounds. Nothing more. Is this related to Charlotte Ansari's abduction in Iraq? No known connection. Who shot the intruders? It's unclear at this time.

Chamomile tea has calmed Charlotte, and Greg has gone to his room.

Charlotte looks over at Mike, who is seated in an overstuffed chair across from her, and says, "Sorry I fell apart."

"Who wouldn't, after all you've been through the past few days."

"I feel—brittle. Like I'd shatter if you touched me."

"Post-traumatic stress, maybe. You're entitled."

As Charlotte swallows another sip of tea, Marcus Elliot walks into the room. The FBI Bureau Chief's tie is undone and his navy blazer is a network of wrinkles. He's hunched over and rubbing a stubbled chin with his hand.

"Didn't expect to see you again so soon, Charlotte."

"Marcus, this is my husband." Charlotte gestures to Mike, who stands. "Marcus is the FBI Bureau Chief."

The two men shake hands indifferently.

"We're pretty rattled here," Mike says.

"To be honest, we're pretty rattled, too," Marcus explains, then looks at a soft chair near a fireplace. "Mind?

"Please," Charlotte says, gesturing for him to sit down.

"I've gotta tell you, we haven't been under this much scrutiny since that Moussaoui thing blew up in our face a few years back. We'd appreciate it, Char—and Mike—if you wouldn't talk to the media about the details here. Would give us a better chance to get a fix on the weirdness."

"Weirdness," Mike repeats, nodding. A good word.

"I've talked to the police, and they're gonna put protection on the house for the next few days at least, so no worries there. I've gotta assume that whatever these guys were after they didn't get."

"What *were* they after, Marcus?" Charlotte asks.

"I was hoping you'd know, 'cus frankly we don't have a clue. At the Curtis place they were clearly after one of the relics and Curtis got in the way. Here, unless you got a secret room someplace I don't know about, beats me. What would make it easier is if we knew. Any ideas?"

"We kind of thought they were after us," Mike suggests.

"What for? You piss off a mullah or something?"

"Honestly, Marcus, you know what I do," Charlotte says. "I piss off people for a living. All over the world. Who'd think they'd follow me to the Land of 10,000 Lakes to call me out?"

"Well, if they came because of a grudge, I've gotta say they planned to do more than call you out. These guys were carrying some heavy metal. But all we've got is theories right now, such as these unfortunate fellows were terrorists, and like somehow you and Jack Curtis are linked, otherwise why the same ritualistic posing of the deceased? I'd say someone's delivering a message and wants to make sure it gets through. But why and to whom I don't presently know. Your boy all right?"

"Greg? Uh, he seems all right," Charlotte replies. "A little shaken like the rest of us, though it's hard to tell sometimes."

"Autism, right?"

"Asperger's Syndrome, it's a little different. Exceptionally bright in some things, gifted in many ways actually. But, uh, emotionally detached."

"We're gonna make sure you're all kept safe now, all right?"

"All right. Thanks for checking in."

Marcus nods and groans as he stands up. "Can I count on you keeping a lid on until we sort this thing out?" He looks at Charlotte, then at Mike.

Charlotte says, "Sure, for now."

Marcus heads for the door, but Charlotte stops him with a question: "Marcus, who's scrutinizing you on this already? It's only been a few hours."

She plays this like a bargaining chip for her silence. He owes her this much.

Marcus turns and stares at her. "If I told you—I'd have to kill you." He laughs halfheartedly at the lame joke and then turns and walks out of the house.

But the cliché cuts like a knife.

Charlotte and Mike enter Greg's room just as the last crime scene investigator is leaving. The shattered glass has been cleaned up.

"Anything?" Charlotte asks the chunky investigator.

"Pulled a bullet from the wall. Same caliber as the guns we found on the perps. Pretty sure one of them shot the window out."

"Okay, thanks."

"I'll get some plastic to cover the window," Mike says. "Be right back."

Greg has not moved since Charlotte entered the room. He is seated in the computer chair and staring at the wall of family photographs. A few faces are circled in green Sharpie.

"Wanna see Grandma Walker's message?" Greg asks matter-of-factly.

"I guess."

Greg reaches into his pocket and pulls out the printout, hands it to his mother. "Simple encryption," he explains. "The first line provides the key."

Charlotte looks at the encrypted message:

```
!@# $ %^=QWE R TY QGDE #RTY*UI=ABCD EFGHIJK
```

It means nothing to her.

"If you remove a couple of spaces," Greg explains, his eyes still on the photographs as if only part of his brain needs to be engaged in this conversation, "the letters QWERTY refer to the standard typewriter layout. Same as computer keyboards. QWERTY takes its name from the first six letters on the keyboard's top first row of letters."

Charlotte approaches Greg's computer and looks down at the keyboard. There they are, the letters QWERTY all in a row.

"Right before the Q in the message is an equal sign. I figured this might signify an equation of some kind. And I was right. The symbols before the equal sign are spaced identically to the QWE-space-R-space-TY. In fact, 1

40

is the key right above the capital Q and on a left diagonal. And the @ is in the same relative position to the capital W. And the pound sign relates to the capital E in the same way. So if you simply put your finger on the exclamation key, which is the shifted 1 key, but then move your finger down one row on the diagonal and type the shifted Q key, you are decrypting. The computer keyboard is the decryption device. Pretty clever. And simple."

"So you just typed out the message one row lower?"

"You have to be careful to use the shift key if the symbol in the message is shifted. And spaces are just spaces."

Greg still has not taken his eyes off the photographs. Suddenly he stands and walks to the wall, studies a photo, and circles a blurry face in the background.

Charlotte looks down at the paper with the decrypted message:

```
Charlotte, you must have wondered why I
disappeared so many years ago. I can't explain
now because I am being watched closely. I am in
great danger.
```

My God, Charlotte thinks, this really is a personal message from her vanished mother, the first communication between them in thirty-one years! And her mother is in some kind of danger. She continues reading.

```
My only hope is that you will decipher this
message and do what is necessary to save me.
There is only one way. You must find the relic
before the others do, and then locate the savior.
Seek and ye shall find. I can say no more. When
you have the proof, reply to this message. Armed
with the truth, I will be saved. But be careful.
There are many who will kill to obtain what you
seek. I have never stopped loving you. Perhaps
some day we will be reunited. Your mother,
Miriam.
```

Relic? Miriam Walker must be referring to the Jack Curtis relic that has attracted so much unwelcome attention. But what does Miriam mean by "locate the savior"?

For more than three decades, Charlotte has been haunted by the remembrance of her mother's longsuffering sweetness, the distinctive fragrance that surrounded her like a mist, and that painful last evening when a screaming husband falsely accused her of terrible things.

Charlotte had been only seven when her mother's tearful face pressed against her own, and when that melodious voice, like wind chimes, told the little girl that everything would be all right, *just go to sleep my darling daughter*. Miriam had rocked Charlotte to sleep that night but was gone in the morning. Vanished.

Charlotte's father has not uttered his wife's name since that day and has refused to talk about what might have happened. Charlotte never believed that her loving mother would abandon her daughter, and so she invented stories to explain Miriam's disappearance. In all of these stories, Thompson Walker was the villain.

No wonder that Charlotte will not answer her father's infrequent phone calls and throws away his letters unopened, although she always notes the countries from which they are posted.

Charlotte looks up from the decrypted message. The world seems to be tilting around her. Abduction in Iraq, a Minnesota neighbor murdered, terrorists shooting out her windows, a coded message from her vanished mother—none of it makes any sense. Nothing connects.

"That was the first e-mail," Greg says. He grabs another sheet of paper, handing it to his mother. "Here's the next one. Different message."

Charlotte looks at the new decrypted message.

```
Dear Charlotte. You must not delay. You have at
best seven days to fulfill your mission. There are
two individuals who can help. One of them is my
grandson, Greg, who will guide you through the
maze. The other one I cannot mention but you know
who he is. He will not want to help but seek him
out immediately and convince him. Without him you
will never locate the savior. Please hurry, I am
counting on you. Your mother, Miriam.
```

Your mission, it says. What mission is that? Find the relic and locate the savior. Why? And how? Charlotte is even more confused now, but she knows that a countdown of some kind has been started. And her mother's life may be at stake.

"Greg," she says, "do you have any idea what this is all about?"

Greg does not acknowledge her question. Again, he is staring at the photographs. Charlotte follows his eyes to a picture of Charlotte at her fifth birthday party at the Como Park Zoo. Someone had taken a picture of her with ice cream smeared all over her beaming face. Miriam is standing next to her with a shrug and an amused look of "not my fault!"

Charlotte remembers that picture, and that party. Such a happy day, filled with comical monkeys and ice cream treats and scary snakes behind glass walls and a picnic in the warm sun and…

Greg interrupts her reverie. He walks up to that very photograph and circles the face of a man in the background, a man just inside the left edge of the picture but seemingly anxious to be outside the margin. The man's face is blurry, but you can make out his features. A sharp nose too big for his face, bushy brows above deep-set eyes, high cheekbones, a dark moustache.

Charlotte looks at this man. He seems faintly familiar, but then again *not* familiar. The kind of man you might have seen at a store and then again at a gas station, wondering if you knew him from someplace.

But then Charlotte scans the other pictures. Greg has circled other faces, too, about six of them. These are also men in the background caught unexpectedly by the lens. But while most of the extraneous faces in these photographs are worn by people going about their own business, looking elsewhere or walking somewhere, the circled faces feature eyes that seem to be studying Charlotte or looking at the camera.

Suddenly Charlotte feels a chill. She has noticed something else about these unknown faces, something that frightens her even before she knows why. All of these faces belong to the same man—not a friend or acquaintance, but a stranger with no clear reason to be with Charlotte or her group.

In one photo, the man is standing near a doorway at Wall Drug in South Dakota when Charlotte was six and the family was driving to the Black Hills. And there he is again in a passing car just as Miriam snapped a picture of Charlotte getting on the school bus for the first time. The man appears again in a picture of 14-year-old Charlotte at a homecoming football game with friends; the man, looking grayer and more wrinkled, is smoking a cigarette in the stands.

The last photo is the most frightening. It was taken at an Irish restaurant in Boston five years ago when Charlotte was celebrating her first Emmy nomination with friends. A waiter took the picture of Charlotte and three others, but in the dimness beyond the reach of the flash, the man with the sharp nose can be seen at a nearby table. His hand is blurred, as if he is moving it unsuccessfully to cover his face before the shutter snaps.

The intersections of her life with this mysterious man are extraordinary, but so is the brain that could extract the unknown face from the chaos of visuals on the wall. This brain belongs to a boy who perceived the outline of a manta ray in the loch when everyone else saw a serpent in the water.

At this precise moment, Charlotte's world turns inside out. Everything else has provoked heart-pounding fear. But now a heaviness, which she recognizes as dread, fills her lungs. She is drowning in it. She slumps into Greg's chair devastated by the realization that since she was a little girl someone has been watching her. And she has no idea why.

That evening, the man with the sharp nose begins to haunt her. Charlotte is floundered by the flow of improbabilities.

As she lies on the bed beside her husband, the rhythm of his breathing rocks her to sleep. But as she begins to doze, through half-opened eyes, she sees the TV screen switch on, hears disconnected snatches of audio as the channels quickly change, and then hears the hoarse, breathy voice of a preacher exhorting the faithful to *persevere in these last days, for Jesus is surely coming soon, but to speed up His return we must do our part to save Israel from the heathens and fight the forces of darkness who have declared war on the One True God and his righteous believers, driving these murderous Islamo-Fascists to the fiery pit of hell and eternal damnation.*

Her last memories of that night are the comforting sound of applause and Amens and Hallelujahs, and the disquieting vision of her Iraqi abductors with demon horns erupting through their scalps and tongues of flame licking their demented faces.

The next morning, after barely three hours of sleep, she wakes up with a clear head, calls Bud Schiebel, news director of CCN, and tells him she needs to get to India as soon as possible. With her son.

Chapter 12

A maze of corridors and tunnels connects thousands of glowing rooms like Christmas lights on a tangled wire. The passageways of Vatican City run for miles, perhaps to infinity, and some say that at the end, if you can find it, are the gates to heaven. Antonio Fortunati knows these tortuous paths well. At seventy-two, he has been walking them for more than thirty years. As prefect of *L'Archivio Segreto Vaticano*, the Secret Archives of the Vatican, he lives within this vast warren.

This morning, however, Antonio Fortunati is returning from a journey into Rome. He had told everyone that he was visiting his banker and celebrating a niece's birthday, but this was a lie, may God forgive him. He has been shopping in Rome, and the shopping bag he carries contains a suit and other items that are practical for many but not for the prefect of the Secret Archives.

It is early morning. Wearing a priest's robe, he enters the great square of St. Peter's and quickly passes the fountains and the obelisk, rousing a soot-storm of flapping pigeons. Lost in thought, he pays no attention to the Leonine walls or the Gate of St. Anne that leads into Vatican City.

"Father!" someone calls out, giving a friendly wave. Antonio looks up but does not recognize the greeter. He waves anyway and continues down an arched road that winds past the *Osservatore Romano* building and on to the Court of Belvedere, the Vatican Library, and next to it the Secret Archives. At three different stations, Swiss Guards ask to see his credentials even though they recognize the prefect.

Over the centuries, the Secret Archives have spread like untamed ivy overtaking the area next to the Library and eventually choking the entire Tower of the Winds and two long corridors, which are now clogged with nearly eight miles of bookshelves. One of these corridors leads from the top of the Tower to the frescoed fifteenth-century apartment of Rodrigo de Borgia, who took the name Pope Alexander VI; this one holds no current interest for Antonio. The second corridor, on the ground floor, leads from the administrative offices to a small prayer room beneath the ornate private chapel of de Borgia. Antonio chooses this passageway.

The prefect passes through the Hall of the Parchments and its thousands of purple documents infected by an uncontrollable, violet-colored fungus. Antonio is sure he can smell the slow erosion of history in this room. When the texts become completely illegible, their secrets will be lost forever.

He leaves the Hall and enters the dim Room of Inventories and Indexes. There are no card files here, no computers, just enormous handwritten books so heavy they are practically impossible to lift.

As Antonio strides down the windowless corridor beyond this room, electric lights switch on and off as he passes, creating the illusion of a glowing capsule moving along the rails of history in the dark. The corridor is stuffed with the records of the senate of cardinals that once advised popes; the proceedings of the conclaves that elected popes; a massive collection of indulgences, the sales slips of ancient sins; and over seven thousand large volumes of petitions for every kind of ecclesiastical grace and favor.

Antonio imagines that his petition for mercy, as yet unwritten, will one day end up somewhere in these archives, for he is about to betray his church. He needs only a few more hours to copy and translate documents that will verify certain relics and bestow upon them the power to change religious history if the relics can be found.

The end of this corridor leads not to the gates of heaven but to a large iron grille that stands beneath a gilded frieze of exotic plants and animals. This is the entrance to the Riserva, an ancient suite of rooms. The iron gate has guarded its possessions since the fourteenth century. The Riserva secures highly classified information about recent and living church figures, contentious political matters, controversial church activities, and a few archival treasures that Antonio has spent over thirty years seeking.

The prefect finds a key beneath his robes and unlocks the gate. Only the Pope has another key, and even the Vatican's secretary of state cannot enter without permission. This is the secret room of the Secret Archives.

Once inside the Riserva, Antonio relocks the gate and marches to an imposing safe that contains the most cherished and secret documents in the Archives. Some of these documents are kept by themselves in a drawer, others are grouped together. Antonio opens the safe and pulls out the third drawer from the top, finding a small sheaf of papers hidden between two other documents. He takes the sheaf to a large carved wooden table and spreads them out.

Here is the proof!

Or as much proof as there will ever be.

Suddenly he is gripped by fear. Does he truly understand what he is unleashing? Will there be any forgiveness of sins for him?

But then he remembers why he embarked on this treacherous journey so many years ago. He loves the church and his Savior, but he cannot abide the hypocrisy that he has discovered. He believes that God is righteous and favors truth; therefore Antonio must be doing God's work. It is time for the church to recognize the *real* Jesus, the one whom Antonio has come to adore, and not the imaginary Jesus of manufactured legend.

If he is wrong, Antonio knows that his soul is lost.

But if he is right…

Chapter 13

He is exhausted. One year on the job and the pressures are high enough to burst a blood vessel. CIA Director William Wyatt was elevated to his position because of the agency's intelligence failures under the direction of his predecessor. Now there is intensified public and governmental scrutiny of this most secret bureaucracy. The president is demanding evidence to support his policies, the vice-president is micro-managing the agency, the White House is leaking, and the giddy press continues to expose the sordid details of botched CIA missions, clandestine prisons, torture, inaccurate intelligence, the shortage of agency translators and human assets, and—even worse—the failure to contain radical Islam and its mutant offspring, terrorism.

Wyatt gulps two ibuprofen caplets for his headache and glances at his calendar. In thirty minutes, a quick briefing for the vice-president. At noon, a helicopter ride to Camp David to consult with the president on the latest clandestine mission. At three o'clock, a news conference to announce the new agency deputy director. *How can a guy get any work done?* he wonders.

Wyatt knows the inner workings of the agency. He is a career spook promoted from within the organization to blunt Congress's criticism of the president's pattern of placing unqualified political cronies in high positions.

At the time of his promotion, Wyatt had thought he knew just about everything there was to know about the agency, but he was wrong. Two weeks after moving into his new office, which occurred ironically on his fifty-second birthday, Wyatt received the gift of secret knowledge. There were, he learned, operations that only the director and two or three other agency department heads knew about. There were unwritten protocols and secret alliances and contract operations and black box technologies of which even the president, for reasons of deniability, was unaware.

The agency, he knew, has many "maintenance" duties to perform, but occasionally the White House requires a special mission. In these cases, the director is issued objectives—called "business objectives" by the vice-president, previously CEO of a large corporation—and the agency is left to craft a strategy to achieve them. Wyatt knows what this means. The director assumes the entire responsibility for accomplishing the objectives, but also for the lawfulness of the strategy and tactics employed. Unfortunately, lawful means are seldom sufficient to achieve the administration's objectives.

If push comes to shove, Wyatt is the fall guy.

A thin voice intrudes into the blessed silence of the office. "Sir, the president is on line one."

Wyatt lifts the receiver and says, "Mr. President, this is Bill."

"We're still on for twelve-thirty, right?"

"That's right, sir."

"Just so I'm not sitting on pins and needles here, are we making progress?"

"I believe so, sir. Yes."

"You don't sound very convincing, Bill. Either we're closer to meeting our business objectives or we're not."

The office door cracks open and Grant Iggers enters without apology. Wyatt looks up at him hopefully, but Grant gravely shakes his head, dashing the director's hopes for good news. At a trim forty-seven, Grant is director of operations. He has the athletic build of a covert agent, which he used to be, and the chiseled face of a model. You wouldn't be surprised to see his photo in a new wallet.

"Are you still there, Bill?" the president asks.

"I'm afraid, sir, that we will need a little more time to work our strategy."

There is an uncomfortable pause before the president speaks. "Dammit, Bill, what's the point in coming out here if there's nothing to talk about? You're not gonna fail me on this, are you Bill?"

"No sir, but it's complicated—and we have competition."

"When is that *not* true, Bill? Well… let's see here… the vice-president will be there shortly, so fill him in and forget about Camp David. Sounds like you've got work to do over there. Whatever's necessary and all that."

"Yes sir, I'll do as you say."

Wyatt knows that "whatever's necessary" is administration code for "legal or illegal." He motions for Iggers to take a seat, which he does.

"Timely intrusion," Wyatt says.

"Helen said you were on with the boss. Thought I'd better intercept before you overcommitted."

"I overcommitted the day I took this job. Grant, you look like a man who just lost his dog. Give me the bad news."

"This Minnesota thing, not good. I passed on your gag request to Bernard at the Bureau and he fired it off to the Minneapolis Bureau Chief, guy named Marcus Elliott. It's been buffered so no one knows it came from the top. I gotta say, the Bureau doesn't like carrying our laundry around."

"Like we've never helped them out."

"This Elliot's a smart guy apparently. Anyway, he put a lid on, but then the damn Arabs attacked a house across the lake from, uh, the rich guy. Unfortunately, it was the home of Charlotte Ansari."

"The CCN Ansari?"

"The same."

"Geez!" The homogenized profanity sounds almost humorous coming from the director of the CIA, but Wyatt is a deeply conservative Christian, which helps explain his promotion over a dozen other well-qualified candidates. Curses just don't form naturally in his mouth. "So why haven't I heard about it on the news?"

"Seems as though Elliot convinced Ansari to stuff it for a while. It's being handled as a local crime deal. They've kept the Arab angle under wraps."

"Buy this Elliot guy dinner on me."

"Another thing. Ansari and her son have just caught a flight to Delhi via Chicago. Probably stopping in the windy city to get visas."

"Delhi? What's in Delhi?"

"The woman is attacked at home last night by terrorists, and this morning she's on a flight to India. I'd say the two things are connected, wouldn't you? Oh, the tickets were charged to CCN."

Wyatt grunts and reaches for the ibuprofen again. "So she's talked to the network and now it's official news business. Well, that didn't take long. Hard way to earn an exclusive, though. But why bring the kid along? And what the hell is in India?"

Wyatt doesn't seem to notice that he has cursed. He swallows another ibuprofen without water.

"Well, we could ask her."

"I think she knows more than we do, and we're the CIA, Grant. This doesn't make me happy. I want to know what she knows. From now on, I don't want her taking a pee without someone watching. And let's not blow it this time. You know the stakes. So what's the deal on all those dead guys up in Minnesota?"

"At the Curtis place? The homeowner, dead. Made the mistake of acquiring the relic. And let's see—three Arabs with al Qaeda links, dead."

"Competition."

"Two Mossad agents, dead."

"Mossad? Geeeez! Those guys are supposed to be on our side. What're they doing free-lancing in our jurisdiction?"

"Whatever it was, they paid for it."

"More competitors? Heaven forbid. The playing field's getting crowded. Get a hold of Yakhim in Tel Aviv and find out what his boys are up to in the great state of Minnesota."

Grant makes a note and continues. "Over at the Ansari residence, two more Arabs, as yet unidentified, probably terrorists, dead."

"And who killed all these guys? Not al Qaeda, not Mossad, *not us*, right?"

"Not us, definitely."

"So everybody else in the world seems to have been at the Curtis and Ansari homes at the same time—*except us*, right? They all knew something was going down *except us*, or we would've been there, am I right?"

"That's, uh, probably true." Grant looks sheepish.

"So our competition clearly knows more than we do. And this Ansari woman knows more than we do. I'll tell you something, Grant. Right now we're sucking hind tit on this thing, but we're gonna catch up, because *you're* gonna see to it. Personally."

Grant raises his eyebrows. He hasn't been in the field for five years. "I'll do my best," he says.

"I hope that's good enough. What really worries me is who killed all these guys."

"Very clean, very professional work. A contractor maybe."

Wyatt stares at Grant for a moment. "When was the last time we...?"

"About a month ago. They never fail, you know that."

"Yeah, but they're dangerous." Wyatt knows the reputation of the contract organization in question. Efficient, global, disciplined, expensive. A year ago, a CIA agent double-crossed one of the contractors who had been hired for an assassination. The agent turned up dead. A week later the agent's family received a $250,000 anonymous gift. With these guys, it was more than business.

"The two Mossad agents in Minnesota—stabbed. That's their signature, isn't it? Daggers?"

"They're ghosts," Wyatt replies. "And they've been doing this for two thousand years, so watch your back."

Chapter 14

Her legs are painfully cramped into the tight space between the seats. So this is how the tourists travel! After several years of first-class tickets, she had forgotten the discomfort and the shoulder-to-shoulder squeeze. On this trip to Delhi, first-class is full and she finds herself instantly resenting the pampered folks beyond the pulled curtain.

Charlotte glances at Greg next to her. He sleeps soundly, head on a bunched-up pillow wedged between the seat back and the window. She pulls a blanket over him suddenly overtaken with a pleasurable flash of motherly affection. But this quiet delight is quickly replaced with a strafing anxiety.

What was she thinking? What sort of dangers is she dragging her son into? What kind of selfishness would cause a mother to expose her only son to unknown peril?

Charlotte knows that her flesh is marbled with the sins of her father. She may never know why or how Thompson Walker drove her mother away, or what emotional or physical tortures he had inflicted on his wife before the day of her vanishing, but using her investigative reporting skills Charlotte had dredged up other moldering skeletons from her father's past.

It seems that Thompson Walker was a Catholic priest before he met Charlotte's mother, Miriam. In 1963, he seduced a 14-year old girl named Mandy while serving in a St. Paul parish. The girl became pregnant and her parents angrily confronted Thompson, who admitted his sin. The church paid the parents a substantial sum for their pledge of secrecy, and the family eventually abandoned their faith and moved away. A retired priest who was involved in the cover-up but who finally confessed the truth to Charlotte— off the record, of course—recollected that Thompson was racked with guilt. Barely a year after the confrontation, Thompson left the priesthood and took a job as an insurance salesman.

In 1967, Thompson met a beautiful, 21-year-old woman named Miriam who had come from Lebanon to attend the University of Minnesota. Apparently, it was love at first sight. Within a year, they were married and in 1969 Charlotte was born.

Charlotte believes she has two things in common with her father. The first is their headstrong nature and their unthinking willingness to use people for their own purposes. The second is their wanderlust. Charlotte travels the world in search of international news. Thompson Walker, since the mid-seventies, has been traveling endlessly to immerse himself in the religions of the world.

For decades, Thompson has studied and practiced Hinduism, Buddhism, Judaism, Zoroastrianism, several distinct sects of Christianity, Islam, Sufism, and the Bahá'í Faith. He has written eloquently about his experiences in best-selling books. Even Charlotte has grudgingly admired his craft, although she prefers to picture her father as less of a spiritual seeker and more of a perpetual penitent struggling to find forgiveness.

He will not find it in his daughter.

Whatever evil her father had visited upon her mother, it was but another link in a long chain of wickedness.

A harsh voice announces that the aircraft will be landing soon, and Charlotte realizes she had fallen asleep. She looks at Greg, who is closing his laptop. Rubbing her temples, Charlotte tries to wake up.

Within forty-five minutes, the plane is on the ground. Charlotte and Greg are herded down a long Jetway, through a crumbling corridor, and into a holding pen. It is an hour before midnight. It takes twenty minutes to move through Passport Control into a small, tightly packed baggage claim area and another twenty minutes of fighting the crowd to locate their five bruised pieces of luggage.

Charlotte has not been to Delhi before. Indira Ghandi terminal is old and disorganized, something out of the fifties. Charlotte looks around for directions but finds scores of confusing signs. Three people passing quickly with suitcase-stacked trolleys nearly run her over.

Greg suddenly takes her hand and leads her across the terminal floor. Just ahead Charlotte can now make out the word TAXIS on a small black placard.

They push through a creaking door to a fume-filled chamber echoing with the groan of engines and grinding gears. Taxis of every description nose through the knot of automobiles like flies swarming on rotten meat. Charlotte spies another small sign, "Pre-Paid Taxis," and gestures for Greg to remain with the baggage trolley. Beneath the sign, a bored Indian with an impenetrable British accent seems to be asking where she wants to go.

"Karol Bagh," she replies, mentioning the district in which she had hurriedly booked accommodations on the Web before their flight. "The Sri Rahul Hotel," she adds.

The ticket seller makes indecipherable scrawls on a piece of paper and then holds out his hand. "Fifty rupees," he says.

She digs in her fanny pack for Indian rupees, left over from a trip to Mumbai a few months ago, and hands them over.

She glances around the teeming chamber and wonders how she will ever get a taxi. There are no lines, just a crush of cranky tourists and businessmen shouting and jostling each other for the attention of the drivers. Normally, a driver would be here to pick her up and escort her to a hotel. But this is not official business. This is personal.

An American voice cuts through the din from just behind her.

"I heard you mention Karol Bagh," the masculine voice says.

Charlotte turns to see an athletic man in his forties wearing a wrinkled suit and an unknotted necktie.

"Karol Bagh, yes," Charlotte says. She is relieved to hear an American accent. "Our hotel is there."

"I'm going near there. Perhaps we can travel together. I can drop you at your hotel on the way to mine."

Charlotte glances at Greg, who yawns. All she wants right now is to check in, find a bed, and go to sleep. "That would be wonderful. We're very tired."

"You look… you look familiar to me. Have we met?"

"I don't think so."

The man raises a finger and points it at her, then seems to realize the rudeness of his gesture. "Charlotte Ansari, right? Cambridge Cable News."

"Well, yes, actually." Charlotte would have preferred anonymity, but at midnight after traveling half-way around the world, who cares?

"I'm a big fan. Watch you all the time. But hey, listen, I promise I won't pester you about it, okay? It's an honor, though. Let me get a taxi."

The athletic man marches through the crowd and finds a tall, wiry Indian who calls a turbaned man who runs to a parked taxi. This latter man gets behind the wheel and aggressively bulls his way in front of several other honking cars to reach a point near Charlotte. The tall man receives a fat wad of rupees for his trouble.

The athletic man has only one suitcase. He helps Charlotte and Greg maneuver their trolley past a throng of shouting travelers to the taxi, which leaves the stinking chamber with two suitcases strapped to its roof. The night is filled with smoke and the surrounding area is blighted with abandoned buildings and broken down cars.

"If you don't mind," Charlotte says to the athletic man, "I'm going to call home and let my husband know we're all right."

"Then I'll call my office. Not that they worry much about me."

Charlotte and the athletic man pull out cell phones and tap in a sequence of digits. Greg sits between them. He stares impassively out the window, watching a boy ride a white horse down the side of the road.

"Mike, thank God you're there. I was afraid I'd get voice mail," Charlotte says into the phone. "No, we're fine. Just a long trip is all. On the way right now to our hotel. Let me give you the number there." She fumbles in her fanny pack for the phone number.

As Charlotte continues to speak, the athletic man connects to his office. "Hi, it's Grant Iggers, I'm in Delhi right now. Put me through to Wyatt."

On the other end, CIA Director William Wyatt picks up his phone. "How's our girl?"

"Just fine," Grant Iggers replies. "I'm on the way to the hotel now. Should be able to take care of things here with no problem."

"Just stay close to her. I want to know everything she does. Everything."

"Will do."

The drive to the hotel takes forty-five minutes. The slum around the airport steadily deteriorates as the taxi reaches Karol Bagh. At one in the morning, the dirt streets and crumbling buildings look like a frontier town in a John Ford western.

The taxi finally takes a hard left into a dark alley, pulls past a series of rusty garage doors and comes to a stop.

"Hotel," the driver exclaims. "Sri Ruhal."

Charlotte looks around. A small buzzing neon sign on a three-story building signals the location. "My God," she says. "This is what I get booking for online." A pack of snarling dogs patrol the alley and circle the taxi. "I'm not sure I want to get out of the car."

"This is pretty scary. Why don't we go to my hotel," Grant says. "I'm sure they can find a room for you."

Charlotte looks at Greg, who is staring at his knees. Greg looks up at her. In a rare moment of silent, real-time communication he subtly nods his head "no."

Charlotte turns to the athletic man. "We're pretty tired. I think we'll give it a shot here."

Grant helps them into the hotel. The front desk clerk is friendly and helpful. And alone.

"We can manage from here," Charlotte says to the athletic man. "I want to thank you for your help."

Grant takes a business card out of his wallet and hands it to her. "If you need anything while you're here, call my cell phone. Works everywhere."

"Mine does too. Thanks again."

The man heads back to the taxi. Charlotte glances at the card, and so does Greg. The name on the card is Jason Hartley, VP Vendor Relations, Opticom Corporation.

Inside the hotel, the room presented to Charlotte and Greg is old but clean. The air conditioner is noisy and smells of mold, but it cools and dries the air. Charlotte whisks back the bedspread and looks for bugs. None.

"All right, mister," she says to Greg. "What's the deal here? You wanted to stay in this place for some reason. Now I'm tired and in no mood to be talking to myself here, so speak up."

Greg walks to the table where Charlotte has placed Grant's business card. He picks it up and hands it to her.

Maybe it's the fatigue, or perhaps just a serendipitous alignment of the stars, but Greg answers her directly. "His name is not Jason Hartley—it's Grant Iggers. He gave his name on the phone. And he didn't call Opticom Corporation."

Charlotte waits, but Greg has stopped talking.

"Who did he call then?" Charlotte demands. "Tell me, Greg."

"I heard the voice through the earpiece. He had it turned up."

"Tell me who he called."

"The CIA."

Charlotte slumps down in a chair. What does the CIA want with her? *Is everyone out to get her?*

"Greg, is that why you didn't want to go to *his* hotel?"

Greg hears the questions but has slipped out of real-time to somewhere in the future. He answers a question that his mother has not yet thought of but would ask later if she had time.

"Tomorrow he will follow us," Greg says.

"Tomorrow… follow us? Are you sure?"

Greg is silent.

"Follow us where, Greg?"

"To the man that Grandma said would help us. That man is here. It's why we came to Delhi, isn't it?"

Charlotte is afraid and confused. She needs to sleep and sort things out, but her mind is racing too fast. Her pulse is pounding. She had not expected anyone to know that she was in Delhi. And Greg is freaking her out with his prescience.

"But maybe Grant Iggers won't follow us tomorrow," Greg interjects.

"Why? What do you mean?"

"If he doesn't follow us, it will mean that others know we're here and stopped him."

Charlotte looks at the bed. So inviting! And yet she knows that she will not sleep tonight.

Chapter 15

The brittle chirp of Charlotte's satellite phone slaps her awake. She lurches from bed, disoriented, stubbing her toe in the dark and cursing. She can't remember falling asleep, and now she can't remember where she is. The blue glow of the phone's screen gives away its location on a dresser across the room.

She navigates unsteadily toward the phone. Before she can reach it, the room floods with light. Greg has switched on the bedside lamp.

The phone screeches her personal ringtone. Only a handful of people have her number. A chill penetrates her as she considers the possible emergencies.

She grabs the phone, juggles it awkwardly, and then stammers, "Ye-yes, hello, Charlotte here."

A hollow silence intensifies her gathering fear, and then she hears a soothing male voice, like melted chocolate, saying, "Charlotte, please listen carefully and do not interrupt. A great opportunity awaits you, if you can move quickly. A very big story. At eight o'clock sharp you must arrive with a cameraman at the Seasons Hotel in New Delhi. Go to room 615 and open the door—it will be unlocked. Ignore the Do Not Disturb sign. You must be gone by eight-thirty because the police will arrive. If you are still there, tell them that you arrived for an interview with Grant Iggers, director of operations for the CIA. The rest is up to you."

A click ends the call. Charlotte turns to see Greg staring at her. "I've got to make a call," she says. "Then I'll explain."

She nervously stabs at the keypad of her phone with an index finger.

"They got to Iggers, so he won't be following us tomorrow," Greg says, almost a whisper. "But someone else will."

As her call connects, she stares at Greg. Why did she think she'd have to explain anything to him? Even though Greg is her son, sometimes the kid spooks her.

A hoarse voice grunts at her from the phone. "Bud Schiebel."

"Bud, it's Charlotte."

"Char! You made it to Delhi all right? Christ… must be, what, two or three in the morning there? What's up?"

"I can't give you the details right now, but I'm onto something I think. Could be big. I need a cameraman in a couple of hours. Anyone free?"

"In Delhi? Uh, no, not that I know of. It's the middle of the night there, isn't it? What's goin' on?"

"Bud, I need someone at the Seasons Hotel before eight o'clock this morning. It's three now. You've gotta have someone…"

"Okay, I'm thinkin' here, all right? I got a guy in Mumbai covering the bus bombing. Maybe I can call our charter service and get a plane fired up in an hour or so. Can't promise, though. Our guy might be out on a drunk, for all I know."

"You'll do it, Bud, you always do. I'll be in the lobby. That's the Seasons in Delhi… got it?"

"Your son with you?" Bud asks.

"Yeah, he's right here."

"Hell of a thing, Char, bringin' your kid with you. We don't pay extra for interns, you know."

"Wouldn't expect it, Bud. Just get me a camera."

Charlotte puts down the phone and looks at Greg. "So what're we gonna find at the hotel, big guy?"

Greg ignores the question. He's already a few steps down a different road. "You set the alarm for six-thirty," he says, "so I guess we were going to meet someone at about eight. The man grandma said would help us?"

It's Charlotte's turn to ignore the question.

Greg continues. "So now we'll miss hooking up with that guy. Was he expecting us?"

Charlotte uncaps a bottle of water and takes a swig. "Certainly not," she replies.

"You have his phone number?"

"As far as I know, he doesn't have a phone."

"So you were going to surprise him?"

"Oh yeah," Charlotte says with a roll of her eyes. "BIG surprise too. In my trade, we call it 'ambush journalism.'"

"How're we gonna help grandma if we lose this guy?"

60

"I'm hoping he'll be at the same place this evening."

Greg has suddenly left the conversation. His eyes are blank now, as if he has entered a different world. Charlotte walks to the bed and sits down next to him, offers him the water bottle. He seems unaware of her presence. She reaches out and touches his hand, but he does not respond. He is somewhere else, but he has left his body behind.

Charlotte takes another long sip of water and curls up next to her son, who doesn't seem to mind, absent as he is from her world. It's not easy being the mother of a special child like Greg. These fleeting moments of conversation are the most intimate experiences in their relationship. Between his Asperger's detachment and her abandonments of family for the sake of career, she hasn't been much of a mother. These few minutes of calm before another storm are precious.

The phone jolts Charlotte awake. *Had she really fallen asleep again?* She sits up, trying to clear her head, then marches toward the phone.

"How did he know your phone number?" Greg asks before she can pick up the call. The boy is referring to the man with the chocolaty voice, and the question unnerves her. She had not stopped to wonder.

"I don't know, sweetheart." She lifts up the phone.

"He knows that you called Bud," the boy says as Charlotte pushes the Talk button.

"Bud, is that you?" Charlotte asks hopefully.

"Strange thing," Bud says. "I called the air charter service, and they already had a plane standing by, just waiting for my instructions. So tell me Char, how the hell—?"

Chapter 16

Antonio Fortunati orders a bottle of wine from the cabin attendant. It's just past midnight in Rome, and Fortunati is travelling on a one-way ticket to New Delhi. He had seen no need for a return trip; he will never be able to return to the Vatican. In fact, he may have to disappear entirely to evade the Vatican agents that surely will be chasing him after news of his treachery reaches the Secretary of State.

The wine arrives. He shifts the frail husk of his body to better grip the cap but has trouble unscrewing it. His weakness makes him feel vulnerable.

Finally he succeeds. He sips the wine and nervously studies the faces of the nearby passengers. Any one of them could be a Vatican spy. It is not inconceivable that his secret collection of papers and relics, plucked from the archives over so many years, had been discovered by someone else earlier and that he was perhaps not escaping the Vatican but leading its agents to his most trusted associate.

More than fear, he sags under the weight of sadness. For decades he has been whipsawed by angels and martyrs on one side, politicians and torturers on the other. It was not always so for Antonio. As a child he had visions of Mother Mary and knew he was specially ordained for spiritual greatness, yet his unassuming nature had prevented him from telling anyone. He never would have let his relationship with the Holy Mother become the kind of tumultuous paparazzi show that other visionaries had unwittingly unleashed.

After seminary, as a young priest in Rome, he was selected as a Vatican librarian because he possessed the gene of orderliness. With misty eyes, he recalls his many prayers of thanksgiving to the Virgin, for surely she had intervened on his behalf for this most perfect calling. Ah, to be a caretaker of the church's most precious traditions, to be immersed in the glorious history of Saints. But the bibliographic riches slowly began to reveal their dark side as Antonio learned the archaic languages and deciphered the pale ink scribblings that had become his life. Drawn into the vibrant stories told by these brittle pages and scrolls, he began to experience a perverse and profane past of petty politics, obsession with property and wealth, papal indiscretion, torture and execution in the name of God. Only through the grace of the Holy Mother was he able to maintain his devotion.

And then, six years after he was named prefect of the Secret Archives, he discovered a document that served as the key to the covert researches of his next twenty-five years. The key had opened a line of inquiry that eventually would destroy his faith and prompt him to plan an act of treachery that could tear apart the church and all the rest of Christianity if the facts could be proved.

When he prayed to the Holy Mother to show him that he was wrong, she remained silent. When he asked for guidance from her, she placed still more evidence in his path. In a dream just last week, he saw the Virgin's face and she was crying—weeping, he was sure, for the sins of the church committed in the name of her Son, and the grievances of the innocent who had been punished instead of praised, and the poor whose pennies had enriched the church rather than feeding their starving families.

And he knew then that he must smuggle the evidence out of the archives and betray the church—which he now believes is the antichrist, if such an entity even exists outside the false mythology of Catholicism. He must do this single heroic act so that the true religion of Christ, which has become so corrupted, could rise again from the ashes of the engulfing flames. This would be the true resurrection!

Antonio Fortunati sips the last of his wine.

And he prays that the Holy Mother will stop crying and smile upon him.

Chapter 17

Gideon sits patiently in the lobby of the Seasons Hotel and checks his watch: seven-thirty. He's sure that Charlotte will arrive as he had instructed at eight o'clock sharp. She's a news whore and wouldn't miss an opportunity for a story.

Instinctively, he studies the opulent lobby, memorizing every door, window, and all possible exits. He scrutinizes each person seated on the overstuffed sofas and chairs, every individual that enters the space, all the employees who buzz past. He looks for furtive glances in his direction, telltale bulges beneath suit coats, nervous fingers, CIA haircuts, Mossad arrogance. He knows the usual signs of peril.

He looks down at his bent knees and notices that his right leg is bouncing up and down like a piston. A nervous tic. He slowly sets the heel of his right foot on the floor and imagines it stuck there, unable to move.

Damn! He has worked so hard on his impatience. One small giveaway like this can call attention to him. The goal is to melt into the environment and give no observer a reason to remember him, no adversary a clue to his presence. It's possible that someone in this very room could be studying its occupants just as he had been doing, searching for the same revealing hints. It is not easy for a man of action to sit quietly; such men almost always give themselves away.

Gideon is startled out of self-appraisal. Into the marble lobby march Charlotte Ansari and her son. But no cameraman. Gideon sifts through several potential scenarios for their early arrival and settles on the most logical one—Charlotte suffers from the same plague of impatience as Gideon. She has arrived early because she can't bear to wait any longer. She plans to meet the cameraman here in the lobby and then converge on Iggers' room at eight sharp.

Yes, he is correct. Mother and son are taking a seat in adjoining chairs about ten paces from Gideon. Charlotte does not have the searching eye of the professional assassin. Instead, her eyes continually turn toward the entrance through which the cameraman will soon enter the hotel.

It's too risky to remain in the lobby, and although he'd prefer another five or ten minutes before initiating his mission, Gideon decides to start now. He reaches for a scuffed brief case and stands, straightening his businessman's suit coat before walking slowly toward the elevators. In a few minutes his morning assignment will be over.

He glances at Charlotte as he moves across the lobby. She pays no attention to him, but the son, Greg, is looking straight at him. Watching him. What could have attracted the boy's attention? Gideon ticks off the possibilities. Gideon is one of a handful of westerners present in the lobby, so the boy may be simply drawn to someone who could be an American. Or perhaps Gideon had stood up too soon after Charlotte and Greg arrived, arousing suspicion. Of course, it could just be the casual glance of a bored youth. Or maybe Greg has some kind of unusual power of observation.

Gideon doesn't want to look back to see if the boy is still watching him. Eye contact, no matter how brief, has an almost magical power to link two people together. Gideon doesn't want that. Not yet.

He reaches the elevators and pushes the UP button. An elevator door opens. He enters and pushes the button for the sixth floor, stealing a glance at Greg as the doors close.

Eye contact.

How astonishing, Gideon thinks, that a boy can so unnerve a professional assassin. It is not that he fears the boy. It's that something in Gideon's appearance or behavior has made him worthy of scrutiny. If the boy detected something, then a dangerous adversary might notice it also.

He gets off and finds room 615. The corridor is vacant. He knocks on the door and hears a faint "What is it?"

In a practiced Indian accent, Gideon says, "Gift basket, sir, from the management."

"All right, I'll be right there!"

He hears a TV in the background—the voice of Tom McKestle of CCN International News. A toilet flushes. There is some scuffling noise like the pulling on of trousers.

Gideon checks the hallway again. Still vacant. He watches the edge of the door. As soon as it cracks open, he puts his weight into it, crashing into the room and knocking Iggers off his feet. Quickly he closes the door.

"Sorry, we're out of welcome baskets."

Iggers grunts, then scrambles across the floor to a desk and opens a drawer, reaching for a pistol. But Gideon kicks the drawer closed on Iggers's hand.

Iggers yelps in pain and manages to extract his bleeding hand. He stands and faces Gideon. As a field agent for over ten years, Grant Iggers is an expert fighter, but he's no match for Gideon. He swings his right fist and Gideon captures his arm in mid-air, deftly cradles it in the crook of his own arm, and twists ever so slight. The overextended elbow tears apart and Iggers cries out in agony, dropping to the floor.

Gideon grabs Iggers by his hair and stands him up, then shoves him into the desk chair.

"Jesus, it hurts!" Iggers says.

"Brought it on yourself, my friend."

Gideon casually opens his brief case and removes a roll of duct tape. With a sticky crackle, he pulls off a few meters of gray tape and binds Iggers to the chair.

Iggers still grimaces in pain, but he looks up at Gideon and grunts. "Gonna kill me?"

"Actually, that's up to you."

"You sound American. Who're you with?"

Gideon bends over and whispers in Iggers's ear.

Iggers nods. "Thought so," he says. "You work for us, dammit!"

"Piece work. Last contract's over. This is a whole different deal and you got in our way. It didn't have to be that way, Grant, but apparently someone thought you didn't need us this time. Anyway, no hard feelings I hope."

"We pay you guys a shitload of money," Iggers says, then grits his teeth as another surge of pain assaults him.

"And we never fail, do we? Worth every penny."

"Kill me and you'll never work for the Agency again!"

"Oh, I doubt that. Sorry to dash your self-esteem, but frankly, Grant, no one really cares about your wish list."

Gideon has been fussing with something behind Grant's back. Now he comes around and faces Iggers directly. He starts to write the number "40" on the man's forehead with a marking pen.

"Now I want you to listen very carefully, Grant. At eight o'clock, you will have a nice, calm interview with Charlotte Ansari. I believe you've already met. She will ask you questions, and you will answer honestly. If you do not cooperate…"

Gideon is holding a joke baseball cap with CIA emblazoned on the crown. The cap also has a fake Budweiser beer can on each side with tubes leading from the cans to the mouth area.

"…I will know immediately, because this cap has a microphone in it. I can hear everything."

Gideon sets the cap on Grant's head.

"Oh, one other thing. The beer cans have radio-detonation explosives in them. Kind of like IEDs in Iraq, but much more discriminating. If you're a bad boy, I just push a little button and your head goes… well, remember that guy in the movie *Scanners*? David Cronenberg directed, right? Always liked that flick. Anyway, it would be unwise to mention this to Charlotte."

Grant is greasy with sweat. His eyes are puckered with pain and fear. "You're a sick son of a bitch," he says. "I don't know much to tell her."

"Sure. The director of ops for the CIA gets put in the field but isn't told why. Tell that to Charlotte and we'll have a real Scanners moment."

Gideon hangs a handwritten sign around Grant's neck. It reads: *Stay far away.* He pulls a small device out of his pocket—it looks like an iPod—and shows it to Grant. "Remember, I just have to push this button." He twists ear buds into his ear canals and plugs the cord into the device. "Say something nice."

"When we find you, we'll cut your heart out."

"Loud and clear. Time to go."

But before Gideon can turn, he feels a cold metal rod pushing into his neck. A gun. How could he be so stupid? Grant was not alone. An accomplice must have been in the adjoining room.

A voice says, "Very slowly now, step over to the window."

"Whatever you say." Gideon says, gliding a few steps to the side of the room. He can now see the accomplice, a stocky young man with blue eyes and pink cheeks. He could be the manager of a McDonald's in Kansas."

"Marty, either kill him now or get this hat off me," Iggers demands.

Marty edges closer to Grant, keeping the gun pointed steadily at Gideon. "I can't believe this stupid cap is a bomb. He's made an ass of you, Grant." He reaches for the cap and Gideon pushes the button.

The small explosion is not loud, but it's messy. Small pieces of Grant's head spatter onto the walls and ceiling. Marty's hand disintegrates, his arm splinters, and the concussion knocks him backward. Barely alive, Marty looks up at Gideon, who is spattered with blood.

"Can't you read?" Gideon says. "The sign said *stay far away*."

Marty's eyes go glassy and still. Gideon searches through the young man's pockets and finds a wad of Indian rupees. He puts the money on the desk. "A tip for housekeeping," he mutters to himself. "They're gonna earn it today."

Gideon's watch shows just ten minutes until eight o'clock. Now that the original plan has literally blown up, Gideon ponders his next move. He takes the marking pen from his pocket, writes on Marty's blood-splashed forehead, and then reopens his brief case, finding a small Bible. He opens the holy book, manages to place a smear of Grant's blood on several pages, and places the Bible on the desk.

Calmly, Gideon looks at the carcass that was once Grant Iggers and decides that he and Grant are about the same size. He walks to the closet and finds a second suit and then retrieves a fresh shirt from a dresser drawer. He quickly washes up in the bathroom, changes into Grant's clothes, packs up the brief case and exits the room, leaving the door slightly ajar.

What a disaster, he thinks. His rating is sure to tumble.

Chapter 18

Charlotte is nervous. It's a few minutes before eight and no cameraman has appeared. She picks up her phone and starts to call the home office, but before she can press the speed dial button a man wearing a safari vest and trailing several metal Anvil cases pushes through the lobby entrance, spotting Charlotte immediately.

"Char, over here!"

Charlotte turns to see the man. "Curt! I'll be damned." She races over to him. "Haven't seen you since Iraq."

"Yeah, like a few days ago. I was just over in Mumbai, so what's up in this neighborhood?"

Charlotte looks at her watch. "Haven't got time to explain right now. Just get ready for an on-camera interview. Camera and sound, available light. We've got like three minutes to get to the sixth floor."

"You were never much for foreplay, my dear."

Curt drops his bags, unzips a carry-on and pulls out a small video camera. "Already locked and loaded," he says. "Was a long cab ride here."

Charlotte orders a bellman to check Curt's bags and turns to Greg, who is stoically watching the action.

"Greg, c'mon. We're going up."

She glances at Curt and explains, "Can't leave him down here alone."

"Well, an interview doesn't seem too dangerous," Curt says. "Also doesn't seem so urgent a man has to lose a night's sleep to get it."

"I'll explain after, I promise. Let's just get up there. And if you don't mind, shoot everything. Tape's cheap."

"You mean, like now? Going up?"

"Just turn the damn thing on and keep it rolling. I don't really know what's going to happen here, but I don't want to miss it." The threesome starts to move toward the elevators.

Curt turns on the camera as they reach the elevators. Charlotte pushes the UP button and they wait. And wait some more. Finally, bells chime and two elevators open. They step in and Charlotte selects the sixth floor.

"You look nervous, kiddo," Curt says to Charlotte.

"Just keep the goddam camera running."

The elevator stops with a jerk and they get out. A businessman is walking down the corridor toward them. Curt stays on the elevator and courteously holds the door for the man.

"Thanks," the man says. "They're running slow today."

Greg turns to catch a glimpse of the man before the doors slide shut. He recognizes the man from the lobby.

Charlotte leads them to room 615. As promised, the door is unlocked and cracked open. Her heart is pounding and her predatory instincts are humming at high velocity. It's time for the media to uncloak Mr. Grant Iggers and dig out whatever story her informant has led her to. She suspects it concerns her mother, All things lately have seemed to orbit around the mysterious Miriam Walker.

Charlotte readies her handheld microphone, pushes Greg to the rear, and grabs Curt by the arm, positioning him directly behind her. Instinctively, Greg reaches into hs pocket and pulls out his digital camera.

And then Charlotte pushes open the door.

Like a fist in the face, the stench of death and the splatter of blood and gore stuns her. She has seen her share of horror in Africa and Lebanon and Iraq, but in this five-star hotel, she was not prepared for a room embroidered in brains and blood. Satan's fascinating art.

With a sharp whistle, Curt pushes past her. The camera has no conscience, no modesty, no etiquette. Curt begins to talk, a nervous mannerism that surfaces during stress. His words sandpaper the horror and fill in the dark empty spaces of the imagination.

"I'd say your interview subject—" Curt now sees a second body— "*subjects*, that is, won't be talking after all."

The second body has no head. The shoulders are mostly gone. A colorful spray of flesh and bone and brain, like rays of a crimson sun, emanates from the space where the headless man sat. Charlotte is both mesmerized and repulsed by the gruesome chaos.

Curt is focusing his lens on the spattered face of the man with one arm. "Char, give a gander. There's a number written on this guy's forehead."

Charlotte comes close, stares at the face. In black marker, the number "40" is scrawled above the man's cold, staring eyes.

"I think we should get out of here," Curt says. "There's gonna be a lot of questions when the police arrive, and I haven't got a single answer."

Charlotte turns around to find Greg standing by the desk. She had forgotten the boy and knows she never should have let him see such a horrifying scene. What a rotten mother she is!

"Greg!" she shouts. "Out." Charlotte grabs Curt by the arm and yanks.

"I don't need encouragement to leave, darlin'!" Curt replies.

They slip out of the room. An elderly lady has just passed their door on the way to the elevator. Charlotte shushes Curt and Greg, quietly closes the door behind, and gestures for them to walk slowly and naturally.

They enter the elevator with the gray-haired American woman, who greets them with a smiling "Beautiful day today. Say, aren't you that woman from TV?"

"I get that all the time," Charlotte says while Curt hides the camera behind his back. "Afraid not."

The woman looks down at Greg, then at the small black object in his hands, and says, "Isn't that sweet? I love seeing a Bible in a Hindu country like this. Carry it proudly, my son."

The elevator spills its occupants into the lobby. Charlotte steers her son to a sofa and sets him down. Curt takes a seat next to them.

"All right, young man," Charlotte says sternly but quietly, "I hope you know that you have violated a lot of laws, even here in India. That Bible is evidence from a murder scene—and if they catch us with it..."

"Settle down, Char, " Curt says. "I'm sure the boy had a reason to take it." He packs the camera into its case. "Anyway, we can't put it back." He gestures toward four Indian police who are entering the lobby. "We'd better get out of here."

"Okay, we'll grab a taxi and drop you at your hotel to check in. I need you to start cutting a two-minute piece out of the footage you got. I'll add narration and a stand-up later."

They begin walking out of the lobby as nonchalantly as possible.

"You're gonna do this story? It'll be like confessing to the world that we were there before the authorities. I smell trouble."

"It's our job, Curt, and this is a helluva scoop." She mimics a likely breaking news story—"This just in—CIA operations director gets blown up in India. Let's go now to Charlotte Ansari…"

"—and Curt Branson—" Curt adds…

"—in New Delhi." Charlotte looks at Curt. "Listen, Greg and I have something else to do while you start working, so we'll meet you at your room when we're done."

"You're the boss, but this is crazy."

"Duly noted. Take this with you."

She takes the Bible from Greg and hands it to Curt, who slips it into a case. They climb into a taxi.

Gideon is the only one watching.

Chapter 19

After a harrowing ride through congested streets, the taxi drops Charlotte and Greg at the "Budha Commemorative Park," a quiet, bird-filled space of stone-lined canals and lush greenery. From the parking lot, Charlotte leads Greg down a walkway toward a glistening golden statue of the Buddha.

Greg follows silently. He watches two Indian women reverently bow in the direction of the Buddha and mimics their movements. Something about this subtle act of veneration calms him. He stares at the blank eyes of the statue and wonders how such a manmade object could have become imbued with God, or some part of Him. In the end, he decides that an idol cannot be God, but only a reminder of His attributes, in this case serenity, judging from the placid pose and expression of the Buddha. Greg stands perfectly still before the statue and closes his eyes, feels a tranquil breeze waft over him like the breath of God, and wonders again…

"Greg!" His tranquility is shattered by the shrill call of his mother, who stands twenty paces ahead of him. "Keep up, fella."

Charlotte calls to Greg but her eyes are searching for something, someone. Greg approaches her as she turns and takes the left fork of a path. They continue to walk, crossing a deep canal by treading on a series of small concrete circles that seem to float on the watery surface, and then meandering up a hillside.

At the crest of the hill, Charlotte bends her knees and leans against a thick tree. "I think we may have missed him," she says. "Got here too late."

Greg sits and crosses his legs. He knows that his mother is talking about the man they came to recruit. Surveying the terrain, Greg notices a tall, well-built man slowly moving across a wide expanse of grass about fifty yards away. The man has a suit coat slung over his shoulder, making him look out-of-place among the joggers and yoga practitioners who dot the landscape. Greg recognizes this man—the man from the hotel lobby, the man from the sixth floor.

"Mother, he's here," Greg says quietly.

"Yes, I see him now," Charlotte replies, but her eyes are looking in another direction. "He's here. I *knew* it."

Greg follows his mother's line of sight to someone else, an elderly man with flowing silver hair. This man is practicing tai chi and his movements flow beautifully from one pose to another, a ballet of perfect balance and astonishing agility. Though the man's skin is bronzed by the sun, he appears to be Caucasian. Charlotte watches the man for several minutes. The exquisite skill with which he renders each move produces a kind of performance art. At last she stands and reaches for Greg's hand.

"Time to make our presence known," she says.

As she leads Greg down the hill toward the old man with the silver hair, Greg is thinking, *Our presence is already known... to the man from the lobby.*

Quietly Charlotte approaches the old man from behind. When she and Greg are several paces away, the man stops his routine. Without turning, he says, "Good morning, Charlotte."

"Good morning, Father," Charlotte replies.

The old man turns now. His skin is crinkly, like thin parchment, and his muscles are sinewy but taut. As he looks at Greg, his eyes smile and he says, "This must be Greg. Good morning, Grandson."

Greg stares at the old man but does not utter a word.

"He doesn't always respond," Charlotte says. "It's rare when he speaks to a stranger. In fact, to anyone."

"A man of few words," Thompson Walker says, still smiling at the boy. "The wisest men always seem to have the least to say, perhaps because they know how few things are worth saying."

"Greg, meet Grandpa Walker."

Greg steps forward and puts out his hand. Thompson takes it and the boy shakes hands deliberately. "Pleased to make your acquaintance, sir."

Thompson glances at Charlotte, who appears moderately surprised at her son's outgoing gesture.

"Thank you, Charlotte, for introducing me to my grandson," Thompson says to Charlotte. "I wasn't sure I'd ever see this day."

"If it had been up to me..." Charlotte says. Bitterness has crept into her voice.

"So what *compels* you, then, to this act of mercy, if not your naturally forgiving nature?" There is more than a hint of sarcasm in Thompson's reply. "And how did you find me?"

"I knew you were in Delhi from your last letter."

"So you read my letters? I always hoped."

"No, I don't. Well, yes—the last one. You mentioned a park and the Golden Buddha and your daily routine. Wasn't hard to find this place. I'm an investigative journalist after all."

"So my predictable nature led you here."

"You were always predictable, Dad. Unfortunately. But I didn't come here for a family reunion."

"Didn't think so. You must need my help in something, I'd guess."

Charlotte doesn't answer. She just stands there and stares at her father, and the longer she stares, the angrier she gets that she has no choice but to seek her father's help.

In the silence, Thompson senses her gathering rage. "Maybe this is enough for one day," he suggests, hoping to defuse the bomb. "I'll be here tomorrow morning if you feel like talking more."

"I got an e-mail from Grandma Walker," Greg blurts out. "She's in trouble and needs our help."

This bald statement changes everything. Thompson turns to Charlotte, who sighs deeply, venting the steam of her anger.

"Miriam contacted Greg?" Thompson asks Charlotte.

"You'd better sit down, Dad. We don't know much, but let me lay it out."

From behind a stone wall, Gideon watches three generations of Walkers seated beneath a large mulberry tree. Charlotte, the consummate on-camera reporter, stabs the air with her hands and stirs the atmosphere as she narrates a story that has captured the attention of the silver-haired man. Greg stares at the dirt as if a suddenly discovered ant mound is infinitely more interesting than revisiting his mother's tale.

Gideon's cell phone vibrates. He knows it is Eve and dreads having to confess the messiness of the morning's confrontation. He presses the TALK button, swallows hard, and says, "Gideon."

"How is the holy family?" Eve asks.

"Father, daughter and grandson are under direct observation as we speak. The trinity has been established."

"And was the news transmitted to them this morning as planned?"

"Transmitted, yes, but not as planned. An unexpected event led to the need to dispatch the informant and accomplice to the netherworld."

"Accomplice?" A pause. "Dispatched dry or wet?"

"Wet... *very*."

"Your job is to anticipate, Gideon. I'm disappointed. Do you need to come in?"

"Negative."

"There'll be hurt feelings in Washington. They don't like losing family."

"I apologize."

"Never mind, I'll take care of it. I'm more concerned about the number of interested parties. Our source inside the Vatican informs us that the prefect of the Secret Archives is AWOL. Vatican agents are looking for him already, so it's possible he has something we all want."

"The Secret Archives is a bunker. We were hoping the evidence was there, weren't we? The Church has every reason to keep it hidden forever."

"But if Fortunati has removed something incriminating, he may be planning to disclose it. At best, the evidence is no longer under the protection of the Archives. The prefect is either a traitor or an idiot—not much difference at this point. If you cross paths, you have permission to terminate if necessary."

"Understood. Anything else?"

"You were trained to anticipate, Gideon. I repeat—do you need to come in?"

"No. It won't happen again."

"Godspeed."

The line clicks and goes dead. Gideon glances at the 'holy family.' The three begin to walk toward a pathway. The old man walks beside Greg, an arm wrapped snugly around the boy. Charlotte trails them by a few paces as she punches a number into her cell phone.

Mike Ansari lies in his Minnesota bed, propped up by large pillows. On TV, a televangelist exhorts him, along with a sanctuary filled with believers, to stand up to the "Islamo-Fascists who threaten our lives, our children, our religion." Pastor John Crate is the founder and president of Millennium Broadcasting Network, a worldwide evangelical outreach with over six hundred affiliates.

Crate's jowls tremble like pudding as he shouts, and his round, cherubic face darkens as he exhorts, "It's in the Bible. Judgment will befall nations and individuals according to how they bless Israel. Genesis 12:3 says 'I will bless those who bless you and curse those who curse you.' And we, my dear brothers and sisters in the Lord, are the agents of God's judgment."

Mike nods in agreement. He feels buoyed by the *amens* and *hallelujahs* of the TV audience.

"God's covenant with Israel is eternal!" Crate shouts, and then takes a deep, wheezing breath, the practiced punctuation of the professional revivalist. "It is exclusive! It will never be revoked! And when the Islamo-Fascists and all the other enemies of God's covenant have been put in their place—and by that I mean *hell!*—then Jesus at last shall come again and restore Israel to her rightful place as the instrument of God on earth!"

"Amen," Mike says just before the phone rings. He mutes the TV and picks up, saying, "Mike Ansari."

"Mike, it's Charlotte."

"Char—thank God. Are you all right?"

"Fine, fine. Bit of a complication this morning—you'll see it on CCN shortly. But we're fine, Greg and me."

"You sound—strange."

"Lot on my mind. I'm with Dad and Greg right now."

"So how is the old guy?"

"Pisses me off as always. He pours on the charm and the 'ancient wisdom of the ages' thing, and makes it practically impossible to stay mad at him. Which really makes me mad when I think about it."

"So what'd he say about the Miriam thing?"

"I told him everything we know, and he said he'd help. I just don't know where to start. Anyway, Curt's in Delhi and I'm going back to finish a piece on an incident that happened here, and then I don't know what."

"I didn't know you were working on this trip."

"Reporters, like cops, are never really off duty. Gotta go."

The line goes dead and Mike says, "Love you too."

He unmutes the TV audio and Pastor Craft continues his rant: "The enemies of Israel are the enemies of America. These enemies seek to destroy life, liberty and the pursuit of happiness. They have drawn the battle line. And I say that we must draw that line around both Christians and Jews... for we are one, united under the covenant of God."

In Georgetown, Virginia, CIA Director William Wyatt is in bed with his wife of eighteen years, Betty. He sips a cup of herbal tea to settle his stomach while watching Pastor Crate on television. Betty munches popcorn.

"When Jesus returns for his millennial reign" Crate bellows, "He's not going to ask the ACLU if it's okay to pray in school. He's not going to ask the churches if they can ordain pedophile priests. He won't endorse abortion or seek permission to put the Ten Commandments in our statehouses. He's going to govern the world by the Word of God. The world will never end, you see. Under Christ's rule, it will become a Garden of Eden!"

The doorbell rings.

"What on earth...? Who could it be at this time of night?" Wyatt mutters as he steps out of bed and wraps himself in a robe.

The doorbell insistently chimes as Wyatt descends a spiral staircase and approaches the door, opening it with a grunt to reveal a dark-skinned man in a cream turban.

"Package for Mr. William Wyatt," the man says, then turns and walks back to a taxi with the driver's door still open.

Wyatt fondles the small package, a fat brown envelope. He closes the door and opens it, finding a stack of thousand-dollar bills. There must be a hundred of them. A taxi driver has just dropped off a hundred thousand dollars.

The phone rings. Wyatt walks to a telephone in the front room and picks up. "Yes, hello."

"Hello, William." The caller is a woman. "You just received a package. Please see to it that the widows of Grant Iggers and his associate receive the contents with your apology. There was no need for this to happen, William. We liked Grant—until you put us on opposite sides. Good night."

The line goes dead.

The *widow* of Grant Iggers? Oh, shit.

Wyatt starts to dial CIA headquarters, but then hangs up. He knows there is no sense in trying to trace the call or find the taxi driver.

They never leave loose ends.

Chapter 20

Gideon stands in the lobby of a small hotel. Through a large window overlooking the street, he stares at the Hotel Indraprastha, the temporary location of Charlotte Ansari and her family. Gideon concludes that the threesome has gone there to meet with the Aussie photographer. It probably will be a long wait.

He opens a satchel and removes a small box-like device that could be a handheld computer game. A tap of the power button illuminates the screen and within seconds a faint grid appears, then a series of gently curving lines at last identified by street names. On this map, a red dot pulses marking the location of the Indraprastha. Gideon smiles; his target is still inside.

Through the curling steam of his tea, Gideon watches the street teeming with small honking automobiles, countless motor scooters burdened by two or three hulking bodies dangling shopping bags, weathered beggars holding up near-dead infants to prick the guilty consciences of tourists, a bored policeman yawning in the heat, donkeys pulling carts of dead flowers and rotting fruit.

A flash of white suddenly floods him with emotion. A bearded man, obviously a Sikh, navigates through the jumble of traffic wearing a traditional kurta pyjama—a loose-fitting, white cotton garment—and a soiled white turban with a blunt, rounded apex at the front. On his left wrist is a steel bracelet called a Kara, one of the five Ks—or sacred symbols—that distinguish a Sikh.

The gleaming white apparition reminds Gideon of the first time he witnessed a gathering of other men in white, also distinguished from all others—the Great White Brotherhood, each member clothed in a seamless flowing wrap of spotless white from which the order took its name. Until then, since his recruitment three years earlier, Gideon and the other recruits had worn only gray shirts and gray pants, the uniform of a janitor or security guard. But finally, at a special ceremony in a Tibetan gompa, Gideon and his eleven fellow trainees, the remnant of over eighty candidates, were escorted from a great stone hall onto an ancient terrace that was visually overwhelmed by the geological siege of the mountains. Greeting them in the buttery sunlight were forty angels in flowing white with smiles that warmed the mountain chill and embraced them like a father's welcome home.

Gideon's training-hardened body had softened and tears had streamed down his face. The dazzling chorus of white nearly blinded him. and for a moment. he thought he might have died unknowingly and gone to heaven.

There had been times during his training that the long days and longer nights seemed like a descent into hell. The physical part had been much tougher than his special forces training, which had broken many men, and the mental training had stretched the outer limits of consciousness and fear.

For three years he had trained seven days a week, fourteen hours each day. He had been tutored in the art of jujutsu, a deadly skill that required no weapons, only contact with one's adversary. If an enemy, armed or not, were foolish enough to come within reach of a jujutsu master, the battle was over. In less than two seconds, Gideon could disarm anyone threatening him with a gun, a knife, even superior strength, and totally disable his attacker by focusing on the many weak points of the human body—the ankles and knees, the shoulders and elbows, the neck and eyes, the bridge of the nose, the ears. Once in Gideon's grasp, an attacker—even one trained in other martial arts— was totally at the mercy of his prey because the jujutsu master could deliver a fatal move at almost any time with astonishingly little exertion.

Jujutsu instruction had been teamed with another ancient discipline, ninjutsu, the black art of the ninjas. This was a system of controlled body movement, deadly striking maneuvers, and weapons throwing skills that Gideon at first believed he would never master. The most difficult of these skills was the ability to move with the balance of a cat, which is to maintain perfect control of one's body at every moment. By the third year, Gideon had been able to climb a tower comprised of three wobbling wooden pedestals without the aid of his hands and then leap from one unsteady tower to another without crashing or falling. While climbing, he could feel the exhilaration of weightlessness and total command of his body, and when jumping fifteen feet to the ground, he could feel the time-stretched sensation of floating, not falling, and was able to land without trauma or sound.

The final layer of his physical training was the art of knifecraft. The favored weapon of the Brotherhood was a small curved dagger. Wielded with a practiced hand and a deep knowledge of human physiology, the dagger was not only deadly but silent. A target could be killed in the middle of a crowd with little mess because a knife thrust between the proper ribs, twisted just so, would produce mostly internal bleeding. Few targets would even utter a sound, occupying themselves with a search for some more innocuous cause of the vague pain—perhaps pleurisy, a heart attack, or even heartburn. Once the victim collapsed, or was helped to a chair, he would be seconds from death, and many targets died sitting up with their eyes open. By this time, of course, the assassin would be long gone.

The unusual mental training centered on the use of meditation to calm the wildfire of one's mind and allow the Brother to see situations, even stressful ones, with less emotion and greater clarity. For hours each day, the recruits would practice mental discipline to block the experience of pain and transform it into energy; to focus one's mind so that no distraction was possible; to imagine one's own death each evening so vividly that familiarity with death conquered any fear of it. In some rare cases, it was reported that a recruit would be able to stop his heartbeat for many minutes without consequence, or even levitate his body.

At that precise transitional moment on the Tibetan terrace, in the giddy high altitude, with cool breezes wafting over his naked body now stripped of the funereal gray gauze of his old life and awaiting the white robe of purity, Gideon had been transfigured emotionally, spiritually, mystically. He had ascended to a new level, a deeper insight, a more profound understanding of his role in the ancient unfolding plan. He had been resurrected from the grave to appear before the face of God revealed in the boundless sky and thrusting mountains.

Gideon had attained unto the station of God's avenging angels.

Chapter 21

Charlotte looks at Curt hunched over his notebook computer and says, "Any chance we'll make the deadline?"

Curt grunts and nudges his mouse, urging a video clip into a new position on the editing timeline. Thompson, Greg and Charlotte crowd behind him for a look at the monitor.

"Look, guys," Curt says finally, "I need some space. Charlotte, move over to the wall where I've set up the lights."

Charlotte walks across the small Indraprastha bedroom and begins to rehearse her lines. Thompson and Greg sit down on the rumpled bed.

Curt stands up suddenly, looks at his watch and says. "Okay, we've got fifteen minutes to get this baby to Cambridge, including the video upload." He races to the camera, which is on a tripod facing Charlotte, and turns on the two lights. "Not too bad," he babbles, "no time for tweaking." He presses a button on the camera. A red light turns on. "It's now or never, sweetheart. I need forty-five seconds of brilliant prose. Go!"

Charlotte, who has been studying her clasped hands, looks up at the camera and begins to speak. Her practiced voice is smooth and professional. She gives a dramatic pause here and there, underscores a thought with an almost imperceptible rise in tone, and in forty-five seconds summarizes the carnage they had found in the room of Grant Iggers.

She concludes with these words: "At the time of his murder, Mr. Iggers was serving as director of operations for the CIA. It is not known at this time what he was doing in New Delhi and whether this was a terrorist attack or something else. As we get more information we will pass it on to you. Donald?"

Curt switches off the camera, removes the memory card, and races back to his computer.

Thompson stares at Charlotte, who is turning off the lights. "So who is Donald?" he asks. "I don't see a Donald in the room."

Charlotte answers matter-of-factly, "Donald Kemp, the CCN anchor this time of day. That's my hand-off to him. Everyone will think that we're

83

having a live conversation. That's how it works. Little lies to get at the truth. How's it going, Curt?"

"I've got the footage into the system. Just have to open up your narration a bit and slide it around. Hush up now so I can finish."

Thompson is still silently staring at Charlotte.

"What?" she asks her father.

"Is it a good idea to expose a CIA guy like that? I remember a flap over a covert agent named Valerie Plame. Maybe this Iggers guy was on a mission or something. Maybe they don't want the world to know he was even here."

"Of course he was on a mission." Charlotte gives her father a sour look. "_We_ were his mission. And I'm not exposing him if he's already dead. You know what? If they're gonna mess with me, it's gonna be in public."

"Wow," Thompson says. "The investigative reporter takes on the world."

Charlotte sighs, and then her face turns red. "This is what I do. What're _they_ gonna do—audit my taxes? Let 'em. I'm within my journalistic rights here. We're in India, not the US. This is a big story. Now it's a CCN exclusive."

"I was just thinking they might do more than audit your taxes."

Curt turns angrily, "Will you guys shut up? I've got less than five minutes to finish this edit and start the upload or we'll miss the broadcast window. Charlotte, call it in."

"Already did," Charlotte replies. "They're expecting it."

For five minutes the room is silent as Curt finishes editing and compresses the piece into compressed Quicktime format. At last he loads his web browser, logs into an encrypted CCN portal and launches the upload.

"On its way!" he proudly announces. "Want to see it?"

Charlotte glances at Greg, who has found the remote control and has powered on the TV. "Not right now," she says. "I don't think we have to relive that bloody scene."

"Fine, but I have something you _will_ want to see. Come over here."

Charlotte and Thompson stand behind Curt as he searches a computer folder for a file.

"All right, here it is. Remember back in Baghdad, after our rescue, when they sent us through interrogation? Really rude, weren't they?"

"To say the least," Charlotte interjects. "They accused me of hiding a video. Wouldn't believe that I knew nothing about it. Those guys were creepy."

"You said it," Curt replies. "Thought I was on my way to Guantanamo. Now here's what I wanted to show you. It's the video they were looking for."

"What?" Charlotte grabs the back of Curt's swivel chair and spins him around. "You had the video?"

"Of course. I shot it."

"But they searched us. Inside and out."

"Yeah, well… I hid the tape in the latrine before they had a chance to find it. Retrieved it right before I left Baghdad."

Curt clicks the PLAY button on the computer monitor and the video starts up. The first sequence, shot through a window, shows a boy on a bicycle.

"That's the bastard that set off the IED. Watch the bugger!"

On the monitor, Charlotte can see the boy take out a cell phone, then slow down and make a gesture as if pressing a button on the phone. A terrible roar emits from the notebook speakers. The camera shakes and rolls violently, then goes black.

"Jesus," Charlotte says. "Thanks for putting me through that again."

"There's more. It seems the camera wasn't damaged. I must have accidently shut it off. Keep watching."

After a few seconds of black, the screen brightens to show a group of Iraqis in a small room. The cameraman speaks in Arabic, the camera trembles, and the men begin to laugh uncontrollably. These are Charlotte's abductors. They are playing with the camera, making their own home movie.

The camera is passed from man to man. Two of the men point the camera at their own faces and grin like children making faces in a mirror.

And then suddenly there is a loud noise, like a door being kicked in. The camera turns toward the door but is dropped, coming to rest on its side. The wide angle lens continues to record an astonishing scene. Four men in beards and plaid shirts have knocked down the door and entered the room. The terrorists begin to grab for weapons. But in the confusion, the attackers have the advantage. Using only knives, they overtake the terrorists, mercilessly slashing their throats. Within seconds, these men, the rescuers, have left the room. The onboard mic picks up the sound of their feet on the stairs.

Charlotte turns to Greg and finds him surfing the TV channels. Curt fast forwards the video to the point where the rescuers are ushering

Charlotte and Curt out of the house. Suddenly, the camera lurches and begins to move toward the open doorway.

"I grabbed my camera on the way out," Curt explains. "Instinct."

The camera moves toward the rescue vehicle and into the back seat.

"I didn't see that the camera was on until we got into the car," Curt explains. "Anyway, I decided to just leave it on."

The onboard mic picks up the brief conversation between a man in the front seat and Charlotte. The picture shifts to see the man's face as he turns fleetingly to look at Charlotte in the back seat. Curt clicks the PAUSE button.

"So here is the face of our anonymous rescuer."

Charlotte stares at the face, which is vaguely familiar. "If I ever see him again, I'll thank him," she says.

"Oh, you've already seen him again. Take a look at this."

Curt cues up another video clip in the editing software, this one from the morning's event with Iggers. The camera switches on and moves into the Seasons hotel elevator. Charlotte can hear the replay of her brief conversation with Curt.

"You look nervous, kiddo," Curt says on tape, his voice tinny in the computer speakers.

"Just keep the goddam camera running."

And then, on the monitor, Charlotte watches the elevator door open. She sees Curt's hand hold open the elevator door for a man.

"Thanks," the man says. "They're running slow today."

The camera tilts up to capture the man's face.

Curt clicks the PAUSE button and aligns this shot with the previous one. Charlotte looks at the two faces, one of them bearded and the other one clean-shaven. Her eyes go back and forth between them. And then she sees it.

"It's the same man!" she says.

Charlotte turns to her father. "The man who rescued us in Baghdad was right here in Delhi this morning—on the same floor that Greg Iggers was..."

Greg, who has been watching TV, speaks without turning toward them. "He was in the lobby when we got there. He recognized you."

"In the lobby, are you sure?" Charlotte asks.

Greg is silent again.

Charlotte continues. "Then he must have killed Iggers while we were waiting for Curt. My God, our rescuer is an assassin. He couldn't be working for the CIA or some other government agency as I thought."

"Obviously, he's working for someone else," Curt says.

"So the CIA and some other group are both following us," Charlotte says. "What the hell do they want?"

"Probably the same thing you're looking for," Thompson replies.

"But I don't even know what that is!"

Greg boosts the TV volume and everyone turns to the screen. A local newscaster speaks in English about a small explosion in a room at the Seasons Hotel.

"Right now," the reporter says, "the authorities believe that the unidentified occupants, who may have been cooking some food in their room, may have inadvertently ignited a fuel source. This is not believed to be a terrorist activity."

Curt turns to Charlotte. "Any idea who might have wanted this story covered up? Like maybe the CIA?"

Charlotte looks at her watch. "Greg, find CCN International."

Greg clicks the remote a few times and stops at CCN. The end of Charlotte's story is playing out. On the screen is a photo of Greg Iggers, inserted by CCN in Cambridge just before airing the piece. Charlotte's voice is saying, "At the time of his murder, Mr. Iggers was serving as director of operations for the CIA."

The piece ends. Charlotte turns off the TV and glances at her father.

"Okay, maybe it wasn't so smart to expose the biggest intelligence agency in the world. But we're safe here for the moment. Iggers and his associate are dead. The assassin fled the Seasons. No one else knows we're here, so we have some time to think this through."

For a moment, they sit silently in the room, staring at each other and trying to be convinced that Charlotte is right.

And then the telephone rings.

Chapter 22

Antonio Fortunati steps from the clattering taxi and pays the Indian driver a fistful of rupees. The old man has shed his clerical garments and accessories for the disguise of a European businessman—tan suit, white shirt with gray pinstripes, red and silver striped tie, and burgundy Italian loafers—the fruits of his foray into Rome. He feels positively worldly.

New Delhi is hot and noisy. The smog stings his eyes. Blinking, he turns toward the apartment building in which his brother lives. He opens the creaking front door and steps into a dusty foyer. The apartment, he remembers from his conversation just one day ago, is on the second floor.

It is mainly while climbing stairs that he feels a sharp arthritic pain shoot through his legs like an electric shock. One by one, he negotiates the stairs, wincing and grunting his way to the upstairs landing, his burning knees crackling like wax paper in a fire. How fortunate that he had traveled light, with only a small suitcase and a satchel that carries the evidence stolen from the Vatican's Secret Archives.

At the top, he surveys five peeling doors that each lead to a different apartment. He identifies his brother's door by its number and drags his rolling suitcase over to it.

He knocks three times. No answer. He knocks again, this time more loudly. Still no response.

With a neatly folded handkerchief, he wipes the perspiration from his forehead and tries to think about his instructions. In the event that his brother is not at home, he should… what? Oh yes, the key. The key is hidden beneath a flower pot on a second floor veranda overlooking the street. He looks around and finds a door leading to the veranda.

Stepping onto the veranda, he finds a dozen flower pots recently watered. The floor is still wet. As he inhales a delightful medley of fragrances, tranquility settles on him like a butterfly. A wicker chair beckons; how wonderful it would be to sit here and rest his painful knees.

In the end, though, he decides that he should first move his things into the apartment. He searches under a massive pot containing a brilliant red geranium plant and finds the key. Of course. Geraniums are his brother's favorite flower. He also finds a note written in his brother's scrawl.

```
Antonio,

Only the most pressing matter could prevent me
from greeting you when you arrive. You will be
safe here until I return. Nevertheless, I urge
you to conceal your evidence well. There are
plastic bags in my kitchen. I suggest you place
the evidence in these bags and hide them in the
geranium pot on the landing, then destroy this
note and scatter the displaced soil. There is
good wine in the cupboard. Help yourself. I am so
anxious to see you again! I hope it will be soon.

Your brother,
Thompson
```

Fortunati smiles. It has been over a year since he has seen Thompson face-to-face. They had met more than twenty years ago when Thompson Walker was in Rome for a promotional tour following the publication of his first best-selling book, *The Evolution of Wisdom and Power*. The author's insights into the progressive (some would say *regressive*) evolution of Christianity and consolidation of religious power had struck a sympathetic chord in the prefect, who had ventured to the public reading in plain clothes.

Moved even more by Thompson Walker's incisive responses to questions, Fortunati waited until the long line of autograph seekers had received their signed books and then meekly introduced himself as a local defrocked priest. Thompson had immediately responded with a grin and a hug—had he not also left the priesthood?—and the two men agreed to have dinner together. Six hours later, with too much wine in him, Fortunati had confided his true identity to the author. Thompson had reciprocated with his own confession, that he had once seduced a young woman in his parish and out of guilt had left the priesthood.

The exchange of secrets had produced a kind of blood bond between the prefect and the author. Over time they had come to think of each other as brothers. Fortunati had even appropriated Thompsons' daughter, Charlotte, as his own niece, though he had never met the young lady; he had only, in fact, seen one photograph of her as a ten-year-old. All he knew of Charlotte were the stories told to him by Thompson Walker.

Fortunati had always wanted a family. His own mother and father had died when he was a child and, lacking other relatives, he had been raised by nuns in a small village in northern Italy. But it didn't matter. He now had a brother. And a niece. He dreams often of some day meeting his beautiful niece, who is so devoted to her adoring father, according to Thompson. Fortunati knows that, once they meet, Charlotte will come to love Fortunati as well.

Family is everything.

It takes fifteen minutes to conceal the evidence in the immense pot. As he stands at the kitchen sink rinsing the soil from his hands, he hears a knock on the door. Without thinking, he walks to the door and opens it.

Three Pakistanis face him. One of them points a pistol and says in heavily accented English, "Antonio Fortunati? You have something we want."

Fortunati sighs and prays that God will claim his soul.

Chapter 23

William Wyatt did not go back to bed after the taxi driver intruded on his sleep. Instead, he dressed quickly and called for a limo with extra security to drive him to CIA headquarters. Within minutes of his arrival, a formal correspondence had been sent to Ajay Sanghvi, director of the IB, India's Central Intelligence Bureau, reputedly the oldest intelligence agency in the world. Wyatt asked Sanghvi to "tamp down" news of the messy assassination business until the agencies could coordinate and then suggested a cover story he had worked up on the way to CIA headquarters in McLean, Virginia.

Sanghvi expressed annoyance with the CIA running an operation in Delhi without his knowledge, but both men knew this was common practice. And Wyatt knew that he now owed a favor to his Indian counterpart.

After this terse exchange, the director instructed agency news auditors to watch for any incident leakage. Shortly before five that morning, a CIA auditor alerted Wyatt about the Delhi TV coverage of the explosion at the Seasons hotel. Wyatt had sent a thank you message to Sanghvi. But ten minutes later the same analyst had called Wyatt, telling him to watch CCN International—monitor eight on the director's wall. Wyatt grabbed a remote and turned up the volume. In horror, he watched Charlotte Ansari narrate gruesome pictures of the assassination and then give away Iggers identity and connection to the CIA.

The cat was out of the bag.

Sidney Goldberg, deputy director, watches the carnage with Wyatt. "Ansari must have been there minutes after the explosion," Goldberg says. "You think she had something to do with it?"

"She's a reporter, dammit, not an assassin!" Wyatt is in a foul mood. "But she was tipped off by the assassin. A messy job he did."

"That would tend to eliminate…"

"Normally I'd agree—those people are very precise. And tidy. A bomb is not their style. But last night I received a package with blood money for Iggers widow. Guess who sent it?"

"We should put extra security on your home."

"Already did that. I've got to tell you, Sidney, I don't like contractors calling me at home."

"*Contractors?* Seems to me they've crossed over the line to enemy combatants. We should take 'em down."

"Right, like we could do that. They're harder to trace than bin Laden, and a lot more professional. Hell, they could probably take *us* apart. Piece by piece. And they'd start at the top, Sidney. That's you and me. They've been doing this for two thousand years. We're still in diapers."

"Maybe, but we've got technology resources."

"Yeah, and that's why we got bin Laden, right? The cretin lives in caves and eats goat meat. I've gotta tell you, Sidney, sometimes I think our reliance on technology has softened our brains."

"You scared of these guys?"

"Scared? You bet. They've never failed a mission for us no matter how tough. And they know where I live. You can sure as hell bet they know about your house too… and your little apartment where what's-her-name, Susan, massages your feet before you go home."

Sidney blanches, then flushes red. He had no idea that director Wyatt knew about his extracurricular activities. "I'm getting ready to close down that operation real soon."

"Might be the best thing for Susan's health."

"Hell, Bill, what do you propose we do here? We're the goddam CIA! We're talking like we're under siege."

"I'm not so sure we aren't."

"So should we call a truce? Maybe we can hire these guys to be on our side. Team up, like in the past. They're mercenary, and we pay well."

"Too late, there's blood on the game table. Right now, let's tend to business. Far as I'm concerned, Charlotte Ansari has committed an act of treason. Let's bring her in. I'll run interference with Sanghvi."

"And we start, like, where?"

"Iggers called in the name of her hotel. If she's not there, search it. I'll bet her news director at CCN will know how to find her."

"I don't think we should play hardball with CCN. If they smell something, they can rat us out."

"Hell, Sidney, they already have. Put the squeeze on CCN—they were stupid enough to air that exposé just to one-up the competition. They made a mistake, which is good for us. So let's scare 'em with some national security BS and threats of subpoenas. You know the drill. They'll buckle if we threaten to muss their carefully coiffed hair, I promise."

Director Wyatt sits alone at his desk now. The ring of his phone startles him though he's been waiting for the call.

"Bill, is that you?"

"Of course, Mr. President."

"Sorry about Grant—a good man."

"Yes sir, he was."

"So explain to me how the CIA director of operations gets himself blown up in Delhi and CCN knows about it before I do and has pictures of it. You withholding from me, Bill?"

"Of course not, sir. I was busy installing counter measures."

"Counter measures against what? Bad PR? Let me tell you something, Bill. When I proposed you to Congress, I believed that you were the right man for the job, but I'm feeling right now that maybe this thing is running away from you, know what I mean?"

"Not a chance, sir. We'll put a lid on it right now. We're looking for this Ansari woman to bring her in. She exposed a covert agent in the field."

"*Covert?* I'm no lawyer, Bill, but seems to me that Iggers was listed as your director of operations on the CIA website. Doesn't seem covert to me."

"At the very least, she interfered with a sensitive mission vital to our national security, wouldn't you agree? You know what the stakes are here."

There is a pause while the president considers this.

"Look, Bill," the president finally says, "you might have something there. I'll check it out with the AG. Meanwhile, maybe it's a good idea to stuff a rag in this woman's mouth for a while. We probably even have reason to suspect she had a hand in the assassination. I mean, how'd she get there so fast if she didn't know it was going to happen?"

"And if she won't cooperate? I've seen her on TV. She's not exactly a fan of the administration."

Another long pause, then the president responds. "Hate to say it, Bill, but this woman's got higher ratings than I do right now so people listen to her. Not good having her blab the wrong stuff all over cable TV. But she's in a dangerous profession, know what I mean? People disappear in that job. Gotta go make my calls. Keep me posted, Bill."

"Thank you, sir."

Wyatt hangs up and immediately places a call to deputy director Goldberg. "Sidney? Listen up, buddy. Seems that this Ansari woman might be linked to terrorist activities after all. When you get your hands on her, the best course is rendition."

"Rendition, really? You actually think...?"

"Sidney, godammit, this is not a consultation."

"Right, well, the nearest detention center is outside Kabul. They call it the Pit."

"Then make a reservation. Sounds charming."

Wyatt hangs up, swipes his sweaty face with a handkerchief, and silently asks God to forgive him for swearing.

Chapter 24

With a worried expression, Curt hangs up the phone and starts powering down his computer.

"So who was that?" There is a nervous twinge in Charlotte's voice. "Say something, dammit."

"That was Bud Schiebel in Cambridge. What I mean is, it was Cindy from the City Desk calling on a pay phone with a message from Bud."

"A pay phone! Where the hell do you find a pay phone these days?"

"No idea, but Bud wanted us to know that he just got a call from the CIA asking about our whereabouts in India."

"Those guys move fast," Thompson says. "Makes you wonder how they missed picking up bin Laden all those times."

"Bud didn't tell them our specific location," Curt continues. "But he suggested we disappear in a hurry. Something about charges of conspiracy to assassinate a CIA agent."

"You're kidding. That's ridiculous!" Charlotte says.

"Cindy said Bud's afraid they're surveilling his cell phone. And the CCN phones too. I don't know how rattled Bud is, but I could hear Cindy's voice shaking. They must be putting some mean pressure on."

"Maybe you should cooperate." Thompson interjects. "You've done nothing wrong—have you?"

Charlotte glares at her father and says, "We have if they say we have. That's all it takes. Ever hear of Guantanamo Bay?"

"Gitmo's a resort compared to the secret rendition camps around the world," Curt adds. "Which only matters, of course, if they decide to keep us alive. You guys can keep talking if you like, but I'm gone."

Thompson says, "Charlotte, where are your things—and Greg's?"

They both turn to Greg, who is now studying the Bible that he stole from Grant Iggers's room.

"In another hotel about five miles from here," Charlotte responds.

Curt is stuffing his duffel bag with clothes. "I don't recommend stopping there on the way to invisibility," he says.

Charlotte rubs her eyes. *What has she gotten them all into?* She picks up the phone and throws it against a wall. "They've got no right to do this!" she yells. "I was doing my job."

"Sorry, sweetheart, they don't need rights," Curt says. "And maybe you went just a teensy bit too far on this latest piece. So tell me, how do I expense the broken phone?"

"To hell with the phone," Charlotte replies as she starts to pack up the camera and lighting gear. "We should be out of here in two minutes. In Delhi traffic, it could take twenty to get to my hotel."

Curt rolls his eyes and mutters, "Dumb idea."

"We've got stuff there I don't want them to see," Charlotte explains. She is thinking of the family photographs with the circled faces and Greg's laptop. CIA forensics would have a field day analyzing her mother's e-mails on that. "C'mon, Dad, pitch in here."

In under three minutes, the foursome has left Curt's room and is standing at the front desk where the attendant, who is busy studying some papers, ignores them.

"Hey!" Charlotte yells. When the attendant looks up, Charlotte grabs the room key from Curt and pitches it to the surprised man. "Room 312. Charge it to his credit card."

She storms out of the hotel and the others follow.

"Okay," she says, looking around at the traffic and the absence of taxis. "How do you hail a cab in Delhi?"

"Good luck," Thompson says.

"No time for this." Charlotte peers at the hundreds of honking cars all entangled in a web of chaos. A pack of young men on motor scooters, weaving dangerously through the small gaps between cars, pass them like a pack of wolves, stopping at a traffic light at a complex intersection a half-block away.

"Follow me," Charlotte yells. She leads the others down the street to the intersection and boldly steps in front of two motor scooters. She reaches into her fanny pack and produces a fistful of rupees, waving them in the air and shouting, "Who wants five hundred rupees for a short ride?"

Three of the young men look at each other and then raise their hands. Charlotte steers Thompson onto the back of one, Curt onto another, and finally she and Greg climb onto a third.

"Hotel Sri Ruhal in Karol Bagh," she shouts.

The three motor scooters putter through the congested streets like San Francisco trolleys with bodies dangling from all sides. In the mad crush of the streets, knees slide against automobiles and pedestrians. The route to the hotel is virtually unnavigable, the traffic an insurgency of movement. Charlotte wonders at the lack of accidents, and then decides, *how would you even know?*

Twenty minutes later they all arrive at the Sri Ruhal. Charlotte pays the drivers who take off, grinning.

Another motor scooter quietly pulls up across the street. Gideon steps off and blends into a knot of shopkeepers raucously hawking shoes and belts and luggage on the broken walkway.

"I want all of you to stay down here," Charlotte tells her companions. "I'm going up to get some things. Won't be more than a couple minutes, I promise."

Curt shakes his head and says, "I say it again, Char. Dumb idea."

"Find us a taxi, okay? Big enough for all of us. If I'm not back in five minutes, Dad, take them to your place. I'll contact you there."

"You don't know where I live," Thompson reminds her. He takes a pen out of his shirt pocket, finds a scrap of paper in his pants pocket, and writes down an address, handing it to her.

Charlotte glances at the address, moving her lips as she studies it. "All right, now I know where you live." She tears up the paper and scatters the pieces. "Don't want anyone to find that address on me."

"I agree with Curt," Thompson says. "This is a really stupid idea."

"I need our stuff! Anyway, who are you to lecture me about doing stupid things? Now get us a taxi. I'll be right back."

Charlotte walks casually into the small lobby of the Sri Ruhal. As her companions become occupied with finding a taxi, Gideon crosses the street and slips into the hotel.

Charlotte rushes past the front desk and steps into the small elevator. Gideon finds a narrow stairway, stepping over a load of laundry on the lower steps as he races upward.

Charlotte steps out of the elevator on the third floor and walks briskly to her room, key in hand. But before she inserts the key into the lock, she hears sounds coming from inside the room. *Housekeeping?* As the sounds grow louder, she is sure that drawers are being pulled from the dresser and chairs are being slid across the floor.

She is too late. Someone is searching her room.

She realizes now that her heart is pounding and her throat has dried up. She should run. Get out of there.

As she starts to turn, the door suddenly opens. Two American men in suits, intent on rushing out of the room, stop in their tracks when they see Charlotte standing there. One of them is well over six feet tall and the other is a stocky bulldog of a man with a buzz cut. The carrying case for Greg's computer is slung over the squat man's shoulder. The tall man is holding Charlotte's carry-on bag, which contains the family photographs and other sensitive material.

Charlotte and the men eye each other, momentarily frozen by surprise. And then Charlotte turns and runs toward the elevator, stopping abruptly when she sees another man blocking her way. This man, though, seems familiar. Yes—the man from the video. From the Seasons Hotel. From Baghdad.

She stands motionless as Gideon moves toward her. Familiarity makes him seem the lesser threat. Oddly, he brushes past to stand between her and the two men. As he passes Charlotte, he whispers, "Count ten, then run down the stairs."

The tall man removes a pistol from beneath his suit coat and says, "Sir, I'll have to ask you to step aside." He drops the carry-on bag and with his left hand holds up a badge of some kind.

"Mind if I see your credential?" Gideon approaches the tall man. Buzz Cut strategically steps aside, lowers the computer case to the floor and moves his hand to his abdomen, shortening the distance to a gun beneath his coat.

"I'm sure you know that American agencies have no jurisdiction in Delhi," Gideon says.

And then Charlotte reaches the count of ten.

She bolts toward the stairway. As both Americans turn their eyes toward her, Gideon grabs the tall man's pistol hand. Using all his weight,

Gideon shifts his body so that the man's arm painfully bends backward against his chest. The elbow hyperextends with a popping sound.

Buzz Cut predictably turns toward his associate, gun in hand, but it is too late. The tall man is heaved into him. Both CIA agents crumple to the ground, the tall man agonizing in pain.

Buzz Cut pushes off the other agent and tries to aim his pistol at Gideon, but the attempt is futile. Gideon kicks the man's wrist and fiery pain shoots down the length of Buzz Cut's arm. The gun impotently drops to the floor.

This only angers Buzz Cut, who roars and lunges for Gideon's ankles. Gideon's heel stubs against the tall man's flailing legs and he falls. Buzz Cut is a cannon ball of fury. He outweighs Gideon by fifty pounds or more. He scrambles on top of Gideon and smashes a fist into the side of Gideon's face.

"That's it!" Gideon mutters. With a swift knee to Buzz Cut's groin, he slows the menace and is able to hook his other leg around the man's neck. By straightening his leg, he is able to pull Buzz Cut backward. This momentarily moves the heavy man's feet forward and Gideon grabs a foot. In less than a second, the ankle joint is broken.

Buzz Cut screams but is not finished. With his other leg he tries to kick Gideon in the chin. Gideon moves and receives only a glancing blow.

Fed up with this tiresome battle, Gideon reaches for his belt buckle. He tears it off, revealing a carbonized plastic dagger. Shifting his entire body to the left, he turns the hulking agent over so that Gideon is on top. He grabs the man's good foot and slices the Achilles tendon with the edge of his knife.

Buzz Cut screams in pain. Gideon stands and looks down at the two whimpering agents. With a kick to their heads, he puts them out. Looking up, he notices that two men and a woman have been watching the mayhem from their doorways. They are now staring at him fearfully.

"Bad tippers," Gideon says, breathing heavily.

And then he takes the men's badges and guns, crushes their cell phones with a stomp of his heel, tucks in his shirt and heads for the stairway, vowing not to skip another workout.

C harlotte, having bounded down the first flight of stairs, stopped suddenly on the second floor. *The pictures! And the computer!* She could not leave them behind. Finding a mop in the hallway, she comically arms herself with the long-handled stick and waits around the corner of the stairs, hoping that none of the assailants would stop on that floor.

She hears the screams of pain upstairs and the crashing of bodies on walls and doors. It is a terrible sound, and she has had no way of knowing which way the battle was going until finally she hears feet scuffling down the stairs. As the sounds pass, she dares to peek around the corner and sees the man from the Seasons Hotel descending.

She feels heartened now. For some reason, this man has protected her from the CIA agents in her room. After the call from CCN, Charlotte was sure those men were CIA. But her protector—she had no idea who he was or why he had intervened.

Charlotte cautiously ascends the stairs and peers down the corridor. Several men have come out of their rooms and are gawking dumbly at the two agents who are still unconscious.

This is Charlotte's only chance to claim her belongings. She walks down the hall toward her room, exchanging a "My God, what happened?" with the chattering onlookers.

She sees the computer case and carry-on bag lying on the floor. As the tall agent begins to gain consciousness, drawing attention toward himself with a loud groan, Charlotte picks up both items and returns to the stairway.

Damn! She has an irrational urge to collect Curt and his camera to document the site, but as she exits the lobby and sees her son so vulnerable in the back seat of a taxi, this impulse disappears.

A cross the street, Gideon watches the blinking dot on the digital handheld map and smiles. He looks up to see Charlotte climb into a crowded taxi with two bags. The woman obviously had gone back to get them.

She's tough, he'll give her that.

Gideon climbs onto his motor scooter and starts the engine.

She's also a pain in the ass to protect.

Chapter 25

The taxi pulls away from the Sri Rahul. Thompson looks at his daughter's flushed face and says, "Complications?"

"You could say that. Two CIA agents in my room when I got there." Charlotte pats the two bags. "But I got what I came for."

"So it's true, then," Curt says. "The CIA is hunting us down."

"Hunting Greg and me, at least."

"What am I, kangaroo meat?"

"Your description, not mine," Charlotte says. "So what's the plan?"

"Plan?" Curt is incensed that Charlotte is putting this burden on him. "You got us into this with that agency exposé of yours."

"And who edited the goddam piece, huh? Who uploaded it to Bud without objection?"

"All right, that's enough!" Thompson's voice booms in the small taxi. He has been listening to the spat from the front seat and suspects there is more behind it than the immediate tension. "You want a plan, I've got one. In case you haven't noticed, I've got a daughter and grandson at risk here."

No one speaks for a few seconds. Curt and Charlotte glance angrily at each other.

"Wait a minute." Curt is the first to break the silence. "Char, you said there were two CIA agents in your room when you got there. So how come you're not in a chopper on the way to some interrogation center?"

"Remember the man from the Seasons Hotel?" Charlotte asks. "Well, he showed up and beat the sh—" She looks at her son, who is absorbed in the pilfered Bible. "—and beat the *crap* out of both of them. I've got no idea how he found me there or why he did it."

Greg' answers the implied question matter-of-factly. "He called you at the hotel last night. He told you to show up at the Seasons. He's everywhere we are."

"Christ, everyone seems to know where we are except me," Curt says. "Where are we anyway?" He looks through the window at the knotted traffic. "And where the hell are we going?"

101

"My father has a plan—right Dad?" Charlotte asks sarcastically.

"We're making a stop at my apartment first," Thompson replies.

"Great," Curt blurts out. "Do I have to remind you what happened last time we stopped for some personal reasons, like five minutes ago?"

"I have no choice," Thompson says. "We can drop you off somewhere on the way and pick you up afterwards if you like."

Curt just shrugs. He sits there like a small, sulking child.

"When I'm done, I know a safe place for us to stay," Thompson says. "A good friend of mine, a Kashmiri. We can gather our wits at his place. Right now, we're running with no purpose, which can get us into trouble."

"I just can't believe the last couple of weeks," Charlotte says. "Such a nightmare. Kidnapped in Baghdad, home invaded in Minnesota, neighbor killed across the lake by Arabs, Mom turning up alive and firing off e-mails to Greg, CIA agents popping up everywhere and getting their heads blown off."

"And suddenly topping Interpol's Ten Most Wanted list," Curt adds.

"Makes you wonder what ties it all together," Thompson says. "There must be a thread."

"I disagree that we're running with no purpose," Charlotte says. "Mom's in grave danger, like I told you in the park. We're trying to save her somehow."

"Hmm-m-m." Thompson sometimes purrs when he thinks. "Maybe saving her will end this nightmare. It's a classical mythic storyline. The damsel in distress and a heroic journey to save her. In the end, everything usually turns out well."

"Sorry, Tommy, but we're not living a myth here," Curt says. "This is reality happening all around us."

"I respectfully disagree." Thompson's rebuttal is gentle but firm. "I believe that most people are living a myth—the myth of their chosen religion."

"I thought you were pro-religion," Curt says. "You've studied them all, spent part of your life living each of them. Sold lots of books talking about them, anyway. You saying now that they're all phony?"

"Not at all. I believe in God, and I even believe that he sends teachers to help us understand His greater truth. But when we as people try to grasp the reality of God, we tend to misinterpret and corrupt his teachings and invent legends to support our manmade doctrines. We turn teachers into gods, or multiple gods. Then we start to base our decisions on these legends, these myths, the same way our ancestors did. As if we haven't learned a thing over the years."

"Save the PBS lecture. Too deep for me," Curt says, shifting in his seat. "It's easier just not to believe in God."

"I wonder if that's true," Thompson says. "We live in an ocean of people, most of whom believe in some particular mythology of God and act accordingly. Their actions often affect us, like when self-righteous Christians publicly burn witches at the stake, or when a radical Islamic suicide bomber blows up a market and kills innocent people. It seems to me that if you're designated a witch, or you're shopping in that market, it doesn't matter if you believe in God or not. You're still dead. The many myths about God and his laws actually rule our lives. So explain to me, Curt, how it's easier *not* to believe in God."

Curt rubs his eyes, buying time to concoct a reply. Instead of responding, he says, "Sorry to say it, mate, but I've gotta pee."

Chapter 26

The taxi arrives at a crumbling two-story apartment building about a mile from the India Gate. Thompson steps out of the front door, massages his stiff knees and turns to the driver. "A hundred rupees extra if you wait," he says. "We need you to take us to another address in a few minutes."

Thompson turns to Curt. "Walk down to the corner and fetch another taxi if you can. We'll need two." He is expecting to retrieve his house guest, Antonio Fortunati.

"*Two* taxis?" Curt asks.

"Just do it," Charlotte says, rolling her eyes. "Don't be difficult."

Curt sighs and gets out on the street side, heading for the corner. Greg and Charlotte get out on the other side.

"I'll only be a minute. You two stay in the taxi," Thompson commands.

"We're coming with you," Charlotte says. "All these years I've wondered how you lived. Now I can see for myself."

Thompson knows it will do no good to argue with his daughter. "You won't see much. I only spend a couple months each year in this place. Mostly I'm somewhere else."

"Living with monks and mystics, getting the flavor of their beliefs, capturing the rhythm of their lives of faith?"

"You quote me, or rather some dust jacket blurb," Thompson says, smiling. "Which means you were interested."

Thompson walks toward a peeling door. Charlotte and Greg follow.

"Not really," Charlotte says as they enter a moldy entrance and start up a flight of stairs. "Except I always wondered how a man who betrayed his church could spend his life writing about faith. Guilt?"

"Perhaps if you had read any of my letters you'd know my answer."

"I threw them away unread, it's true. Just wasn't *that* interested."

At the top of the stairs, Thompson halts his daughter with the broad palm of his hand. Something is wrong; Charlotte can see it in her father's face.

Thompson puts an index finger to his lips, signaling for his daughter and grandson to be quiet. Slowly he walks to one of five doors, the one that is partially open. He slowly cranes his neck to look through the doorway.

"My God," he whispers before pushing the door open to reveal a landfill of trashed possessions—scattered books, heaps of broken furniture, cushions ripped apart, draperies bunched in mounds, the contents of kitchen cupboards smashed on the tile floor.

Charlotte and Greg rush to his side. He restrains them again.

"We don't know if the intruders are gone," he whispers, picking up a smashed lamp and yanking the electrical cord out of a sparking outlet. He steps into the front room of his apartment wielding the lamp like a weapon. Slowly, he moves into the bedroom, opens the armoire, then searches the bathroom.

The vandals are gone.

As Thompson reenters the front room, he sees Charlotte kneeling beside a dark spot on the mussed Kashmiri carpet.

"It's blood," she says. "Whoever did this hurt himself badly."

"No," Thompson replies as he squats next to her, his knees cracking. "My friend Antonio arrived today from Italy. He was going to stay with me for a while. My God, they must have found him here and—"

"There's mud in the sink," Greg says, interrupting. He has wandered into the kitchen and is peering into the stained basin. "I think someone washed their hands after playing in the dirt."

Charlotte and Thompson enter the kitchen.

"There's a few small leaves here too. I think your friend was gardening."

"My God, the geranium," Thompson says. He races out of the apartment and bursts onto the veranda, sighing when he sees the flowering plant sitting contentedly in its large pot. Charlotte and Greg watch him through the doorway to the veranda.

With a grunt, Thompson uproots the geranium, tossing it aside.

"What are you doing?" Charlotte asks.

Her answer comes as Thompson reaches into the pot and plucks out a parcel wrapped in plastic.

"They were after this, I'm sure of it," Thompson says. "Antonio would have never told them where he hid it."

"What is it, Dad?"

"I honestly have no idea. But we'll find out. Just not here."

"I agree. Let's get out of here."

"Get into the taxi now. I'll be right down."

Charlotte gives her father a glaring look that says *waiting is a stupid idea*.

Thompson ignores the rebuke and shoves her toward the stairway. "Just one minute, I promise. Now hurry!"

Charlotte ushers Greg down the stairs. Thompson races back into his apartment, finds a large carry-on bag and stuffs it full of books and papers. Two minutes later he steps into the taxi.

"You broke your one minute promise," Charlotte says. "How can I ever trust you?"

Thompson thinks he can see relief at his safe appearance in his daughter's eyes, and this pleases him. He sees that Curt and Greg are in the back seat with Charlotte.

"Charlotte paid off the taxi I wrangled," Curt explains. "Together again."

Thompson gives the driver an address and the taxi eases into the traffic, which is suddenly congested due to a minor collision down the street.

Chapter 27

A willowy Pakistani man with a severely scarred jaw watches the taxi pull away and smiles, revealing a gristly gum line that is missing three teeth, the result of a bullet entering his mouth and exiting the back of his neck. It was God's will that he was not killed or paralyzed in that tumultuous battle against the infidel Americans in the bleak mountains of Afghanistan, a clear sign that he should continue his sacred duties.

Or perhaps his survival was a celestial reward for saving the life of Osama, who later praised the young man's courage for "trying to catch a bullet in his teeth."

Scarface plucks a cell phone from his shirt pocket, taps in a number, and begins speaking in Pashtun. "The old man and the others have left the apartment," he says. "Yes, in this traffic I can easily follow them. I will call again when I know their destination."

He terminates the call and puts the phone back into his pocket. As he steps onto a motor scooter and starts the engine, he notices a westerner settled into the seat of an idling scooter across the street. Westerners always attract the attention of Scarface.

The infidel hesitates before pulling into traffic. But then, instead of easily slipping through the narrow seams of traffic to pass the taxi, as a swarm of other riders do, the westerner pulls up behind the vehicle separated from it by one small truck.

Scarface is no idiot. He immediately understands the meaning of this behavior. The westerner is also following the old man and his family. The rider is certainly not a Jew. This means he is not Mossad. Which means the westerner must be CIA or MI5, or…

The alternative sends a chill down Scarface's spine.

God willing, may this infidel be CIA, he mutters to himself.

With less confidence than he had felt just seconds ago, Scarface mutters an Islamic prayer for protection and slips into the traffic behind Gideon.

The vehicles begin inching forward. Scarface is only thirty feet behind the westerner but feels perfectly camouflaged by his dark skin,

Pakistani features, and banged-up scooter. Scores of other dark-skinned riders are navigating their motorbikes through the constricted spaces between cars and trucks. Here and there, knees scrape doors. Handlebars clip side view mirrors. An occasional fist angrily raps an intruding fender. The percussive chirp of horns provides an orchestral score for the slowly unfolding drama.

Scarface has no intention of slipping through the traffic and closing the gap between him and Gideon, so he lets other motorbikes pass him. Finally, the congestion eases and vehicles slowly begin to move forward. Scarface is suddenly nudged to the left by an aggressive truck, and he bellows a Pashto curse at the Indian driver, a Hindu infidel by the look of the man's turban. In retaliation, the Indian jerks his steering wheel to the left, bumping Scarface even harder.

The Indian laughs, feeling invulnerable in the cab of his truck.

Scarface takes the driver's action as a sign of Indian hatred for Pakistanis. Instinctively, his hand moves to a pistol in his waistband. He intends to put a bullet through the infidel's head, but his training gains the upper hand. He must try to maintain his composure and stay focused on his mission. Shooting a Hindu in the middle of traffic will not advance his cause.

He cannot restrain his anger entirely, though. He pulls out the pistol. Using the barrel of it, he imprints a deep scratch along the side of the truck.

The Indian furiously opens his door to confront the vandal, but the door slams against the motor scooter. Frustrated, the Indian repeatedly slams his door against Scarface's scooter. The tantrum ends when Scarface smiles and lifts the pistol so the truck driver can see it with suddenly round eyes.

Scarface turns his attention to the vehicles ahead. A sudden panic erupts. While the taxi can still be seen about two hundred feet ahead, the westerner has disappeared. The Pakistani's eyes slide left and right, futilely searching for the westerner. Suddenly a car bumps the rear wheel of Scarface's scooter, rudely suggesting that he is blocking traffic.

Scarface realizes that his heart is pounding and his throat has dried up. Yes, he wants to move forward now. In fact, he wants to get away. Seconds ago he was the hunter, but now he fears that he has become the prey.

Just before he accelerates, a man jumps onto the back of the motor scooter. An arm insinuates itself around Scarface's chest and a very sharp object pokes his back. A soft voice speaks the Arabic word for "Drive."

Scarface speaks Arabic as well as Pashto. It is the universal language of al Qaeda. As his abductor gives further instructions, Scarface realizes that they are following the taxi.

Scarface knows that he had made fatal mistakes in front of the old man's apartment. He had hovered too closely to the building and had failed to adequately disguise his intent, never anticipating that a competitor might be tailing the family. After blending into the traffic, he had undermined the value of his natural camouflage by failing to imitate the behavior of the other motorbike drivers.

Instead, he had lagged behind while the others had flowed like water through the traffic. He had made himself stand out. And then he had shifted his focus away from the westerner to an ignorant Hindu, losing track of his adversary. Even worse, he had shown his gun. If the westerner had fostered any doubts about his role, the pistol would have given him away.

The sharp dagger in his back was the only calling card Scarface needed to identify his adversary. A Mossad, CIA, or MI5 agent would have shoved a gun into his back, not a dagger.

This was the worst case scenario.

Traffic picks up and Scarface contemplates martyrdom. He reminds himself of the rewards to come in Paradise with a prayer to remove fear: *Oh, Lord! Help us to hold fast all together to Your path, even in the shaky times...*

And then he wrenches the handlebar to the right, swerving in front of a honking automobile. The car crashes into the scooter's rear wheel, narrowly missing Gideon's leg and tossing Gideon onto the trunk of a taxi.

Scarface is thrown from the scooter and skids onto the roadway. The pavement peels skin from his elbow and back. The searing pain sends a rush of adrenaline through his body. He pulls himself to his feet and sees a circle of spectators rushing toward him.

This is not Paradise, he realizes, so I must not be dead.

He still has a holy mission to perform. Pushing his way through the crowd, he searches for the westerner. He is no longer afraid of this man, no longer afraid of anyone. He will tear the man apart with his bare hands!

But then his legs begin to tremble and he drops to his knees, coughing. *What is happening?* He is suddenly lightheaded. The street begins to tilt and he is now looking up at a sea of faces that are looking down at him. He can't move. Can't talk. Can't even think clearly, except to know that his life is draining away.

In death, his eyes continue to stare upward, as if searching for a Paradise that he will never see.

Gideon is in a taxi before the police arrive. It will be more than a day before the Indian authorities discover the slender knife wound, an accidental result of the collision. They may never find it on the skinned back of the victim.

Gideon is holding Scarface's cell phone, which had been flung from the man's shirt pocket. He presses a few keys, finds the last number called, and smiles.

With a press of a button he could summon the voice of evil.

Chapter 28

Thompson's taxi finally enters a Kashmiri market in South Delhi. The hilly streets are lined by restaurants and shops selling silver cutlery and utensils, hand-carved wooden furnishings, CDs of Kashmiri music, woolens and pashmina textiles of all descriptions, and carpets of wool, silk, and blends of both.

The taxi pulls up in front of an upscale shop called Kashmiri Carpets and Thompson hurriedly urges his companions out of the vehicle, up eight cracked steps, and into the shop. A gray-haired man with thick glasses immediately spies Thompson and rushes toward him, clasping the author in a bear hug.

"My dear friend!" the man says.

"Mohan, it's so good of you to take us in like this," Thompson replies.

"For you, anything, Tommy."

Thompson turns to his companions and introduces his friend with a dramatic flourish. "May I present my good friend Dr. Mohan Bhatt, our host for the evening."

"And for as long as you need to stay," Dr. Bhatt adds. "Please, all of you, come in. We're preparing tea."

Mohan Bhatt leads the small group into a large showroom ringed by mirrors and scores of rolled-up carpets. A young man enters the room bearing a silver tray with a steaming pot of tea and many small cups. "Please, my son Sushil brings tea. It will refresh you after a tense day."

Dr. Bhatt pours a cup of tea for each of his guests. Three other dark-eyed Kashmiri men stand protectively along the walls of the showroom. They are ready in an instant, Charlotte presumes, to show their wares.

Charlotte samples the tea and widens her eyes with pleasure. "Delicious," she says, glancing around the room. "Are all the carpets here from Kashmir?"

"Yes, my dear," Dr. Bhatt replies. "It is my mission in life to present the fruits of my people's handiwork to the world and help support the families that produce these magnificent works of art."

111

Dr. Bhatt motions for Sushil to unroll the first of many carpets on the wooden floor. The silk fibers shimmer in the soft light. There are red patterns and blue, earth tones mixed with muted greens, geometric shapes and abstract figures—a kaleidoscope of color and imagery.

As the carpets roll out in layers, Dr. Bhatt explains: "You see the beauty of these designs? It is nothing compared to the beauty of my country—the lush valleys and waterways, the majestic mountains. Truly a land of milk and honey. Some say that Kashmir is the inspiration for Shangri-La. Once upon a time, tourists from around the world came to imbibe our beauty, our spirit, our good nature. And they bought our handmade goods. In those days, life in Kashmir was indeed *heaven on earth*."

He refills Charlotte's cup and continues, looking at Curt now. "But today, India and Pakistan have a bitter dispute over Kashmir, which is mostly Muslim, you see, but ruled by the secular government of India. The armed forces of India and Pakistan maintain a truce along an invisible border we call the 'Line of Control' that divides our regions, but this truce is frequently violated."

Curt, who has been seated cross-legged on the floor, moves to a freshly unrolled carpet at the beckoning of Sushil. "I've read about it, but never been there," he says.

"Ah yes, you are a photographer, correct? Tommy informed me."

"I am," Curt says. "Shoot video, actually. So are you saying the armies clash over this so-called boundary?"

"Oh yes, from time to time. But mostly Islamic terrorists wage a holy war to unite Kashmir with Pakistan. Naturally, this has frightened off the tourists. And so the government of Kashmir asked me to be their ambassador of trade and set up this village to find a market for our goods."

"Are you Muslim?" Charlotte asks.

"Yes, of course, but a very moderate one. I despise the terrorists who are destroying my country and corrupting the teachings of my faith. Unfortunately, I am but a modest rug merchant, as your father knows."

Thompson smiles and says, "He is a devout Muslim, that is true, but not so modest as a merchant. He can't afford not to be good at his job. If he were not selling carpets and carvings in this village, several hundred families in Kashmir would lose their livelihood."

"How is that so?" Charlotte asks Dr. Bhatt.

The Kashmiri walks to a thick layering of carpets on the floor and begins to lift the fringed edges one at a time, revealing the myriad designs.

"You see how different these carpets are? Each one is woven by a Kashmiri family. The large carpets can take an entire family over a year to weave. These carpets are their sole source of income. And each design and color combination is exclusive to a particular family. It is their unique design. Point out any carpet in this room and I can tell you the name and the sad tale of the family that wove it. A carpet tells its family story with unsurpassed craftsmanship. You see, the Kashmiri double-knotted technique of weaving produces the finest, most durable carpets in the world and has never been duplicated. But what about Persian rugs, you ask? Or Turkish carpets? Even the finest of those are crude by comparison."

Dr. Bhatt walks over to Greg, who is seated on the wooden floor engrossed in his stolen Bible.

"Perhaps I should also mention," Dr. Bhatt says to the others, "that every carpet here has a certificate from the government stating that no child labor laws have been violated in its making. We do not force our children to do the work of adults."

Dr. Bhatt fixes his gaze on Charlotte with such intensity that she guiltily gulps the rest of her tea.

"But enough about my merchandise," Dr. Bhatt says with a smile. "Is there anything I can do for you besides offer my hospitality?"

Thompson now stands and solemnly looks at his friend. "I'm afraid I haven't been exactly forthright, Mohan."

"With you, Tommy, there is always more to the story. Are you in trouble?"

"Quite a lot, actually. I should not have dragged you into this affair, but truthfully, I didn't know where else to turn."

"I come from Kashmir, Tommy. I have learned to live with quite a lot of trouble. But I would like to know what kind is following you, and why."

"So would I, Mohan. Are we safe here?"

Dr. Bhatt stares at his friend for a moment. Then he glances at his son and the other three Kashmiri men. He nods slightly and each of them takes a step or two. Sushil reaches into the top end of a rolled carpet, which is propped against the wall beside scores of others, and extracts an AK-47 assault rifle. From beneath his baggy shirt, he plucks a cartridge case and snaps it into place. The other three men simultaneously produce weapons from nearby hiding places. With much clicking of metal and practiced pageantry the men stand with weapons at the ready—a Hechler and Koch G36, an M14, and an M24 SWS. In less than ten seconds, the mild-mannered Kashmiri rug merchants have transformed themselves into an armed militia.

Curt whistles softly and proclaims, "I'd say we'll be safe here… wouldn't you, *Tommy*?" He says the name with a sarcastic familiarity.

"This is a side of you I didn't know, Mohan" Thompson says. "It seems you were expecting trouble before we arrived."

"We're always expecting trouble," Dr. Bhatt replies, gesturing to his men to put down their arms. "Even though we are Muslims, we have many Muslim enemies. Perhaps some of our enemies are yours as well."

"Perhaps."

"Our enemies are the radicals and terrorists who wish to transform our country into an Islamic backwater of the harshest sort. There are many of us who are no less devout in our Faith but wish to be part of the twenty-first century. Our enemies see our trade with India and the west as a betrayal of Islam, and they will stop at nothing to destroy us. And yet they offer no alternatives to keep our families out of poverty."

Charlotte studies the gray-haired Kashmiri whose gently smiling eyes obviously hide a deep frustration. "Your enemies apparently are from your own country," she says, "and probably neighboring Pakistan. Our enemies are from our own country as well. For some reason, the CIA is out to get us."

"The CIA? Well, of course, that does not surprise me. Your intelligence agency is all tied up, like a Gordian knot, without a clue as to how all the sides line up these days. Your country chooses to arm one side against another, and within a few years the sides have traded places and all those weapons are being used to kill Americans. Too many marriages of convenience, in other words, with no long-term strategy. Or commitment. Which is the basis of any worthwhile relationship. Forgive me for talking about marriage, but are the two of you…?"

114

Dr. Bhatt glances from Charlotte to Curt. Charlotte catches his meaning and blushes like a school girl. "Curt and me, you mean? Married? Good heavens no. We're just associates… a news gathering team."

"Mates, in the sense of working together," Curt adds.

"Sorry for my bluntness, but I need to know how many rooms you will need. So the two of you are good friends, drawn closely together by the tribulations of covering world events, I imagine."

"Good friends, certainly," Charlotte adds. "Though he's a bit hard to get along with at times." She laughs nervously. The others merely smile.

"*Committed* friends, I'm sure. Nevertheless," Dr. Bhatt continues, "if the CIA is after you, they must think you have turned against them—or against one of their friends."

"You're right, I'm sure, but I can't begin to reason what we might have done to piss them off," Charlotte says.

"How badly do they want you?"

"They followed Greg and me to Delhi, then set up a meeting. When we arrived, we found two agents dead. Blown up in their hotel room. Afterwards, I found two other armed agents searching my room."

"And yet you are not in their custody."

"No—another man saved me."

"So you have a guardian angel," Dr. Bhatt says. "And now you have five more." He gestures broadly to the five Kashmiris, including himself, and they bow gracefully.

"I am a very poor host," he continues. "Let me show you to your rooms upstairs. You must all be exhausted. After a short rest, we will have a wonderful dinner together and you can start at the beginning. God willing, I may be able to help you make sense of your predicament."

Greg looks up from his Bible and flings a question at Dr. Bhatt. "Do you have Internet access?"

Chapter 29

The next hour is a merciful pause in the day's lurching violence. Two rooms above the shop are hurriedly prepared for the exhausted guests. Curt and Thompson are given a room with a large window and two beds. Charlotte and Greg are placed in a small room with a single narrow bed.

Lying in the dark, Charlotte struggles to remember the last time she had slept in the same bed with her son; he must have been four or five years old, the night of his terrible earache, and she had held him close and stroked his head until the ear drops finally softened the pain and he went to sleep. She remembers the smell of his hair, and the warmth of his skin, and the way he nuzzled his face into her shoulder and held her hand.

Held her hand.

Was that the last time?

She remembers crying as her son slept, not because of Greg's pain but because he had already become a phantom, a presence disconnected from her plane of existence, so difficult to touch, except for that one night when he had reached out in misery and taken her hand.

Or had *she* become the phantom? This is the fear that haunts her—that *she* is to blame. Had she not withheld her love for the boy, her mother's presence, by her unceasing travel? In her desire for distance from her husband, hadn't she separated herself from Greg as well? What child would not suffer from a mother's abandonment?

The sight of Greg reminds her of her failure as a mother, and the guilt rises like a cold mist around her. She shivers. She wants to touch the arm of her son, who is lying with his back to her. In a complicated geometry, as if by conscious design, they are not touching. She reaches out her hand until there is the thinnest space between her fingers and Greg's skin—she can almost feel sparks leaping through that lonely synapse—but she cannot close the gap. Her fingers are trembling, and she fears that they will accidentally brush against her son, and so she withdraws—as she always has done—cursing her cowardice and yielding to the familiar instinct to flee, to be someplace else.

Anywhere but here.

"Greg, are you awake?"

Greg responds to his mother's words by sitting up. He rubs his arm. Had he felt her hand through that sliver of space?

"I'm so tired, but I can't sleep either," Charlotte says. "I'm going downstairs for a while to pace. Too wound up, I guess."

Greg stands up, allowing his mother to climb out of bed. Both are still dressed, as if they are two strangers sharing a room.

Charlotte brushes her hair, smooths her clothing, and leaves the room with a timid, "Try to get some sleep."

Without looking at his mother, Greg walks to a small table holding the laptop. He powers up the computer. Using Dr. Bhatt's WEP key, he connects to a wireless access point down the hall and begins searching the Internet.

Lying next to the computer is a color printout of the digital picture he took of the dead Arabs on the lawn. He picks up the picture and studies it. The photo clearly shows the men's faces, their eyes staring eerily into the camera as if they were looking directly at Greg. On their forehead is the number "40," most likely scrawled there by the killer.

Greg finds a website called Digital Online Bible and enters the numeral "40" into the site's search box. After a day of obsessively reading the Bible, with its many references to forty this and forty that, he wonders if there is a connection. A page displays with hundreds of references to "40," most of them chapter or verse numbers.

He tries another search, this one for the word "forty." The monitor flickers as another page displays, a long scrolling page that returns over a hundred matches. Apparently, the word "forty" is a favorite of Bible writers.

Greg electronically copies the many Biblical references and pastes them into a document, storing it in a folder called Bible-Stuff on his computer desktop.

Near the computer lies the Bible that Greg confiscated from the exploded man's hotel room. In reading the book, Greg had come across several pages that were stuck together. In peeling these pages apart, he had discovered that in each case a smear of blood had glued them. The smears seem to have been made deliberately, as each one points to a specific verse on a different page.

The assassin must have marked these verses with the victims' blood shortly after the explosion—which was just before Greg and his companions entered the room. Greg tries to imagine a murderer who blows up two victims and then takes the time to carefully mark a Bible with their blood. Such a man would be extremely fearless and patient. Experienced. And on a mission.

The assassin—the man Greg had seen at the Seasons Hotel and who had saved his mother at the Sri Ruhal—had left a message: three marked Bible passages. Intent on organizing his clues, Greg types the first passage into his document.

> Matthew 2:1-2: Now when Jesus was born in Bethlehem of Judaea in the days of Herod the king, behold, there came wise men from the east to Jerusalem, Saying, Where is he that is born King of the Jews? for we have seen his star in the east, and are come to worship him.

This passage is the familiar story of the wise men and the Star of Bethlehem. He can see no other meaning in it, so he types in the second passage.

> Luke 2:8: And there were in the same country shepherds abiding in the field, keeping watch over their flock by night. And, lo, the angel of the Lord came upon them, and the glory of the Lord shone round about them: and they were sore afraid.

This is another familiar part of the story: the shepherds in the field. But with this verse, Greg feels a tingle, the slight recognition of some hidden meaning when this second verse is read after the first one. He begins to interchange and compare various words and phrases in these two passages, a frantic and dizzying exercise performed just below the threshold of consciousness. An interesting juxtaposition suddenly flashes in his mind.

In Matthew, the wise men saw a star shining in the east. And in Luke, the glory of the Lord shone upon the shepherds.

A star shining.

The glory of the Lord shining.

Of course! The star in the east *is* the glory of the Lord. One and the same. You could interchange the phrases "his star" with "the glory of the Lord" and the meaning of each verse would remain the same though illuminate the other.

The phrase "glory of the Lord" is familiar to Greg. He has come across it many times in his reading of the Bible. He is tempted to plunge back into the Digital Online Bible and explore that term, but decides to complete his task of recording the blood-marked Bible passages, the third of which is:

> **Luke 2:21: And when eight days were accomplished for the circumcising of the child, his name was called Jesus, which was so named of the angel before he was conceived in the womb.**

This verse jumps forward eight days to the circumcision the infant Jesus, obviously a big moment in the life of a Jewish baby. But Greg can see no connection to the first two passages, no relationship to a star, the "glory of the Lord," or the number forty. He begins to type in the fourth and last passage.

> **John 20:11-12: But Mary stood without at the sepulchre weeping: and as she wept, she stooped down, and looked into the sepulchre, And seeth two angels in white sitting, the one at the head, and the other at the feet, where the body of Jesus had lain.**

Again, Greg can make out no connection except that these Bible passages define three important events in the life of Jesus—his birth, circumcision, and resurrection. But then a line from his grandmother's email suddenly makes sense:

> You must find the relic before the others do, and then locate the savior.

According to the Gospel of St. John, Mary, called "Miriam" in Hebrew, peered into the sepulcher and saw two angels seated there.

As if in a vision, Greg sees another Miriam—Greg's grandmother, Miriam Walker—enter the tomb of Jesus. She looks around.

But where is the savior's body?

Chapter 30

Gideon glances at the glimmering screen in his palm and sees the Charlotte dot. The woman is across the street in a carpet shop that is closed for the evening. Obviously, the woman and her companions have found shelter there. Very resourceful.

The street is quiet but well-lit. Gideon scoots his motorbike into the shadows of a bumpy side street that runs along the south edge of the shop, leaning it against a wall. He squats, looks down the street and back the other way, then finally sits down beside a large stack of splintered crate-wood. It will be a long evening, but he's well hidden here. If anyone approaches the shop, he will know.

Gideon removes the dead Pakistani's cell phone from a pocket and looks at it. He desperately wants to call the last incoming number, which is the same as the last outgoing number—probably the terrorist's main contact. He wants to hear the greeting on the other end, to announce the Pakistani's unfortunate accident, to hear the contact's voice rise in anger and impotently shout curses into the phone.

He smiles, thinking about the considerable pleasure such an act would give him, but in the end he puts the phone back into his pocket.

The door cracks open and a hulking shape silently enters Greg's dark room. The shape stands behind the boy, who concentrates fiercely on the computer screen as his fingers tap-tap-tap the keyboard.

"Mom's gone downstairs," Greg says matter-of-factly. He can see the half-lit face of his grandfather reflected in the monitor.

"Thought so. Curt went down too, leaving me all alone." Thompson yawns and shuffles his feet.

"They're together right now. My mother loves him."

"Who? Curt?"

Thompson swivels Greg's chair so he can see the boy's face.

Greg does not look directly at Thompson. Instead, he glances at an array of family photographs he has stuck to the wall.

"Greg, I know that having a conversation may be difficult for you, due to your, uh…"

Suddenly Greg's eyes meet Thompson's. "Asperger's Syndrome," Greg says, completing Thompson's thought. "A pervasive developmental disorder related to autism named after Hans Asperger, a pediatrician who called many of his patients with the disorder 'little professors.'

"Right, Asperger's. I've studied up on it."

"Good. Though I don't see it as a disorder. Do you?"

"Well… not really, judging from you. But I'm a little surprised that you picked up on your mother's…"

"…predilection for a man other than her husband? Pretty obvious, the way she tries not to show it. She doesn't love my dad. They fight."

"To be honest, I hadn't picked up on that. Must be getting old. But I thought that Asperger's kids had trouble noticing nonverbal things like that—social cues and subtle interactions…"

"Maybe I don't have Asperger's, then. Does it matter?"

"Not to me. It's just that you surprise me. I thought you were one way, and it turns out you're quite something else. Here you are having a normal conversation with me."

"I like talking to you."

"Thank you, Greg. I can honestly say that I like talking to you too."

Thompson bends over and gives Greg a hug, expecting the boy to pull away and is surprised when he doesn't.

"I'm smart in some ways," Greg says.

"That's what your mother says. Good at puzzles and figuring things out."

"Sometimes I don't talk to people because they bore me."

"I share your sentiment, but I've never had the courage to voice—I mean *un*voice my sentiments. Even though there are plenty of times I'd rather pull into my own shell and focus on something more interesting than the small talk of the people I'm with. Is that what you do?"

Greg thinks about this and then says, "Sometimes. But maybe it's the Asperger's. If a person has a mental condition that he can't always control, can he be aware of why he's doing the things he can't control?"

Thompson has no answer. To fill the empty space, he shrugs his shoulders and sits down on the edge of the bed.

Greg asks, "Can you keep a secret?" Thompson nods yes. "Usually, my brain goes into a different gear when I'm thinking about something and everything else just disappears for a while. That's pretty bad, huh?"

"I wouldn't say so. I think maybe it's a gift."

"My dad hates it. Mom's not around enough to... I mean, she never says she hates it, because she feels guilty about being gone so much, but she does hate it, because it reminds her of my Asperger's, and she feels responsible, like it's a really terrible thing. I come from her womb. Half of me is her—she thinks it's the bad half."

"Personally, I don't think you have a bad half."

"I was pretty young when they diagnosed me. They took me to a psychologist, and since then they stopped harassing me about ignoring them. I guess they figured there was no use."

"You're not ignoring me."

"But I'm intentionally disobeying Mom's orders. I'm not supposed to talk to you because you're a bad influence."

"So the only reason you're talking to me is to disobey your mother?"

Greg thinks about this "I don't know," he says. "Maybe I just want to see what kind of bad influence you'd be."

"Fair enough. So, maybe I should get it over with and be a bad influence right now." Thompson leans toward his grandson and with a serious face says, "Wanna smoke a joint with me?"

Greg stares at Thompson for a moment, not sure what to say.

Thompson can't keep a straight face any longer. Suddenly he laughs. Greg, relieved beyond measure, laughs with him, though he really doesn't see the humor.

"Do I have to call you Thompson?"

"You can call me Grandpa."

Greg considers this for quite a while. He seems to be trying out the word in his head before saying it. Finally, though his eyes timidly wander back to the wall, he says, "Grandpa, can you tell me about Grandma Walker?"

I n the shadowy grayness of the shop downstairs, color sleeps on the supple carpets of Kashmir. Charlotte spots Curt silhouetted against a window glowing with orange streetlight. Like a warm breeze, she wafts across the hardwood floor and embraces him, her arms a hushed whisper around his chest, her eager hand slipping beneath his unbuttoned shirt.

Curt winces in pain as she squeezes him.

"Sorry, Luv," he says, turning to face her. Three broken ribs and a bunch of bruises from our little sortie in Iraq. Not healing as fast as I'd like, got to admit. Still feel like I been kicked by a troop of kangaroos."

Charlotte withdraws her hands. "Didn't know—sorry," she says.

"Been a bit of a hard time of late."

"How's Barbara?"

"As in *my wife Barbara*? Wouldn't know. She left me right after she visited me in hospital with the cracked ribs. Said something about the loneliness and the worry that goes with supporting my career choice." He pauses and instinctively prods the Ace bandage that wraps his chest.

"I'm sorry about Barbara," Charlotte says, taking Curt's hand and gently stroking the knuckles. She's not really sorry, though. She is worried. Will Curt now press her to leave Mike? Abandoned men become desperate to reattach.

"And how is Mike, pray tell?" There is an edge to Curt's voice, and Charlotte doesn't like it.

"As in *my husband Mike*?" She tries to give her voice the same sharp edge that Curt had used, but it comes off sounding phony. She lets the pretense fall. "You know how he is, I've told you countless times. His head is still buried in his pathetic little restaurant, which was fine until all this bloody business started, and now he's just scared like me. Having terrorists killed in your front yard does that to people."

"Maybe this shared horror will bring you two closer together."

"Never," she says, putting his hand on her cheek. "But you and I, Curt, have shared a real horror. In Iraq. You saved my life."

Curt pulls his hand from her cheek. "More like the other way around, unless mimicking a punching bag counts, which I doubt."

Charlotte takes his hand and kisses the palm. "It's not much of a relationship, is it, every few months when we're thrown together on assignment."

Curt closes his eyes and whispers, "It's what I live for."

"A few days here and there."

"Am I the only one, Luv?"

"The same question every time." She tenderly kisses his cheek.

"I'm insecure. I need to hear it," Curt says.

"There are no others."

He cups the back of her head with his palm and pulls her close, kissing her—the desperate kiss of a soldier leaving for the front, of a dying man saying goodbye to his lover. He inhales her soul and she yields, breathless and dizzy with the danger of it.

Light suddenly floods the room, startling them. Quickly, they separate as the sound of footsteps intrudes. Charlotte turns and finds Dr. Bhatt descending the stairs. The Kashmiri sees them and smiles.

"Dinner is served in the upstairs dining room," he announces.

"That's good, good…" Charlotte replies, "we were hungry. Thank you."

Dr. Bhatt stares at Curt and Charlotte for a moment, his lips curling into a faint smile. "Hunger must be fed," he says at last. "We'll expect you in about fifteen minutes?"

He turns off the light and walks upstairs with a bounce in his step.

Chapter 31

Two automobiles pull into the silent street fronting Kashmir Carpets. The silver Alto Bharatt and the green Maruti 800 are among the most common vehicles in India. Each car parks within a block of the shop and ejects three Pakistanis like spent cartridges from an automatic weapon. The wiry Alto driver, Mostafa, whispers in Pashto to his men, who are dressed in dark shirts and pants.

"Remember, we must take him out before the others, but be careful. Do not try to do this by yourself."

A stocky, pock-faced man spits into the street. "He killed my brother. You must let me do this, Mostafa. It is my right."

Mostafa pats the stout man on a muscular shoulder. "Zawaar, this man we hunt may not be an ordinary man. It is possible that he has the strength and cunning of a hundred men."

"And I have the strength of Allah," Zawaar replies. "A hundred men do not frighten me."

"You are brave, my friend, but our mission is most glorious, and this is only the beginning of it. We do not seek martyrs tonight, and a martyr you would be if you tried to do this by yourself. This is only the first stage, so be patient, Zawaar, and obey your superior."

Zawaar kicks a stone in frustration. "If I see the infidel, can I kill him?"

"Of course. He has fulfilled his purpose in leading us to the others. The difficulty will be in seeing him."

With a motion of his hand, Mostafa sends his team into the shadows.

The upstairs dining room is larger than Charlotte had expected. In the center is a long table that could seat ten or twelve, though only Dr. Bhatt and his four guests are currently seated there. The remnants of roast lamb, brown rice and fresh fruit mark Curt's plate as he pushes it away.

"No more, not another bite," Curt says.

"But we have a special dessert for you," Dr. Bhatt suggests, smiling. "You must try it or our cook will be insulted."

"Later, then. Like maybe next week."

"May Allah bless us with your presence until then."

Charlotte looks weary. She sighs loudly to signal her frustration and the others turn toward her, then says, "Look, for the last hour we've hashed over the events since my visit to Iraq and looked at the evidence and the clues, but we're no closer to deciding what to do next than when we came here."

Dr. Bhatt, who is seated next to Charlotte, pats her wrist and says, "I believe we have made considerable progress. We've nourished our bodies at the same time all five of us learned the facts of this mysterious quest of yours."

"I didn't mean to suggest…"

Dr. Bhatt interrupts. "No, my dear, you are right. Time is short and we must now consider what we know. May I summarize?"

The others nod their heads in agreement.

"Charlotte, your mother sent a message to Greg that she was in jeopardy. She asked that you gather up your father and son to help find some sort of relic before other unnamed parties did, and then 'locate the savior,' whatever that means.

"The important questions seem to be, first, what is this relic? Then who are the other parties searching for it and why do they want it? From your report of the attack on your neighbor, who was a collector of religious relics, and the violent episodes that occurred today, it seems there are several parties interested in this relic, which apparently was the bait that attracted all of them."

"All true," Charlotte says. "And I thinkr that terrorists are one of these parties. We have bodies to prove that."

Thompson adds, "And the FBI told you that there were dead Mossad agents at your neighbor's home."

"The CIA definitely has an interest," Curt suggests. "They followed Char and Greg to India."

"Terrorists, Mossad, the CIA," Dr. Bhatt summarizes. "But there is someone else, or some other group, that also has an interest, isn't there?"

Charlotte takes a deep breath. The question prompts a memory that relieves her anxiety. "Yes, the man who killed the CIA agents, and saved me at the hotel a few hours ago. He's not CIA, unless he's some sort of rogue agent. And he didn't look Semitic, so I don't think he's Mossad or part of an Islamic terror group."

"It seems we have a fourth party involved—this *guardian angel* of Charlotte's, and whatever group he represents," Dr. Bhatt suggests. "And for all we know, there may be other parties. This relic is very important to many different factions."

"Including the Vatican," Thompson interjects.

The others turn to him, stunned.

"The Vatican?" Curt asks. "This is getting too weird. How do you know this, Tommy?"

"A good friend of mine, Antonio Fortunati, is—or *was*—prefect of the Secret Archives of the Vatican. He came to visit me today."

Charlotte blanches. "Fortunati was the visitor at your apartment? Oh my God—the blood stains…"

"We don't know what happened to him," Thompson cautions, "but I do know that he removed some relics from the Archives and brought them here to show me. He hid them in a potted plant—one of the precautions I suggested to him. I would have to say that we should consider the Vatican as another player in this unfolding drama. Throughout history, after all, which other organization has had a greater obsession with religious relics than the Vatican?"

"Do you have these relics with you?" Dr. Bhatt asks.

"In my room. Documents, mostly. To be honest, I haven't had a chance to inspect them closely."

"I suppose that a document could be the relic everyone is looking for," Charlotte says. "Still, I don't really understand how I fit into this. What's the link? Mike and I happened to attend a Christmas party at Jack Curtis's house—that's about my only link to him. Except for…"

"Except for what?" Dr. Bhatt prods.

"The FBI agent told me that Jack Curtis was found with a bullet in his head and copy of Dad's book, *The World's Great Wisdom Traditions*, in his hands."

Everyone at the table turns toward Thompson, suggesting through their intense gazes that he should respond.

"Look, over fifty thousand copies of that book were sold. Apparently, this Curtis fellow bought one of them. That shouldn't be surprising if he were an ardent collector of religious relics. I must say, though, it's quite a coincidence that he bought my book, owned a relic that people will kill to obtain, and lived across Lake Minnetonka from my daughter."

"This relic is a magnet for trouble," Curt says.

"But the relic is only half of your mother's instruction," Dr. Bhatt says, staring at Charlotte. "You were also asked to *locate the savior*."

"That part's easy, right Dad?" Charlotte says. She has found the sharp edge she had been lacking an hour ago in her discussion with Curt. "Jesus is in heaven, seated at the right hand of God. At least according to the Catholics and Evangelicals."

"If that's true," Curt says, "we know where he is—in heaven. But your mother makes it sound like locating hime is a physical thing. Maybe finding his bones or something."

"Impossible," Charlotte retorts. "Christians hold that Jesus was crucified, rose again, and then ascended bodily into heaven. So no trace of him could ever be located."

"Maybe we should review what we know about this *Savior*," Thompson says. "Does anyone know his actual name?"

"Tommy, are you kidding?" Curt says. "Jesus Christ."

"Certainly we call him that," Thompson answers. "But Jesus is a Greek name, and the Savior was born a Hebrew. In fact, the name Jesus did not even exist until about five hundred years ago, and the letter "J" did not exist in any language at all until the fourteenth century in England. The Savior's Hebrew name was Yahshua. Today we would pronounce it Joshua. In other languages, such as Arabic or Persian, he is called 'Isa' with one 's' or 'Issa with two.' How he came to be called 'Jesus' is too long a story, but I have another question for you. Where was Yahshua or Issa born?"

Almost to himself, Curt begins singing "O little town of Bethlehem, how still we see thee lie." He stops, then sheepishly looks down at his plate. "Yes, yes, in the little town of Bethlehem," Thompson says, "though it's a bit early for Christmas carols. But *where* in this town was he born?"

"In a stable. Apparently the local inn screwed up the reservations." Curt replies.

"Ah, yes, the familiar verse from St. Luke: 'And she brought forth her first-born son and wrapped him in swaddling clothes and laid Him in a manger.'"

"Because there was no room for them in the inn," Greg adds.

Charlotte is surprised her son knows this.

"Very good, Greg," Thompson says. "A manger, of course, is a wooden trough used for feeding horses or cattle, and one would think it was located in a stable. But are you really sure that Jesus was born in a stable?"

The thin, reedy voice of Greg intrudes again. "The Gospel of Mark talks about the wise men visiting Jesus in a *house*," he says.

"Oh my—I believe you're right, Greg." Thompson smiles proudly at his grandson. "Mark says, 'And when they were come into the <u>house</u>, they saw the young child with Mary, his mother, and fell down and worshipped him.' Adding to this confused narrative, in the early days of the Christian faith there was a firm belief that Jesus was born in yet a different place. Eusebius, the first ecclesiastical historian, wrote that Jesus was born in a cave, and that in the time of Constantine a magnificent temple had been built above it so all Christians could worship the site of Jesus's birth. Even Jesus's brother, James, referred to a cave when he wrote the Protevangelion, one of the apocryphal gospels. He wrote, 'On a sudden, the cloud became a great light in the *cave*, so their eyes could not bear it.'"

"So we don't really know where he was born, is that what you're saying?" Curt suggests.

"I'm saying that our commonly held beliefs are often misinformed and based more on legend than fact. The truth is that Jesus was born in a cave, but Matthew was very nearly correct when he mentioned a house. The cave of Jesus's birth was actually a well-developed grotto that served as a rescue house and hospice. There were three of these grottos in Palestine, all of them administered by a cultish group we call Essenes.

"These people lived communally, were deeply spiritual, took vows of poverty, swore to the secrecy of their cult under penalty of death, and wore white robes made of one seamless piece of material. For this they were known as the Brethren in White Clothing. And because they were so often silent, and when speaking exhibited an unusual control of intonation, they were sometimes called the soft-speaking men."

Chapter 32

In a shadow, Gideon is seated on a slab of wood with his back against a stone wall. The heat of the day has dissipated and a humid chill has now settled in. A rust-colored dog, hungry and filthy, sits at his feet seeking a handout. Gideon slaps the side of his leg and the dog timidly approaches. With gentle fingers, Gideon scratches the dog behind the ears. The dog sighs, inching even closer. A frayed piece of rope is tied round the dog's neck, evidence of a vain attempt to restrain the mutt's movement.

"So you broke out of jail, huh?" Gideon whispers to the dog. He finds a granola bar in his pocket and breaks it, giving half to his new friend. "Might be the only food we get tonight, pal."

The dog munches the bar and squeaks a thank you, or so Gideon thinks.

Gideon looks at a second-floor window across the narrow street that separates him from the carpet shop. For over an hour, this window has been illuminated. Gideon guesses that Charlotte and her companions are dining in that room, or maybe discussing with their host the events of the day.

The most difficult part of Gideon's work is not the stress of an assassination attempt in impossible circumstances, or the occasional altercation, or the long stretches without sleep. The hardest part is boredom.

Gideon has learned that certain forms of meditation enhance his awareness of surroundings while allowing his brain and muscles to rest. He thinks of it as conscious sleep, a kind of self-hypnosis with dual benefits. He has gone for seven days without traditional sleep by periodically entering into this immensely pleasurable altered state. He has also learned that between episodes of meditation, he can improve his mental agility by playing cerebral war games, imagining every scenario that may occur in his current environment and planning a winning strategy for each one.

This evening he plans to meditate. One thing, however, prevents him from entering into that blissful state—he is still tempted by the Pakistani's cell phone. He holds it in his hand, staring at the cool glow of the screen. The on-screen indicator shows that the battery is almost dead.

Go ahead, do it! The voice in Gideon's head urges him to call the terrorist's contact. Gideon knows the impetuous tone of this internal voice all too well. It is the voice of a younger Gideon. It is the voice that prompted him to disobey a military order, an act that saved innocent lives but landed Gideon a dishonorable discharge and a new life as a school janitor.

He knows the danger of placing this call. He has not been authorized to initiate contact with any Islamic terrorist organization because such an act could heighten the group's alertness and jeopardize other operations. Rules always have a logical reason. And yet his instincts tell him to violate the rules and make the call—for personal gratification, perhaps, or for some clue to the mother organization behind the search for the relic. It doesn't matter. No one will know.

Gideon decides to use his random number generator to make the final decision. He knows this is a cowardly cop-out because there is no strategic or tactical need to ask the question, but he asks anyway. Should he make the call? Odd number *yes*, even number *no*. The number comes up odd.

Gideon scrolls through a menu on the cell phone and presses a button to call the last incoming phone number. Holding the phone to his ear, he waits for the other phone to ring. And it does—about thirty yards away.

A surge of terror-stoked adrenaline rushes through Gideon's body. The Pakistani's contact is here. Now. Just down the street, though Gideon can't see him.

The terrorists must have embedded a tracking device inside the cell phone. Gideon has led them right to Charlotte's neighborhood.

The call is terminated at the other end. The contact had made a serious tactical error by forgetting to silence his phone. Gideon imagines the man's mute Arabic curses. Tonight, boredom will not be a problem.

"Wait a minute," Charlotte says. She has been slumping in her chair, impatiently enduring her father's pedantic history lesson. But now her curiosity is piqued. "Weren't the Essenes the people who lived in, what's-it-called?—Qumran—and left behind the Dead Sea Scrolls? I did a piece on the Scrolls a few years back. A kind of secretive mystical sect of Judaism, right?"

Thompson snaps his fingers and points at his daughter. "Almost correct. But the Essenes were not really a *Jewish* sect. They were an ancient mystical society established by the ancestors of a Pharaoh named Amenhotep IV. Those of you who have prayed or said grace before a meal have unintentionally paid homage to the god after which he was named every time you said *Amen!* Amen-Ra was the god, and the name Amenhotep means 'Amen is satisfied.'

"The secret society grew over time and the Essenes of Heliopolis spread into Palestine, eventually forming a great center of learning at Mount Carmel, the Mountain of the Lord as the Old Testament refers to it. The Prophet Elijah, who dwelled for a time in a cave on this holy mountain, was in fact one of these Essenes, according to the old Jewish records. In Greece, members of this mystical cult took the name 'Therapeuti,' and there were many other branches. The overall organization became known as the Great White Brotherhood, not because it was racist, but because its members preferred to dress in pure white garments.

"Pharaoh Akhnaton, an ancestor of Amenhotep, modernized the Brotherhood with new rules and regulations. He established the world's first monotheistic religion, laying the foundation for many of the doctrines of Judaism and Christianity. If you don't recognize the name Akhnaton, I'm sure you know him by reputation. He was Pharaoh when the children of Israel dwelled in Egypt."

Charlotte interrupts. "So the man who propagated the belief in one God turned into one of the greatest villains of all time."

"Sometimes a good man just gets a bad rap," Thompson says, gazing directly into Charlotte's eyes. "In other words, he wasn't fairly portrayed by Yul Brynner in 'The Ten Commandments.'"

Charlotte bristles at this metaphoric appeal to reconsider her father's reputation. "This is getting us nowhere," she complains. "Just a waste of time. Mom's life depends on us *doing* something."

"I believe we are doing something," Dr. Bhatt interjects. "We're trying to get at the meaning of your mother's message. If we don't understand what she's asking of us, it's impossible to know what to do. We must reason first."

Charlotte bites back. "This history lesson, according to the Gospel of St. Thompson, isn't helping me understand Mom's message at all."

Ignoring the previous exchange entirely, Greg inquisitively urges on his grandfather. "Akhnaton," he says, rolling the word over his tongue. "Akhnaton was a good guy?" he asks.

Charlotte slumps in her chair, overruled by her host and her son.

Thompson nods at Greg. "After he was adopted into the Egyptian royal family, Moses was initiated into the Great White Brotherhood, and this is where he learned the fundamentals of monotheism, which he later introduced to the tribes of Israel. After many adventures, he appealed to the Pharaoh for assistance in leading his people out of Egypt. But the heathen priesthood at that time had power and influence that rivaled, sometimes even exceeded, that of the Pharaoh, and they were threatened by the radical religious notions of Akhnaton. They also wanted to keep the tribes enslaved. It was through the aid of Akhnaton, and the secret assistance of the Great White Brotherhood, that the people of Israel safely escaped."

"Okay, it's all very interesting, but I tend to agree with Charlotte now," Curt says. "This is all pre-Christian history. How does it relate to Jesus?"

"It relates directly," Thompson says. As he speaks, he becomes more animated. "You see, Mary and Joseph were both devout Essenes. In other words, they were members of the Great White Brotherhood. Mary was raised in the Brotherhood's Temple of Helios just outside Jerusalem.

"The Brotherhood had determined that Mary was to be the mother of a Holy Child, and so when she was twelve and yet a virgin they appointed the widower Joseph to be her guardian, though he was much older than Mary and had two children from his previous marriage. He took Mary into his house in Galilee.

"About a century earlier, Aristobulus, the first king of the Jews, had forced all those living in Galilee to adopt circumcision and the Mosaic law. So even though Joseph and Mary were Essenes, they were required to follow the laws of Judaism. And if you followed Judaic law, you were considered a Jew, even if you were not ethnically Hebrew."

"While Joseph was away on a building project, Mary became pregnant with Jesus. This presented a problem. Eventually, to help Mary avoid community censure for an apparent indiscretion, the Brotherhood arranged for her and Joseph to travel to an Essene grotto, a hospice near Bethlehem, for the delivery of the child. And that is how they arrived there—not by accident, but by design. So you see, Curt, their reservations were *not* screwed up at all."

"Did the Magi actually follow a star to find them?" Greg asks.

"Think about it, my boy. How can you *follow* a star, which is so high in the heavens? Ever try it? And how can a star pinpoint the location of an infant, a town, even a country, unless it descends to hover directly over a specific location? Of course, today we know this is impossible."

"So now you're debunking the Star of Bethlehem?" Curt asks.

"Not at all. In fact, an astronomer friend of mine claims that in the year 7 BCE, which could be the actual year of Jesus's birth, there was a brilliant conjunction of Venus and Mercury, and this would have appeared as a very bright star in the sky.

"Maybe you don't know that the births of many of history's 'Messengers' of God, or 'Avatars,'" have been accompanied by an astronomical event—at least according to tradition. And the mothers of these Holy Ones are also said to have been virgins like Mary. Krishna, the founder of Hinduism, was born of the virgin Devaki, who was called the 'Mother of God.' A great star announced his birth, and immediately several Magi came bearing gifts of sandalwood and perfumes. Sound familiar?

"A great moving star also directed wise men to the birthplace of Buddha, where they presented the infant with gifts. Buddha's mother, by the way, was a virgin named Maya or Mary, and the infant Buddha was called the 'Begotten of God.'

"If you look, you can find stories of a bright star guiding wise men to the birthplace of Confucius, Mithras, Socrates, Bacchus, Romulus and many others. Tradition holds that virgins gave birth to the Siamese savior Codom, the Chinese god Lao-Tsze, the Egyptian gods Horus and Ra, the Persian prophet Zoroaster, as well as Cyrus, the king of Persia. Even Plato was believed to be the Divine Son of God born of a pure virgin named Perictione. Pythagoras, the father of geometry, and Appolonius, who lived during Jesus's lifetime, were said to have been born of virgins. So was the Aztec god Quetzalcoatl. Should I go on?"

"So the star and the virgin birth were not unique to Jesus," Greg says.

"And maybe that's why the historical record, other than the Bible, lacks references to either event regarding Jesus," Thompson replies. "Perhaps these 'miracles' were not seen as miracles at all in that day but something much more commonplace."

"But the star…" Greg says, hesitating for a moment. "You say there probably was a Star of Bethlehem. But how did the Magi follow it to Jesus, since you can't literally follow a star?" He is unusually engaged in this conversation.

Thompson squints his eyes and stares at Greg. "Another good question, Greg. The title of Magus was given only to those who had attained the highest level in the mystery schools of the day. They were very learned men who had studied for years the arts and sciences, including astronomy, history, natural and spiritual law, and so much more. They were the oracles for the learned class.

"For months, even years before the birth of Jesus, they had been watching the heavens, perhaps charting the coming conjunction of Venus and Mercury, which they fully expected to herald the birth of a Holy Infant as it had in the past. Several weeks before this celestial event occurred, they began their journey to pay tribute to the infant. And they knew just where to find the newborn Jesus, because the Brotherhood had revealed to them its plan to move Mary and Joseph to the Essene hospice."

Greg jiggles his chair a few inches closer to his grandfather. "Maybe that's how we'll locate the savior this time," he says.

"How's that, my boy?"

"By following a star."

Chapter 33

Gideon finishes tying the terrorist's cell phone to the dog's neck with the frayed rope. "Off with you now," Gideon whispers. "Take that phone down the street."

The dog cocks its head.

"You owe me for that granola bar."

Gideon pats the dog on the butt. The dog sits there staring at him.

"All right, pal. This could be the end of a beautiful friendship, but I've gotta do this."

Gideon pulls out a dagger and pokes the mutt with it. The dog yelps and scurries down the street away from the hidden terrorist. Gideon huddles behind a smashed crate and waits for his adversary to make the next move.

Within a minute, footsteps approach Gideon's position. From his crouch, Gideon can make out two pairs of legs. They stop just past his hiding place. One of the men, Mostafa, is holding an electronic device that displays a moving blip, the cell phone.

In Arabic, Mustafa hoarsely speaks to his companion. "He's heading towards Zawaar. Allah may grant our brother his desire to kill the infidel."

From behind, the two Pakistanis hear another voice.

"Allahu Akhbar!"

Mustafa and his partner turn just in time to see a short blade gleaming in the streetlight. And then all is silent again.

"Greg has some novel ideas," Charlotte says.

"Insightful ideas, I submit," Thompson counters. "Who's to say he's not correct? If we only knew which star to follow! But to pick up my line of inquiry…"

"You mean your homily," Charlotte suggests.

Thompson ignores his daughter. "We may learn something interesting if we look at the life of this savior. He was born in Bethlehem, but does anyone know where he was raised as a child?"

"Jesus of Nazareth," Curt says. "I went to Sunday School, okay? He was raised in a town called Nazareth. That's in Galilee, I believe, unless this is another trick question."

Thompson stands, stretching muscles stiff from sitting. "As it happens," he says, "there was no town called Nazareth in Galilee, or anywhere nearby, at the time of Jesus. Translators mistakenly changed the phrase 'Jesus returning to the Nazarenes' into 'Jesus returning to Nazareth'."

"So? Isn't a Nazarene someone from Nazareth?" Curt asks.

"Therein lies the problem. That's just what the translators thought. But 'Nazarene' was a name given by the Jews to people outside their own religion who belonged to a secret society or cult. In the Bible, even John the Baptist was called a 'Nazarene.' And in the book of Acts 24:5, we find another man who is called a 'ringleader of the sect of the Nazarenes.' You see, when Jews came across someone in their own country who had a different religion and seemed to have a mystical understanding of the things of life, they usually called such a person a Nazarene."

"But there is a town called Nazareth in Israel. I've been there," Curt says. "to cover a Christian pilgrimage to the site of Jesus's birth."

"Of course there is a town called Nazareth. In the fourth century, it became necessary to identify the place of Jesus's birth, but since there was no place called Nazareth, the searchers attached that name to a small settlement called En-Nasira. Thus, the town of Nazareth was born. Unfortunately, this town has none of the physical attributes mentioned in the Bible."

"So, what's your point?" Charlotte asks, still exasperated with the history lesson.

"I believe your father is saying that legends take on a life of their own," Dr. Bhatt says.

"If Jesus wasn't born in Nazareth, the way the Bible says," Greg interjects, "then maybe he didn't die in Jerusalem, as Christians believe. Isn't that possible, Grandpa?"

Thompson seems to be the only one who notices that Greg has called him Grandpa in public. As he smiles at his grandson, Charlotte suddenly stands up. Greg's comment has stirred an insight.

"The crucifixion!" she says. "It's the cornerstone of Christian belief."

"No, the crucifixion isn't," Thompson asserts. "The cross is just the set-up. The resurrection is the payoff. If Jesus did not die on the cross in Jerusalem, then there could be no resurrection. A healing, perhaps. Or a convalescence. But no rising from the dead."

"Christianity would be in serious trouble," Curt says. "If this were true, and it could be proven, Christianity would disintegrate. Along with its powerful institutions."

"Wouldn't the terrorists love to exploit that!" Charlotte adds. And then, after thinking about it, she adds: "And wouldn't our Christian president, and his CIA—and the Vatican, too—love to cover it up to keep Christianity intact."

"Talk about fertile ground for the rise of Islam," Thompson says.

Dr. Bhatt waves his hand. "It is true that Islam does not believe in the resurrection. The Qur'an teaches that another person was substituted for Jesus on the cross. We believe Jesus was a great teacher, a Messenger of God, as was the Prophet Muhammad. But His Holiness Jesus is not God and was not resurrected."

Charlotte rubs her temples. "'Locate the savior,' my mother said. If Jesus did not die after the crucifixion, he certainly would have died later. In some other place. Without a resurrection, there could be no ascension, and so his bones would be lying somewhere in Israel."

"Unless he traveled elsewhere," Dr. Bhatt adds.

"It may surprise you," Thompson says, "that a number of people besides Muslims believe that Jesus survived the crucifixion and recovered from his wounds. I have to admit that after traveling the world and studying many different faiths, I find the tale of crucifixion, death, physical resurrection and ascension to be rather hard to swallow."

"But if he survived," Curt says, "and died sometime later, wouldn't there be records? Wouldn't his bones have turned up somewhere over the past two thousand years?"

"Maybe they have," Dr. Bhatt suggests. "On the other hand, who's been looking?"

Chapter 34

Firecrackers. That's what the shots sound like at first. But after hearing the odd sequence—three in rapid succession, then two more, then another three—Dr. Bhatt rises from the table with a stern look.

"Please, you must come with me. There is trouble," he says, waving his hands to hurry his guests along.

"What is it?" Thompson asks.

"Gunshots, Tommy. Keep movin'," Curt replies.

"Do not worry, we have guards," Dr. Bhatt mutters as he efficiently ushers the others down the hall and into a small room with bolted metal plates fish-scaling the walls.

When everyone is inside, Dr. Bhatt closes the heavily armored door and slides a thick steel bolt across the doorway. "It is safe in here, unless they have RPGs. We have canned food and water, you see? And candles."

"Mohan, what in heaven's name is going on?" Thompson asks.

"We will know shortly," Dr. Bhatt explains. "It may be some of our misguided Islamist brothers who have been swayed into a life of terror. They don't appreciate moderate Kashmiri business people like us, as I explained before. Of course, the shots may also originate with one of the many organizations that are after Charlotte."

Five more gunshots are faintly heard through the steel-lined walls.

"We got the idea for this safe room from a Jodie Foster movie," Dr. Bhatt continues. Badly dubbed, unfortunately. This is the first time we've used it."

"We're honored," Curt says sarcastically.

After spotting two men coming toward him, Gideon pulls a Glock from his waistband and rolls behind a steel dumpster. From this spot he can see the men approaching on his right. They stop and raise their weapons.

Three shots ring out in rapid succession, the first one surprisingly from Gideon's left, the next two from the oncoming pair. Gideon looks to his left and sees a Pakistani—Zawaar—lying in the street next to a parked automobile. Gideon watches the two men cautiously approaching Zawaar's body. They slowly walk past Gideon's hiding place and stop to kick the dead man. Obviously, they do not suspect Gideon's presence.

The men speak to each other. The language is not Hindi or Urdu, not Sindhi or Gujarati. It has distinctive vowel and consonant sounds not typical of other Indian languages. In this neighborhood, the men are likely speaking Kashmiri. Perhaps they are part of a local militia. In any event, Gideon has no quarrel with these men.

Suddenly, another shot sounds on Gideon's right, and the window of the car nearest Zawaari's body shatters. The two Kashmiris duck behind the car. Another shot rings out on Gideon's right.

The shape of a head appears above a small truck about thirty yards from the two men. One of the Kashmiris—Dr. Bhatt's son, Sushil—raises an automatic pistol and fires three shots that strike the man's head. The young man is deadly with a pistol, obviously better trained than a typical militia member, Gideon notes.

Sushil and his companion race to the body and find this man dead as well. Sudden movement causes them to look up. Another man dashes across the street before Sushil can fire. The sound of a car starting is followed by screeching tires. The fleeing man has decided against martyrdom.

As the Kashmiris watch the car fishtail down the street, Gideon spots another man, the sixth Pakistani, sneaking up behind the Kashmiris. The Pakistani raises a gun, points it at Sushil, and…

Pffft. Gideon's silenced Glock whispers in the night air. The Pakistani's lower leg bursts open and the man howls, dropping his gun. The shouting turns Sushil's head. The Kashmiris rush to the wounded terrorist, look around frantically for the shooter, then seem to decide that anyone who would shoot their enemy is an ally.

Sushil angrily kicks the Pakistani in the head, yelling a particularly vile Kashmiri curse. With help from his companion, he picks up the bleeding man and drags him toward the carpet shop.

Gideon looks up and down the vacant street. He counts faces in three windows overlooking the gun battle. And then he decides to leave the neighborhood before the carrion is scooped up for disposal.

Whoever is protecting Charlotte this evening does not need his help.

The booming voice of Sushil penetrates the armor of the safe room, though faintly. "Father, it's Sushil. It's safe to come out."

Dr. Bhatt opens the door and a cool draft whisks into the room. "Are you all right, my son?"

A shrieking groan spirals up the staircase to the safe room.

Sushil nods yes. His face is slick with sweat. "There were six Pakistanis. Four dead, one escaped. The last one is downstairs, wounded."

"And your cousins?"

"No one is hurt, father. But there is something else of importance."

Overwhelmed with relief for his son's safety, Dr. Bhatt does not wait for Sushil to deliver more news. He reaches for his son, embraces him fiercely, then strokes Sushil's face with broad, calloused hands.

"You are safe, that is the most important thing."

Sushil looks deeply into his father's eyes. "Listen to me, father. There was someone else on the street. He shot the sixth Pakistani in the leg. On purpose, I think."

Dr. Bhatt lowers his hands. "Did you see this seventh man?"

"No, the man is a *prith*." Sushil uses the Kashmiri word for *ghost*. "But the evidence of his marksmanship is downstairs. He just as easily could have shot Ashok or me, so he is most... *atha-rochi*."

"Generous? Perhaps, or more likely motivated by some other purpose. Maybe to provide us with an interview subject."

Charlotte steps forward. "I think this seventh man may have been my Guardian Angel."

"That seems the most logical explanation, in which case we needn't worry about him for the moment," Dr. Bhatt says. "Sushil, we are going downstairs. Bring our wounded guest to the safe room for treatment and, shall we say, a personal interview. Make sure your cousins gather up the bodies and dispose of them in the usual way."

Thompson is startled by Dr. Bhatt's inference. "The *usual* way?"

"Yes, we have had infestations of vermin in the past. We simply transport the carcasses to another part of the city where the police know how to take care of them. In our neighborhood, dead vermin are bad for business."

ideon settles onto the seat of his motor scooter and starts the engine. The scooter coughs and then emits a soft purr. He smiles. Tonight he will have a good night's sleep in a hotel room he thought he would never use—but only after he completes two important pieces of business.

First, he inspects Mostafa's cell phone, which he had taken from the victim. He finds the last several calls neatly logged, including the incoming call from Gideon a few minutes ago. Good. Without hesitation this time, he pushes a button to call one of the listed numbers. It rings and a man's voice answers in English.

"Mostafa, I was worried. Have you completed the mission?"

Gideon is startled by the American-sounding voice tinged with a Boston accent. He was expecting Urdu or Punjabi, even Pashto or English with that distinctively clipped Pakistani accent.

"Mostafa, are you there?"

Gideon pushes the SPEAKER button and moves the phone closer to the scooter's engine. He begins to speak, doing his best imitation of Pakistani-English and hoping that the motor's whine will mask his voice. "Yes, yes, the mission was successful, but bad connection. I will call you back."

There is a pause. Gideon wonders if his ruse has worked.

After a few seconds the voice returns.

"No, I must get details from you. Meet me at the usual place."

What place is this? Gideon wonders, then sets the phone directly on the scooter's metal frame, intensifying the noise.

"What? I cannot hear you. Say again."

"Dammit, Mostafa. Meet me at ten tomorrow morning."

"Did you say ten?"

"Yes."

"Okay. Where should we meet?"

"The usual place."

"Where?"

"For Chrissake, Mostafa. The India Gate."

"Okay. See you then."

Gideon ends the call. He has established that the man is from the Boston area or has spent considerable time there. Now, Gideon has just one other task.

Putting the cell phone in one pocket, he reaches into another and retrieves the electronic locator that Mostafa was using to track the cell phone. It is still powered on. As Gideon presses a key, the screen illuminates and displays a blinking dot about two blocks away.

Gideon drives off in pursuit of the dot. Within minutes, he has found the dot's source attached to a mangy mutt hiding beneath a parked truck.

"Hey fella," Gideon says, trying to coax the dog into the open with gentle words. "Forgive me, okay? I didn't mean to hurt you back there."

The dog seems to recognize the man's voice. He slowly creeps out from beneath the truck. Gideon reaches into the scooter's storage compartment and takes out a bag of beef jerky he had been saving. He is addicted to jerky—has been since his service days—but it's tough to find it in a country that worships cows.

"Here fella, got something for you," Gideon says, tearing open the bag and dumping the tantalizing contents on the ground. "This is my apology."

For both the dog and Gideon, the aroma is irresistible. The dog scuttles over to the pile of jerky and fills its mouth with the chewy treat, looking up periodically with round eyes of gratitude.

Watching his cherished jerky disappear, Gideon contemplates the meaning of sacrifice.

Chapter 35

The cries of the wounded terrorist, though muted by the steel walls of the safe room, betray acts of torture. Head in her hands, Charlotte listens to the tormented wails. She is desperately trying to justify Dr. Bhatt's tactics by conjuring the demonic brutes who had abducted Curt and her.

She envisions the attempted rape and Curt's savage beatings. She replays the crisp sound of sharpening blades as the terrorists prepared for their beheadings. She remembers experiencing waves of exquisite gratification when she saw the bloody corpses of these vile men, even though the ordeal's horror was still spreading like venom over her vulnerability.

The reverberating screams intensify her memories. On the air, she had frequently denounced the use of torture, but now she recognizes the acid taste of bloodlust. And because of fatigue, fear and anger, she feels powerless to control herself. In fact, she doesn't want to. She wants vengeance. But first, she wants answers.

"I'm going upstairs," she says.

Thompson and Curt see her flushed face and determined eyes. Greg does not hear her; he has brought his computer downstairs and is lost in some esoteric exploration of the Web.

"Char, listen to me," Thompson says. "Mohan lost his oldest son in a terrorist attack two years ago. I don't approve of his tactics, but please don't interfere right now."

"I don't want to interfere," Charlotte says. "I want to help. Curt, get the camera."

With a glance at Greg, who seems oblivious to everything but his computer, Charlotte marches upstairs.

"What does she think she can do?" Curt asks Thompson as he retrieves his camera bag.

Thompson shrugs. "I must admit I'm feeling a bit unsettled—like Moses, I suppose, after he killed an Egyptian slave-master and had to flee. What I need right now is a burning bush to set me on the right path."

"Burning bush?" Greg asks.

Thompson could not have guessed that the boy was even casually aware of the conversation. *The oddest things attract Greg's attention. He is like a bird scavenging twigs and gum wrappers that soon become a nest.*

"You know who Moses was, right?" Thompson asks.

"Of course."

"After Moses fled, he became a shepherd. And then one day, forty years later, he was tending his flock on Mount Horeb when he saw a strange sight. A bush seemed to be on fire, yet the fire was not destroying the bush. As Moses approached the burning bush, the voice of God came out of it and give him a specific mission—namely, to bring the Israelites safely out of Egypt. Of course, Moses had a credibility problem in Egypt, so God showed him how to perform impressive miracles to get the Pharaoh's attention."

"We could use a miracle or two ourselves, mate," Curt says. And then he climbs the stairs, camera bag slung over one shoulder and carrying a tripod with the other hand, pausing only briefly as a muffled howl escapes the safe room.

"Moses was a shepherd for forty years, then the burning bush appeared?" Greg asks.

"God's arithmetic," Thompson replies. "He likes things in groups of forty, twelve and seven. Particularly forty."

"I know. I found over a hundred of them in the Bible."

Thompson stares at Greg, impressed. *The boy is way ahead of him.*

"So you probably know that Moses was forty when he fled his Egyptian family and became a shepherd," Thompson continues. "Forty years later he encountered the burning bush. And he was in the wilderness with the children of Israel for forty years. Just don't ask me why all of these forties. It would be simpler to explain the burning bush."

Greg has been avoiding eye contact as usual, but now he looks deeply into his grandfather's eyes, a tacit challenge to explain.

"Okay then, the burning bush," Thompson says, interrupted briefly by another loud groan from upstairs that Greg does not seem to hear. "Many religious scholars believe that the burning bush was a mystical phenomenon called the Divine Shekinah, a mysterious light that shows the presence of God. The Bible sometimes calls it the Glory of God. This Divine Shekinah is said to have appeared at the birth of Moses. It appeared again in the burning bush, just before the Israelites began their exodus from Egypt. And again when God presented Moses the Ten Commandments."

Thompson stares into Greg's eyes; they seem to be looking through him, flickering with sparks, peering into another dimension.

Suddenly the eyes focus on Thompson. "In other words, the Shekinah appeared to Moses every forty years or so," Greg says.

"Or so it is written."

"Did it come back, you know, after Moses?"

"It has appeared many times since." Thompson sees an urgency in Greg's eyes, and this propels him forward. The questions come now in rapid succession. Thompson struggles to dredge up the facts demanded by Greg, but he feels exhilarated by the boy's quest.

"When did it come again—the Shekinah?" Greg asks.

"I don't know exactly—let's see… it shone in the Holy Tabernacle built by Moses, but then disappeared for a time. The Jews believed that it came and went depending on God's will. It appeared again at the dedication of Solomon's Temple, when the foundation stone was laid."

"When was that?"

"Most scholars say the year 967 BCE."

For Greg, each scrap of new information is a pulse of clarity. "And how long was that after the exodus began?" he asks.

"Let me find an online Bible on your computer."

Greg hands the computer to his grandfather. Thompson's fingers fly over the keyboard, launching BibleGate.com, according to the Home page a "ministry of the Millennium Broadcasting Network".

He begins searching the text of the Bible. "Okay," he finally says with a satisfied smile. "Here it is, in the First Book of Kings chapter six, verse one: 'And it came to pass in the four hundred and eightieth year after the children of Israel were come out of the land of Egypt, in the fourth year of Solomon's reign over Israel, in the month Zif, which is the second month, that he began to build the house of the Lord.'"

"Four hundred and eighty years after the exodus," Greg repeats. His brain churns and Thompson can see in Greg's eyes a sparkle like the firing of a billion neurons.

"Any other intervals?" Greg asks.

"What?"

"Intervals—in years. Like so many years between the start of the Temple and something else."

Thompson pinches the bridge of his nose as he searches his memory for more clues to a puzzle he can't define but Greg seems close to solving.

"I think in Josephus—do you know Josephus, Greg?"

The boy shakes his head.

"Josephus—a Jewish historian who lived around the time Jesus."

Thompson searches Google for Josephus and finds a link to the digitized works of the famous historian.

"Here it is," Thompson says. "In the book called 'Antiquities' by Josephus—Solomon began to build his temple… let's see here… after the deluge one thousand four hundred and forty years."

"The deluge?"

"Noah's flood."

"So, 1,440 years," Greg says slowly, as if inserting the number into a calculator. "Jesus was born in the year zero?"

The question comes out of the blue and startles Thompson. The boy is hungry for data.

"Probably not," Thompson replies. "First, there was no year zero because the calendar makers mistakenly and went right from the end of year 1 BCE to the year 1 CE. In other words, they skipped a year. Kind of like figuring that the day you were born, you were one year old, even though we all know that you're not a year old until your first birthday. Secondly, most Biblical scholars now believe that on this flawed calendar Jesus was probably born sometime between 8 and 4 BCE."

"What do you think? What year?"

"What I think isn't important."

"It is to me," Greg says.

Those four words vibrate in Thompson's soul. *He is important to his grandson.* A great surge of emotion, like Noah's flood, rises within him. For a moment, he cannot speak, so drunk is he with the wine of astonishment.

At last, provoked by Greg's ravenous gaze, Thompson feeds the boy another morsel. "I would vote for the year 7 BCE."

Greg breaks into a sunny smile, the first one that Thompson has seen on Greg's usually stoic countenance. The intensity of the boy's serious demeanor momentarily disappears.

"I agree," Greg says. "It *has* to be 7 BCE.."

"Why is that, Greg?"

"Don't you see?" Greg's tone is unintentionally patronizing.

Thompson shrugs off the condescension and plays along. "Sorry, but I don't see at all."

"You said it—'God's arithmetic!' His basic intervals are forty and twelve. The big one here is forty—a cycle of forty years. Forty times twelve is what?"

"Uh, 480. Right?"

"Okay, twelve forty-year cycles is 480. An interval of twelve cycles. Sort of an epoch! And how many years between the start of Solomon's temple and the deluge?"

"The deluge? Well, 1,440 years."

"Now do you get it?"

Thompson still doesn't see where this is going. He shakes his head and Greg sighs, frustrated that his grandfather isn't keeping up.

"You see, 1,440 years is three epochs. Do the math, Grandpa. Three times 480 is 1,440 years."

"Okay, now I'm with you."

"So, if you start at 967 BCE. and go forward 960 years, which is two epochs of 480 years, you get to…"

"…the year 7 BCE. The year that Jesus was probably born."

"And if you go backwards from the birth of Jesus exactly 1,440 years, whicih is three epochs, you get the year that Moses led his people out of Egypt and through the Red Sea."

"So, everything is based on a forty year cycle?"

Greg nods excitedly. "Which is the basic building block of a 480-year epoch." He pauses, then says, "I think I know where that forty year cycle comes from."

"A lot of Biblical scholars think the forty years represents a generation."

"Then they're stupid. A generation would be more like twenty years. The forty year cycle is all tied into appearances of the Shekinah. Think about it—the answer is in the heavens."

"The heavens?"

"The Star of Bethlehem. Maybe it was some kind of celestial phenomenon that also happened at the birth of Moses, the exodus, the start of Solomon's temple. I think it happened at the birth of all those other people..."

"Confucius, Mithras, Cyrus..."

"All those guys, including Jesus." Greg stops and thinks for a minute. "And maybe more to come," he adds.

And then he reaches for the computer. Thompson gently surrenders it and Greg summons a folder containing digital images from his camera. He double-clicks one of the pictures and launches a viewer displaying the image full screen. Swiveling the computer so Thompson can see the image, Greg says, "They're saying that '40' is important. It's written on the faces of the dead guys."

Thompson studies the image of a dead Arab on the lawn in front of his daughter's house. The numeral '40' is scrawled on the man's forehead.

Greg taps the **PageDown** key and the image changes. Thompson is now staring at a dead man in a hotel room. The man's face is spattered with blood and the numeral '40' is written on his forehead.

Thompson looks away, disgusted by the carnage. "I see the messages, but who are they talking to?" he asks.

"Whoever can decipher the meaning," Greg says.

Thompson considers this before speaking again. "Right now, that's you, Greg. Your grandmother sent you coded emails, and this... this assassin sent you a message in body art. You seem to be a very popular young man."

Greg suddenly closes the computer. The color drains from his face. He stands and looks nervously around the room.

"Grandpa," he says. "I thought everyone was after mom. But they're not, are they?"

Thompson reaches out and silently takes Greg's hand.

And then, squeezing his grandpa's hand, Greg says, "They're after *me*."

Chapter 36

Mike Ansari finishes his lunch at the restaurant. *His* restaurant. The only venture he has ever done completely on his own that has come close to success. But what does it matter now? In a few days he will be gone, leaving behind the fruits of his labor. His wife will reap the rewards. Or, more likely, she will have to untangle a web of liabilities.

From the beginning, of course, Mike knew that there was no long-term future for the two of them. (The *three* of them, he reminds himself.) Never any hope, really. It probably was this utter lack of possibility, known only by him, that prevented even the remotest chance of a genuine, honest relationship. When hope is absent, desire dies.

Not that his relationship with Charlotte was devoid of meaning. The true meaning of it is deep and immeasurable—to others. For Charlotte, unfortunately, the meaning will remain veiled. There will be no waking from the nightmare she entered nearly fourteen years ago.

Mike shoves aside his plate of lamb and saffron rice. There is a heaviness in his gut; not the byproduct of tainted food, he knows, but of the resurrection of guilt that he had kept buried all these years.

He marches to his office, where the fluorescent lights make him look sickly green. Staring into a mirror, he studies the dark smudges beneath his eyes and the creases on his forehead. He has not aged well during these years of his sentence.

So here he is. Sliding open a desk drawer. Fumbling with a bottle of vodka. Pouring a glass of odorless oblivion, then impatiently moving the bottle's neck to his lips. Pouring the anesthesia directly down his gullet.

Sighing. And sitting down.

Waiting.

The cherished effects come and bring with them dark memories. Of seeing Charlotte in the Boston pub radiating intelligence and energy. Of their light-hearted conversation half-shouted into the storm of music and laughter. Of Charlotte in the car, legs splayed, and Mike awkwardly hunched between her naked thighs, frantic and joyless, lunging into her until…

He tilts the bottle and gulps. The fire of the vodka is gone, the bitterness now sweet. Sugar and spice, and everything nice.

He could have loved her.

Could have. But he had to finish what he had started.

Darker memories come now. The fear on her face when she told him she was pregnant. *Impossible*, she said, *I was a virgin!* But it was true, and Mike explained how she was drunk and they had made love and he's so sorry, but how can she not remember the passion, the sweet words, and how she urged him on?

All the time, of course, he knew the truth. That she was unconscious. And he had done this to her, this unbearable indignity. This cowardly, loveless, rohypnol-laced betrayal. He had had no choice, really. From the beginning he knew that she was the one. And now there was an unbreakable link—Greg.

Out of fear and panic, perhaps, she had agreed to marry him. Even thanked him for doing the honorable thing. Raising a child alone? *Unthinkable!* She was not yet a famous news celebrity. *Maybe this guy can help support us, anyway.*

Yeah, right.

So bring it on. We'll make this work. We'll raise this child together.

Mike closes his eyes. The alcohol is doing its job. The dark memories are fading to white and the shimmering whiteness makes him smile.

Soon, very soon, he will disappear into this bright, white heaven.

William Wyatt, the beleaguered CIA Director, sips soup in a box through a straw. Lately, he's had trouble keeping down solids.

Wyatt has no window in his office, so he works in a perpetual twilight. It would be easy to lose track of time if his computer didn't display the exact time in eight zones around the world. Until two days ago, Delhi time was not one of them. When it's noon in Wyatt's office, it's eleven-thirty in the morning in Delhi. He wonders if his adversaries there are asleep.

An intercom buzz asks permission for Allison Timms, a bright analyst that he had personally recruited four years ago, to enter the office. He approves, hoping for some good news.

Allison is an imposing woman, about thirty pounds overweight and wearing an unfashionable suit that probably fit well forty pounds ago. She is in her early forties and very smart, though her doughy face has a slightly cartoonish look that camouflages her incisive mind. For this irrelevant reason, she is not taken seriously by some. Wyatt, however, trusts her implicitly.

"What have you got for me, Allison?" Wyatt asks.

Allison glances at her watch and says, "Just over three minutes ago we intercepted an alert from the police in Delhi." She is precise about the timing, as she is about everything else. "Thought you should know that four Pakistanis, probably terrorists, were found dead in a back street. One of them bore the distinctive knife wounds of a previous contractor."

Wyatt stares at Allison for a moment. "So Delhi's still a hot zone."

"Seems so, sir."

"I would guess that the bodies were dumped there, so it would be a waste of time to search that neighborhood."

"Something else, sir. We know that Curt Branson, who was with the Ansari woman in Iraq, was diverted from another assignment to New Delhi. We suspect he is teaming up with Ansari. We haven't had any luck tracking Ansari or her son—they've managed to lose us at every turn—but we did find out that Branson carries a cell phone. I've got his number."

She pauses and Wyatt leans forward anticipating the punch line to the story. "And...?" he says.

"And it seems the cell phone company has a couple of favors they want, so they decided to cooperate and we've been able to track its location, a Kashmiri shopping district. Been there for several hours now. I don't have any real authority to direct our agents in the field, but..."

"But you alerted them anyway?"

Allison briefly studies her scuffed shoes and then looks up. "I thought that time might be important here. Hope I didn't overstep..."

Wyatt leaps from his chair and rushes to Allison, wrapping his long arms completely around her and kissing her on the forehead. "Allison, you are beyond doubt my best recruit ever. And you've literally made my day. Probably saved the entire Christian world as well."

Wyatt looks at his watch.

"We've got just enough time to stage a midnight surprise party in Delhi."

Chapter 37

The safe room door is closed, so Charlotte knocks. Dr. Bhatt's voice, faint through the steel, tells her to come in. She enters to find the Pakistani prisoner seated, his forearms duct taped to the wooden arms of a chair. The man's right pants leg has been cut away and his leg is oozing blood. Muscles and bits of bone protrude through the flesh. The man is perspiring heavily and his whole body seems to vibrate with shooting pains from his injured leg.

Dr. Bhatt is seated stoically in front of the man. He does not look up as Charlotte enters, but instead stares at the captive without blinking. He seems unbelievably calm. There is no blood or perspiration on him, so Charlotte figures that Bhatt has not been physically torturing the prisoner.

"What are you doing?" Charlotte asks Dr. Bhatt.

"Watching," Dr. Bhatt replies quietly.

"Has he told you anything?"

"Nothing yet, but he knows the questions. So I am waiting."

"Have you… I mean, did you…"

"Torture him? I am not a torturer. His pain is torture enough. And so I am watching. And enjoying his pain. I almost hope he does not talk, because then my satisfaction will know no bounds."

The Pakistani looks up at Charlotte. At first, the sight of her frightens him, but then as another wave of pain overtakes him, he vomits all over himself.

Charlotte looks away in disgust, using a hand as a shield against the sour stench. The prisoner's weak voice in broken English intrudes.

"Please…"

Charlotte remembers her own pleas for mercy in Iraq, and the mocking laughter of her abductors. This prisoner's ridiculous plea angers her. The man taped to the chair is the same man, the same *kind* of man, who dragged her into a cold stone torture room and prepared to rape and behead her. These men deserve no mercy. No compassion. They know nothing but hate and violence and terror. They are one species that should be made extinct.

Charlotte turns back to the sweat-drenched man, who moans uncontrollably and thrashes his body against the back of the chair in a vain battle with the unbearable pain.

No longer disgusted, but just plain pissed off at the whole idea of this man, Charlotte approaches and stares into his reddened eyes. She wonders if she can see a demon in there, or some dark place behind his eyes where evil resides, but finds nothing but pain. And hate. She can feel the hate exuding from the man's pores. From his soul. He is a manifestation of hatred, as she is.

Charlotte moves her lips close to the man's left ear.

"We're going to have some fun, you and I," she says. "Some fun on camera. And you are going to answer my questions, because my subjects always answer my questions, and always tell me more than they intend. So prepare yourself well for your television debut."

Curt steps into the safe room, recoils at the stench, then sets down his camera bag. Charlotte steps away from the Pakistani with a heady sense of power. She is not sure what she will do next. Her intention had been simple—to interrogate this beast on video—but now she knows that she is capable of much more.

She watches Curt remove the video camera from its carrying case. He begins attaching it to the tripod head.

She turns back to the prisoner. His face has been transfigured from a mask of pain to one of pure terror. His eyes, now round with fear, are fixed on the video camera, and Charlotte suddenly understands.

The video camera.

For a terrorist, this is preparation for a beheading.

Charlotte moves until her eyes are barely six inches from his. When she speaks, her voice is almost a whisper, and her hot breath fans his eyelashes.

"Do you understand English?"

The man nods nervously.

"Have you ever watched a beheading?"

The man's eyes flash, then his lids close, quivering.

"I thought so. Now I have some questions. If you answer them, we will treat your leg and you will live. Otherwise..." She pauses ominously. "Understand?"

The man opens his eyes and nods again.

"Curt, start the camera please," Charlotte says in a normal voice before backing away from the prisoner.

"First, tell me about the Italian, the man from the Vatican. Is he still alive?" She is guessing that this Pakistani has knowledge of her father's houseguest.

The prisoner glances at her, then quickly averts his eyes and turns his head downward.

"I am not a patient woman," Charlotte says. She boldly steps behind the bound man and takes a fistful of his hair, raising his face so the camera can see the fear in his eyes. In a strident voice, she begins a pronouncement. "I condemn this man for crimes against humanity and his complicity in the murder of innocent people."

Curt is startled by Charlotte's aggression. She has gone over the line. His thumb moves toward the camera's STOP button, but Charlotte shakes her head no, continuing her denunciation.

"His silence is his confession without shame or remorse," she says. "May his soul burn in hell for eternity."

She yanks the fistful of hair upward. The man's chin rises. With her right hand, Charlotte places the edge of a small knife against the man's throat and his eyes flash with panic.

Seven men and one woman rattle through the narrow New Delhi streets in two dark vans. The CIA field operatives have been gathered on a moment's notice by an urgent directive from CIA headquarters in Langley. The oldest man, forty-eight-year-old Brad Henderson, strangles a radio in one hand as he speaks.

"Goddamit, I need a specific address. There's twenty people per square foot in Delhi. How do you expect me to find three out of millions without an address?"

"We're working on it."

The radio spits and crackles.

"We're less than ten minutes from the neighborhood," Henderson says. He can hear the metallic clacking of automatic weapons being readied. "So hurry up your ass."

Henderson lowers the radio and turns toward the driver next to him. "Slow down, big guy, we don't want to attract attention. This little sortie hasn't been cleared by IB."

The van slows down.

"Much better," Henderson says. "Goddam headquarters's got its head up its ass trying to find us a target. Makes you proud, doesn't it, working for such an elite organization?"

The radio interrupts. "All right, it's a shop called Kashmiri Carpets on Gagan Vihar…"

Charlotte's knife makes a bloodless crease in the prisoner's neck. Dr. Bhatt does not flinch at Charlotte's act, but Curt instinctively starts to rush forward to stop this madness.

Before Curt can take a step, he catches a glimpse of the object in Charlotte's hand. It is not a knife at all.

It is a nail file.

Curt stops, looking up at Charlotte.

She stares back, her eyes wide with terror and disgust. Even though this is stagecraft, the performance of it shocks and sickens her. She knows it is torture, which she abhors—or thought she did—and yet she cannot stop herself from scraping the edge of the nail file against the prisoner's neck while she hisses *I will make it slow.* The most subtle movement of her hand makes the man's body grow rigid, and she draws from this a depraved but exhilarating sense of power.

The prisoner loses all desire for martyrdom. He screams and then mouths in heavily accented English, "Okay, okay! Stop! I tell you everything!"

Charlotte is drained. Sweat cascades down her neck and her hair sticks to her forehead, creating an even more savage appearance as she steps in front of the prisoner.

"Tell me everything now!" she yells. "The Italian."

"Okay, the Italian." The man grimaces as another wave of pain rips through his body from his shattered leg. "The Italian, yes."

"Is he alive?"

"Yes, alive."

"What did he tell you?"

"We tortured him. He said nothing."

"Where is he now?"

"I don't know. They move him."

"Why did you want the Italian?"

"They just said to get him."

The man groans again and his body starts to shudder. His eyes roll up, showing only the whites. Charlotte slaps him. The man coughs and sputters. His eyes roll back, pulling him into consciousness as he tries to focus.

"I think they take him… Italian… to Desi Khana," the man says, and then starts to sob. "Please… for the pain."

Desi Khana means nothing to Charlotte. She glances at Dr. Bhatt, who says, "A local Pakistani restaurant."

She turns back to the prisoner, grabbing his shirt and shaking him violently. "What do you want with me and my son?"

"You are messenger," the man says. "The boy is guarantee."

Before Charlotte can shout another question, a cell phone rings out the first notes of Beethoven's Fifth. With their eyes, Charlotte and Dr. Bhatt trace the music to Curt. Embarrassed, Curt reaches into a pants pocket and pulls out a cell phone, glancing at the display screen.

"You have a cell phone?" Dr. Bhatt is indignant.

"Sorry. It's my boss."

Dr. Bhatt bolts from his seat and snatches away the cell phone.

"You idiot!" he screams. "Your location can be tracked through your cell phone! Hurry, you must leave now."

Charlotte grabs Dr. Bhatt's iron-hard arm. "What's the deal?"

"Does anyone else have a cell phone"

"Not anymore. Wait, my dad…"

"Get it and give it to me. Now hurry! You must all leave now. I'll have Sushil drive you away in the van."

Dr. Bhatt's urgency and the glint of terror in his eyes are enough for Curt and Charlotte. They grab the camera equipment and rush down the staircase.

Halfway down, Curt spins and shouts, "My phone!"

"I will take care of it. Now go." And then he yells for Sushil.

A dark blue van stops two blocks short of the target. Another van parks two blocks on the opposite side. From inside his van, Henderson barks into a headset microphone, "Messiah Two, do you copy?"

"Messiah Two, we copy."

"Surprise is our friend. No shots unless absolutely necessary. Copy?"

"Roger."

"We walk to the target. Drivers, stay alert for our signal."

Henderson and the other two black-clad agents quietly climb out of the car. As their feet land on the pavement, they reposition body armor and reach inside the vehicle for their automatic weapons. Slowly, they begin to walk toward Kashmiri Carpets, leaving only the driver. It takes two minutes and seventeen seconds. Henderson's team works its way to the rear, hiding behind a dumpster as a green van maneuvers down the narrow alley and innocently sweeps the shadows with its headlights.

The Messiah Two team posts itself by the front door. The team leader, Gloria Sykes, whispers into her microphone, "Messiah One, we see lights on in the shop."

"A good sign, I think," Henderson replies. "At this hour, if they knew we were coming, they would've turned out the lights. Prepare to enter, but wait for my mark."

Henderson motions his two men forward to the back door. One of them inserts a pneumatic pry-bar device into the door jam and then turns to wait for a signal. At the front door, an identical device is readied.

"Messiah One, move now." Henderson's voice betrays his excitement. This is what he lives for.

With a loud *whoosh* and crack, the front and rear doors splinter and fly open simultaneously. Both Messiah teams pour into the shop with weapons pointed ominously at five individuals seated passively on carpets in the show room.

Chapter 38

Sushil slows the green van. The four American troublemakers are lying on the rear seats hiding from unseen enemies. The bound Pakistani, finally unconscious from the pain, is stuffed into the storage space behind the seats.

In the rearview mirror, Sushil can see Curt's head rising.

"Keep low," Sushil says. "Someone may see you."

Sushil is certain that he saw movement in a shadow on one side of the alley. As Curt lowers his head, Sushil can make out three dark phantoms crossing the alley and approaching the rear door of the shop.

"We got out just in time," Sushil says.

He grabs a pre-paid cell phone from his shirt pocket and savagely attacks the keypad with a thumb. After a few seconds, he speaks. "Yes, please, I want to report a robbery... No, it's in progress as we speak... Yes, Kashmiri Carpets, 18 Gagan Vihar... that's right. Please hurry, the men are armed and holding prisoners."

Sushil suddenly terminates the call.

Thompson starts to unbend his large frame to sit up, but Sushil shouts, "I said stay down! We are not out of danger yet."

Thompson collapses back into his hiding space.

Sushil turns the van into the main street and heads west, passing the dark blue CIA van now parked with its lights off. Sushil can just make out a figure seated in the driver's seat. As the green van's headlights spray across the man's face, Sushil can see the driver—obviously a look-out—turn his head to study the passing van.

Moving slowly down the street, Sushil checks his rearview mirror. The blue van remains parked. Good news so far.

With a sigh, Sushil is now free to worry about his father. The old man is clever but not omniscient, and the escape plan was thrown together on the spur of the moment.

The police are likely to approach the carpet shop by coming east on Gagan Vihar, which means they will pass the van, and the look-out will alert his associates. This is no good. Once alerted, they may react violently, jeopardizing his father and cousins.

Sushil jarringly swerves the green van to the right, pulling into an empty parking space. The tangled bodies slumped behind him complain.

"We have a problem," Sushil explains. "I have to correct it. Stay hidden."

Sushil checks the 9mm pistol in his waistband and opens the door. "Keep your heads down," he reminds the others, imitating bad dialogue from a dozen American movies.

He slides out of the driver's door and crouches beside the van. His plan lacks detail. He knows only the goal—kill or neutralize the look-out. And he understands the peril. If he kills the target, the powers who sent him will have verification that Sushil's father is part of a broader scheme, and this could jeopardize Sushil's family. Overpowering the target temporarily would send the same message. Yet leaving the look-out unneutralized will certainly allow him to alert his associates with potentially lethal results.

If only he knew which enemy faction this look-out represented. He had not been able to see any telltale clues when passing the blue van. If the driver is a terrorist—well, Sushil is prepared to take him out. The local streets are already flowing with terrorist blood. But if this man is Mossad or CIA, there are too many political ramifications to consider right now. He'd rather have the local constabulary sort that out.

There is only one way to get answers.

Looking the part of a Kashmiri local, which he is, Sushil stands and walks down the worn and buckled sidewalk toward the blue van. He turns once to glance at his own van and sees two heads raised up, apparently watching him. Stupid Americans!

When the blue van is in sight, he moves the pistol behind his back and tucks it into his waist band. His heart thumps loudly and his mouth is dry as a sack of salt. He prays to Allah that this man is not CIA. Terrorists are not as well trained and are more easily fooled.

Thirty feet to the blue van. Then twenty.

At last he is facing the blue van's window. The target's face is heavily shadowed behind the glass. He can't just stand there, so with bare knuckles he raps on the window.

The driver seems startled. He jumps slightly, as if he had not seen the Kashmiri. Slowly, the driver rolls down the window. His face moves toward the opening. The street light now paints a definition on the man's face. He is definitely American. He wears a black shirt, and Sushil can just make out the top edge of black body armor. An earpiece dangles from the man's left ear. The man's hands are out of view and Sushil guesses that one hand is ready to fire a gun through the door if necessary. The driver says nothing, just gives Sushil a look of annoyance.

"So sorry, sir…" Sushil says. "I'm with the local militia. We had reports of gunshots in the neighborhood earlier. Are you all right?"

"Just fine, thank you.

"Might I inquire as to your presence here this evening?"

The man squints his eyes and says nothing. He seems nervous.

"At this hour, I mean," Sushil continues. "It does seem odd."

"Waiting for a friend," the man says. "We're driving to Agra this evening… to see the, uh, you know…"

"Taj Mahal," Sushil offers.

"Right. Want to be there at dawn. Hear it's pretty then."

"Most beautiful," Sushil says. "Have a safe journey."

The man gives an uncomfortable smile. "Thank you."

And then, as Sushil starts to turn away, the man relaxes slightly. A big mistake. Sushil swivels powerfully. His fist flies through the open window and viciously strikes the man directly on his ear, knocking him unconscious. Another hand tears the earpiece away from the man's body, disabling radio contact.

Sushil opens the door and yanks the man out of the vehicle, then goes through the man's pockets. He finds a wallet and takes the rupees and ID that are stuffed inside, flinging the wallet into the street to stage a robbery scene.

He rolls the man over—he's heavy! He binds the man's wrists with the wire from the earpiece. Finally, he turns on the emergency lights and reaches through the vehicle to push open the street-side door.

This should catch the attention of the police.

All of this takes less than two minutes.

Sushil walks briskly to his van and climbs in. "We're safe now," he explains. "But stay down."

"I've got a cramp," Thompson says.

"Better a cramp than a bullet in your head," Charlotte says.

"Point well taken."

Four Delhi police cars suddenly roar past. One of them stops at the conspicuous blue van. Sushil sighs deeply and maneuvers the green van out of the parking space, proceeding slowly down the street.

H enderson is the first agent inside the carpet shop. His automatic weapon points at everything his eyes see. The other five agents are now with him in the showroom. They stop suddenly. Before them, Dr. Bhatt and three younger men are seated cross-legged on Kashmiri carpets. It appears that they have been affixing sale stickers to various items.

"The sale doesn't begin until tomorrow," Dr. Bhatt says to the intruders.

Henderson ignores the old man.

Silently directed by vigorous hand gestures, two of the armored agents force the Kashmiris to their feet and push them against a wall. Henderson and the remaining two agents slowly climb the stairs, weapons at the ready.

Dr. Bhatt, facing a plaster wall, can hear American voices barking the word "Clear!" as the agents search the upstairs. Within minutes, the searchers are back in the showroom. Henderson grabs Dr. Bhatt by the shoulder and spins him around. Dr. Bhatt can smell the American's stale breath as the agent leans close.

Henderson says, "Where are the Americans?"

Dr. Bhatt turns his head left and right, seeing the other four agents, and then replies sarcastically, "They are here with you, sir."

Henderson points the barrel of his automatic rifle against the underside of Dr. Bhatt's chin. "Don't be cute. You know what I mean. We know the Americans are here, so where are they?"

"Sir, we have many American customers. Which ones interest you? Perhaps we sold them a carpet."

Henderson jerks the barrel of his weapon. It strikes Dr. Bhatt on the temple opening a wound. Bhatt flinches, but his demeanor does not change.

"You're pissing me off, old man. We know more than you can imagine, so cooperate."

Henderson backs away and speaks into his headset. "Are we still good at the carpet shop?"

The voice in his ear replies, "The phone is still there. Hasn't moved."

Henderson turns to the female agent and says, "You, guard these bastards. The rest of you, tear the place apart. The phone's still here."

Dr. Bhatt seizes this opening to save his shop. "Excuse me, sir," he says. "Did you say phone? Are you meaning a cell phone?"

Henderson turns to the old man and grabs him by the throat, slamming him against the wall. "What do you know about a cell phone?"

"May I show you, sir?"

Henderson releases his grip on Bhatt's throat and says, "This better be good."

Dr. Bhatt slowly walks to the desk at the front of the showroom. He stands and stares at a cell phone in open view on top of the desk. "I don't want to make any provocative movements," he explains, "but as you can see, there is a cell phone right here."

Henderson picks up the phone, an American brand.

"Four Americans—perhaps the ones you are interested in—came into the shop just before closing," Bhatt explains. "They seemed very nervous. Distracted. But they inspected carpets and drank some of our sweet tea before leaving. About an hour later, I found that cell phone beneath a stack of Kashmiri shawls. For what purpose someone placed it there, I can't imagine. Please, if it's the cell phone you want, take it. Don't worry about my doors. We'll take care of it."

Henderson looks confused. He speaks into his headset. "This is Messiah One. Call the cell phone now."

"Are you sure?" the voice in his ear asks.

"Do it now."

Twenty seconds later, the phone rings in Henderson's hand. He answers and with apparent disappointment speaks into it. "We have the phone—repeat, we have the phone, but that's all. They ditched it in a carpet shop, possibly to throw us off."

"Roger. Any casualties?"

"Two doors are dead, that's all."

"Then vacate the premises immediately."

At CIA Headquarters in Langley, a Messiah project control room has been set up. Director William Wyatt observes an array of screens as he listens to the radio transmission from New Delhi.

Henderson speaks. "We should interrogate the shopkeeper and the…"

"Vacate immediately!" Messiah mission coordinator Jane Frick shouts. "That's an order."

"Roger that."

Frick turns to Wyatt and complains. "Cowboys," she says. "This is supposed to be a lightning strike. Bad things happen when we dally."

Wyatt focuses on one of the monitors as blurry video of Delhi roofs pass by. The overhead camera is circling a quadrant of the shopping district.

"We're taking the shopkeeper with us," Henderson says.

"All right. The drone shows no activity outside."

Another monitor shows the POV of Henderson's helmet cam as hands begin to bind Dr. Bhatt's wrists with a plastic tie. Wyatt watches as the shopkeeper turns suddenly and the tie drops to the floor. An open hand smacks the old man across the face and Bhatt drops to his knees.

"Move it!" Frick barks.

Henderson's hands pick up the tie and begin again. "Okay, we're outta here in a minute."

As Henderson yanks Bhatt to his feet, Frick's eyes are drawn to movement in the drone monitor. "Pull back on five," she shouts to the young operator who is controlling the drone camera. "Back!"

The view from the drone widens to reveal Delhi police, probably eight of them, surrounding the carpet shop.

"Hold it!" Frick shouts. "We have company."

"Geeez," Wyatt mutters. This is bad news. His agents could easily take out all of these police officers, but a fight would surely backfire. US relations with India are too sensitive to sustain an unsanctioned act of CIA aggression inside the country.

Frick is looking at Wyatt with a look that demands a direct order. Wyatt shakes his head and says, "Back down."

Wyatt knows that this whole thing will now get bumped up to Ajay Sanghvi, director of India's Central Intelligence Bureau. Wyatt had chosen not to get clearance from Sanghvi, who will be furious.

Henderson's voice fills the silence. "Messiah Control, what's up?"

"Delhi cops front and back," Frick says.

"Shit! How many?"

Wyatt grabs the headset from Frick and speaks into the microphone. "Doesn't matter. This is director Wyatt. Put down your weapons and surrender. No one gets hurt, understand? No aggression."

"Roger that. What do we tell them?"

"Tell them…" Wyatt finds it galling to say the words. "Tell them to contact Ajay Sanghvi at IB and have him call me. Got that?"

"Copy that. What about us?"

"They'll ream me out and send you all home."

Henderson's camera pivots to point at the other Messiah team members. "All right, listen up," Henderson says. "Everyone, lay your weapons on the floor and put your hands up. That means now!"

Henderson's monitor shows his weapon being placed on the floor. The camera swivels to show five Delhi police entering the front door with a lot of shouting. Suddenly, Henderson's camera tilts down and the floor moves upward until the picture is a blur of shadows.

"He's lying face down, sir," Frick says.

"I'm going to my office to wait for a phone call." We got nothing, Wyatt thinks. We look like the Original Amateur Hour. Could things have gone worse?

"Sir," Frick calls out, causing Wyatt to pause. "We just got word that one of the Messiah drivers was attacked."

Wyatt turns and faces Frick incredulously. "Attacked?"

"Yes sir. And robbed."

Yes, things could get even worse.

Chapter 39

Gideon sits next to Rahul Pradesh, who is driving a silver Opel Vectra. Rahul is tall and wiry—*springy* may be a better word—with a long face and sad eyes made sadder by the dark pouches that cradle them. Headquartered in New Delhi, the native Indian is a reliable support to the organization's migrant assassins. As clandestine chief of Delhi operations, he provides field agents with a safe house and hospice, money in every currency, counterfeit passports, logistical assistance, and technical equipment. He has facilities for intercepting local communications and transmitting encrypted, untraceable messages.

Pradesh is also highly skilled in firearms and marksmanship.

For the mission this morning, Pradesh has chosen a long-range pistol, the Savage Striker, chambered in .243 Winchester and outfitted with a red dot laser scope. From a hundred yards or less, the weapon is deadly in Pradesh's hands but easy to conceal.

The Opel quietly maneuvers through the traffic on the Rajpath, the ceremonial avenue of the Republic of India that originates at the India Gate, a monumental arch commemorating the ninety thousand Indian soldiers who died in World War I and the Afghan Wars. As the vehicle crosses Mansingh Road, Gideon motions for Pradesh to move into the right lane. A park filled with families and souvenir hawkers looms on the right as they approach the final cross street, which loops in a hexagon around the red stone Gate.

Pradesh stops the car. Gideon adjusts his nearly invisible earpiece and microphone, then pulls a baseball cap over his head. Wearing an unbuttoned khaki shirt over a white tee and blue jeans, he looks like your average American tourist. As a final touch, he hangs a cheap digital camera around his neck.

"Can you read me?" Gideon says.

Pradesh taps his earpiece and nods, smiling. Tucked barrel-down between his thighs, the butt-end of the Striker looks like a metal cod-piece.

"Work the plan, my friend," Pradesh says. "You will be protected."

Gideon climbs out of the automobile. There are over a hundred people in this section of the park, and on the other side of the cross-street—open only to foot traffic—are several hundred. And this is just the Rajpath approach. Like the spokes of a wheel, eleven other streets converge at the Gate. It seems an impossible task to find one man here without knowing his likeness.

Gideon checks his watch—9:50 a.m. He begins to walk through the park. Quickly, he dismisses all the men with families or female companions. Certain that his prey will be alone, he also discounts men with male companions. This reduces the immediate field from a hundred to about fifteen. Of these, some are too old to match the voice that Gideon heard on the captured cell phone, and several are too young. This leaves about five candidates—two Indians and three who are either Europeans or Americans.

Gideon knows, of course, that there is no guarantee the target is even in this sector. Surrounding the Gate are vast fields of trees and lawns scorched by drought and hot sun. The man could be anywhere.

The five men scrutinized by Gideon all disqualify themselves by various behaviors. Two of them hook up with friends and start chatting. One hails a taxi, another loosens his shirt and lies down on the grass, not the behavior of a terrorist awaiting a secret meeting. The last one answers his cell phone just as Gideon is passing, and speaks in a shrill, nasal voice unlike the one Gideon heard the previous evening.

"I'm moving closer to the Gate," Gideon says.

Through his earpiece, Gideon hears the reassuring voice of his partner. "I have the binoculars on a man in a cream, short-sleeved shirt about halfway down. He's been standing near the Rajpath for about five minutes. Okay, he's glancing at his watch now."

Gideon looks at his own watch—10:03 a.m.

"I'll check him out," Gideon says.

Dancing through a crush of traffic on the cross-street, Gideon walks briskly toward the man. "I see him now," he says. "Is he in your range?"

"Barely. There's no wind, so probably. Wait, he's coming toward you."

"Okay, so he was checking his watch. Maybe he's our guy and he hates tardiness."

"He's taking out a cell phone. Still walking, looking at the phone. Putting it away now. Checking for messages, you think?"

As the man in the cream shirt approaches, Gideon grabs a souvenir book peddler and holds up a fistful of rupees. "What's your best booklet?" he asks.

The peddler grins and begins a well-rehearsed patter about the colorful Delhi Historic Sites book. He flips through the pages, calling attention to the quality of the printing, the variety of stunning pictures, the English text. With good grammar, yet. And it's on sale today!

If the man in the cream shirt is their target, Pradesh's only shot will be through the windshield of the Opel. There is no opportunity on the Rajpath to park diagonally for a sideways view.

Hurriedly, Pradesh loosens three thumb screws that hold the Opel's false windshield in place. With these removed, the windshield hinges downward to lie across the dashboard, forming a stable platform on which Pradesh places his left hand palm-up. Like a ball joint, his cupped palm cradles his right fist, which is firmly grasping the scoped Savage Striker.

The thick Delhi smog blurs the image of the man in the cream shirt, but the image through Pradesh's high-powered scope is good enough to see the red laser dot on the man's chest as he walks.

Gideon nods as the souvenir peddler works to earn a sale, but he keeps the man in the cream shirt—a well-groomed semite, perhaps Arab—in his peripheral vision. With the man now about fifty feet away, Gideon stuffs rupees into the peddler's hand and takes the booklet.

"Thank you, I'll take this one," he says.

The man in the cream shirt passes within five feet of Gideon, who presses the recall button on the cell phone he had taken from Mostafa.

He hears a faint ring.

The man in the cream shirt stops and plucks a cell phone from his shirt pocket. He speaks into it.

Through Mostafa's phone, Gideon can hear a bitter voice drizzled with a broad Boston accent. "You better have a good explanation for standing me up!"

Gideon smiles. Speaking to Mostafa's phone, he says, "Good morning, this is your wake-up call. Remain motionless if you want to stay alive."

The man stands motionless as directed.

"Now look down at your chest."

The man does this. A vibrating red dot appears on his shirt.

"Checkmate," Gideon says.

"What is it you want?"

"You may now continue walking. Straight ahead."

The man laughs. "You think you are so smart? You think that I couldn't tell last night that you were not Mostafa? You will not leave these grounds alive, my arrogant friend. And now your red dot has betrayed the location of your associate. Tell me, how many men do you have? Are you foolish enough to bring only one? I am prepared to bargain for your life."

Either the man is bluffing, or Gideon has stepped into a trap. One thing is clear—continuing to speak into the cell phone will disclose Gideon's identity. He terminates the call, puts the phone into his pocket, and speaks into his headset microphone.

"Rahul, redeploy now… Are you there?"

Silence. Now Gideon is worried.

He's even more worried when he looks down at his khaki shirt and sees a dancing red dot. He knows that the decision he will make in the next few seconds may save him—or cost him his life. The alternatives zip at light-speed through his brain. Move to avoid the laser dot and give himself away. Or do nothing and wait for his chest to explode if they have identified him.

The muscles in his jaw tighten. He forces a smile on his face, enough perhaps to confuse the sniper. He takes the cell phone from his pocket and mimics a happy greeting. "Hello, Sweetheart. Thought it might be you."

He's still alive. Glancing down, he can see the red dot move to his left and vanish. It reappears on the street peddler, then moves again.

They have not identified Gideon.

"Gideon!" Rahul's voice echoes in Gideon's ear.

"Rahul? My God, man, I thought you were dead."

"No, just my damn radio. It's back now, after a little jiggling."

"Listen, they're onto us. Enemy sniper just painted me. Don't know how many there are."

"I know of one. Across the Rajpath from me, a guy with a telescope pointed in your direction. I don't think it's a telescope."

"Let's hope there's just one, then. You take the peeping tom and I'll take the target in ninety seconds. Now!"

"My man!"

Rahul glances at his watch, marking the time, then deftly removes the scope from the Striker and tucks the pistol into his belt beneath a loose shirt. He darts across the street, dodging a Honda Civic. Crunching across the crispy brown lawn, he approaches the man with the telescope.

The man, an Indian, is so intent on viewing his subject that he does not notice Rahul behind him until a hand clasps his mouth and the barrel of a gun pokes him in the ribs.

"Be silent now," Rahul says, "or you will die right here."

The man grows still but Rahul can feel him trembling. This is not right. A seasoned sniper would not be quivering in fear.

Rahul spins the man around. The young man cowers and drops to his knees. Holding the pistol against the man's throat, Rahul quickly looks through the telescope, which is pointed at a young couple embracing in the grass.

"My wife!" the terrified man exclaims.

Rahul barks into his microphone, "Gideon! He's not a sniper."

Gideon stands behind the man in the cream shirt, his sharp dagger piercing fabric and creasing the skin of the man's back.

"Great," Gideon says just before a red dot appears on his arm.

In a flurry of motion, Gideon grabs the man's collar and jerks him to the right, using him as a human shield.

A jarring *thwack!*

The man's shoulder shoots a fireworks display of blood and bone. Gideon falls onto his back, protectively pulling the man on top of him.

Rahul hears a faint cracking sound from a cluster of trees about fifty feet away. He starts to run toward the sound, but a stout Arab with a scoped rifle is racing toward him. An unfortunate choice of direction.

The Arab never sees the gun being raised by Rahul.

A hundred yards away, Gideon shoves aside the man in the bloody cream shirt and rolls to his feet amidst the chaos of people screaming and running. The disorder is in his favor.

"Rahul, where are you?" he shouts.

"On my way, Gideon. You okay?"

"Just hurry!"

Gideon kneels by the wounded man, who groans and searches the sky with glassy eyes of terror.

"I'm dying!" the man shouts.

"If you die, I'll kill you with my bare hands!" Gideon yells back. He pulls the man toward the street, leaving a bloody smear on the pavement. Within seconds, the Opel skids to a stop next to him. Rahul leaps from the vehicle and frantically helps Gideon hoist the man into the back seat.

"I figure we have about thirty seconds to disappear," Gideon says, climbing into the front seat.

The tires smoke and the Opel does a one-eighty, heading for the congested intersection. Just when it seems the Opel might broadside a yellow Mahindra, Rahul eases the gas pedal, cranks the steering wheel to the right, and miraculously slips into traffic so dense the Opel becomes but a silver drop in a vast, flowing river of vehicles.

Hidden in plain sight.

Chapter 40

Pastor John Crate exhorts his fervent followers to hold fast to their faith. Mike Ansari wonders if he has lost his. The prophecies don't hold the same sway over him, and the zealous admonitions fail to stir him as they once did. It's time to go home.

He fondles the remote, intending to switch off the TV but unable to press the POWER button. Something about this preacher captivates him as always. Despite his denials, the message still resonates faintly, as if thrumming a strand of his DNA. The preacher's passion fans dying embers lying somewhere in Mike's soul.

Pastor Crate's face fills the television screen. His ruddy countenance darkens as he outlines the signs leading to the return of Jesus Christ.

"The scriptures have told us these signs," Crate says, his voice quivering with emotion. "The first sign is the establishment of the state of Israel and the return of the Jews. Did we not see Israel's birth pangs in 1948? It is astounding to me that most so-called Christians see no prophetic significance in this event, and many of them have actually become hostile to Israel. They are siding with her Islamic enemies by declaring that the world's problems can be solved through compromise and appeasement. They put forth their anemic peace plans, but the truth is that that you cannot negotiate with the Antichrist!"

The camera pulls back to reveal Crate standing in front of a giant mural. Along a timeline, vivid apocryphal images depict the vast sweep of prophetic signs and coinciding world events. The mural's audacious splendor makes the fulfillment of these prophecies seem inevitable... and the timing precise.

"Have the Jews been returning to Israel?" Pastor Crate asks. "My friends in Christ, since its birth, Jews have been flowing to this new nation established by God. They started coming from the east, then the west. And then they came from the north, and finally the south. My friends, this is the exact order foretold in Isaiah 43:5-6. Praise God for keeping his promises! But I ask you, how many Christians have taken notice?"

Mike sets the remote down, leans back in his living room chair, mesmerized by the emerging logic set forth by this man of God.

"Another plain sign is the rise of the Antichrist and the massing of huge armies to attack Israel." Crate is animated now, marching along the timeline and gesturing to the obvious signs emblazoned on it. "Are your heads in the sand, my friends? Have you not noticed the rise of Islamo-Fascism? Did you not hear the call of Iran's president to destroy the state of Israel? Did you not witness on every news channel and in every newspaper the missile attacks on Israel by one of the Antichrist's armies called Hezbollah? Can you not taste the bitter venom spit out by those who worship the false god Allah, who is actually Satan in disguise?

"And yet another sign has been given to us—the rebuilding of the Third Temple in Jerusalem. My friends, listen carefully. In Israel today, plans are underway to construct this temple. The Jews have re-established their Sanhedrin, an assembly of seventy-one men. The Sanhedrin, which was not in existence for 1580 years, is once again the supreme religious authority in Israel. And this great institution's first order of business is to determine exactly where the Third Temple should be built.

"These plans for the Third Temple need our support to become reality. Our political support. And more importantly, our *financial* support. On the screen right now is a phone number and a Web address. This is how you can contribute to the fulfillment of God's prophecy, and the hastening of Christ's return."

The doorbell rings, startling Mike. Can it be eleven o'clock already?

Clicking off the TV, he walks to the door, stepping around five suitcases. He opens the door and smiles benignly at the familiar visitor.

"These are my bags," he says. "You can take them. I'll be with you in just a minute."

The visitor, an athletic man of about thirty who looks faintly Greek, steps into the house and begins hauling the luggage to a parked BMW.

Mike turns and looks at the inside of the house he helped design. The door to his home office is open; he'll leave it that way. No use for an office now. He glances into the dining room and sees a sheaf of papers on the table, each document bearing his signature; all the assets have been assigned to Charlotte, and if she should not return alive, to Greg. And if Greg should not...

Mike had not expected to feel such sadness upon leaving. After all, he had been given fourteen years to prepare for this day. So why the grief?

"We're ready, sir," the Greek says.

Mike turns solemnly and forces a smile.

It doesn't fool the Greek. "Do you need another minute?"

"No, I'm ready."

Mike follows the Greek out of the house, closing the door behind. A hot, crampy ball of regret balloons in his chest.

"With a little more time, I could've made the restaurant work," Mike says, and then immediately knows how pathetic he sounds.

"We know sir. But it doesn't really matter, does it?"

Mike agrees by shaking his head, but he is lying. For him, it does matter. It really does.

"You should go home, sir," Allison Timms says to CIA Director Wyatt. They have been seated in the Messiah project room for hours waiting for fresh intelligence from New Delhi. "We can call you if something comes in."

Wyatt ignores her. "Tell me, Allison, how the greatest intelligence operation in the world suddenly can't seem to touch its own nose and walk a straight line."

"Six billion people in the world, sir. Not that hard to go off the grid if you pay by cash, use pre-paid cell phones, and keep your head down. I might also add that India doesn't have thousands of surveillance cameras per square mile like we do. And even if they did, Ajay wouldn't…"

"Ajay!" Wyatt exclaims, taking the name of India's intelligence chief in vain. "That sonofabitch really reamed me out, didn't he?"

"We went around him, sir. A calculated risk."

"I could feel him smirking as he spanked us. Just who does he think he is? Damn third rate intelligence force that couldn't find Ajay's mother at her own birthday party. Sorry for the language, Allison. Not like me."

"It's all right, sir. A tense time here."

Mission project coordinator Jane Frick interrupts. "Sir, we've intercepted something from New Delhi. A reporter we track just contacted his station with news of a shooting near the India Gate."

"Why are we tracking him?"

"He's a Hindu, but he did a segment on Delhi TV last year that was sympathetic to the Iraqi insurgents. Seemed strange, I guess."

Wyatt rolls his eyes. "No wonder we can't get real intelligence around here. Hindu TV correspondents take up all the bandwidth."

"It took place near the India Gate. One man shot, probably wounded, fell on top of another guy. The man he fell on pulled him into a car with an accomplice and they disappeared."

"Disappeared? The victim?"

"I'm just the messenger here. Blood on the street, they're suspecting terrorism, but they don't know who the victim was so they can't be sure."

Allison turns to Wyatt and cocks her head. "Sounds more like a messy kidnapping than an assassination attempt."

Wyatt nods. "Or both. I'd say Delhi is still in play."

Frick, excited, turns to Wyatt. "There's more coming in, sir."

"Give it to me."

"Turns out the reporter was in a nearby park when all this happened. A man with a rifle, a Pakistani, was shot to death a couple hundred yards from him right after the first shooting. Could be the shooter got himself killed trying to get away? Anyhow, the reporter found an eyewitness to the first shooting who videotaped the whole thing. An American, Jason Wells."

"Probably wants to sell the footage to America's Most Violent Home Videos," Wyatt says.

"This is why we watch Hindu TV reporters," Frick says.

Wyatt gives her a hard look and says, "Get someone on this Wells character now. Maybe he hasn't turned over the tape to the police or the media. With any luck, we'll get a picture of our biggest pain in the ass."

Wyatt is pacing the room now. "At least the guy's an American," he adds. "That means we can really put the fear of God into him."

"Makes me glad to be an American," Frick mutters to herself.

harlotte wakes up with sunlight slanting into her eyes. She jumps. Can't remember where she is. Draws her knees up to her chest, heels digging into a hard mattress. And then recalls.

Early this morning, Sushil had brought them to a friend's home in northern Delhi. Depleted by last night's adrenaline rush, she had fallen asleep within minutes. She still doesn't recognize the room, but she recognizes the shape of her son lying on the floor.

This is the start of day two in India. Seems like a month.

Charlotte is still in her clothes and she desperately craves a shower. The bed squeaks loudly when she climb out, so she moves slowly, trying not to wake Greg.

"I'm awake," Greg says, sitting up.

"I'm going on a quest for a shower," Charlotte replies.

"No shower. Just a bath. Last door on the left. They put in towels."

"And how do you know so much?"

"Couldn't sleep last night when we got here, so I stayed up for a while and talked with Sushil and his friend, Ashok. They figure we should leave before noon 'cause whoever's after us will probably check out all the friends and relatives of the guys who work at the carpet shop."

"Hmm, they sound experienced. You okay?"

"Fine. But I kinda sweat through my clothes."

"You and me both." Charlotte suddenly realizes that she is having a genuine mother-son talk with her Asperger's child. She finds this comforting until she remembers that they are fugitives.

"Greg, can I ask you a question?" she says quietly.

"Sure."

"Do you suppose you could talk your friend Ashok into going out to buy us some clothes? What we got, we're wearing."

"Already asked. I gave them some rupees I found in your…"

"No problem. We can get more money on my credit card."

"Ashok says we shouldn't use any credit cards or do anything where we show passports. Traceable."

"By who?"

"Probably the CIA. And he says we should stay away from anyplace that might have surveillance cameras. Local markets are usually okay."

"You had quite a talk with, uh…"

"Ashok. He's trying to get us food for an American lunch. I wish we could stay here with him."

"It's great that you made a friend," Charlotte says.

And she means it. It has been years since Greg has called someone a "friend," and now he has two—Ashok and Thompson.

"Have you heard anything about Dr. Bhatt and the others?" she asks.

"They're okay for now, but we're not supposed to contact them because they might be bugged."

A sharp rap on the door launches Greg to his feet. "It's Ashok," Greg says, opening the door.

Ashok is a fiercely handsome Kashmiri about thirty-five years old. Charlotte's eyes feast on the man's dark eyes and athletic build. She had paid scant attention to him last night, but this morning she is infatuated by his sweeping eyelashes and delicate lips and… and embarrassed by it.

Greg hugs Ashok. The boy seems practically normal here.

"Good morning, young man," Ashok says. And then, turning to Charlotte, he says, "We barely met last evening. So glad to see you fully awake."

Ashok reaches out his hand, and Charlotte takes it. The feel of his skin sends a shower of sparks over her body.

"So nice to meet you when I'm fully awake," she replies.

"Look! I bought you clothes," Ashok says, holding up an appalling dress, blouse, and slacks clearly several sizes too large. "Do you like it?"

"Very much," Charlotte says, touched by his sweetness but worried that he believed she could fill out those slacks. She desperately wants to find a mirror. "Did you have to go far to find them?"

"The local market, just down the street," he explains. "Well, I am going downstairs to make your lunch," he says, withdrawing his hand.

Had she been holding his hand all this time?

"Greg, you come and help, okay?"

Greg smiles and nods. "Be there in a minute."

Charlotte immediately begins to plot how to avoid wearing those clothes.

Inside the secret hospice, which is tucked behind a women's handbag shop in a busy Indian market, Gideon studies the injured man in the cream shirt. The elderly hospice physician inspects the gaping shoulder wound. The patient looks vaguely Arab, or even Afghani, but then vaguely not.

The painkiller injected by Mohandas Chauhan, the physician, has the additional effect of causing one's mind to slip gears, to blur the past and the present. When this confused state takes over, a skilled interrogator can guide even the most reluctant patients to betray their secrets.

"The joint is badly damaged," Mohandas explains to Gideon. "If you wish, I can call for an orthopedic surgeon—we have a fine one in Mumbai. For now, I've applied the Ointment of Jesus to stanch the flow of blood and keep the wound aseptic, which is the best I can do at the moment."

"Well, it worked for Jesus."

"And He was more damaged than our fellow here. Should I call for the surgeon?"

Gideon nods yes. "Make the call. Until then I'll take advantage of our visitor's disoriented state."

Mohandas leaves to make the call. Gideon pushes a chair close to the drugged man and whispers quietly, "My friend, are you in pain?"

The man has been staring at the ceiling, but now turns to view the face of Gideon. "No pain," he says. "Am I dead?"

"No, you are alive. We were fortunate to find you before your enemies did. I need to verify your identity now. Can you tell me your name?

"My name? I'm not supposed…"

"You must identify yourself so we can inform your superiors. They will be glad that you survived."

"My name?" The man pauses for a moment, and then says in Hebrew "My name is Michael Levy."

Gideon is stunned. This man is a Semite, but not an Arab. He is a Jew. A Jew who controls a cadre of Pakistani terrorists. How can this be? There is only one plausible explanation.

Gideon speaks Hebrew fluently, an absolute requisite for his position. In that expressive, throaty tongue, he says, "Michael, who is your commander in Mossad? I must contact him at once."

"My commander… is Ibrahim Weiss. I must tell him that we failed."

Gideon knows of Weiss, the chief of *Kidon*, which in Hebrew means *bayonet*. Kidon is the name of Mossad's department for assassinations and kidnappings.

Levy's story instantly becomes clear to Gideon. A young man in Boston becomes a Zionist and either moves to Israel or is recruited by Mossad in Boston. He is trained for many years in arms and languages, and his indistinct Semitic appearance allows him to pass for an Arab or, better yet, an Afghan. The Pashtuns of Afghanistan are thought to have descended from the exiled Lost Tribes of Israel, so possessing a physical hint of Jewishness would fit in.

Once his training is complete, Levy infiltrates a Pakistani terrorist cell providing an ideal assassination team untraceable to Mossad. And then Charlotte Ansari enters the picture and all hell breaks loose. Levy's in the perfect position to help out.

Gideon speaks a bit of Pashto, the language of the Pashtuns who are commonly found in an area from southwestern Afghanistan to western Pakistan. Guessing that Levy must speak Pashto, he switches to that language.

"Michael, we have not failed yet. But you must explain the mission more clearly so I can succeed."

Michael grimaces as white-hot pain streaks through his shoulder. He moans loudly, and Gideon is afraid that Michael is going to pass out. But the highly trained Kidon agent fights through the pain, grits his teeth, and says in slurred Pashto, "You must kidnap the boy and bring him to me."

Gideon sits back, astonished. He had not expected this.

They want the *boy*!

Daggers of fear stab him. This information changes Gideon's plans entirely. Either the Mossad knows more about the boy's true value than Gideon's organization thought, or it wants the boy for some other reason.

What other reason?

Of course! Ransom. Not for money, but for Charlotte's cooperation. Gideon earnestly hopes this is the reason they want Greg, for if it is not…

His phone rings and he picks up. "Gideon," he says.

"It's Eve. Charlotte has moved."

"I know. I'm heading out to intercept right now." He briskly heads for the door. "But I have some news for you. Guess who our visitor works for?"

Chapter 41

Around midnight, Allison Timms convinces Director Wyatt to leave the Messiah project room and go home. Walking with him down the long colorless corridor to his office, Allison puts a question to him, one that has been nagging her since she was abruptly snatched from her job analyzing extremist Hindu activities and dropped into the Project Messiah team by Wyatt.

"Sir..."

"Will," he instructs. "It's midnight and we're on the dogwatch. You can call me Will."

"Yes sir—Will. As you recall, I was not briefed with the other members of the team, so I have some gaps in my knowledge."

"Gaps? Allison, smart as you are, it's hard to believe that you have *any* gaps in your knowledge."

"Thank you, but I do. For example I know that someone or something out there frightens the Agency more than run-of-the-mill terrorists. It would be helpful to know who we're really up against."

Director Wyatt stops walking. He looks at Allison with weary eyes but says nothing, as if words suddenly have been banned inside the Agency.

Allison nervously blurts, "I do have the proper security clearance..."

"That's not the issue," Wyatt says curtly. "Good God, we're moving too fast here. You certainly have a need to know. Just not... not out here."

"But this is CIA Headquarters."

Wyatt nods. Of course it is.

"Few people here have a need to know this particular information," he says, then leads her another fifty yards down the stark corridor and into his office.

The bottle of single malt scotch should not be here, according to the Agency's strict policies, but it is, and Wyatt pours some into a glass for Allison and himself, a sign that listening to his story requires some fortification. He motions for Allison to sit on a leather sofa, and he slumps into a soft, forest green chair to her right. He has left the harsh fluorescent lights off and has switched on a single lamp. The shadows add to the mystery of the moment, and Allison's imagination begins to conjure all sorts of horrors soon to be revealed. Agency moles. Dirty bombs. Long-range missile attacks. A new strain of mutant super-terrorists. Even worse—Dubai and China now own America, and they want us out.

"You want to know who we truly fear, who we would dearly love to exterminate, and who is better at our job than we are?" Wyatt solemnly asks these questions before taking a large swig of scotch.

Allison nods yes too many times, betraying her nervousness.

"Then I have to go back more than two thousand years, because that's when they began. Many believe they flamed out a few decades later, but they didn't. They've continued to this day, mutating like a virus, until they finally became a worldwide clandestine operation."

"Worldwide? Sounds like us," Allison suggests.

"In our dreams," Wyatt replies. "This secret society began innocently enough. Ever hear of the Essenes?"

"Qumran… Dead Sea scrolls… right?"

Wyatt nods. "But much more than that. The Essenes were a secretive religious cult with a community at Qumran. But around the time of Jesus, the Essenes splintered into factions. A radical offshoot was born called the Fourth Philosophy. Today we call it the Zealot Movement, and it was fiercely opposed to Roman rule."

"Zealots," Allison says. "Doesn't the New Testament refer to the Apostle Peter as a Zealot?"

Wyatt's Evangelical upbringing has made him well-versed in the Bible, particularly the New Testament. In college he entertained the idea of entering a fundamentalist seminary, but life got in the way.

"Good, you know your Bible, Allison. Luke refers to Simon the Zealot. In those days, no one called someone a "Zealot" simply because they were "zealous" about something. The label Zealot had a specific, well-known meaning. So we know that in Jesus's inner circle there was at least one Zealot."

"There were others?"

"My Evangelical brothers would argue with me, but the truth is that Judas was not only a Zealot, but an extreme version. Within the Zealot

Movement itself, a smaller group began to perform acts of extreme violence against the Romans. They became particularly skilled in assassinations and often used a short Roman dagger, called a Sica, to murder their victims. This secret death squad of Zealots became known as *Sicarii*, named after their weapon of choice. Judas was a Sicarii, which is why he's referred to by the Bible writers as Judas *Iscariot*—meaning Judas the Sicarii. Switch the first two letters of his epithet, "Iscariot", and you'll see what I mean. Judas the Sicariot, or in Greek, the Sikariotes."

"So the Sicarii go back to the days of Jesus."

"Many historians say no, that the Sicarii did not exist before 40 or 50 CE, but they are mistaken. As a secret death squad, the Sicarii existed decades earlier but were a small, super-secret group. Early on, as assassins, they terrified the Romans because a Sicarii could conceal his small dagger and work his way close to a target, and then stab in such a precise way that the wound would cause little immediate pain but enormous internal bleeding. By the time the target collapsed, the Sicarii would be some distance away and beyond suspicion.

"By 50 CE, the Sicarii had become a large movement dedicated to the overthrow of Roman rule. The book of Acts refers to an army of 4,000 Sicarii. This visible massing into an army became their downfall. A couple of decades later, the Sicarii stormed a Roman garrison at the top of Masada, a large rocky mesa overlooking the Dead Sea, and established its headquarters there. But within months, the Romans assembled a fighting force of over ten thousand solders—some say fifteen thousand. The sheer cliffs guarding the Sicarii compound thirteen hundred feet above made a direct attack impossible, so the Romans launched a siege that lasted about three months. Over ten thousand Romans against less than a thousand Sicarii, if you counted their women and children.

"During the siege, the Romans built up a massive embankment and eventually climbed up the man-made ramp. When they reached the top, they found a wall made of wood and soil—the last defense of the Sicarii. They burned it down. With all hope gone, the Sicarii—all the men, women and children—committed mass suicide rather than surrender. Only two women and five children were found alive. They were hiding inside a cistern."

Wyatt pauses to take a long gulp of scotch.

"Quite a story," Allison says, "but if the Sicarii were wiped out..."

"Ah, but they were not." Wyatt leans forward confidentially, and Allison instinctively leans toward him. "Remember the seven who were hiding in the cistern? One of these women, we believe, kept the Sicarii secrets and tradition alive and was eventually able to re-launch the movement. But she learned from the mistakes of the past. Having seen the error of building a visible army, she kept the new Sicarii cult secret. All but invisible."

"Are you saying they survived to this day?"

"That's exactly what I'm saying. They were copied, of course, as they eventually dispersed geographically. Ever hear of the Assassins, an eleventh century Islamic cult of suicide murderers?"

"I think so."

"Well, the Sicarii were the originals, but the Shi'ite Assassins in the Middle East adapted the Sicarii ways and set out to murder prominent Sunni leaders who were persecuting them. Eventually they established a network of fortified settlements. They even used strange rituals to induct new members—much like the rituals used in many mystery cults, including the Essenes. But like the Sicarii, once they concentrated en masse, they could be fought and defeated. Which they were."

"So all this time, the Sicarii still existed."

Wyatt nods. "And continued to evolve into its present unholy form."

"Which is?"

"Actually, we don't know. We don't know where they're headquartered or how they're organized. We don't know their purpose or mission. But we do know how they are funded, at least in part. Contract services."

"You mean they're assassins for hire."

"The elite of the elite. Very expensive too. But if you want the job done, and done right..."

"And we've used them?"

"Four times that I know of, for extremely difficult and sensitive operations. I can't speak for previous administrations, as this is one area where we don't keep records, you understand."

"What have we used them for?" Allison asks.

"Can't tell you that. But I can tell you that they're picky. We've tried to hire them for nine jobs. They've turned down five. And it wasn't the money."

"Well, they started out as zealots for a cause. Maybe they still have a cause and some of your jobs didn't match up,"Allison suggests.

"Are you kidding? They're paid killers, not Robin Hood."

"So why turn down large sums of money then?" Allison says. A rhetorical question. She scrunches against the soft back of the sofa, full of questions. "Do they only work for us?"

"No. From what we can tell, they've worked for many different sides, except for Muslims or terrorists. Don't know what's up with that. Otherwise everything from Mossad to Vatican Intelligence. One thing that frightens us is that we have no clue as to their allegiances. They might work for us on one job, and against us on another. They might report to me this week, and have me in their sights next week. And believe me, you don't want to be on their hit list."

"They really scare you?"

There is a long pause as Allison and William Wyatt look at each other. For the first time, Allison feels frightened too.

"Don't get me wrong," Wyatt says, breaking the silence. "Our operatives are the best in the world. Except for theirs." He reevaluates his statement. "Frankly, there's basically no comparison. In Minnesota, we think one Sicarii took out four Arab terrorists and two Mossad agents. We laid a trap in Delhi, and he blew up our operations director, Iggers, one of our most experienced operatives, along with a second agent. Very disheartening. The same day, we believe that same Sicarii single-handedly crippled two of our best trained agents hand-to-hand, two against one. And a few hours later a bunch of Pakistani terrorists were discovered dead in a Delhi street. No coincidence, I assure you. If this guy is working alone, as they usually do, he's a one-man wrecking crew."

"So you believe this Sicarii organization is working Project Messiah."

"Absolutely. But not for u," Wyatt says.

"Then who?"

"God knows. With these secretive Sicarii bastards, pardon my language, even God might not know. Who's left when you eliminate Mossad, Islamic terrorists, and us? The Vatican."

"Actually," Allison reports, "we picked up a little chatter from Vatican Intelligence that the director of the Secret Archives is AWOL."

"Wouldn't be surprised if this Sicarii fellow snatched him too."

"Well, we've got everyone in India working this thing," Allison says, trying to console her director.

"With a little luck ,that American tourist in Delhi might have a picture of this guy. I don't doubt that a Sicarii was in the middle of that India Gate dust-up as well. I want that footage, no matter what we have to do." Wyatt stands. Obviously the briefing is over.

"I'm all over it," Allison says. "Go home and I'll call you with news."

"You should get some rest too."

"I'm fine. Now go home."

Wyatt is stalling. He doesn't relish going home alone.

They know where he lives.

Chapter 42

Charlotte knows it is stupid, but she feels somehow invincible. Her Guardian Angel won't let anything happen to her, so what's the problem? It is not until she is more than a block from the safe house that fear-induced nausea rises like an acid tide in her throat and she has to swallow down the bile.

What the hell is she doing out here alone? Is her vanity so great that she would risk her life to buy a fashionable garment or two just to impress Ashok, the new Kashmiri god of divine eyelashes?

Furtively, she looks around, then worries that her glances are too obvious. The street is a mash-up of humanity, and every one now seems suspicious. Charlotte tries to walk forward, but like a drunk driver walking a straight line, every move is self-conscious and forced. She must look like a marionette with tangled strings, she thinks.

Her heartbeat is a crescendo of thumps. Surely everyone can hear it.

At last she staggers into the market. Perhaps she can hide in a shop while she gathers her wits.

Feeling eyes on her back, she turns to find the source. None. And then someone grabs her arm. She gasps and pulls away but can't free herself. They are after her right here in broad daylight, in front of hundreds of people, emboldened by the chaos of the market. She is about to cry out, to make a scene, when she notices that the hand still grasping her wrist belongs to a pleading Indian woman cradling in her other arm a withered infant that appears dead.

"Please miss, for the baby," the brown woman begs, releasing her vise-like grip on Charlotte and holding out a pink palm for alms. "For the baby."

Charlotte nearly collapses from relief. She finds some rupees in a pocket and hands them over—not alms, really, but a show of gratitude for not being a terrorist. Or the CIA. Or any of the other bad guys.

More beggars see the exchange and encircle Charlotte, hands grabbing and toothless jaws jabbering a babble of demands. Charlotte pushes her way through the briar of bony appendages and crippled bodies to a tiny shop displaying scores of knock-off lady's handbags. The corpulent shopkeeper, an Indian woman with yellow teeth and thinning hair, shoos away the beggars, claiming the American woman for her own.

"We have many fine handbags, lady, all famous brands, guaranteed original, very cheap," the woman says. "Which one do you like best? This one is made by Coach, you know it? Very popular with Americans. Are you from California?"

Charlotte feels faint. It occurs to her that this entire city menaces her; the entire *country*. She gathers some rupees and offers them to the shopkeeper, saying, "No handbag, thank you. But please help me get a taxi."

The shopkeeper studies the rupees and nods, ushering Charlotte toward the back of the shop before marching through the stream of pedestrians passing by. The woman has a daunting presence and within a minute has commandeered a taxi in the middle of the clogged street.

"Lady, over here!" she shouts. "Hurry!"

Charlotte wades through the first wave of pedestrians. She is nearly overcome by the sour stench of body odor and rotting fruit, and then is besieged once again by the beggars who seem intent on ripping the clothes from her body until they receive alms.

The shopkeeper raises a fat palm at the taxi driver, wordlessly commanding him to stay put. Like an icebreaker, she powers her formidable bow through the crowd and pries Charlotte from the clutching beggars. She shoves Charlotte into the back seat of the taxi with a grunt, slams the rear door, and rubs her hands together in a gesture of good riddance.

The taxi lurches forward but stops suddenly. The other rear door swings open. A muscular man clambers into the back seat. A strong hand slaps the driver on the shoulder, urging him on.

Charlotte's body stiffens. She knows she is being kidnapped but dares to turn and look at the face of her abductor.

It is Gideon.

A sharp intake of breath betrays her astonishment. "It's you!" she says.

Gideon does not make eye contact. Instead, he looks straight ahead. He is not comfortable making contact with the woman, but there is no choice, really.

"What are you doing in the market alone, Charlotte?" Gideon's question is abrupt but softly spoken.

Charlotte remembers this gentle voice on the telephone in her hotel room. *Was it really just yesterday morning?* And then she remembers something Thompson had said the previous evening about the Essenes— what was it? Oh yes, they were also called the *soft-speaking men.*

"How did you find me here?" she counters.

Neither of them speaks for a few seconds, a test of wills. And then Gideon breaks the silence, giving the taxi driver instructions to take them to a cross street near Ashok's house.

"I know you're protecting me, but why in the world would you do that?" Charlotte asks.

"Because you're obviously incapable of protecting yourself," Gideon replies. "Do I have to point out that you're alone in a Delhi market while some very bad people are out to get you?" Impatience darkens his voice. "Stupid."

"I needed to do some shopping," Charlotte says, knowing how feeble this sounds. She mimics Gideon's straight-ahead gaze.

"Did you know that two terrorists were within fifty feet of you at the handbag shop?" Gideon asks.

Charlotte turns to look at Gideon, horrified. "You're kidding!"

"Yes. But you can never be sure."

Charlotte punches Gideon in the arm. Hard. Like a schoolgirl. She immediately regrets it.

"Look," she says, "I don't have a clue what's going on, or why anyone would want to hurt me or my son, or what anyone expects of me except my mother. And I can't figure out what she really needs from me either."

She has said too much. She clenches her eyes and purses her lips as if this will erase her last words. But then, maybe she hasn't revealed too much. Perhaps her Guardian Angel knows more than she does.

She glances out the window and realizes that the taxi has stopped. They have driven less than two blocks. She had forgotten how close the market is to Ashok's house.

"What do you want from me?" she asks. "Just tell me, please."

"I want you to be smart. And safe. And I want your son to be safe. The rest is up to you."

"Will you keep protecting me?"

"It would be better for you not to rely on anyone else, including me. I'm just one man, not a Guardian Angel."

Damn close, Charlotte thinks. Then she says, "You know my name. Do you have a name?"

Gideon hesitates, as if weighing the wisdom of a reply, then finally says, "Gideon."

"Gideon, You know what we're supposed to be doing, don't you?" Charlotte asks.

Gideon is silent.

"Why can't you just tell me?" she continues.

Gideon still does not speak.

"Which side are you on?"

The taxi driver is getting edgy. For such a small fare he doesn't want to sit around while this pair verbally dukes it out. He turns his head, a hurry-up signal.

Gideon raises an index finger, holding off the driver for one more minute. "I'm on your mother's side," he replies. "You want to know what to do? Your mother told you—listen to her."

"Where is my mother?" Charlotte asks, confrontationally turning her body toward Gideon.

Gideon holds up a palm, dismissing the question, then hands a fistful of rupees to the taxi driver. He steps out of the vehicle, then bends down to say one more thing through the open door. "I'll wait until you're safely inside, but then I can no longer guarantee your safety. By the way, what were you doing in the market?"

Charlotte studies the man's expression, an enigmatic blur of kindness and coldness that slowly resolves into detachment as he awaits her answer.

"I was just going to buy some pretty things to wear." She looks down with disgust at the ill-fitting outfit given to her by Ashok. "This... this is pretty much what I have right now, so you can understand my desperation."

Gideon's eyes smile, but his lips don't. "Consider this carefully, even in your desperation," he says. "Your past is buried. As you exhume the future, you must be your own guide and protector."

"And my son's," Charlotte adds.

"Be brave Charlotte, but very wise—particularly in who you trust."

He closes the door and walks to the other side of the street. Charlotte exits the taxi feeling suddenly vulnerable in the open air. She heads toward Ashok's front door, turning once to catch a final glimpse of Gideon, but he has vanished into the Delhi smog.

Chapter 43

Before she can grasp the handle, the heavy door swings open, the gaping mouth of a beast. A strong arm darts from the darkness like a tongue, grasping her hand and pulling her in. As her eyes adjust to the murkiness, a face emerges, unfamiliar and menacing. The creaking door snaps shut and Charlotte shudders with the fear that in her absence this house has been seized by her enemies.

"Come with me quickly," the man says. He is angry but oddly respectful.

"Who are you?" Charlotte asks, still trembling.

"Ashok's brother, Ravinder."

Looking closely at the man's face, Charlotte can see a familial resemblance. The tightened spring of her body relaxes suddenly and the recoil practically knocks her to the floor. Ravinder steadies her. Embarrassed by her display of weakness, Charlotte pushes him away and attempts to project a more commanding presence as she speaks.

"You scared the hell out of me," she says. "What's going on here?"

"Please come with me. Ashok will explain."

Ravinder leads her into a room with layered Kashmiri carpets and crumbling plaster walls. Ashok and her companions are seated on the rugs in a small cluster. They rise as Charlotte enters.

"My God, Charlotte, where have you been?" Thompson asks.

"Do you have Greg with you?" Curt adds.

Charlotte studies the figures in the room and notes the presence of Ashok, Thompson, Curt and Sushil, but the absence of Greg.

"I went to the market." Charlotte says. "Where is Greg?"

"You went *shopping*?" Curt is plainly angered by her answer. "Dammit, Char, have you lost your senses?"

Charlotte ignores Curt's outburst and stares at Thompson. "Dad, where is Greg? He wasn't with me."

Thompson sighs. In his eyes, the light fades. He slumps visibly and says, "He's missing, Char. Disappeared."

"My God, no," she says. "Who took him?"

"We only have a theory, Charlotte." The voice belongs to Ashok. "We were hoping that maybe he was with you, but since he is not…"

"Then how did they get him? You were supposed to protect us!" She focuses her gaze accusingly on Ashok and Sushil.

Thompson steps forward and wraps his arms around Charlotte. She lets him. "Charlotte," he whispers, "remember that they have put their lives at risk, and they don't even know us."

"I know," Charlotte says. Pushing away from Thompson, she turns to Sushil and Ashok. "I'm sorry, it's just that…"

"We are all very worried," Ashok says. "We don't understand how anyone could have entered the house without our knowledge. We checked all the rooms and there is no sign of any disturbance."

"Well, I left the house without anyone noticing. Maybe Greg went out by himself."

"For what reason?" Thompson asks.

"Maybe to go shopping, like his mom." Curt's sarcastic tone earns a sharp look from Charlotte.

"I don't know what goes on in that boy's head most of the time," Charlotte says. "Maybe he noticed I was gone and went after me."

"We can't take any chances," Sushil says. "We have to assume that the boy has been kidnapped, which means that someone knows our location."

Charlotte doesn't like Sushil's inference. "What do you mean we can't take any chances?" she asks. "What does that mean exactly?"

"It means we must leave at once. Staying here is too dangerous."

"I'm not leaving without my son. No way!"

Sushil steps closer to her. "The fact that Greg may have been kidnapped is not our only risk. You returned from the house by taxi. You were in the back seat with another man, My brother saw you. This is very important now—who was this man?"

"No one you should worry about," Charlotte answers, taking a step away from Sushil.

"Whoever it was knows that you are here, in this very house," Sushil says. "That is something to be very worried about. Now you must tell us— who was it?"

It should be easy to tell them about Gideon, Charlotte knows, but it isn't. Selfishly, she wants to keep the conversation with her Guardian Angel a secret. Some things are no one else's business. When the Prophets of old spoke with angels they did not tell everyone else about it unless they were instructed to do so. To reveal such an intimacy would seem almost to breach a sacred trust.

"He's right, Charlotte, you should tell us," Thompson says.

Curt nods. "We're all at risk here, Char."

Her mind whirls. Everything is spinning out of control. She has to be the strong one now, that's what Gideon was telling her. "All right," she says, "but first, let's go back an hour. I spoke with Greg when I woke up, and Ashok brought some clothes to my room. I took a quick shower and decided to sneak out to... to accessorize."

"*Accessorize?*" Curt says incredulously.

"I don't expect you Neanderthals to understand, but sometimes a woman needs to feel like a woman. I wanted something to go with the, uh, the outfit that Ashok gave me."

Charlotte gives Ashok a furtive glance that betrays her infatuation with the handsome Kashmiri. Seeing this, Curt glares at Ashok.

"I went to a handbag shop and then got kind of scared, realizing all of a sudden how foolish I was to go out alone, so I hopped in a cab and... someone else... okay, it was my Guardian Angel in the taxi."

"How in the world did he find you?" Curt asks.

"No idea," she responds. "He just climbed into the taxi and told me that he might not be able to protect me any longer. So that's my story. Now tell me how in hell you lost my son?"

Ashok speaks first. "Your son and I have established a friendship. We were talking about how worried he was for your safety. He needed to talk about it with someone, and his grandfather was talking on one of our disposable cell phones."

Charlotte struggles to keep focused even though her mind wants to chew on the gristle of Greg's abduction, the grisly possibilities, the horror.

"Wait," Charlotte says to Ashok, reigning in her thoughts. "You said that Thompson was making a call." She turns her eyes on her father as she recalls Gideon's admonition to *be brave but very wise—particularly in who you trust.*

"Who were you calling, Dad?" Her eyes narrow. "I told you about my conversation in the taxi, now it's your turn."

Thompson squirms under her gaze. Finally, the weight of everyone's eyes squeezes out a confession. "I was speaking with the Vatican."

"The Vatican! What on earth for?" Charlotte asks.

"First of all, Greg was not missing yet, all right? Secondly, in case you've forgotten, my good friend Antonio Fortunati is still in the hands of the terrorists. I got through to an acquaintance in Vatican Intelligence and told him that Antonio was mostly likely being held prisoner at the Desi Khana restaurant here in Delhi, as you told me after your interrogation of the prisoner last night."

"You expect the Vatican to rescue your friend?"

Thompson grows angry. "I don't know, Charlotte. I don't know anything anymore, except that we're certainly not going to launch a rescue mission. And I can't just let my friend be tortured and probably killed, if he isn't dead already."

This speech, which catalogs the reality of a terrorist kidnapping, makes Charlotte's legs tremble and her gut erupt hot lava into her throat.

She sits down to steady herself. Curt rushes to her side, distressed by Charlotte's suddenly flushed face.

"I'm all right," Charlotte lies. "Just need a minute to think."

She spends the next minute not thinking but swallowing down the bile. The others sit down around her. She becomes aware that everyone is waiting for her to make sense of this senseless circumstance. To issue a command. To set them going in some productive direction. This, after all, is what she was born to do, what she has done for years as CCN's most aggressive correspondent. She is a producer, the frontline dictator who commands the news gathering team even in the most dire situations, and there have been many of those.

"Okay, everyone sit down." This is all Charlotte can think of saying right now. While she remains standing, maintaining a position of superiority, everyone follows her direction.

"I just can't figure out how this angel guy keeps finding us," Curt says.

"Gideon," Charlotte says. Curt stares at her quizzically, so she adds, "That's his name. Gideon."

"So you're on a first name basis now with a guy who blows the heads off CIA agents."

"Trying to protect us, I think."

"You *think?*"

The quarrel heats up. Sushil interjects, "He must have been the *prith*, the ghost who helped us defeat the terrorists. I want to know how he found us at the carpet store last night."

"Cell phones, maybe." Curt suggests. "You said they have GPS chips that can be tracked, right?"

"Not pre-paid disposable phones." Sushil says. "That's all we have with us now. So how did he track us here?" Sushil turns to Charlotte. "How did he track *you* into the market?"

Charlotte looks even more flushed. She is perspiring now, and starts to wobble. Curt bolts to his feet and helps her sit down. "What's the matter, Char?"

"Just got dizzy, that's all,"

On his hands and knees, Thompson crawls the five feet to his daughter and says, "You're sweating. A fever maybe."

"No, it's just… I'm experiencing some… it's high blood pressure. Be all right in a minute. Damn device is supposed to not let this happen."

Ashok stares at Charlotte, confused by her explanation. "What device?"

"A pulse generator. Implanted right here…" Charlotte's fingers find a small lump to the left of her right shoulder.

Ashok touches the lump above her right breast. He doesn't intend any intimacy by his action, but Curt brusquely pulls his hand away.

"I suffer from hypertension, not good in my line of work. So they implanted this thing, which is supposed to send activation energy to the carotid baroreceptors when my blood pressure goes up, and this somehow reduces the blood pressure. Hell of a thing to get through airport security if I forget my doctor's letter."

Curt stares at the small lump and cocks his head. "So you've got an electronic device inside your body… and this Gideon character is able to track you wherever you go. Quite a coincidence, wouldn't you say?"

Charlotte stares up at Curt. "That's not possible. A tracking device… inside of me? How could they do that? My doctor was a well-respected… Actually, I never met him before the implant. He was a specialist. But my internist... shit! Was not around. But this would mean that they've been watching me... tracking me for... it's been almost two years since my implant."

"More than two years, I think," Curt says.

"What do you mean?"

"Those family photos that Greg marked up, remember? The face you didn't know, all those years growing up..."

Charlotte tries to grab the lump, but her fingers can't get at the edges. "I want this damn thing out of me!" She shouts.

Curt fights her hand away from the device. "Don't be an idiot!" he says. "You can't dig that thing out without hurting yourself, so be reasonable."

Charlotte gives Thompson a pitiful look. "Do something, Daddy." Her words are not a taunt, not an accusation, just an honest plea. She feels invaded. Marked. "I'm a fuckin' transmitter!" she says. "How do I turn it off?"

Thompson puts his arms around his daughter for the first time in decades, and she lets him. He had never dreamed this would happen, but his daughter needs his comfort.

She gasps and rubs her head, feeling dizzy, disoriented, full of anxiety. Thompson helps her lie down and whispers, "Be quiet now, Char, I'm here with you. We'll find Greg and bring him back, I promise."

"I'm such a wimp." She is panting.

"You just need to calm down now and you'll be all right. We'll figure things out, really." He shifts his body to cradle her head.

Charlotte reaches out and touches her father's arm. Strokes it. Closes her eyes. "Thanks, Daddy." She seems to have entered another world, but her breathing is now slow and shallow.

Thompson doesn't know if Charlotte at this moment is an adult talking to her estranged father or a child who doesn't yet know the full gamut of his sins. But he doesn't care. For ten minutes, he holds his daughter close.

And then there is a knock on the front door.

Thompson looks up and Charlotte opens her eyes as Ashok and Ravinder silently approach the door. Ashok peers through a peep hole, then turns to his brother, astonished. In Kashmiri he says, "You won't believe this."

Ashok opens the door and finds Greg staring at him. The boy stiffly enters the house carrying a shopping bag.

"Clothes for mother," he explains.

Chapter 44

Less than an hour ago Charlotte had quietly left the safe house under Gideon's surveillance. Leaving his parked car in the hands of Rahul Pradesh, he had followed Charlotte on foot toward the market.

Two minutes later, Rahul called Gideon on a disposable cell phone. "The boy has just left the house with a backpack," he said. "He's headed in the opposite direction."

"The fleas are leaping off the dog," Gideon replied. "Keep him in sight and find out what's going on."

Gideon had followed Charlotte into the market and watched her grow increasingly agitated. In this frantic state, she was particularly vulnerable. Even though there was no identifiable threat nearby, Gideon knew that he needed to intervene, so he jumped into the taxi and tried to warn Charlotte to be careful. Clearly, she had no idea what was really at stake.

As Gideon watched Charlotte reenter the safe house, Rahul called again. "The boy found a four-star hotel two blocks away," he said. "He walked into the lobby and found a vending machine. Paid for a bottle of water with a credit card."

"Probably his mother's, but I doubt he went there for water."

"You're right, the bottle's still in the machine. So what's he doing?"

"He figured out a way to use his mother's credit card without having to show an ID, so I think he's trying to turn himself in."

"How is that?"

"Using the credit card will flag the computers. She's a fugitive, so I don't think it will take long for the CIA to get the location of that machine and have an intercept team on the spot. Obviously, we can't let them get the boy, am I clear?"

"Very clear. Want me to pick him up?"

"No, I'm just a couple of minutes away. What's he doing now?"

"Sitting on a chair about twenty feet from the vending machine."

"Waiting for them to show up. Probably has figured out that he's the prize, and if he gives himself up it'll save his mother. Trouble is, they'll just use him as a hostage to get Charlotte. Together, they're are an even bigger prize."

"I thought he was an Asperger's kid. Emotionally distant and all that."

"Yeah, well… listen, I'm on the move. Just don't lose the kid."

Five minutes later, Gideon pulled the gray car into the hotel's reception parking circle. Sitting there for a moment, he studied the other cars, the people moving in and out, the uniformed help. A black Toyota Corolla pulled up behind him. In his rearview mirror, Gideon noticed two American men talking inside the Toyota. After a brief exchange, the driver nodded to the passenger who stepped out of the vehicle, glanced suspiciously left and right, then instinctively reached beneath his unbuttoned suit coat to check what almost certainly was a concealed handgun.

Gideon called Rahul. "Incoming, American, gray suit. I'll take the driver and meet you for a bottle of water."

Gideon left his vehicle running and walked toward the black Toyota. The driver was watching the lobby door. Through the open driver's window, Gideon said, "Excuse me, but you'll have to move your car. We have a VIP coming in."

"Are you kidding me?"

"Just back up, sir, and you can pull into a parking space over there." Gideon gestured to a full guest parking lot.

The man expressed frustration with his hands. As the driver placed his left hand on the steering wheel and his right hand on the shifter, Gideon thrust a fist through the window. It struck the man like a piston behind the left ear, instantly knocking him out.

Gideon reached into the car, turned off the ignition, and pocketed the key. From the same pocket, he removed a plastic tie and bound the man's left hand to the door rest. After maneuvering the slumped body into a more natural pose, Gideon casually walked into the hotel lobby where two uniformed men were attending to an unconscious American guest.

Playing a curious spectator, Gideon asked Rahul, "What happened?"

"Slipped and hit his head on the floor. They're getting help."

"Ouch."

Gideon glanced around and saw the boy seated in a nearby chair, eyes glued to the commotion. He walked up to the boy and leaned down.

"Do you know who I am?" Gideon asked.

Greg nodded and said, "But I was expecting someone else."

"You don't have to do this, Greg."

"Yes I do."

"You know that I've protected your mother?"

Greg nodded again.

"Then come with me, and I'll explain why staying with her is the best way to help her. Will you do that?"

Greg looked uncertain. He glanced at the unconscious man on the floor.

"He's the one you were expecting," Gideon said, "and he's not a nice man. Come with me, son, and I'll explain things while we do some shopping for your mother. She needs clothes. Any idea what size?"

Now, as Gideon looks at the closed door of the safe house and imagines Greg reunited with his mother, he wonders if Charlotte will ever know how her son had tried to sacrifice himself for her. And for just a moment Gideon allows himself the exquisite bliss of imagining himself reunited with his own mother, though he can't recall her face.

Chapter 45

Charlotte stares at Greg. He stands in front of her, pinioned by her stare. She wants to yell at him, tell him how stupid he was to leave the house alone—but hadn't she done the same thing? Fragments of accusations blister her tongue, but she remains silent, as do the others who await the outcome of this mother-son showdown.

Suddenly, she feels an unfamiliar effervescence, a warm and voluptuous sensation bubbling up through her skin. A mother's relief. Her son was not abducted. He is safe! Her baby is back.

Fighting the urge to wrap him in her arms (where did this aberrant maternal impulse come from?), she simply rises to her feet and extends a hand. Cautiously, Greg approaches her. She wants to touch his shoulder, his face, make sure he is real, but Greg has misinterpreted her gesture and hands her the shopping bag containing the new clothes.

Disappointed yet grateful for the emotional distance, she grips the string handle and says, flatly, "Thank you."

She continues to stare at her son, but his eyes never lock onto her gaze. He is looking perhaps into some other Asperger's world that she cannot enter. Over the past several days their worlds had intersected, as if he had found a portal from some parallel universe into hers. They had communicated. He had established relationships—with Thompson and Ashok, at least. But now Greg seems to have drifted back through that fickle wormhole and left only his physical husk behind.

Ashok breaks the tense silence. "We need to go!"

"Go where?" Curt asks. "I feel like a pinball here."

"Ashok is right," Thompson says. "Charlotte, are you up to moving?" He's worried about her hypertension.

Charlotte turns to her father. "You know, I think that blood pressure business was a crock, just something to explain the implant. Trouble is, I believed it and made it real. There's nothing wrong with me except my damn suggestibility, so let's get the hell out of here."

"What about that transmitter in your chest?" Curt asks.

Charlotte has come to think of the implant as a lifeline to Gideon. But she knows that her companions don't see her Guardian Angel as a reliable ally, so she offers a feeble "Maybe we'll get out of range."

Thompson senses Charlotte starting to take charge. "With that in mind, I can suggest a destination—the Hemis monastery in Ladakh."

"Where the hell is Ladakh?" Curt asks.

Thompson gives the geographically challenged photographer a professorial stare, the kind that usually wilts ignorant students. "In the western Himalayas, *where it's always been*."

"I have no quarrel with you, Mr. Levy," Gideon says, "even though you tried your damndest to kill me. I understand it's just business. We are both very good at what we do, but I am just a bit better. So how is David Weiss these days?"

The Boston-born Mossad assassin stares up at Gideon from his bed, surprised that Gideon has used the name of his boss, the chief of Kidon. The painkillers are beginning to wear off and fiery bolts of pain shoot through his shattered shoulder.

"So, I told you things," he says, bravely assuming a *doesn't matter much* expression. Levy's drug-distorted mind is becoming unclouded. "I did not need to interrogate you under drugs to know who you represent. The knife said it all."

"Then we can have a polite conversation, you and me—two professionals comparing notes."

"And then what? You kill me?"

"It depends on how polite our conversation is. There is no need for you to die. Perhaps some day in the future we will work a job together. We do not hold grudges."

"You know Weiss. By reputation?"

"We've never met in person, only through an intermediary. That's how it works. But in the past, I had the honor of serving the cause of Kidon, so we are only temporarily on opposite sides."

"Muaz," Levy says, saying the name of a Wahabi Mujahid that Kidon had desperately wanted assassinated. "That was you?"

"Muaz, yes. Ironically, the name means 'protected,' but in his case obviously a misnomer."

"We were never able to get close to him, and we feared that a missile strike in Saudi Arabia would provoke, well, unfortunate consequences."

"You sound like a diplomat. No matter—the man is dead and his chief rival was blamed for the assassination, causing all sorts of internal strife, as Weiss intended." Gideon smiles sardonically and adds, "It hurts me that I never received a thank you."

"I'm sure your organization was well compensated."

"So you see, our differences are only temporary, and when this business is finished we may end up on the same side again."

"That may not be so easy. How about our two agents in Minnesota?"

"It was so unfortunate they were there. Why is it, Michael, that Mossad can't leave this matter alone? Why compete?"

"I think you know. We can't risk having it fall into anyone else's hands, even a friendly." He grimaces again as the pain worsens. "You may as well kill me now, or Weiss will do it later. He has a low tolerance for failure, and I bungled this one badly."

"Just one small screw-up at the end. I have to admit some admiration for how an American Jew could end up directing a team of Pakistani terrorists in India. Care to share?"

"Three years, that's all you have to know. Hell of an investment to go up in smoke. You weren't our mission until Ansari arrived in Delhi. I had another objective entirely, but then you came here and priorities changed. We had to improvise, and we both know how that turned out."

"I'm going to be honest with you, Michael. It would be much easier to kill you here and dispose of your body than to treat your wounds and get you back to your employer. But contrary to what you may have heard, we don't like killing. Unless our hand is forced, we only kill strategically. We will get you safely home if you honestly answer a few questions for me. Is that fair?"

"And if I don't?"

Gideon exposes a 9mm Glock clutched in his right hand. "Then my hand may be forced."

"What's the first question?"

"Do you know where the relic is?"

"How will you know if I'm telling the truth?"

Gideon moves his face close to Levy's and stares so intently into the man's eyes that Levy squirms, averting his gaze.

"I'll know," Gideon says.

Levy take a deep breath and looks squarely into Gideon's eyes. "No," he says. "I have no idea where it is. And neither does anyone in the organization. That's why we want Ansari and her son."

"To kill them, I imagine. They're competition like me."

"Are you nuts? Weiss thinks they're the only ones who can find it! We targeted you because we thought you wanted her dead."

Gideon laughs without meaning to. Both Mossad and the Sicarii have been trying to protect Charlotte and Greg, hoping that these two can uncover the secret and locate the relic.

"How did Weiss decide that Charlotte Ansari is the key?"

"Are you kidding?" Levy says.

Gideon lowers the pistol.

"We tracked the terrorists to the Curtis house in Minnesota," Levy continues. "It was my job to know their plans—but now that my cover's completely blown, that'll never happen again."

"So you tracked them to Curtis and sent agents to intercept the relic."

"Curtis was a fool. He dared to show it off to the wrong people, including an al Qaeda sympathizer. After you killed their team and our two agents, we believed for a short time that the relic had fallen into someone else's hands. But hours later another terrorist team hit the Ansari house. That was quite a surprise. I knew nothing about it. But it told us the relic was still in play."

Gideon thinks this through. Once he had taken care of matters at the Curtis house, Gideon had worried about the proximity of this violence to Charlotte and Greg, so he went back to his primary mission—protecting mother and son. He had saved Charlotte from a random kidnapping in Iraq and worried that she had become a lightning rod for more violence.

When another al Qaeda team showed up, Gideon disposed of them and used the opportunity to plant a bold message for the Ansari clan, one he hoped they would be able to decipher.

Still, he had not known at the time why the terrorists had come after Charlotte and Greg. How could they have tied Charlotte to the relic?

"All right, Michael. Tell me why al Qaeda hit the Ansari residence."

Levy grimaces in pain. "Another dose, please," he begs."

"When we're done. Now tell me why they hit Charlotte's home that night."

"Look, I don't know everything, okay? All I know is the chatter I heard come through my guys, which was that Jack Curtis had been under surveillance for a couple of weeks, and during that time Mike Ansari was seen visiting Curtis at least three times. The last time was the day before Charlotte arrived home, and Mike Ansari was seen leaving the Curtis house with a package. It might've been the relic, right? The fact that Charlotte's father is into all kinds of religion crap led them to believe that Mike could have obtained the relic for the old man. Bought it, you know? Or taken it for authentication. Or even worse, maybe Charlotte was going to do a big exposé about it on CCN! So in desperation they went to Charlotte's house with guns blazing. Real subtle."

For Gideon, this has the ring of truth. It also makes him question Mike Ansari's role in the unfolding events.

Levy squirms and pants. The pain is overwhelming him. He yells and pleads, "Kill this fuckin' pain or put a bullet in my head."

Gideon touches his arm. "One more thing. How did Mossad get involved in this thing?"

"You guys don't know? Shit, you work for all of us and you don't know?"

"Tell me and I'll give you the painkiller right now."

"The CIA... leaked it to us. We're buddy-buddy, you know? Close allies. Idiots can't keep a secret... never thought we'd be a competitor. Whole damn thing was an al Qaeda idea... got spilled to the Americans by a soft-belly in Guantanamo."

Levy bellows in pain. His eyes widen in desperation.

"All right, my friend," Gideon says. "Here is the painkiller."

With a deep and grateful sigh, Levy closes his eyes. "Thank you," he whispers. "Thank you." And then receives his wish—instantaneous relief.

A bullet in the head.

The irrevocable penalty for attempting to kill a Sicarii.

Chapter 46

Jason Wells, a wiry man in his late twenties, is still spooked by the violence near the India Gate, but not so spooked that he has failed to consider the value of the video he captured. Unlike American news gatherers, the Hindu reporter who interviewed Jason offered a handsome amount of money for the footage, but Jason turned him down, certain that the tape would fetch a higher price in the US if he could get out of India before the police confiscated it.

He throws the last of his possessions into a suitcase and backpack, checks the dresser drawers for any forgotten articles, and then makes sure his passport is secure inside the ID holder that swings from a lanyard around his neck. There has been no time to change his flight, so he intends to do this at the airport.

He just wants to get out of India.

His traveling companion, Hector Galvez, watches meekly. Hector is a handsome man about the same age as Jason. "Wish you wouldn't do this, blow off the last week," Hector says. "You never even got to see the Taj Mahal."

"Take some good pictures, okay? See you back in Houston."

Jason lugs his belongings across the room then sets down the heavy suitcase to open the door, which swings wide to reveal two men blocking his way. Jason's heart plunges. Indian police? No—these men are clearly Americans, one of them tall with blue eyes and sandy hair, the other shorter and thicker with dark eyes and hair. Both are much bigger than bony Jason Wells, an art student who has exhausted his savings on this trip-of-a-lifetime to see the artistic treasures of the East.

"Jason Wells?" the sandy-haired man asks.

Jason is confused and scared. He hesitates briefly, considering whether he should lie. Hector rises to his feet.

"Mr. Wells, may we have a word with you inside?" The thick man has removed Jason's quandary. He takes a step toward Jason, forcing the young man to back up, nearly tripping over the suitcase.

The sandy-haired man closes the door behind them and pulls an identification card out of the breast pocket of his suit coat. "Glen Jardace, CIA," he says, "and my associate George Ford."

Jason backs up a few more steps, putting more distance between himself and the two CIA agents. "What's this about—that shooting?"

"It is, sir. You videotaped the incident?" the thick man says.

Jason can see his future windfall disappearing. "I did. Do you need a statement or something?"

"No sir," the thick man says, moving closer. His presence grows more threatening. "We need the videotape. Do you have it here?"

Jason is incensed. Despite his precarious position, he resists. "Far as I know, it's my property. And this is India, not America. You have no jurisdiction here."

"Jason, I want to be very clear here," the sandy-haired man says as he hoists up the heavy suitcase as if it were weightless and throws it onto the unmade bed. "We have jurisdiction over Americans everywhere. And you're in a pile of trouble, my friend. One of the men in your videotape is a clandestine CIA operative and your footage is jeopardizing his safety."

"This is stupid," Hector says nervously, walking toward the two men. "I think you should leave now."

The thick man elbows Hector so viciously that the young man flies into a wall, knocking over a floor lamp. Jason's eyes grow round with fear.

"Fact is," the sandy-haired man says, opening the suitcase, "it really doesn't matter what you think. If you resist, you may end up going through a period of prolonged interrogation to determine why you did not cooperate. Frankly, it's already making me wonder why you wish to expose one of our agents."

"What? You're kidding, right?"

"We have no sense of humor about these things," the thick man solemnly replies, moving even closer to Jason.

Will he ever get a full night's sleep again?

Director Wyatt bolts upright in bed and answers the phone. "Yes, what is it?" His mind is still clogged with the debris of a nightmare.

206

"It's Timms, sir. We've scored big."

"Don't you ever sleep, Allison?"

"Not during times like these."

The debris in Wyatt's brain is settling. "So tell me the score."

"We got the videotape of the India Gate incident. Apparently, the patriotic tourist who shot it voluntarily surrendered the tape to our agents."

"Right," Wyatt says sarcastically.

"The Delhi office digitized the analog tape and uploaded it over a secure channel to Headquarters. Our analysts here found three clear frames of the injured man, and five clear frames of the second man. Are you logged in, sir?"

"Just a minute."

Wyatt leaps from bed, lumbers over to a desk, then wiggles a mouse connected to a laptop. The screen lights up. Over a virtual private network, this computer can securely access CIA files. Wyatt places himself so that he can see his own eye's reflection in an iris scanner. Three seconds later, he is logged in. Two people appear on the screen.

"All right, I'm in. I see two faces here—speak to me."

"On the left is the man who was shot. Face recognition has shown him to be Michael Levy, a Jewish native of the Boston area who was recruited in college by Mossad and eventually assigned to Kidon."

"So, someone popped an Israeli agent. And the other guy?"

"He's the one you think might be a Sicarii agent. He seems to be an American, but face recognition has turned up nothing."

Wyatt studies this face. "Sicarii—I'm sure of it. Can feel it in my bones."

"You're probably right, sir. The local police discovered a small dagger at the location of the incident."

"I knew it! These guys are in league with each other, you think?"

"I've looked at the tape, sir. It seems clear that they were adversaries. Hard to say if Levy or the Sicarii agent was the target of the hit, but we do know the would-be assassin was an Arab, and the escape vehicle—the one both men ended up in—seems to have been driven by a man with Indian features, according to witnesses. No clear picture of him, though."

"Escape vehicle?"

"You can see in the video that the Sicarii helped Levy into a car."

"If they were adversaries, why would he do that?"

"To extract information from him later? Pure conjecture."

"So an American Sicarii, an Israeli agent, an Arab, and an Indian all meet at the India Gate. Sounds like the start of a bad joke. How do these pieces all fit together?"

"No idea yet."

"Okay, here is what I want you to do. Contact Ajay Sanghvi…"

"The head of India's Intelligence Bureau? Sir, he's really pissed at us right now, as you know. That Kashmiri Carpet fiasco—"

"Timms!"

"Sorry sir."

"Tell Sanghvi that we have a known terrorist at large in India right now and we need help in getting him off the streets and into our hands. Send him the photograph. Those guys are very efficient."

"And you think he'll cooperate with us?"

"Apologize first. These guys love it when America grovels. Then let him know we're willing to make concessions for their assistance. He can name his price. I guarantee he'll cooperate."

"Consider it done, sir."

"Timms, I want this Sicarii bastard in a Langley interrogation room where I can sit across the table and look him in the eye. He's got answers to a lot of our questions, and I intend to get them."

"All right sir, but you called this guy a *ghost*."

"Ghosts don't have faces, Timms. This phantom has suddenly become flesh-and-blood."

"And if he changes his appearance?"

"Why would he do that? He still thinks he's a ghost."

Chapter 47

The green van has been traveling through Delhi traffic for over forty-five minutes. Ashok, the driver, turns to Thompson with the universal palms-up shrug of confusion. "I have no idea where we are," he says.

"I've got directions here," Thompson replies. "In about a mile we veer left and then we're almost to the site."

"I don't understand why we're going to Ladakh," Curt says. "Are we just escaping to someplace remote?"

"We don't have time for retreat," Charlotte replies tersely. "According to Mom's emails, we're on the clock."

"Look, a close friend of mine may have given his life to return something to the Hemis monastery." Thompson turns from the front passenger seat to face the others. "I'm bloody well going to see that his mission is accomplished before Mossad, the CIA, or a bunch of terrorists kill me."

"Your friend from the Vatican," Curt says.

"Once again, his name was Antonio Fortunati. We were like brothers."

Thompson glances at Greg, who is lost in reading the Bible, and then at his daughter, who averts her gaze as if she is not interested in anything personal about her father.

"For some years Antonio has been suffering a crisis of faith," Thompson explains. "No, that's not quite right. His faith in God never wavered, but he was experiencing a crisis of *the* Faith—the Holy Roman Church. You see, his work gave him access to all the secret treasures and documents that the Vatican had collected through legitimate and sometimes illegitimate means. He came to believe that the Church had deliberately concealed or destroyed evidence that refuted many of its teachings, particularly the doctrine of the divinity of Christ, his resurrection, and his ascension to heaven."

For the first time, Greg looks up at his grandfather.

"Just before Antonio flew to New Delhi," Thompson continues, "he stole a couple of artifacts that he had found in the Secret Archives. He hid them in a geranium pot at my apartment. Now it's my duty to return this particular artifact to its true owner in Ladakh."

Thompson holds up a leather satchel.

"So what is it?" Curt asks.

"A true story," Thompson replies.

The van suddenly veers left.

Ashok's excited voice announces, "There it is—the construction site."

Two minutes later the van pulls into a littered construction area and noses up alongside a weathered Bell 214 helicopter parked about fifty yards from a rising office tower.

As soon as the van stops, Thompson jumps out and races to a paunchy, silver-haired man who is standing next to the chopper. The other occupants of the van exit slowly, unsure of what to do next. Charlotte watches her father warmly embrace the silver-haired man, pat him on the back several times, and then hold the man at arm's length to get a good view of him before giving another bear hug.

The group meanders toward the two old men.

"Herb," Thompson says to his friend, "meet my daughter, Charlotte."

The big man steps toward Charlotte and takes her in his arms, nearly crushing her with a hug, and then starts to dance around the gravelly field with her. She can't help but smile at the man's good humor and fancy footwork.

"Your father has done a lot of bragging about you, my dear," Herb whispers into her ear just before the unheard music stops and the dance ends.

"Most of what my father says is untrue," Charlotte replies.

Herb laughs, but Charlotte isn't kidding.

"Herb Rossi, chopper pilot extraordinaire," Thompson says, more formally introducing his friend. "I want you to also meet Curt, a CCN photographer—works with Charlotte—and my grandson, Greg."

Herb reaches out and nearly shakes the hand off Curt's arm, then turns to Greg, who is staring at the helicopter. Sensing that the boy is shy, he pulls back on the enthusiasm throttle and quietly says, "You like it, Greg? She's like a daughter to me. The Bell of the ball!" He laughs at his own joke.

Thompson walks over to his friend and puts his arm around the big man's shoulders. "We got trouble following us, Herb. Might be a good idea to be airborne as soon as possible."

"Then I suggest you use the porta-potty over there," Herb says loudly to the assemblage. "I'll put your things in the belly of the beast."

"We're traveling light," Charlotte explains.

"Had to leave quick, huh? Okay then."

Curt, Charlotte and Greg head for the porta-potty. Thompson stays to speak to his friend. "This is good of you, Herb. Like I said on the phone, everything that's dear to me is going to be on your bird today. I'm afraid I haven't got enough cash on me to pay for the trip, but I can…"

"Don't worry, my friend. If you can cover the fuel, the rest of the trip's on me. Haven't been to Ladakh since, well, I got you out just before the snows. What was it, three years ago?"

"Five."

"Gotta say, Tommy, you are a real idiot sometimes for such a smart guy."

"And getting dumber by the minute."

"Hell, forget about the gas. If it hadn't been for you, Angie would never have gotten into that school, you smooth talkin' devil. She graduates next spring!"

"I'd like to be there. You know she was like a granddaughter to me."

"Yeah, but now you got your own daughter and grandson to look out for. See how things work out? And you thought Charlotte would never speak to you."

"Things haven't quite worked out all the way, Herb."

"When she sees what a great guy her old man is, it'll work out, guaranteed. Now if you're so hell-bent on gettin' out of here, I've got work to do. This is gonna be a whole lot more fun than ferrying heavy construction equipment."

Ashok has set their bags beside the van. Herb and Thompson walk to it.

"No flight plan, right?" Thompson asks Herb.

"Off the books and flying low. Invisible as a zephyr. I hope you know what you're doing."

"I hope *you* know what you're doing. You're the pilot. Herb, I'd like you to meet Ashok, from Srinagar. Saved our butts over the past few hours."

"Kashmir. Beautiful country. Too bad about all the conflict." Herb extends his hand and Ashok takes it.

"Pleased to make your acquaintance," Ashok says.

Herb starts to carry the bags to the helicopter.

Thompson gives Ashok a hug and tells him, "Thank you. It was beyond the call. I think we'll see each other again, my friend."

"I'm sure of it. Take care of that headstrong daughter of yours."

"I'm hoping she'll take care of me."

Chapter 48

"The target has moved," Eve says. Her voice sounds thin and brittle over the cell phone.

"We knew she would," Gideon replies. "Where is she now?"

"The map shows an empty plot—the most recent satellite photo shows the beginning of a construction project. She's been there for about twenty minutes."

"Want me to intercept?"

"No, we'll just see where she goes from here. Hold on—she's moving again. Awfully fast."

"Still by van you think?"

"Too fast for the van. I'd say a plane, or if they took off from a construction site, more likely a chopper. They're off-road."

"That should dust their trail pretty well. Let me know where they set down—they'll soon be out of range for me. In the meantime, I've got a little piece of business to take care of. I'm moving to the next number now."

"Be careful. You're in everyone's crosshairs."

He terminates the call and rips the battery out of his disposable cell phone. He restarts his motor scooter, darts into the flow of traffic and hurls the phone into the back of a passing garbage truck. Then he plucks another phone from his shirt pocket and switches it on, moving to the *next number* at which he can be reached.

After about twenty minutes, Gideon arrives at a local market full of small shops and big smells. He chains the scooter to a metal post and pushes his way through a mass of bodies to the unassuming storefront of a money changer. As he approaches the shop, he replays the single unretrieved message from Michael Levy's cell phone in his mind, a message probably left during the India Gate melee.

"Michael, it's David. It's urgent that we meet at six," the man had said, "at the money changer's in Chandni Chowk. Delete this message now!"

The voice betrayed a pale tinge of Hebrew, probably recorded by a Mossad associate of Levy, perhaps even the dead man's commander. How brash, choosing the stereotypically Jewish occupation of money changing as the Delhi front for clandestine Israeli activities.

Gideon checks his watch. It is 5:52. He begins to study the leatherwork in a nearby shop as he keeps an eye on the money changer's storefront. It's possible that David is already inside, although Gideon suspects the man will not show up until the appointed time. Agents don't usually arrive early or leave late for announced meetings.

The leather goods dealer pesters Gideon for a sale. After trying to brush him off, Gideon finally buys a cheap wallet to gain some peace. *How will he expense that?*

At 5:58 a stout, balding man with jowls that jiggle with each step steers a course for the money changer's shop. The man could be Jewish, possibly Afghani, even Kashmiri—there were many physical similarities between these ethnicities. Gideon watches the man motion to the Indian money changer who sits behind a thick window accessible from the long market corridor. The Indian subtly nods, leans forward as if reaching for a switch, and then a door opens.

If Gideon is to make a move, he must do it now.

Gideon begins to walk toward the stout man, who is about to step through the unlocked door.

"David!" Gideon calls out.

The man stops and turns. Gideon can see the man's reflexive response to the name, a sure betrayal. Yes, this man is David.

"David, I found your wallet," Gideon says, holding up the newly purchased wallet and waving it so David can't get a good look at it. He approaches David with a smile.

"Do I know you?" David says, scowling.

"Don't you want your wallet?" Gideon hands the wallet to David, who is about to say that it is not his property, but instead feels the cold, sharp point of a blade in his belly.

Quietly, Gideon whispers to David, "Be quiet now, my good man, and take me through the door."

David has been a Mossad agent for over twenty years and few things frighten him, but a *Sicarii*—! He is quite certain that he no longer has the skills to overtake this adversary. He smiles, though his blood is running cold. Nudged by the sting of the dagger's point, David steps toward the door followed by Gideon.

The Indian money changer sees Gideon's right hand at David's back and starts to reach for a pistol in one of the drawers.

"Huh-uh," Gideon says. "David will be dead before your finger touches the trigger, so be smart now and close up shop for the day."

The Indian hangs a CLOSED sign in the window and lowers a blind so no one can see in.

With his left hand, Gideon pats down David and finds a Glock beneath the man's suit coat. He looks around the small inner chamber.

"Are you the one who killed my men in Minnesota?" David asks.

"There are many of us. We're all over the world," Gideon replies.

"You have worked for us in the past. Why turn on us now?"

"Another firm contacted us first. The real truth, however, is that this other firm had interests that were more aligned with our own."

"I didn't know your organization had interests."

"Then you've not been paying attention. Who else will be joining us this evening? Certainly you and Michael Levy were not planning a romantic evening."

"Ah, *Michael Levy*. I see the connection now. No one else will be joining us, to answer your question."

"I was wondering if I would ever meet the head of Kidon in person. I'm deeply honored."

The Indian still sits at the window, intently watching the unfolding conversation. Suddenly, he lurches for the drawer, reaches in, and pulls out a Glock 9mm pistol. It is a blur of motion, well-practiced and nearly faultless, except that before the Indian can raise the pistol, a flung dagger slices into his left eye. The man slumps backward onto the counter.

"You have no weapon now," David Weiss says, staring at Gideon's dagger protruding from his associate's head.

"Neither do you," Gideon says. "Care to try a little mano-a-mano?"

"At my age, no thank you. But twenty years ago I could've *whupped your ass*, as they say in your country." He taunts Gideon with a mimicked southern accent.

"No weapons—no witnesses either. So maybe we can just have a nice intimate little chat. My boss doesn't like it when I knock off our customers. Says it's bad for business."

"Glad to hear it. But you may as well kill me now. You know that I'm a stubborn old man and won't give you any helpful information. Besides, you keep killing my staff. Not very civil." David's tone is mockingly casual.

"Very well. I appreciate you saving me some time."

Gideon walks the five short steps to the Indian and pulls the dagger from a bloody eye. He finds some Indian rupees on the counter and uses them to wipe the blade. All this time his back is turned toward David, who considers pulling a small revolver from his ankle holster, but decides that the Sicarii would hear the rustle of clothes and that would be the end of the Kidon chief.

Gideon turns, smiling. "Decided not to go for the gun down there?" He glances at David's ankle. "Too bad. You would have had a chance."

Gideon walks toward David. "So, are you a religious Jew or a secular one? In other words, do you want to pray before we finish this conversation?"

David Weiss suddenly loses his cockiness.

Gideon stalks to a position behind David. "Okay, then. Because you've been a good client of ours, I can promise that this won't hurt very much. At first it will feel like a touch of pleurisy—a little finger of pain through the lung." He shoves the point of the blade into David's back far enough to draw blood and the man flinches.

Gideon leans forward and whispers into the man's ear. "Next, you'll get very sleepy—not an altogether unpleasant feeling. And that's about it. The transition into the next world will be a lot like going to sleep. If you think about it, the end of someone in your line of work could be much more agonizing, but you don't have to thank me. No one ever does. All right then—ready?"

"Wait!" David is perspiring heavily now. His mind is scavenging for some piece of harmless information to feed this assassin, or some diversion to buy time. "You took me far too seriously when I said you should kill me now. What will that get you? Just a dead client."

"*Ex*-client. While we were chatting, I remembered that your agent, Michael Levy, was sent to kill me. Now, who might have given that order? Oh yes, it turns out that the chief of Kidon happens to be in Delhi. I take attempts on my life very seriously, David."

"What the hell do you want from me?" David growls.

Gideon steps around the stout man and stares into his rheumy eyes.

"I want you dead. But I'd settle for something a little less dramatic."

"For God's sake, what?"

"For *God's* sake? You're onto something there." He pauses for a moment and David watches him expectantly. "Mossad has been trying to protect Charlotte Ansari and her son—Levy told me that."

"The sonofabitch!"

"And if he hadn't, you'd be dead right now."

"Is Levy dead?"

"Yes. I killed him."

"Well—if you hadn't, he would've shown up here tonight and I would've killed him."

"He's your man! Why would you do that?"

Gideon lowers his dagger.

"He's not my man," David says. "He's a rogue agent, and unfortunately he's not alone. There's a breakaway group of Mossad agents who've become very suspicious of the US. Levy was one of them, perhaps the chief instigator. These disloyal agents have taken it on themselves to capture the same relics that you and I are after. But for quite a different purpose. They fear that the US is faltering in its commitment to preserve the security of the Israeli nation, and they want to use these relics to blackmail the US into unwavering support."

"So the Mossad agents who were killed in Minnesota—?"

"Were rogues. Good riddance."

"Thank you. But where do *you* stand in all this?"

"You asked if I were a religious Jew or a secular Jew. The answer is—I lost my religion as a young man. I'm no religious zealot like these rogues—I'm a realist. And while I have the same apprehension about the US that these rogue agents have, I'm not stupid enough to try to blackmail the most powerful government in the world. That would be an act of suicide for Israel."

"Levy was leading a cell of Pakistani terrorists."

David nods. "He was a chameleon. Gifted that way. We set him up in that role to infiltrate al Qaeda, but we suspect he departed from his orders and was hunting down the relics instead."

"By following Charlotte."

"Now let me ask you a question," David says. "The Sicarii began as Jewish zealots. Two weeks ago I stood on top of Masada where the Sicarii were savaged by the Roman army. Standing there, even knowing that most of the legend of Masada was just that, I was still thrilled by the stories of that last battle. So, how did a non-Jewish American end up as a Sicarii assassin?"

"Probably much the same way a college physics professor with a Jewish father and an Irish mother ended up as the head of Kidon."

"So, where do we go from here?"

"Well, I did you a favor and took out Levy. Seems like you owe me."

Chapter 49

The Bell 214 chopper deftly maneuvers around the jagged slopes of the western Himalayas. Through the cabin's square windows, Charlotte and Thompson gawk at the geological fatigue of the landscape. Despite the persistent vibration of the helicopter, Curt tries to capture on video the majesty of the countless white peaks set like uncut diamonds against the dark sapphire sky. Greg alone ignores the sweeping vista. His Asperger's brain is far more fascinated by the mysteries of the stolen King James Bible in his hands. With a crisp rattle, his fingers flip the onion-skin leaves back and forth in search of hidden meanings and obscure connections.

Modest turbulence causes Curt to set down his camera. He turns to Thompson, who is gazing serenely out the window, and says, "So, Fortunati left you something you need to return to someone. Gonna keep it a secret?"

The spoken words seem to pull Thompson out of a meditation. "Sorry," he replies, "what was that?"

"The thing in your bag," Curt says. "Must be really important to carry it all the way up into these mountains. You said it was a story?"

"A true story, yes. I'm sorry—I was meaning to tell you about it, but my mind slipped a gear."

Charlotte turns to face the center of the cabin. "Well, I appreciate a good true story," she says. "I am a journalist, after all. And up here you've got a captive audience, so let's have it."

Thompson picks up his satchel from the floor and sets it on his lap. Like a small boy protecting a personal treasure from covetous friends, he cradles it with his arms.

"All right then, "Thompson says, "the story begins one hundred and twenty years ago with a Russian aristocrat who was also a journalist like you, Charlotte. His name was Nicolas Notovitch. In 1887 he decided to study the culture in India. He was twenty-nine. His wanderings eventually took him to Ladakh, the most sparsely populated region of Kashmir. The remoteness and rugged beauty of the region intrigued him, so he launched an expedition into the higher elevations above the hamlet of Wakkha where an ancient gompa—a Buddhist monastery—seemed glued to the flank of an isolated rock—Notovitch's own colorful description. I believe you can see it below, out the window on your left."

Greg silently sets down his Bible. Without making eye contact with the others, he repositions his body to stare out the window, as do the others. Below them, impossibly stuck to a massive gray outcropping, is a Buddhist gompa.

"Herb—that it?" Thompson says to his friend, the pilot.

Herb nods.

"That is indeed the first gompa Notovitch visited in 1887," Thompson explains. "To reach it, the Russian and his translator had to climb a long, narrow stairway carved into the face of the rock. The Russian was a lot younger than me when I made my first visit there. Almost killed me. At the top of the stairway, Notovitch was greeted by a very fat *lama*—the chief priest of the gompa."

The helicopter banks and the gompa disappears from sight. Everyone settles back into their seats.

"The lama led Notovitch through a maze of low, dusty chambers decorated with images of the Buddha, and finally they emerged on a terrace overlooking the mountains and sat down on a long stone bench. Monks brought them a type of homemade beer known as *tchang*."

Thompson's warm, growly voice smears the story with the patina of reminiscence, as if he had been an eyewitness to the unfolding events. He is a master storyteller, and the hint of an extraordinary secret about to be exposed ensnares his listeners.

For Charlotte, hearing her father tell the story is like revisiting her once-happy home before the troubles. Charlotte dimly recalls the blissful excitement she felt when Thompson would vividly spin tales from the Bible for his young, wide-eyed daughter, and she would pepper him with questions—a journalist in the making. *Why just two of each kind of animal?* she remembers asking about Noah's ark. *What if they had families too—were they split up?* She had been troubled that God could be unfair.

"Through the translator, Notovitch and the lama engaged in a spirited discussion of religion," Thompson says. "In a sense, I've always considered Notovitch to be my surrogate in this amazing interfaith discussion, which was held long before my time. According to Notovitch, the lama said that in his occasional contacts with Muslims, he had found little common ground between their faith and his. The lama expressed regret that the Muslims often converted Buddhists to Islam by force and that it took such great effort to return those tortured souls to the path of the true God."

"And Christians?" Charlotte asks. "How did the lama view them? As I recall, the Church has a rather malodorous history of conversion by force."

"And yet the lama had not seen this in his land," Thompson replies. "He saw a remarkable similarity between the teachings of Christ and Buddha, and the sacred rites of Christian priests and Tibetan lamas. In fact, he attributed this to Christians having adopted the great doctrines of Buddha. The lama assigned only one fault to Christianity—that it had cut itself off from Buddha by creating for itself a different Dalai-Lama, whom the monks believed to be the only intermediary between heaven and earth."

"A *different* Dalai-Lama?" Charlotte says. "He was referring to Christ?"

"Notovitch asked that question," Thompson replies. "The lama shook his head and said: 'No, we too respect him, and revere him as the son of the One and Indivisible God, though we do not see him as the Only Son, but as the excellent being who was chosen among all.' Clearly, what the lama meant by another Dalai-Lama was the Pope.

"They knew all about Jesus since long before Christians traveled to Tibet. I can recall the thrilling words of this lama to Notovitch as if I had been there: 'Buddha incarnated himself, with his divine nature, in the person of the sacred Issa, who without employing fire and iron has gone forth to propagate our true and great religion among all the world.'"

"Sacred *Issa*!" Charlotte says emphatically. "Who the hell is *Issa*?"

Thompson winces at the mild curse in such close proximity to the mention of Issa. "Once again, Notovitch anticipated us all and probed to find out. The lama's eyes opened wide as the interpreter translated the Russian's perplexity into the Tibetan language. And then the lama replied: 'Issa is a great prophet, one of the first after the twenty-two Buddhas. He is greater than any one of all the Dalai-Lamas, for he constitutes part of the spirituality of the Lord. His name and his acts have been chronicled in our sacred writings. And when reading how his great life passed away in the midst of an erring people, we weep for the horrible sin of the heathen who murdered him after subjecting him to torture.'"

"Sounds like Jesus," Curt says.

Charlotte flashes Curt a startled look, and then returns her gaze to Thompson. "Issa is Jesus?" she asks.

"Notovitch suspected as much. Today we know that the Buddhist name Issa, with a double 's', and the Hindu and Islamic name Isa, with a single 's', are derived from the Syrian name Yeshu, or Jesus. In some Islamic writings, Jesus is also referred to as Yuz Asaf, which loosely translated means healer of lepers."

"Okay, so we sideswiped the story of Notovitch on the patio of a Buddhist gompa that is glued to the side of a rock," Charlotte says. "A real cliff hanger."

"Notovitch, with the tenacity of a CCN reporter, kept pushing for more information, and the lama revealed that the Buddhist gompas throughout Tibet contained many scrolls about the life of Saint Issa, or Jesus. The ancient scrolls, in the Pali language, were written in India and Nepal shortly after many of the events happened, and then were moved to Lhasa, the traditional seat of the Dalai-Lama. But the lamas who visited Lhasa often made copies of the scrolls, usually translating them into the more common Tibetan language, and then distributed the copies to other gompas during their travels as custom dictated."

"The gompa entertaining Notovitch had some of these copies?" Charlotte asks.

"Unfortunately, no. And very soon Notovitch was sent away, his mind reeling with the possibility that Jesus, known as Issa, was a great prophet of the Buddhists. The Russian vowed to visit other great gompas in search of the scrolls about Jesus, even though as a Russian Orthodox Christian he knew such evidence would blow the lid off his faith."

"He traveled to Lhasa?" Charlotte asks.

"He set out at once with a loose plan to visit as many gompas as possible. He traversed Namykala Pass, which is at thirty thousand feet of altitude, and descended into the valley of the River Salinoumah, then headed toward Leh. He visited a number of gompas, and the lamas all told him the same stories of Issa and the scrolls, but none of them had copies.

"After an arduous journey, he finally reached the Hemis monastery near Leh, a much grander gompa than the others. He arrived in time to witness a major festival with loud trumpets and drums, hundreds of dancers in vibrant costumes, and frightening masks resembling animals, birds, devils and monsters.

"Following this celebration, the chief lama invited Notovitch to a large veranda where they were served pitchers of tchang. The Russian asked about Issa and was astounded at the depth of knowledge that the lama possessed of the political and religious history of Jesus's time and the life of the great prophet. I can imagine the hair on Notovitch's head standing straight up when the lama told him that a copy of the scrolls pertaining to Issa was in this very gompa."

"So, Notovitch was given the scrolls?" Charlotte asks.

"Again, unfortunately no. The lama explained that he didn't know exactly where these particular scrolls were, and that his duties during the festival made it impossible for him to seek them out. But the lama promised that he would show the scrolls to Notovitch if the Russian should ever visit again.

"Notovitch, who was staying in Leh, sent some presents to the lama with a note saying that one day he would return to see the scrolls, and then he departed for Kashmir. But while traveling, his horse tripped and the Russian was thrown from the saddle. He broke his leg below the knee. His guides brought him back to the Hemis gompa, which was only a half-day's ride away. During his convalescence at Hemis, Notovitch pleaded with the chief lama to show him the Issa manuscripts. At last, two books were brought to him, their leaves yellow with age.

"The Russian's interpreter read from these books and Notovitch carefully wrote down the Russian translation. It was, indeed, the story of Jesus and his travels to the east during the so-called lost years of his youth, and it described how Jesus was tutored by Buddhist lamas."

"Did he bring the scrolls back with him?" Charlotte asks with a journalist's hunger for corroborating evidence.

"I'm afraid not," Thompson replies. "The scrolls were considered sacred by the monks and could not be taken. But Notovitch did return with the transcriptions. He desperately wanted to publish an account of his travels along with the Issa documents, but when he consulted Church leaders, he was predictably urged not to publish because the story would cause problems for the Church and confusion among believers.

"A year later he showed his manuscript to a cardinal in Rome. The Cardinal explained that publishing it would create many powerful enemies for Notovitch—a not-so-veiled personal threat. The Cardinal even offered a sum of money, which Notovitch considered a bribe, to turn over all of his notes to the Church. Finally, though, he did publish his work as 'The Unknown Life of Jesus Christ,' and the book immediately unleashed a torrent of vicious attacks from all corners of the globe. Even today, the ridiculous and unproven charges about Notovitch and the manuscript, though completely disproven, are still accepted by scholars and religionists alike.

"His attackers said that no such scrolls ever existed, that Notovitch had never traveled to Hemis, and that when investigators traveled to the gompa to seek out the Issa manuscripts, the lamas said the scrolls did not exist."

"I've got to admit," Charlotte says, "without the scrolls themselves, the credibility of the Notovitch manuscript is questionable. I'd never be allowed on CCN to make claims about the scrolls without producing them."

"But you see, the lamas at Hemis had become very suspicious of the many people who came looking for the documents. The lamas feared for the safety of the precious manuscripts, so they answered questions with denials."

"So *you* say," Charlotte suggests dismissively.

"Not just me. In 1922, after the fervor had died down, a well-known scholar named Swami Abhedananda traveled to Hemis and inquired about the Issa documents. He persuaded the chief lama to show him the ancient books, and the lama, who spoke English, translated some of the passages for the Swami, proving that Notovitch's translation was in fact based on the same books."

"Okay, but let me guess—the Swami did not return with the Tibetan books either," Charlotte says. "Right? It's a great story, though."

"Yes, it is," Thompson agrees. "And the ending is even more interesting. It seems that the Issa documents were eventually stolen from Hemis. This was in the mid-forties."

"How convenient," Charlotte says, raising her palms arrogantly. "Now nobody can wonder why the manuscripts are not in the gompa. It's the makings of a hoax, Dad."

"Except for one thing," Thompson replies.

He opens his satchel and plunges a large wrinkled hand into the bag's dark interior. He pulls out one large book, then a second one. He opens the first and shows the brittle, yellowed leaves onto which an alien script has been inscribed.

"I have the Issa manuscripts," he says calmly. "Antonio found them in the Vatican's Secret Archives."

Chapter 50

Gideon walks away from the Kidon storefront. He feels unsettled about the truce negotiated with Weiss. The Israelis, like the CIA, have often proven to be untrustworthy. Yet if Weiss's claim of a schism within the ranks of Mossad are correct, then the Brotherhood can use an ally to control the contagion that would make their mission more difficult.

Who would've thought that by killing Mossad agents in Minnesota, Gideon was actually serving the interests of Mossad? He should send them a bill.

Gideon's disposable phone chirps and he picks up the call.

"Give me your status," Eve says.

"I met David, the head of Kidon."

"David Weiss? Interesting. Did you kill him?"

"No, but I had to take out one of his men at the shop."

"All right. Weiss will clean up, I'm sure. Is he upset?"

"About his man? Didn't seem to be. We had a nice discussion about a rogue element within Mossad."

"Hmmm—makes sense. Radical Muslims on one side, radical Jews on the other. What we call balance."

"The guy who tried to take me out at the India Gate was a rogue brain. I traded him for some cooperation."

"So Weiss owes you one. Just don't expect more than one."

"Still tracking our quartet?"

"They just put down."

"So they didn't go too far. Where are they?"

"Ladakh. The Hemis gompa."

"And you want me nearby."

"There's a flight in three hours. And while you're at it, we have another small assignment."

"Never been to Leh."

"Something to tell your grandchildren about. The highest commercial airport in the world—but the lowest spot in Ladakh."

"Why can't I get a chopper like Charlotte?"

"You killed Weiss's associate, which means you didn't manage the scene, so now you're flying coach. And try to stop killing people. It attracts attention."

Allison stares at CIA Director Wyatt, waiting for a reaction.

It comes.

"The sonofabitch! Pardon my language, but *going public*?"

"Sanghvi said he can mobilize all of Delhi in thirty minutes if we agree to a news conference right after the arrest. He's sure CCN will agree to conference you in by video. Not often that a high-value terrorist gets busted. Do we have a choice, sir?"

"Of course not. But *Judas Priest*! If Sanghvi goes public with capturing our phantom, and I cough up evidence that he's a terrorist, how long do you think it will take the Sicarii to figure out I was behind the order. Sanghvi will be a hero and I'll be a marked man."

"I've thought of that, sir. For obvious reasons, we haven't told Sanghvi who the target really is, just that he's a terrorist of American extraction. Quite a novelty. Anyway, in this case I think we should let Sanghvi take *all* the credit for tracking this guy down. After all, the target killed two Americans in a hotel—no one knows they were our agents. He wounded two others that same day. And there's reason to believe he caused that bloody scene near the India Gate. Instead of making this a joint operation, I think we should step aside. Let Sanghvi get sole credit—and become the marked man."

Wyatt ponders this. "We still want interview privileges if the target isn't killed. But under wraps."

"I'm sure he'll agree. Sanghvi has two other high-profile terrorist incidents with no arrests. He needs this."

"Then make the offer."

"Do you really think they'd try to assassinate the Director of the CIA?"

"For these guys, Allison, I'm small potatoes."

Cradled in a gorge near the Indus River, the Hemis gompa spreads out horizontally like a theatrical backdrop, its stage a large stone courtyard used for festivals and mystery plays. The Bell 214 lands about a hundred meters in front of the gompa's imposing façade with its impressive wooden *rabsaals*, or balconies.

The Bell's rotor shuts down and Charlotte is the first passenger to set foot on Ladakh soil, followed quickly by Greg, Thompson and Curt. A grinning monk in a red robe rushes toward Thompson. The man is short and round, about forty years old, with thick glasses that give him frog eyes. He wraps his arms around the old man and giggles.

"My good friend, welcome back to Hemis. So good to see you!"

Thompson whispers something in the monk's ear and then turns to face the others. "This is my friend Jamyang Urgyen, the manager of Hemis while the Rinpoche is away."

"So good to meet you!" Jamyang says with a voice like water bubbling.

"Jamyang, this is my daughter, Charlotte, and my grandson, Greg. Over here is our photographer, Curt."

Charlotte's hand rises to her chest and her eyes widen. "My," she says, "the air certainly is thin up here."

Jamyang rushes to Charlotte and takes an arm. "Let me escort you inside. Many people experience altitude sickness when first arriving. You must drink frequently to avoid dehydration."

Jamyang begins to walk Charlotte toward the gompa.

"I will have some tea brought to you, or maybe some tchang?"

"Tea, please. You're very kind."

"Our gompa is also known as Chang-Chub-Sam-Ling—the Lone Place of the Compassionate Person."

Thompson looks down at Greg, who is staring at him. "I lived here for nearly a year," he says. "This is like coming home."

"You didn't tell him about the books," Greg says.

"All in good time."

Herb has unloaded the baggage. "Tommy!" he yells. "I'm going to Leh for fuel. Think I'll spend the night there. When do you want me back?"

"I'll call you on the sat phone you loaned me," Thompson says. "How long to get back here?"

"About twenty minutes, once I'm in the air. Don't sweat it—I'm good. Got a friend might be in town."

Herb gives Thompson a sly wink and climbs back into the chopper.

Thompson grabs a suitcase and his book-heavy satchel. He glances at Greg standing by him, then at Charlotte up ahead, and wonders how he will ever be able to apologize for what he is doing.

He takes a deep breath of the cool mountain air and stares up at the virile mountains that tower above him. Suddenly he feels very old and very small.

Chapter 51

Gideon arrives at Indira Gandhi airport, pays the taxi driver, and walks into the terminal carrying a small backpack and a suitcase. He always travels light; whatever else he needs will be provided to him at his destination. To pass through security, he is unarmed, except for the carbonized plastic dagger disguised as a belt buckle.

Twenty feet inside the terminal, a stout man bumps into him. Gideon has been trained not to make a scene but instinctively glances at the man.

David Weiss!

Gideon immediately senses danger. Certainly this is no coincidence. But if the head of Kidon were merely following Gideon, he would not have made his presence known so obviously. And he would have had agents doing the dirty work. Was this a warning?

Gideon avoids direct eye contact with Weiss but stops and mimes receiving a cell phone call, an excuse to stop walking in case anyone is watching. He needs time to think.

Weiss has walked away. Gideon turns and braves another glance in the fat man's direction. With his eyes, Weiss steers Gideon to the exit where he casually leads the Sicarii outside and toward a maroon van. The side door to the van opens and Weiss steps in to join two others.

Gideon studies these men. One is the driver, a mid-forties Indian with prematurely gray hair. The other man is older, a Jew of sixty or so who sits in the rear seat wearing a rumpled tan suit. This threesome is not a typical Kidon abduction team, so Gideon stuffs his bags into the side door, climbs in beside Weiss and closes the door. The van pulls away.

"If this is a trap, David, I'm going to be very disappointed in you," Gideon says calmly.

"This *is* a trap," Weiss replies, "but not one of our making. I'm referring to the airport."

"So I'm in danger there?"

"We intercepted a communiqué between the CIA and India's Central Intelligence Bureau. We have men inside the IB."

"Jews in Indian Intelligence?"

"There are many people of Jewish ancestry in India. Many of them do not even know it. Ever hear of the Lost Tribes of Israel? A few of our cousins know of their heritage, however, and wish to help us."

"And this communiqué…?"

"…requested IB assistance in capturing you. They have a photograph of you apparently taken during that little kerfuffle at the India Gate."

Gideon ponders this. "Shit!" The word sums up the mess he's in. This is not only a temporary inconvenience, but a permanent dilemma. Despite his precautions, the CIA and IB—probably other agencies as well—now have his likeness. It will be more difficult for him to travel in the future. Forged passports will have to match his disguise of the moment. The risk of detection has grown markedly.

"Why are you helping me?"

Weiss pauses and lights a cigarette. "Because you took out a rogue agent, which solves one of our problems. And because you didn't kill me."

"And?"

"And because I need something from you in exchange. I might also add that not all my colleagues are in favor of saving your ass. After all, you killed one of our loyal agents, too."

Gideon leans back in the lumpy seat. "What is it you want?" He is not in control of this situation, which makes him feel uneasy. He is embarrassed by his ignorance of the trap—by having tarnished the Sicarii's reputation of omniscience and coordination. And by having to be rescued.

His phone rings. Weiss nods for him to answer, which he does.

"Yes," Gideon says, and then listens. "Got it. Thank you. I'll call when I'm in Leh. No, I'll find a way there."

He hangs up. "I've just been told not to enter the airport."

"Hmmmm," Weiss replies. "That call was about two minutes too late. Without our intervention, you'd already be in custody." He pauses. "Or dead, depending on how you played it."

"So I ask again, what do you want?"

"In a way, the same thing your client wants."

These words startle Gideon. "You could not possibly know who we are working for."

"But I do, because your client leaked it. Not on purpose, of course—they're too stupid for that. But they are friends of Israel, you know. Staunch defenders of the state for their own selfish reasons."

"It doesn't matter if you know who we work for. Everyone in this scrum wants the same thing."

"There are too many competitors, I agree, so I am proposing that we reduce the number by one and join forces, even if temporarily."

"I'm curious—how did Mossad get pulled into this?"

Weiss studies the younger man for a moment, considering how much he should reveal. "A CIA leak," he finally says. "The world is full of leaks these days. Pity, how that once proud organization has depreciated over the past decade under the current administration. Nevertheless, with so many resources dedicated to counter-terrorism, even the CIA was eventually bound to come up with something valuable.

"Quite by accident they apprehended a brilliant young al-Qaida operative named Tamir Nassif. The Saudi lad turned out to be a brilliant mullah of the extreme Qutbian brand of Islam. Naturally, he wound up in Guantanamo Bay. Most of the detainees there are innocent, which means they have nothing useful to reveal. The rest are too hardened to crack. But seventeen-year-old Tamir was, how shall I put it, *terrorized* by Gitmo and bargained for gentler treatment. He offered up details of an imaginative plot supposedly invented by himself and personally endorsed by bin Laden in the mountains of Pakistan.

"This ingenious plot became the picture on the box of a jigsaw puzzle. Suddenly bits and fragments of intercepts from the usual terrorist channels started to fall into place and make a new, horrifying kind of sense. The pieces were confirming that al-Qaida was pursuing the plan.

"Then, one day, Nassif's chief interrogator completed his military service and got drunk to celebrate, or perhaps to gain a few hours of freedom from his personal ghosts. In any case, he ended up thoroughly soused and blabbed the general outline of the insidious plot to a very close friend, Billy Stewart…"

Gideon interrupts. "Who was a Mossad agent, I would guess."

Weiss nods. "Spent three years befriending the interrogator. During that time he picked a few juicy plums off the Gitmo tree—but never anything like this."

"So now, Israel knew what al-Qaida was after," Gideon adds. "If they could find the relics, they hoped to prove that Christianity was a fraud."

"Yes! Christianity would implode and a severe form of Islam would fill the vacuum," Weiss declares. "But this much you already know, because your client shared it with you. And he heard it from the president of the United States himself, a fierce loyalist to your client's cause. But what the president failed to comprehend before violating every canon of intelligence practice and breaking countless laws was that his trusted friend would actually become his competitor by hiring you."

Weiss laughs. "We both hold important cards, don't we? So now I am showing mine and hoping that, as a man of honor, you will reciprocate."

Gideon had never understood how the field of competitors had become so crowded. Now the picture was filling in, and he could guess at the motives. Tamir Nassif, in a feat of creative brilliance, had concocted a plot to destroy Christianity and, with it, the United States. Whether inspired by legends or facts, Nassif and bin Laden had set in motion a plan to find two relics that would irrefutably prove the Christian fallacy.

Having uncovered this plot, the CIA had desperately launched a mission to secure the same relics for precisely the opposite purpose, to preserve Christianity, the religious cornerstone of the nation it was sworn to protect.

Ironically, Israel also has an enormous stake in defending Christianity. Its fate as a nation remains inextricably linked to its super-power ally. If core beliefs of Christianity could be disproved, Israel's protector could collapse, leaving the tiny nation alone to defend itself against an emboldened Islamic force.

And yet Israel mistrusts its powerful ally, partially because of the messiness and unpredictability of democracy; in America, the political winds can shift suddenly (hadn't a Muslim been elected to Congress?) and the current president seems unable to prevent the opposing political party from gaining control. Will the new administration continue the old policies of support for Israel, or introduce peace initiatives that would demand unthinkable Israeli compromises?

As for the CIA, Mossad doubts that this once respected organization can successfully compete for the relics. The Agency and its diverse sister groups within Homeland Security have become highly politicized and largely ineffective.

And even if the relics should end up in American custody, that government is obsessed with the preservation of everything. Archived relics would always pose a future threat to Israel. Therefore, the relics must be destroyed, which means Mossad must find the relics first so they can be preserved.

Then, of course, there is the unnamed client of the Sicarii. This powerful individual understands the menacing vulnerability of his dim but devoted friend, the lame duck President. He also sees in the future an almost certain shift in political power, which will erode much of his own influence. The true motives of this individual are murky, but the values and beliefs of the man's organization are closely aligned with the Sicarii's, so an alliance is understandable. While most Sicarii contracts are purely mercenary, this contract merges a high fee with a cause close to Sicarii hearts.

"You know that I am a man of honor, because all Sicariis are," Gideon replies. "So you must know that I will never betray our client."

"If we are to get you on that plane safely, we must move quickly," Weiss urges, looking at his watch. "I've shown some of my cards, so now it is your turn to show some of yours. Then I will tell you what I want."

"What can I possibly know that you don't?"

"Since your organization got involved in this craziness, every move you have made has been followed. You decided to put Charlotte Ansari in play. Why? Is she one of your agents?"

"You ask a lot in exchange for helping me avoid a trap."

"I am bartering. Full disclosure—I have withheld one bit of information that may change everything you believe. What I ask is to receive fair value in exchange."

Gideon decides to confess certain facts that he is quite certain Weiss already knows. If this is a test, the truth may win Weiss's confidence.

"The Ansari woman is not a Sicarii agent," Gideon replies. "In fact, she doesn't even know about our organization. She is a pawn."

"And her son?"

"Same. He knows nothing about us."

"But you have been protecting them."

"For many reasons, not just for the relics."

"Conjecture is that they know where the relics are, so they must be working for you."

"How can they work for us if they don't know of our existence? The simple fact is that we—the Sicarii, in fact everyone who is competing for the relics—has come up empty-handed. We believe that these two don't know where the relics are, but are able to figure it out."

"Even though all the rest of us have failed?"

"Don't ask why we believe this. I can't tell you. For the time being, we protect and watch them. And wait for results."

"You protect them against assassination?"

Gideon shakes his head. "Who would kill them before the relics were found? The greater danger is abduction. If either of them—or both, heaven forbid—were kidnapped, they could be persuaded to work for the abductor."

"Frankly, we had sketched out a kidnapping ourselves. But now those two have recruited a third person, Charlotte's father, a religious scholar."

"Well, three heads may be better than two."

"Are they close to finding the relics?"

"Actually, they don't yet know what they are looking for."

Weiss laughs heartily. "I see. And still you have confidence in them?"

"We do, provided we can keep them in play."

"And if they produce the relics for you…?"

"We will honor our contract and turn them over to our client. We'll be paid handsomely and the relics will be destroyed."

"And that's what you want?"

"As a Sicarii, yes—if the relics turn out to be genuine. Of course, if fakes, then it wouldn't matter. Our collective worries will have been in vain. If that is the case, perhaps you and I will meet in Jerusalem, share a cigar and celebrate together."

"But if the relics are genuine, they should be destroyed?"

"Of course," Gideon confirms. "Personally, though, as a man of faith, I believe it is impossible for them to be genuine. Still, our contract pays well, so we win regardless."

"It's time for me to show you another card. I hate to be the messenger of bad news, but if you turn over the relics to your client and they prove to be genuine, they most certainly will not be destroyed. How do we know this? Because your client is so confident in your success he jumped the gun and betrayed his true intent. Would you like to know more?"

Gideon nods and listens to the older man. There is no clear way of immediately corroborating the story now spun by David Weiss, but pieces of it fit into a pattern of plausibility. If true, then the Sicarii client has betrayed the organization, and the penalty for that is death.

When Weiss is finished, Gideon stares at him as if expecting to find some nervous tic or pulsing vein to measure the man's veracity. Instead, the man merely sags, his plump carcass pulled deep into the worn seat cushions by the weight of his words. His eyes are watery and his breath stinks of cigars. But there is no hint of either honesty or deceit. The old man has learned to guard his emotions, except for his impatience.

"You have no response," Weiss says after revealing his secret. "All right then, we will take you back to the airport. I was hoping we could be a team for a while. Now we will return to being enemies. A pity."

"You didn't tell me what you wanted," Gideon replies.

"It doesn't matter. Unless we teamed up, you couldn't deliver."

"I'm impressed by your intelligence capability. It exceeds my expectations."

"And as the head of Kidon I must admit some envy of your organization. We could've made a good team."

"All right then," Gideon says, "I believe your story about our client. Of course, we'll have to check it out."

"Of course."

"So on the condition that you are right, perhaps I can do something for you. If you tell me what you want."

"I will explain while Aviram helps you with your disguise. We must hurry or you will miss your flight."

In the rear seat, Aviram unzips a garment bag and then opens a case filled with nose putty, make-up, glasses and hair pieces. "They will be looking for a man who resembles the photograph," Aviram mumbles. "Fortunately, you will not be that man."

Weiss hands Gideon an American passport. Gideon opens to the photograph of a Jewish man fifteen years older and wearing thick wire-rimmed glasses.

"The new you," Weiss says, smiling for the first time. "The first Sicarii was a Jew, you know. The picture will match your new look, which I chose myself from a variety of computer-enhanced portraits. I must say it's quite an improvement over the original photograph, which was taken during your visit to our office a few hours go."

Thirty minutes later, the van drops Gideon back at Indira Ghandi airport and pulls away. A bit of padding between the shoulder blades of his too-large suit coat gives him a slight hunch as he walks to the ticket counter, checks his bags, shows his passport, and purchases a ticket with Indian rupees.

Walking toward the security line, Gideon notices a half-dozen Indian police scrutinizing everyone within sight. He walks past one very tall officer and smiles. The officer, looking very crisp in his peak cap, bush shirt, gabardine slacks and cloth belt, smiles back.

Gideon is still astonished that Kidon had actually photographed him during their previous meeting. Those guys are good! Unfortunately, there are now two pictures of him floating around.

The security check is impressively disorganized and takes twenty minutes, but finally Gideon is at the gate. About forty others are also awaiting the flight to Leh. Out of habit, Gideon studies each of them one by one. A young Pakistani couple. A Buddhist monk in a crimson robe. Three older gentlemen, British or Americans.

His eyes continue to scan his future cabin-mates. But then he stops on one of them, a man seen only from the rear.

The man turns and faces Gideon—looks right at him, in fact—then moves his eyes to a clock on the wall. The plane to Leh is late arriving.

Without the disguise, Gideon would have been recognized instantly, but with it he has the luxury of observing Mike Ansari, Charlotte's husband, without fear of detection. His secondary mission has begun.

Chapter 52

Jamyang Urgyen's red robe pulsates like a beating heart as he leads his guests on a dizzying tour of the gompa. He loquaciously describes the large murals of the Wheel of Life and the Lords of the Four Quarters that decorate the verandahs; the Dhu-khang, or main worship room, adorned with images of the Buddha and important events in His numerous incarnations; the library and its countless books of loose-leaf pages held between wooden boards and wrapped in silk. Each golden Buddha or jewel-encrusted stupa possesses a meaning, a story, a mystery, a provenance. Jamyang is compelled to speak of each one.

Curt has been freely documenting the tour on videotape, a habit of electronic news gatherers. But now, as a murky wooden door swings open behind Jamyang's broad hand, the monk courteously gestures for Curt to put down the camera.

I apologize, my friend," Jamyang says, "but we prefer not to have our private quarters photographed."

Curt nods and turns off the camera.

Jamyang leads the group down a dark, stone stairway. "The gompa was built on the site of a twelfth-century cave monastery, so there is a small underground village here. Many of our three hundred monks live below ground, and this is where your quarters are. I hope none of you are claustrophobic."

Charlotte wasn't until she was asked.

By Curt's estimation, they descended about two stories before emerging into a long, wide corridor well-illuminated by electric lamps.

A few robed monks move silently down the hall toward them, nodding slightly to acknowledge their guests.

"It's so good to have you back, Tommy!" Jamyang says as he opens a door to a small room and clicks on a light. "Your room is just as you left it. We have been hoping you would return to us."

Thompson smiles sincerely and replies, "This is my second home, Jamyang. But if you don't mind, I'll accompany you to the other rooms."

238

Driven by curiosity, Charlotte pushes her way into the small room revealed by Jamyang. "So this is where you live when you're not in Delhi?" she asks her father.

"Quite often. I find a measure of peace here."

Charlotte scans the room. The walls are hewn from stone and there are only three pieces of furniture—a narrow cot, a wooden chair, and a small table containing a framed photograph of Thompson with a long arm curled around a young woman, Charlotte's mother, who is holding a baby.

She walks to the photograph and picks it up, then turns to Thompson. "I'm surprised that you still have a picture of mother," she says bitterly.

Thompson stares at his shoes.

Inspecting the photo more closely, Charlotte sees that Thompson and Miriam are looking at each other with unmistakably loving expressions. "So you were once happy together," Charlotte adds.

"We were, yes," Thompson replies.

"Shall we continue then?" Jamyang urges the group down the corridor. "I'm sure you will want to rest before dinner."

Mike Ansari wearily descends the steps from the plane and trudges toward the austere Leh terminal, looking only once at the mountains that jut upward like crooked teeth around the flat tongue of tarmac. He pays no attention to the older Jewish man with wire-rim glasses who follows immediately behind him.

Inside the terminal, Mike switches on his cell phone and enters the MEN'S room. The Jewish man follows. Standing at a urinal, Mike watches his phone make a connection. He taps a key with his thumb and waits for a call to go through. The Jewish man steps toward a urinal to Mike's right, smiles at the younger man and says, "Shalom aleichem."

Startled, Mike reflexively blurts out a stuttered "Aleichem shalom," and quickly turns away, not wanting to start up a conversation. Still waiting for his call to go through, Mike begins to consider why the older man addressed him in Hebrew. Even though Mike is a Persian Jew, almost no one guesses his Jewish heritage. He steals a glance at the older gentleman, who is now staring benignly at the stream splashing into the urinal.

Perhaps the man only speaks Hebrew.

The call goes through just as Mike backs away from the urinal and zips his fly with one hand. Approaching a sink, he cradles the cell phone between his shoulder and ear and begins speaking quietly. "I'm in Leh… yes, just arrived… No, they're sending an escort… All right, I'll be in touch, don't worry."

Gideon backs away from the urinal and adjusts his wire-rim glasses. As Mike's appointed escort, he is troubled by the fact that Mike has checked in with another party. Mike had said, "*they're* sending an escort," which means that he had been talking to some other party, a clear violation of his instructions. Absolutely no one was to be told where he was going or how he would get there.

Mike Ansari and Gideon are now alone in the rest room. Mike is washing his hands as Gideon steps up behind him.

"Mihad," Gideon says, using Mike's real name.

Startled, Mike wheels around to face the Jewish man.

"You know my name?"

"I am your escort," Gideon says. "But I'm afraid you will have to give me your cell phone."

Mike's eyes twitch with nervousness. The escort must have overheard his conversation. Had he said anything incriminating?

Impulsively, Mike tries to shove the older man backwards to clear a passage to the door. But he succeeds only in knocking the spectacles off the man's face. Before Mike can react, his wrist is locked in a vice-like grip behind his back and he is facing the mirror. He has no idea how this had happened.

A voice behind his ear calmly says, "I need your cell phone now."

Mike's wrist is suddenly released, but his heart is pounding through his chest. Is this how his life will end, in a men's rest room in Leh?

He plucks the cell phone from a shirt pocket and hands it to Gideon without turning around.

Gideon takes it. "I'm hoping that I will have to apologize for my rudeness," he says. And then he presses a button to review the phone's history log. He taps another button to recall the last number dialed. And waits.

Mike can hear a faint voice rattling in Gideon's ear. He closes his eyes. His body begins to shudder, anticipating his fate.

Gideon terminates the call. "A professional would never have kept incriminating evidence on him."

Mike turns desperately and says, "So I called them. What's the big deal? You're working for the same people."

"Only Eve has an official reason to speak with them. You know the rules. So what was *your* reason? I would guess that they want you to watch us from the inside. Whatever happened to *trust?*"

Mike is trembling. "So what now. You kill me here?"

"I have no authority to kill you because of your infidelity. That will be up to others. I'm your escort, so I will see that you arrive safely at your destination. But tell me one thing... *why?* For money? We know your restaurant was failing."

"It was *not* failing!" Mike shouts, defending his honor. "We were on the verge of... I didn't need anyone's money. But you have to choose sides. I thought we were on *their* side, but apparently not, or they wouldn't have worried about our motives. Our loyalty. I don't know when we lost it, but we did. Now they're on the right side and we—*you*—are not. Sometimes you have to choose."

This is why Gideon hates fanatics.

It may have been the stress, the flight, the altitude, dehydration, or all of the above, but the effects put Charlotte, Curt and Thompson into a virtual coma despite the gompa's hard cots.

Now, though, a timid tap on the shoulder wakes Thompson. At first he is confused, but the whisper in his ear steers him back to reality.

"Grandpa, come and see."

Thompson's eyes feel pasted shut. The lids slowly peel back and soft light reveals a boy's blurry face.

"What is it, my son?" Thompson asks, amazed that he has found a voice.

"Come and see!" The whisper is more urgent. Soft hands tug at Thompson's arm.

Slowly, achingly, he sits up. Greg's face grudgingly comes into focus. "All right, all right, I'm coming. I just need a minute..."

"I found something," Greg says excitedly. "Come on!"

The hands pull Thompson from the cot. He staggers the first few steps then finds himself moving slowly out of the small room and into the corridor. Greg leads him down the hall, around a sharp corner, and into a large domed room decorated by many frescoes and statues. Hundreds of candles bathe the room with a flickering glow. Thompson knows this room, has spent countless hours meditating in it. He can understand Greg's excitement about discovering it for the first time.

"It's magnificent, isn't it? Many of these artifacts go back centuries."

"Over here," Greg says, tugging again on Thompson's hand, leading the old man to a large golden Buddha sitting atop a silver stupa encrusted with jewels.

"My old friend," Thompson says to the Buddha. "Good to see you again." He bows reverently.

"Do you see it?" Greg asks, interrupting Thompson's meditative moment.

Thompson looks up. "See what? I see the Buddha, the candles..."

"There—on his hand. Do you see it?"

Greg is pointing at the Buddha, who is seated with His legs crossed in the lotus position, right foot on top of the left calf. His left hand cradles a bowl, and out of it a plant emerges. The right hand hangs over the right knee, palm facing outward; the index finger and thumb are joined in a circle. From this hand a larger plant originates, growing outward to the knee and then upwards.

"Yes, I see now what you mean," Thompson replies. "The Buddha's left hand is in the classic meditation pose, or *mudra*, and holds a medicine bowl. Growing out of it is a Tibetan medicinal plant called myrobalan. You can see another of these plants growing from the right hand, which is in the charity mudra, palm forward, as if offering us healing."

"In the palm, don't you see it?"

Thompson's erudite explanation has missed the mark. He steps forward to inspect the Buddha's palm more carefully. A large ruby is embedded in the center of it.

"I see a ruby, yes. Many Buddha's are decorated with precious stones."

"In the palms of the hands? With rubies?"

"Actually, I don't think I've ever seen that before, but…"

"It looks like a wound. Like a stake was driven through the hand."

These words stun Thompson. Yes, it is true, the ruby looks like a bloody hole in the palm.

"And look at the foot," Greg urges.

The Buddha's right foot lies on top of the left thigh, sole facing upward. In the center of the sole is embedded another large ruby.

"My God," Thompson exclaims. "Why did I never see this before? This Buddha has been crucified!"

A third voice says, "I didn't know they practiced crucifixion in Tibet."

The voice comes from behind Thompson and Greg. They turn and see Charlotte facing them.

"I woke up when you two wandered down the hall," she says.

"Crucifixion was never practiced in Tibet, or India, or…" Thompson pauses. "Of course, they could have heard stories about Jesus. The Apostle Thomas evangelized in India."

"But how could stories of Jesus turn into a crucified Buddha?" Charlotte asks.

Greg is studying the rubies, fingering them. "Maybe they saw the wounds," he says. "That Russian said Jesus came to India when he was a kid. They called him Issa, right? You've got the writings, Grandpa. Maybe Jesus came back here to see his friends after the crucifixion and they saw the wounds all healed over. Maybe he didn't die in Israel after all."

Thompson considers this. "I think it's time to give my friend Jamyang a present," he says.

"You have no idea how complicated this is," Eve says.

Gideon holds the cell phone close to his ear and answers, "I think I do. The guy is…"

"Don't say it, even on a secure channel," Eve barks. "We need to handle this delicately, precisely according to our laws. There will be some who'll oppose severe action because of the… the *connections* here. I must admit, I'm also torn. But we need to get him back here right now. We can't risk having him escape, not with everything he knows."

"Trust me, he's no professional. I've got it under control."

Gideon turns to look at Mike, who is seated next to him in a worn chair at an unused terminal gate.

"It's not under control until he's back here!" Eve is rattled. Gideon can hear it in her voice. "There's a chopper waiting to pick you up. A charter, so don't say anything incriminating. Here is the pilot's cell number…"

Gideon memorizes the number and then dials it. After three rings, a husky voice answers.

"Herb Rossi."

Chapter 53

We have books that say your Jesus was here," Jamyang says, offering his guests tea. "But they are scattered throughout our gompas and difficult, maybe impossible, to find today. Some have been stolen from us."

"Jamyang, tell us about Nicolas Notovitch," Thompson says, passing a cup of steaming tea to Curt.

"A most famous guest. He brought upon us much undesirable attention, but that was long ago. What can I tell you?"

"The book that he claimed to have discovered here, the one about Issa," Charlotte says. "Many called it a fraud, at least according to my father's account."

"Many people came here trying to disprove that book. Very few came to prove it. The last party was a delegation of four monks from Rome. They were here on a mission to foster understanding between our faiths, or so they claimed. My uncle was here at that time. The monks from Rome were particularly interested in the Issa manuscripts, and because they were monks like us, my uncle showed them the writings. The monks were here for several weeks, and everyone felt that they were indeed brothers in spirit, just as Issa was. But a short time after they departed, my uncle discovered that the books were missing. We believe that these monks from Rome managed to steal them."

"And now I have the privilege of returning them to you," Thompson says, pulling the books from his satchel and handing them to Jamyang, whose astonishment fills the room.

"Is it true?" Jamyang asks. "Can these be the stolen books?"

"As I understand it, these are copies of the original, translated from Pali into Tibetan. Can you read them?"

Grinning broadly, Jamyang pages through the leaves. "You have brought great happiness to our gompa, my friend. Yes, I can read them. Would you like me to read for you?"

Curt switches on his ever-present camera as the group nods yes and Jamyang begins his eloquent translation of the Tibetan text.

"A marvelous child was born in the land of Israel," he begins. "God himself spoke through the mouth of this child… The parents of the infant were poor people, who belonged to a family of, of great, umm, great piety."

The room is silent except for the reverent, melodic tones of Jamyang, which sound like chanting as he occasionally lapses into Tibetan and then repeats the words in English to the delight of his guests.

"When Issa was thirteen years old," he continues, "…Issa secretly absented himself from his father's house, left Jerusalem, and in a train of merchants journeyed to the Sindh…"

"…which is now one of the Pakistani provinces," Charlotte interjects. "I've been there."

Jamyang nods and continues. "He traveled there with the object of… of perfecting himself in the knowledge of the word of God and the study… the study of the laws of the great Buddhas. In his fourteenth year, young Issa, the Blessed One, came this side of the Sindh and settled among the Aryas, in the country beloved by God."

Jamyang continues to read about how Issa traveled south, all the way to Ceylon, and then north into the holy cities of India to teach the people of the lower castes. But he was quickly condemned by the Brahmins and others of the upper castes, who considered the less fortunately born to be their slaves. Issa stood up to his detractors, denouncing the divine inspiration of the Vedas and Puranas on which the priests relied for their authority, and announcing that there is but one law from the One God, which was given to guide all men's actions.

The writings reveal that Issa continued traveling northward, to Nepal and Kashmir, where he was also much loved by the common people. But the priest and warrior classes sought to kill him and so he was forced to depart. During his travels in the east, Jesus had learned the Pali language and studied the sacred scrolls of the Sutras. He had learned to heal through medicines and prayer. He saw how the core spiritual teachings of the Buddha supported and gave depth to the scriptures of the Jews.

After many years of studying and teaching, Issa finally began a journey west toward Israel, crossing Afghanistan and Persia before finally arriving in Jerusalem. For three short years, he continued his teaching only to find the same kind of hostility among the priestly and ruling classes as he had seen in the east. Finally, he was arrested.

"By order of the governor," Jamyang continues, "the soldiers seized Issa and the two robbers and led them to the place of... the place of execution, where they were nailed upon the crosses erected for them..."

Greg is listening intently, mentally comparing this version of the crucifixion story to the one he has just read in the New Testament.

"Pilate was afraid for what he had done," Jamyang continues, pausing to read ahead. "Pilate ordered the body of the Saint to be given to his relatives, who put it in a tomb near the place of execution... Three days later, the governor sent his soldiers to remove Issa's body and bury it in some other place, for he feared a rebellion among the people. The next day, when the people came to the tomb, they found it open and empty, the body of Issa being gone. The rumor spread that the Supreme Judge had sent His angels from Heaven to remove the mortal remains of the saint..."

Jamyang looks up at his guests. "I never thought I would have the privilege of reading this text in the Tibetan language."

"The golden Buddha downstairs," Charlotte says, "has rubies marking the kinds of wounds that Issa would have suffered. Very surprising, to find crucifixion wounds on a Buddha."

"Of course," Jamyang says. "The great Buddha is the soul of the Universe. In the course of his earthly life, when he is a human manifestation, he creates a new world in the hearts of men but eventually leaves to reenter the invisible world. Three thousand years ago, He incarnated as the celebrated Prince Sakya-Muni. Twenty-five hundred years ago, He incarnated anew as Gautama, the one that westerners think of as Buddha, but who was only one manifestation of that universal soul. About two thousand years ago, the Perfect Being—in Christianity, you call him the Word of God or the Son of God—awakened again as the newborn child of a poor family in Israel, only to be persecuted and crucified by those he came to teach. So explain to me why are you perplexed that a statue of the Buddha should exhibit the wounds of crucifixion?"

"The golden Buddha has plants growing out of a bowl and out of the Buddha's hand," Charlotte says. "Medicinal plants, I understand."

"Healing plants," Jamyang adds. "Myrobalan is the Buddha's chosen herb and is known to cure many ailments, including leprosy. Issa was known to be a great physician."

"So maybe Issa—Jesus—healed lepers by using this myrobalan plant," Curt replies, putting down his camera.

"Tommy," Jamyang says, turning to his old friend, "how did you come to possess these stolen manuscripts?"

"Not all the monks from Rome are thieves, Jamyang. One of them was my friend, and he discovered these writings in the Rome archives. But I fear that he may have paid for the book's return with his own life."

"I'm sorry," Jamyang says sadly. "A book is not the equivalent of a life."

"A book," Thompson replies, "is sometimes all we know of a life."

Jamyang studies the faces of his guests for a moment and then says, "Perhaps I can repay this great favor"—he clutches the returned book lovingly—"by returning something of value to you. But what might that be?"

Jamyang removes his thick glasses as if removing a barrier.

Charlotte leans forward and peers into Jamyang's eyes. In them she sees a gentleness and understanding that penetrates her soul, sifts her heart's strata from bedrock to doubt, and warms her like a council-fire.

"It's possible, isn't it, that Issa returned here after his crucifixion?" Greg says, his first words of the conversation. No one suspected he had been listening.

Jamyang replies, "In your Bible, Issa said he would come again. And he did—he returned to *us*, just as he promised. And he died in the Promised Land of Kashmir. All the lamas know this, even though the people don't. His tomb is still there."

"Do you by any chance know where this tomb is?"

"The tomb is no secret, but most people believe it is merely the resting place of a Muslim saint. You can find the tomb in the Khanyar district of Srinagar. It's called Roza Bal."

Chapter 54

Twisting his wrist proves futile. The skin is frayed and bleeding beneath the plastic tie that binds him to the toilet plumbing in the airport MEN'S room stall. Even if Mike Ansari could free himself, he doesn't know what he would do. Just outside the closed stall, the Jewish man is doing God-knows-what. All Mike can hear is a rustling noise.

At the sink, Gideon removes his disguise—the nose putty and fake eyebrows, the oversized suit, unfashionable shirt and old man's tie. Opening his carry-on bag, he removes a pair of jeans and a cotton shirt, hurriedly putting them on. Gideon takes the carbonized plastic dagger from his belt and begins to cut up the suit, searching through each strip with his fingers. In the fake hunch of the suit coat he finds the object of his search, a damning contrivance that he hoped would not be there.

A GPS transmitter.

He has been set up by that damn David Weiss. Obviously, Kidon wants to track Gideon, perhaps locate the Sicarii headquarters.

Whatever happened to *trust*?

Now he knows. It's dead.

Gideon combs his hair and takes a deep breath. It's good to be himself again. In Leh, he has few worries about being recognized. He turns and approaches the stall. "Open the door, Mike," he commands.

The door opens and Gideon steps in, holding the dagger. Mike gasps, certain that he is going to be killed. But the sharp blade slices through the plastic tie, freeing Mike's arm.

"So they sent their best man to bring me in," Mike says. "I'm flattered."

"Whatever," Gideon replies flatly. "Ironically, my job is to keep you alive long enough to be executed."

"You know as well as I do that I pose a significant dilemma for the Great White Brotherhood." Mike says this name with great disdain.

"What on earth turned your head like this, Mike?"

"Jesus Christ. He spoke to me through…"

"Jesus? So now you're fighting a battle where Jesus leads both sides."

"The Brotherhood has a corrupt view of truth, Gideon. You follow a Jesus of the Brotherhood's invention. The Brothers use this false Jesus to justify their own perverted system. I follow Jesus, the Son of God."

Gideon stares at this man, whom the Brothers had always recognized as one of the pure ones, and whose mission was far more important than any to which Gideon had ever been assigned. There, cowering on a toilet seat, his face greasy with sweat, is—*was*—the hope of the Brothers. Trained in patience and obedience. Deepened in the Brotherhood's most esoteric mysteries. Privileged beyond measure in the organization's clandestine society. Ready to be welcomed home to a hero's tribute.

But obviously left too long on his own.

Gideon grabs Mike by the shirt and lifts him off the toilet. "You disappoint me, Mike," Gideon says. "Go wash your face."

A t the baggage claim, Gideon finds a young American man and woman, each with a backpack. "From the States?" he asks.

"Colorado," the young man replies. "I'm Ned, and this is my wife Heather. You from the US?"

"Yeah, Vermont," Gideon lies. "Some mountains, huh? Looks like you're heading out for some trekking."

"Taking a bus out to a couple of the nearby monasteries, Sankar and Matho, then trekking from there. Got two months to explore the top of the world."

"So you've graduated from the Rockies. Wish I had the time," Gideon says.

Ned sees a large duffel bag tumbling down the baggage chute. "That's ours—excuse me." He dashes off to retrieve it. While he and Heather wrestle with the duffel, Gideon places the Kidon homing device into a pocket of Ned's backpack.

Watched carefully by Gideon, Mike claims his baggage. He begins making his way to the far door of the terminal, which leads to the taxi stand. He climbs into a metered jeep, followed by Gideon, and the vehicle takes them to a small, squat structure that serves private aircraft.

"I'm looking for Herb Rossi," Gideon says to the only person there.

"You found him," Herb says. "You the two going into the mountains?"

"That would be us."

"Well, give me a destination. I'll file a flight plan and we'll be off."

"The flight plan will say Alchi gompa."

"Alchi? That one's abandoned." Herb looks down at Mike's expensive suitcases—not exactly what you'd take camping in the Himalayas.

Gideon hands Herb a fistful of currency and says, "Who knows, maybe we'll change our mind in-flight."

Herb pockets the money and says, "Seems there's a lot of that goin' around these days."

D inner at Hemis is satisfying—balep korkun, a thin coin-shaped bread; thenthuk; Tibetan dumplings and chicken in a rich vegetable broth; and po cha, the traditional butter tea. The meal warms the body from the inside, an important attribute in this high, cold climate.

After dinner, Charlotte and Curt walk out into the courtyard. The sky is already purple and darkening quickly. As Charlotte speaks, her breath makes tiny puffs in the chill. "Are you thinking what I'm thinking?"

Curt shoves his hands into his pockets. "About the tomb, you mean?"

"When he mentioned Roza Bal, I had a vague recollection."

"Me too, and then I remembered Reggie Hoskins, the BBC producer. Remember him?"

"Reggie, of course. His documentaries. What?—it was 2002 or something when it aired—that piece on Roza Bal. Wish I had paid more attention."

"Same here."

"Seemed ridiculous at the time. Like one of those cheesy Great Mysteries of the World shows that rehash legends and never prove anything."

"Millions of people must have seen it though, right?

"Right. So it's no secret.

"It just seems too obvious. If the bones of Jesus are in the Roza Bal, and suddenly everyone wants them, why doesn't everyone just go there and take them? The goddam BBC told the world where they are!"

"Obviously, no one took the story seriously. Except for a handful of radicals, maybe…"

"…and a couple of authors." A new voice intrudes—Thompson's. The old man walks up to the couple, hands in pockets. "I've read their books. They have a plausible premise and lots of circumstantial evidence—enough, I suppose, to convince conspiracy theorists and new age lunatics—but nothing close to scientific proof."

"Well you should know all about religious lunatics," Charlotte says bitterly. "I don't suppose you've been there, to the Roza Bal? You've been just about everywhere else in your pathetic search for atonement."

Thompson stares at Charlotte but says nothing, just shoves his fists deeper into his pockets.

"Where the hell did *that* come from?" Curt asks Charlotte.

"Nowhere—*that's* where it came from, because that's exactly where we are!" Charlotte detonates like a fragmentation bomb. "Just how is this trek to the Himalayas getting us any closer to saving my mother? Because some monk in crimson bed sheets tells us a story about Jesus's tomb that he probably saw on the Discovery channel? Hardly. Because some mildewy parchments in a scribble we can't read tell the story of Jesus? If I may remind you, Curt, good stories get repeated. So maybe a teen-age Jesus came to Tibet for summer camp. How the hell does that help us? We're not making a fucking documentary here. We're trying to save my mother!"

Curt ignites from the heat of this blast. "Don't shoot your friends because you're pissed at your father. So who the hell are you, anyway? Not the Charlotte Ansari I used to know. That Charlotte always dug to get the story. And she always got it!"

Charlotte sighs, just a bit calmer now. "Not always."

"Always! Sometimes it wasn't the story she thought she'd get, but she always got *a* story… and got it before the competition did. So what's the story here, Char? What's different about this one? Too personal? Then get out of the way. Tommy and I'll go after it. Too tough? Maybe it's time to retire. Shit, I think we *should* do a documentary on this. Then maybe we'd remember some of our investigative skills. We've been amateurs on this thing from the beginning. We're better than that!"

Curt confidently folds his arms across his chest. Charlotte painfully looks away from him, wounded by his charge. Fortunately, it is only a flesh wound.

She looks up at the crescent moon emerging from the twilight. This is what's been lacking—passion to get the story. And to do that, she has to stop *being* the story.

With an expression of grim resolve, she turns to Curt and says, "The story is about Jesus. That's what mother's been telling us. 'Locate the savior,' she said. So it's about getting physical evidence that he survived the cross and instead of ascending bodily to heaven left his mortal bones on earth."

She turns to her father. The anger is gone, replaced with a lucid stream of reasoning. "'Find the relic,' mother said. So it's also about getting corroborating evidence. This second relic is something that will prove the bones are from Jesus—otherwise, how could you ever prove it? You need two data points to have incontrovertible proof that the Bible was wrong and Jesus was human, not God."

Curt nods. "Every story needs corroborating evidence."

Charlotte thinks for a minute. "Maybe that's why no one has bothered to collect the bones from Roza Bal. They're not going anywhere. And without the second relic, they don't prove anything."

Her mind is made up now. "Dad, get Herb on the phone. Tell him we need to go to Srinagar. "

She turns to Curt. "Some stories you can only write by knowing the ending. Then everything else starts to make sense."

Chapter 55

The wrinkled mountains whisk by like bunched-up bed linens. Many of the peaks are too high to fly over, so Herb Rossi navigates the chopper around them, zigzagging a course toward assigned coordinates.

Gideon alternately changes his focus from the sharp crevices of the mountain slopes to the creases of Mike Ansari's stony face. Mike is roughly the same age as Gideon but his body lacks the muscular angularity of the Sicarii's. His expression is oddly calm, not anxious as one would expect from a man about to be tried for treason. *Does he think his high position indemnifies him from punishment?*

At last the chopper banks steeply and arcs around a jagged peak, dropping several thousand feet to approach a magnificent gompa that appears to have grown directly out of a rocky outcropping in a flat, flowered valley. At first glance, the large white Dhukang and the two temples above it could be a medieval European castle, with the boxy huts of a village stuck precariously to the sides of the rough slope below like barnacles on the hull of an overturned boat.

The chopper lands on the valley floor near a small band of yellow-robed monks standing near a group of yaks. Mike is the first to exit, followed by Gideon and Herb.

Two of the monks approach Gideon and embrace him warmly. The tallest one smiles and says, "Glad you are safe, my brother." The man's face is partially hidden behind a pair of round, thick-rimmed spectacles. The man turns toward Mike and coolly says, "It has been many years. You've changed."

Mike merely shrugs.

Herb offers his hand to the tall monk, saying, "Herb Rossi. Quite a place you got here. Didn't know it existed."

The tall monk shakes Herb's hand and glances at Gideon before saying, "We must give you some refreshments. It's a steep climb to the Dhukang. Would you like a ride?" He gestures toward the yaks.

"We'll walk," Gideon says. "I need the exercise."

A jarring ring causes Herb to pluck a satellite phone out of his pocket. "Excuse me just a minute," he says.

Turning his back on the others, Herb speaks into the phone. His buzz-saw voice is still audible to Gideon. "Hello, Herb here… yes, just finishing a charter… when is that?… Well, I could, I think, leave in a couple of hours, be there in, say, four?… Who is it?… okay, be there in a bit."

Herb wheels and finds all of the men staring at him. "Sorry about that," he says.

"Tourists?" Gideon asks.

"Government—American. Their chopper's on the fritz… damn politicians can't take care of infrastructure any more, know what I mean?"

"You do a lot of work for the government?" Gideon asks.

"That's what's so odd. I'm not on their list. Not since, well—it's a long story." He decides against sharing it.

Gideon shows no reaction, but he knows that Herb is on the government's list now, and he suspects the timing for this charter is no coincidence.

Herb's phone rings again. He answers and mumbles a simple, "You sure?" Then he stammers an agreement to something and hangs up.

"Damndest thing. You go days sometimes without a charter, then it suddenly gets crazy. I got a group over at Hemis that wants to go to Srinagar now. If I leave right away, I could do that and still pick up those government folks on schedule. So maybe a rain check on that hospitality?"

Gideon does a quick mental calculation. Herb is going to fly a "charter" for a group of government agents, probably CIA. Herb now knows the location of the Sicarii headquarters. Plus, he's going to pick up Charlotte and family at Hemis. Added together, these elements add up to a heap of trouble.

Or opportunity.

Gideon nods his understanding, and Herb smiles.

"Turning to his associates, Gideon says, "Take Mike to the Dhukang. I have some business to take care of down here."

The men nod.

"Herb," Gideon says, putting his hand on the older man's shoulder, "I have a business proposition that I'm sure you'll appreciate."

He gestures to the tall monk to remove his yellow robe. The monk nods and pulls off the robe, revealing pure white slacks and shirt beneath. Gideon points at the man's face. The man removes his spectacles, pulls a Glock 9mm pistol from somewhere behind his back, and then hands everything over to Gideon.

Herb stares at the pistol, his eyes round as the full moon in the day sky.

Gideon steps toward the helicopter. "Come into my office," he says to Herb, "and let's talk terms."

Allison Timms looks up at CIA director Wyatt and says, "They reached Rossi and he's coming back to Delhi."

"Are we sure about Rossi?"

"Ninety-nine percent. We know that Thompson has used Rossi before, and we know that Rossi took off from Delhi without filing a flight plan. Sounds like an escape to me."

"Intimidation only, understood?"

Allison understands this remark in two ways—as a direct order not to harm or kill Rossi, but only to intimidate him into revealing where he took Charlotte and family; and as a deniability statement, not to be taken literally.

"Yes sir, understood," Allison replies.

"Only the agents on this mission are to know its purpose?"

"Correct. I gave them orders myself through a secure channel, no intermediaries."

"Search and capture."

"Yes sir, and then alert you immediately."

"Charlotte and her son will be held in place. I will personally handle the interrogation. Am I clear on that?"

"Absolutely. We have a plane on hold to transport you as soon as we have a destination."

"Good work, Timms. We may be at the end of this messy business."

He says this hopefully, lacking conviction.

David Weiss puffs on a foul-smelling cigar and watches CCN on his hotel TV. The disappearance of star international correspondent Charlotte Ansari, along with a scrubbed version of her possible involvement in a Delhi murder, dominates the news. Four pundits pollute the airwaves with their theories about what is going on, two of them defending Charlotte's honor and the others providing the obligatory argumentative view. Weiss has learned, however, that Charlotte has now become the subject of a global search. But it is still unclear whether this is to rescue the correspondent… or arrest her.

Weiss wrestles his bulk out of a soft chair, lumbers to the mini-bar, and wrenches open a small bottle of scotch. He doesn't bother to pour it into a glass. The golden liquid trickles down his throat and he sighs. Better already!

His cell phone rings. Still standing, he pulls the phone out of a shirt pocket and speaks into it. "This better be important," he growls.

"It is," the voice replies.

Immediately, Weiss recognizes this voice. "Gideon, my friend. So good to hear from you." He is not happy at all, of course; this call is interrupting a modest attempt at inebriation.

"Perhaps you shouldn't be," Gideon responds. "By now you should know that I am not at the Sankar or Matho gompa. But your device is."

Weiss pauses, then speaks. "Gideon, you're talking gibberish. I have no idea…"

"I found the homing device in the suit you gave me. I'm disappointed in you, David. I thought we were friends."

"I'm a man of my word, Gideon, as you are. And I'm telling you straight up that I have no knowledge of any homing device." Weiss can hear the muffled thup-thup-thup of a helicopter between the verbal exchanges.

"You'd like to know my whereabouts, I can understand that. Would be useful, wouldn't it, David, since I'm guarding Charlotte? I'm sure that you can understand why I no longer consider our agreement in force. But you've also created a quandary for me—what to do about my betrayer."

Weiss stumbles back into his soft chair and drains the scotch from the small bottle.

"Are you still there, my friend?" Gideon asks.

"Listen, Gideon—you're jumping to the wrong conclusion here."

"I'm listening."

Weiss drops the empty bottle on the floor and nervously reaches for his gun on the night stand. Even though Gideon apparently is in a chopper, another Sicarii could be close.

"Aviram."

"What?"

"Aviram, you dunce!" Weiss chambers a cartridge in his pistol. The action calms him down. "I'm sorry, Gideon. But since I have no knowledge of this homing device, there is only one other explanation. Aviram made the suit for you. It must have been Aviram who placed the device in it."

"The old man…"

"In the car, yes. Aviram. Listen to me, Gideon, Aviram must be one of the rogue agents."

Now it is Gideon's turn to hesitate.

"Did I lose you, Gideon?" Weiss asks.

"I'm here. But as I think about this now, I can't believe you would be that naive, David. Sorry."

"What do you mean, sorry?"

A knock on the door startles Weiss. "Did you send someone for me, Gideon? Is that what you're trying to tell me?"

"You can't talk yourself out of this one, I'm afraid."

"Excuse me for a moment, will you?"

Weiss sets the cell phone down on the arm of the chair and quietly approaches the door just as the knocking begins again.

"Who is it?" Weiss asks irritably.

"Room service, sir."

Weiss is confused because he remembers ordering room service earlier.

"What did you bring me?" he asks.

"The sea bass, sir. And wine."

Correct answer. But those damn Sicarii are clever bastards! The best at this assassination business.

Weiss opens the door a crack, standing in a space that the door will conceal as it opens.

"All right, bring it in."

A thin Indian attendant timidly carries a large tray into the hotel room. As the man clears the door, Weiss slams it behind him, pointing a pistol at the man's head. The man turns slightly and sees the pistol. The tray rattles in nervous hands.

"Set it down over there," Weiss demands, "then raise your hands."

This man doesn't look like a Sicarii, but that could be a ruse. Weiss approaches the tray and removes the lids from the dishes. Sea bass. Asparagus. A bottle of Chianti.

He approaches the man and pats him down. Nothing.

A false alarm.

Weiss reaches into a pocket and produces a fistful of rupees—much more than a normal tip. He forces the rupees into the trembling man's hand and says, "This is for saying nothing... to anyone. Understand? Nothing happened here."

The man looks down at the fistful of money. His eyes are wide, but clearly he likes the tip. He nods yes. Without turning around, the man leaves, slamming the door behind him.

Weiss picks up the cell phone.

"Aviram," he says again.

"Rather nervous, aren't you?" Gideon asks. Clearly he has heard the entire event over the phone.

"My dinner is getting cold," Weiss says. "Frankly, I don't care if you believe me or not."

"Yes you do."

"I have bigger problems inside the organization."

"Problems, yes, but none bigger than me."

"All right. How can I convince you?"

"That's another one of your problems."

"Here's an idea. I'll send Aviram to meet you. And you can take him out."

"A sacrificial lamb?"

"A job. Bill me."

Gideon is silent.

"Do you really think I would send an innocent man to you for execution?" Weiss says. "I may have faults, but I would never betray one of my loyal agents."

"Send him to Srinagar on the next commercial flight," Gideon says. "Tell him I have news to pass along, and I need a different disguise. Enjoy your meal, David. You did bring a taster, right?"

The phone goes dead.

Weiss marches over to the serving tray. He lifts the plate of sea bass, carries it into the bathroom and dumps the food into the toilet.

Damn Sicarii!

Chapter 56

Greg watches the sky from Rossi's chopper. He and his companions anxiously stand near the presumed landing zone. Charlotte is having an animated conversation.

"We're on a hunt for evidence, don't you understand?" Charlotte says to her stern-faced father. "Theories abound—they always have—but where's the evidence that Jesus somehow survived the crucifixion? So far we have impeachable evidence that maybe, just maybe, he came to this part of the world as a young man. That's it."

"The Issa documents are about an older prophet…"

"…But maybe they are confused with the younger prophet. Even today, with electronic global news gathering, we get our facts wrong."

"You saw the Buddha statue."

"Sure, with rubies that may represent hand and foot wounds. Interesting, I admit. But this could have resulted from crucifixion stories that traveled here from Israel along the Silk Road. An attempt by Buddhists to tie their prophet to a new incarnation, maybe? That's easier to believe than Jesus traveling down the Silk Road to prophesy in Kashmir after surviving the crucifixion."

"For your mother's sake, let's hope that he survived and his bones are in Roza Bal."

"I hate to be pessimistic," Curt chimes in. "But Charlotte's got a point. Most likely we're on a wild goose chase. The more I think about this, the harder it is to believe that Jesus didn't die on that cross."

"And if there were an eye-witness account of his survival?" Thompson asks.

Greg sees a helicopter—just a faint dot, really—in front of the wide expanse of mountains.

"More hypotheticals," Charlotte says. "No offense, but that's your territory, Dad—religious theories. We're looking for facts."

"All right, try out this fact." Thompson is stirred up by his daughter's jab. "Some years ago, a member of the Abyssinian Mercantile Company discovered in Alexandria the remains of an ancient house once occupied by Grecian friars. Archeological investigations showed that this same house was previously owned and occupied by the Order of Essenes. In the library of this house, they discovered an old parchment written in Latin that contained an eye-witness account of the crucifixion and the survival of Jesus."

"Sounds like bad conspiracy fiction," Curt says.

"But it's true," Thompson continues. "A Jesuit missionary tried to destroy the document, but a French literate, who was there accidentally, somehow was able to protect it. For years, the Vatican continued its attempts to gain custody of the document, but eventually the parchment found its way to an Order of Freemasons in Germany.

"In 1873, a translation of the parchment was published in Germany and under intense pressure was immediately withdrawn. All plates were destroyed and all published copies were rounded up and burned—or so it was thought. Even the copies deposited in the Library of Congress went missing. But one copy ended up in the hands of a Mason in Massachusetts. Understanding the controversial nature of the document, he hid it well. After the Mason's death in 1907, the German manuscript was discovered by his daughter, who had it translated into English."

"So that translation is actually available?" Charlotte asks.

"It is."

"And the original?"

"I made friends with a high-level Mason in Germany, who told me that the original was missing—probably stolen."

"Maybe he was just trying to protect it," Charlotte remarks.

"I have good reason to believe him," Thompson says, reaching down for his satchel. He pulls out a slender metal case and opens it. Inside the case are brittle pages of parchment. They almost shimmer in the sunlight.

"No way," Curt says.

Thompson reaches into his satchel and removes three slim, bound volumes. "Behold the three copies deposited in the Library of Congress," he announces.

Greg's attention has been drawn to the conversation. He inspects one of the volumes and finds the Library of Congress stamp inside.

"So what was so threatening about this document?" Charlotte asks.

"Let me read one short passage for you," Thompson says, pulling a last document from the satchel—the English translation. "This is written by an Essene brother to the leader of his Order.

"'When the timid servants of the high-priest saw the white-robed Brother on the mountain slowly approaching and partially obscured by the morning mist, they were seized with a great fear, and they thought an angel was descending from the mountain…' and then this, from later in the letter: 'Entering, we perceived the white-robed novice kneeling upon the moss-strewn floor of the grotto, supporting the head of the revived Jesus on his breast… Then Joseph embraced him, told him how it had all come to pass, and how he was saved from actual death by a profound fainting fit, which the soldiers on Calvary had thought was death.'

"The writer explains that Jesus ate some dates and honey, and then writes: 'Then it was that he became conscious of the wounds in his hands and in his side. But the balsam which Nicodemus had spread upon them had a soothing effect, and they had already commenced to heal. After the byssus wrapping had been taken off, and the muckender was removed from his head, Joseph spoke and said: This is not a place in which to remain longer, for here the enemies might easily discover our secret and betray us.'"

These closing words—*this is not a place in which to remain longer*—are underscored by the rhythmic thumping of rotors as Rossi's helicopter rapidly approaches the landing zone. The weather-beaten Bell 214 hovers and then gently touches down. Even before Rossi can shut down the engine, Charlotte leads the others to the aircraft. They are in a hurry to get going.

Charlotte wrenches open the chopper door and enters as Curt begins loading up the luggage. Charlotte looks toward the rear of the passenger compartment and sees a yellow-robed monk hunched into a seat. The man seems to be unconscious.

She turns to Rossi with a questioning look.

Above the whine of the rotor, Rossi says, "A sick monk. I'm taking him to the hospital in Srinagar. I wouldn't get too close—don't know what he has."

The others finish boarding and the chopper lunges into the air.

Greg has taken a seat behind the others. After a few minutes, he unbuckles his seat belt and turns around to stare at the monk. The man has pulled a portion of the yellow robe over his head, as if he is chilled, and the robe partially obscures his face. From behind thick-rimmed glasses, the man's eyes flash open. The suddenness of it startles Greg, but he knows these eyes.

His protector.

Gideon sees the boy's eyes sparkle with recognition. He brings his index finger to his lips, silently asking Greg to keep the secret.

Greg stares at Gideon. He sees no reason to reveal his discovery, and so he turns around and opens his Bible for more study. There is so much to learn.

Aviram nervously punches the CALL button on his cell phone. A hoarse voice barks into his ear: "Shalom!"

"Shalom," Aviram says. "I am at the airport now. The flight has been delayed for two hours—why didn't someone tell me?"

"My apologies, Avi," David Weiss replies sarcastically. "Our entire operation, of course, centers around you. Do you have the disguise?"

"You think my memory is gone, David? Of course I have it. What I don't know is why I'm the courier. I'm no field agent."

"What can I say, Avi? He likes you. He bonded with you in the back seat of the limousine. You remind him of his father. How the hell do I know why he wants you? Can you just do this without the questions for once, Avi? This whole affair has us stretched thin."

"Am I in danger, David? Just tell me that. Am I being set up?"

"Don't be an idiot. I wouldn't send you if there was any danger. You saved this fellow once—I think he trusts you is all."

"Two hours, David. What do I do here for two hours?"

"Contemplate your navel like those fuckin' Buddhists—why are you asking me? Buy a magazine. Learn Hindi. I'm no goddam tour agent."

"Sorry, David—just this... this whole thing has unsettled me. Not my SOP, you know?"

"We're all in a little over our heads on this one, Avi."

"The man's a Sicarii. He scares me."

"Just do the job and come home. You're what—three months from retirement? There'll be a little something for you when you get back... something to make retirement come a little early, all right?"

"Of course, David. I know you wouldn't send me out if, if… there was any chance of a…"

"You're right, Avi. See you soon."

David Weiss replaces his cell phone into his breast pocket and continues to stare at Aviram, who is barely twenty paces away.

The old Jew is not aware that he is being observed. He is obviously nervous. With great effort, his frail arms push his wiry body upward from his seat and he begins pacing.

Weiss hates lying to an old friend, but he has no choice. And in this business, he has no friends, either. This is a business of compromises and sacrifices. Avi is one of the sacrifices.

Weiss pulls the cell phone from a pocket and taps in a number. "Weiss, here," he says when the connection is made. "You can back off my departure by an hour."

He pauses, listening to a question, and then replies, "That's right, our destination is still Srinagar."

Migraine-provoking, is what Charlotte thinks of the trip to Srinagar. Lumpy mountain air had buffeted the chopper all the way to Srinagar where the helicopter was met by grim-faced Indian security forces. The group had been escorted rudely to customs and immigration. *What had happened to the sick monk?*

As Charlotte and the others enter the main terminal, a legion of sturdy Indian soldiers with automatic weapons angrily contains—but just barely—a storm of arriving Muslim travelers and their greeters, striking taut nerves like flint on steel.

Thompson guides his family and Curt through the shouting mob. "I don't know what's going on here!" he shouts. "Never seen it so busy. And the military…"

An Indian soldier pushes Thompson and Charlotte forward, separating them momentarily from Greg and Curt.

"Excuse me!" Charlotte cries out. She reaches into her travel lanyard and holds up her news credential. "Press! Press!"

"Ah, CCN," the soldier says in a crisp British accent. "Follow me."

Curt and Greg manage to reconnect with the others, and the four of them muscle their bags through the crowd, following the soldier toward an exit.

"Maybe it's good it's so busy," Charlotte says to Curt, who is immediately behind her. "In case they were looking for us."

Outside, the Indian soldier guides them to a taxi stand. "I'm so sorry I cannot grant you an interview." He beams a wide grin at Charlotte. "But if you would like to take my picture…"

"Yes, of course," Charlotte says. "Curt?"

Curt catches her meaning. He sets down an aluminum case, unsnaps the lid and removes the video camera, preparing it for a shot.

"No interview, I understand," Charlotte says to the Indian. "But perhaps you can fill me in on what's going on before we shoot."

"Yes yes, of course, of course," the soldier says. "My name is Captain Durjaya Gutta." He smiles proudly, imagining himself on the international news network. "Srinagar is not always like this, but the protests… So now there are more soldiers here than civilians, and more militants than both"

"More militants than both," Charlotte repeats. "And they are coming in from…?"

"From Pakistan, chiefly. And other Muslim nations. Separatists. They want Kashmir free of Indian rule, and we are here to assert India's right to rule."

"Ready, Char," Curt announces. The camera is on his shoulder.

"Captain, we would like a picture of you containing the crowd over here, if you would, please." Charlotte gestures to a mob that is spilling out of the terminal. She can't understand the words being shouted, but she imagines that they are curses aimed at the soldiers.

"Yes yes," the Indian says, no longer grinning. "But hurry. You should remove yourselves from this area as soon as possible. I cannot guarantee your safety here."

Gutta turns and rallies a half-dozen other soldiers to the new mission of managing the spillage of humans from the terminal and protecting the CCN "crew." Suddenly a number of Pakistanis rush the soldiers. One large man lunges for Durjaya before being rifle-butted by another soldier. The outmanned army quickly establishes a holding formation that seems to temporarily discourage the angry crowd, which continues to hurl insults at the Indians.

Charlotte leads her companions to a white taxi, but Curt instinctively continues to shoot video of the mob. Captain Gutta moves his men into a new position to protect the four Americans as they load bags into the vehicle, but the mob has seen the camera and begins to chant undecipherable slogans in its direction. Defiant fists punch the air.

Just as the final bags are loaded and the four have been seated in the taxi, the crowd overwhelms the soldiers, surrounding the vehicle and pounding on the windows and hood.

"Go! Go!" Charlotte yells.

The frightened driver cautiously backs up, trying not to run anyone over, but as the pelting of fists on the taxi becomes thunderous, he guns it, zipping out of the parking space. An angry growl of gears propels the vehicle forward. The taxi delivers a glancing blow to three militants, who tumble to the pavement, then speeds toward Aerodrome Road, the main thoroughfare into Srinagar.

Thompson sighs heavily. Curt checks the lens of his camera for dirt. In the front seat, Charlotte turns to look at Greg, who is expressionless.

Glancing at Charlotte, the driver speaks in heavily accented English. "News?"

"CCN," Charlotte replies.

"Okay. You are safe now. My English learned in Mumbai."

"Yes, very good."

"Your destination please," the driver says, suddenly very formal.

From the back seat, Thompson's baritone intrudes. "A houseboat on Dal Lake." He hands a slip of paper to the driver.

Charlotte gives Thompson a quizzical look.

"Arranged for by Jamyang," Thompson explains. "We'll need a base of operations. For whatever we're going to do."

Charlotte sits back and looks out at the ring of mountains surrounding the lush valley that cradles Srinagar.

Kashmir! The inspiration, some say, for the legend of Shangri-La. So peaceful once. But now in the crosshairs.

Just like Charlotte and Greg.

267

Chapter 57

Mihad "Mike" Ansari is seated in a gray robe on an open balcony surrounded by mountains. The majestic view summons a succession of voluptuous memories. Each pulse of clarity, each rippling image makes him shiver with delight.

It was here, in this secret Himalayan monastery, that he had been reared in the comforting bosom of the Great White Brotherhood. He had been trained in purity, spirituality, and the ancient truths. Thrilled by the heroic tales of his ancestors, he had imagined himself growing up to be a great Defender of the Order, an Assassin of Evil. After all, was he not one of the few young men of pure Sicarii blood?

The Brothers were seldom allowed to marry, and so there were few purebred offspring. Most were recruited members, and many of those were "adopted" children raised by the Brotherhood. No Brother would have sexual relations out of wedlock—except, as Mihad knew, when directed by the Council for a purpose of such importance that the usual rules of morality could be set aside.

Women chiefly served the Order as Associates, not full members, with one exception. Ever since the great tragedy of Masada, a Woman of the Lineage has led the Brothers whenever such a woman was present—and when there was no Divine Light to serve as leader of the Order. For almost two thousand years, the Sicarii has been a matriarchy.

Masada had nearly brought about the end of the Order, the longest-surviving branch of Essenes. Roman rule had radicalized a splinter group of Essenes comprised of those who were critical of the organization's monastic withdrawal from civilization and sought a more active response to unjust government. The Zealots, as they came to be called, established a death squad to carry out its most violent acts. And so the Sicarii had quickly evolved from the peaceful Men in White to an Order of Assassins that was still, however, deeply religious at its core, embracing most of the Essene Traditions but with a distinctly different mission—the eradication of evil personified by Roman rule.

The Sicarii Brothers established its own strict code of governance to prevent anarchy among its ranks. It became the single coherent unit of the Zealot movement. By rule, every assassination would have to be approved by a Council of the wisest Sicarii Brothers. Evidence of personal evil-doing would be gathered and presented to the Council, which would find the accused guilty or innocent. A guilty verdict could result in an order for execution or amnesty, depending on circumstances. Council orders quickly became indistinguishable from "Divine" decrees. In this way, assassinations could be justified as conscious, rational acts of Divine justice to help defeat evil, which would bring about the "Kingdom of God on earth," a theme frequently repeated by Jesus.

Though they had separated themselves from their mild Essene cousins, who were dwindling in number, the Sicarii still greatly revered one of the dominant Essene leaders. Yeshua, who came to be known as Jesus, had become known as one of the wisest of them all. He had been sent to Egypt and the Far East for training as a youth and had returned with a wisdom both spiritual and worldly. The Sicarii had hoped that this great leader would break from the quiet, cloistered traditions of the Essenes and aggressively declare himself a leader of the fight against Roman oppression.

Their hopes were stirred as Jesus left the insular confines of the Essenes and began a public mission to shake up the established order. Had this Jesus not invited two well-known Sicarii Brothers, Judas the Sicarii and Peter the Zealot, into his own secret order of Apostles? Had he not said, "I did not come to bring peace, but a sword," words preserved in Matthew 10:47? And at the Last Supper, in Luke 22:36, had he not told his Apostles, "… he who has no sword, let him sell his garment and buy one." Sword was a code word, the Sicarii believed, for "sica," the small dagger favored for assassinations, and from which the Brothers drew their name.

After the crucifixion of Jesus, the Sicarii had come to see him as a great martyr for their cause. Their studies of ancient scriptures convinced them over time that this man, Jesus, had been sent by God to lead *them*. And the greatest evidence of this, they believed, was the date of his birth: 7 BCE. Like other God-sent prophets and kings, the proof was in the stars. And the stars bore witness to the Divine mission of the Sicarii. The Brothers believed that their first great leader was Jesus himself.

Two women survived the tragedy that occurred at Masada some forty years after the crucifixion. One of these women, Sarah, was the wife of the Sicarii Council leader and a descendant of John the Baptist; the other woman was Sarah's sister, who died shortly after her capture by the Romans. They had been hidden in a cistern, a kind of improvised Noah's Ark. Five surviving children were given to various ruling families so they could brag to the other elites about owning the last living remnant of the savage Sicarii.

In a rare display of generosity, General Cornelius Flavius Silva of the conquering Roman 10th Legion gave Sarah to his siege-master, Rubrius Gallus, as a reward for devising the earthen ramp that breached the mountaintop stronghold. Gallus soon became obsessed with the beautiful enchantress and eventually took the widow as his wife. Two years after the Masada siege, in 74 CE, Sarah bore him a son, Paternius, but never forgave Gallus for his role as chief engineer of the Masada catastrophe.

Three years later, Sarah assassinated her husband with a sica and fled into the Jerusalem hills with Paternius and a large cache of money pilfered over the years from the household account. She adopted a new identity and set out to free the five surviving children of Masada from their bondage. A skilled assassin herself, she began a campaign of terror aimed at the families who owned the child slaves. Because of her actions, rumors spread that the Sicarii had not been eradicated, and that the most ferocious dagger-men were out to avenge anyone who enslaved their children. Before long, the children, now a liability, were sold for a pittance to a woman who seemed oblivious to the new Sicarii threat.

Sarah.

She had succeeded in gathering all of the Sicarii remnant together.

Sarah transported Paternius and the older children to a large Essene monastery near the cave of Elijah on Mount Carmel. This compound was situated on one of the world's most historic sacred sites. Since the earliest days, a temple or monastery had always been located on this spot. When the prophet Elijah first visited Mount Carmel, he discovered an ancient temple and altar already there. After Egyptian Pharaoh Thothmes the Third conquered Carmel, he pledged to maintain a library and monastery there for a great Mystic School, the first Essene center of learning established long before the secret Essene Temple and Library in Alexandria. Pythagoras spent part of his life at this mystical place on Carmel. And as a child, Jesus was brought here to study before traveling to India and Kashmir.

The introspective Essenes had remained passive during the first Jewish-Roman War, and so the Romans had not destroyed the monastery as they had the Temple in Jerusalem. The surviving Masada children—four boys and one girl—were raised as Essenes, but Sarah secretly taught them the passionate dogma, urgent mission, and eventually the unique skills of the Sicarii.

Sarah's new identity, Eve, symbolized her role as the first woman of the resurrected Order, and since that time all of her direct descendants had been Women of Lineage, seats of respect and authority in a brotherhood of men.

The grand sweep of history and flood of personal recollections cause Mihad to reflect on his choices. Perhaps he had been left alone too long, had forgotten his sacred duties, had become disconnected from the Brotherhood and influenced by the forces of evil he had originally pledged to defeat. Looking back, he can see how his selfish desire for self-controlled success led him further away from the principles of the Brotherhood and down the blind alley of materialism and failed businesses.

Had he really sold out the Brothers for money and then invested it so unwisely into another stupid business idea that had left him with nothing but debts?

He had been so happy here, so stirred by a vision of future heroism for the cause. So in love with the Brothers who showered him with love and appreciation.

And now he was undone by his own actions. He had thought that he could escape his failures and return to this secret monastery with his sins hidden. But he had been found out, and here he was, on the Judgment Balcony, awaiting the verdict of the Council.

He still believes that amnesty will be granted. He was, after all, of pure blood. It was for this reason that he was assigned his life's mission, which he had accomplished. Surely the Council will consider this fact. And had his betrayal led to any serious consequences for the Brotherhood? Certainly not. So what was the great harm?

Not enough to merit executing one of pure blood.

Eve steps out onto the balcony, her dazzling white robe fluttering in a gentle mountain breeze. Strikingly beautiful and stately, she looks about sixty, with long dark hair that ruffles in the wind and contrasts with the brilliant whiteness of her robe.

"The Council has decided," she says calmly. "It was a difficult decision because of your heritage."

"Am I to be exiled? That would be worse than death."

"Then you will be very pleased with the decision. No exile."

Mihad sighs with relief. Now that he had returned to his boyhood home, this Shangri-La, he could not imagine being apart from it again. The past fifteen years in the "world" now seems like a nightmare. He looks out at the mountains, the same mountains that protected him growing up, the snowy peaks that entranced him with their mystery when he was a boy. He is home at last. Among family.

But then he looks again at Eve and sees the sica in her hand. In a blue-white flash, he understands.

No exile.

He sighs again, but this time with resignation. It is not fear that seizes him at this moment, but regret.

He turns his back on Eve and leans on the balcony wall. Leans out toward the mountains. Hears soft footsteps behind him. Takes a deep breath of the sweet, crisp mountain air.

His last.

Chapter 58

Like a timid mosquito afraid to land, the Bell 214 flutters momentarily over the Delhi tarmac before dropping the final few feet with a jarring thud. As the rotor begins to slow, two men rush the chopper with hard-shelled black cases.

"They're in a hurry," Herb Rossi says to Gideon, his counterfeit co-pilot now rescued from the monk's robe.

"So am I," Gideon responds.

Like zephyrs, the two men board as Rossi restarts the engine. The first man, bald with an oddly smashed-in nose, is about forty-five. His gut bunches up slightly as he climbs into the cabin. Definitely past his prime. The second man is fifteen years younger. Sleek as a sparrow. Gideon can imagine the chiseled musculature beneath his clothes. The eyes of both men are obscured behind aviator sunglasses. It's clear they aren't interested in small talk.

"How long to Hemis from here?" the bald man says, shouting above the whine of the rotor.

Herb silently turns to Gideon who replies, "Couple of hours, depending on weather. Buckle up."

The chopper lifts off and lunges north. After forty-five minutes of smooth flight, Herb fiddles with a control, purposely making a light begin to flash in the cockpit. Gideon turns to the passengers and says, "We're having a technical issue up here. We're going to put down in Srinagar and check it out."

"We're in a real hurry!" the bald man yells angrily.

"Crashing in the mountains is not exactly a speed-up strategy. Sorry."

The two CIA agents have no options but consult furiously with each other anyway. At last, the bald man pulls out a cell phone and punches in a number. Gideon sees him.

"Hey! Turn that off! Phones can interfere with our navigation."

The bald man pulls his sunglasses down slightly and peers at Gideon over the top of the rims.

"Too fuckin' bad," he says.

Having arrived in Srinagar a half-hour before the commercial flight from Delhi, David Weiss watches Aviram emerge from immigration with a small suitcase. Aviram plunges into the crowd, navigates to the ground transportation area, and looks around. No unoccupied chairs. He leans against a wall and pulls out a cell phone.

Weiss's phone buzzes. He answers. "Aviram?"

"You knew it was me?" Aviram replies.

"Of course. According to the schedule, you landed a few minutes ago."

"So here I am. What now?"

"You wait. He will find you there. Give him the suitcase with the disguise and then come home."

"I've been thinking, David. What if he found the homing device? This could be a trap."

"Trust me on this, old friend."

"But how can you be sure…?"

"We have ways. I'll personally meet you at the Delhi airport when you return, all right?"

Weiss hangs up. He watches Aviram try to tuck his phone into a pocket, miss the opening, and then try again successfully. "He's nervous," Weiss says to Layak, a dependable Indian contractor.

"Of course he is," Layak says. "He's not a field agent. Do you really think he'll betray you to the Sicarii?"

"Of course, if we let him. That's why you're here."

Layak glances away. Weiss senses some hesitation in the tall, wiry contractor. "You fear him?" he asks.

"The Sicarii?" Layak replies. "I'm no match for a Sicarii. Who is?"

"Just follow the plan. If I can't distract him, abort the mission. I have plans for you, Layak. I don't want anything to happen to you."

"It's Gordon calling from the chopper, sir," Allison Timms says, switching on the speakerphone for CIA director Wyatt.

"From the chopper? What the hell…?" Wyatt turns in his chair and barks: "What's going on out there, agent?"

"Problem with the helicopter, sir," the bald agent replies. "We're going to Srinagar to fix it."

A boxcar of profanity unloads in Wyatt's brain, but he constrains himself to one word. "Damn!"

"If we can't fix it quick, should we commission another ride, sir?"

"Listen to me carefully, son. You must *not* fly with another pilot. Understood? You are to go to Hemis as quickly as possible and complete your mission. When you are finished, the pilot becomes a liability. Am I clear on this?"

"Yes sir. The co-pilot too?"

"Absolutely."

"I'll let you know as soon as we balance the books."

Wyatt switches off the phone. "Idiots!" he says to no one in particular.

"It's a dynamic situation, sir," Allison reminds him.

"Do we have assets in Srinagar? Besides these two clowns, I mean?"

"I'll have to check. But I think we have maybe half-a-dozen men monitoring the conflict there."

"Okay, the protests are mainly around the Old City, which is not far from the Khaniyar district. I want all our assets deployed in Khaniyar, except two. I want two men at the airport now."

"What's going on, sir?"

"The chopper is diverting to Srinagar. Just too much of a coincidence. Srinagar is ground zero for this operation. I'm telling you, Allison, something's in play—and it's not happening at Hemis."

"Then why send Gordon there?"

"Trust me. They're not going to Hemis."

"Then we should warn our agents that..."

"No! If someone is onto our agents, they'll be watching their every move. I don't want our guys giving away that we're on alert in Srinagar."

Suddenly he looks up at Allison with a revelation. "Damn!" The mild curse erupts so suddenly that even Wyatt is surprised by it. "Gordon said there was a co-pilot in the chopper."

Allison's brain grinds into action. "Far as I know, sir, Rossi never flies with a co-pilot. He's a lone eagle."

"Allison, I think our Sicarii nemesis is in that chopper with Gordon and, and…"

"And Troy, sir."

"I want that Sicarii bastard, you understand?"

"I do."

"The chopper'll be landing anytime. It's our best chance to pick this guy up. Pull whatever strings to make it happen."

"That means calling Sanghvi at IB again."

Wyatt sighs. Another chance to grovel at the feet of the head of Indian intelligence and beg for a favor.

"Whatever it takes," he says. "Offer him an audience with the president. He's a fan."

"We can do that?"

Wyatt glares at Allison. "Just make it happen. And Allison, have them saddle up the horses. I'm going to Kashmir."

Boulevard Road runs along the south edge of Dal Lake. Colorful houseboats float like confetti on the serene water—hundreds of them with names like "Rick's Place," "Serengetti," "Buckingham Palace," and "Mona Lisa."

"Over there!" Greg shouts. His eyes are focused on a large houseboat with a nameplate that becomes legible as the taxi slows down.

"Yes," Thompson says. "A houseboat named 'Desire.'"

And so it is.

The taxi stops and unloads passengers and baggage. Charlotte overpays the driver, who summons a shikara—a canopied, flat-bottomed longboat resembling a gondola. They load up the shikara and climb in. Skimming past crimson lotus blossoms adrift on the placid water, the shikara quietly glides toward the houseboat.

Thompson notices the heart-shaped paddles used by the three oarsmen to propel the vessel. He turns to Charlotte behind him. "You see the oars?" Thompson says. "The blades—shaped like hearts. You see that?"

Charlotte rises from the brocaded cushion on which is she lying. She gives Thompson a confused look punctuated by a dismissive shrug.

276

"You can find such oars only in two other places on earth," Thompson explains. "On Lake Kalundia near Jerusalem, and on the lower Euphrates, homeland to Jewish descendants thought to be one of the Lost Tribes. Many people believe the Kashmiri people, like the Afghanis, also descended from one of the Lost Tribes."

"And your point is...?"

"That maybe, just maybe, this is why Jesus came here."

"That's too big a leap for me," Charlotte says, turning her gaze again onto the beautiful heart-shaped oar.

Thompson's sigh disappears among the watery sighs of the oars.

Greg breaks the silence. "Christ said, 'And other sheep I have which are not of this fold; them also I must bring, and they will hear My voice; and there will be one flock and one shepherd.'"

Charlotte quizzically looks at her son. *Where did that come from?*

"John 10:16," Thompson says. "Jesus is the Great Shepherd. The fold refers to Judah—the Jews living in Judea. The tribe that was *not* lost." He glances at Charlotte and adds, "Your son has made good use of his study time."

Charlotte quickly gathers her thoughts. "So, you believe that these *other sheep* who are *not of this fold* are the Lost Tribes?"

Her father replies, "In the Gospel of Matthew, Jesus says I was not sent except to the lost sheep of the house of Israel."

Greg, suddenly engaged, adds: "Jesus said to his Disciples at the Last Supper... 'And you will sit on thrones judging the twelve tribes of Israel.'"

Thompson again turns to his daughter. "Photographic memory?" he asks, referring to Greg.

"Eidetic memory, to be precise—but only for information that he's interested in. I wouldn't be surprised if he's memorized the New Testament."

Thompson turns to Greg, who is staring out at the golden water. He begins quoting another Biblical passage: "And I have other sheep, that are not of this fold..."

Thompson pauses and Greg completes the passage for him. "'I must bring them also, and they will heed my voice. So there shall be one flock, one shepherd.' John 10:16."

Thompson turns to Charlotte and says, "So maybe it was necessary for Jesus to go all the way to Kashmir to seek and save the lost tribes of Israel—to return them to the faith of Abraham and Jacob. As a youth, traveling throughout Afghanistan, India and Kashmir, he had found some of the Lost Tribes at least partly absorbed into the local cultures. Clearly, he must have known where they were. Otherwise, how could James have written in his book…"

Thompson turns to Greg, who hesitates slightly and then produces the intended verse: "'James, a servant of God and of the Lord Jesus Christ, to the twelve tribes which are scattered abroad, greeting.' James 1:1."

"How could James write a letter to the twelve tribes if he didn't know where they were?" Thompson asks. "And how did he know this? Well, Jesus certainly knew. And Jesus directed each of his apostles to reach out to them. In the Gospel of Matthew, what does he tell them, Greg?"

"'Go not into the way of the Gentiles, and into any city of the Samaritans enter ye not: But go rather to the lost sheep of the house of Israel.'"

"And so he assigned his disciples to reach out to the tribes of Israel in different regions. We know, for example, that St. Thomas went to India and founded a church in Taxila. If Jesus came to Kashmir to gather up some of his Lost Sheep, we could be within minutes of his final resting place. And a lot closer to saving your mother, Char."

The shikara reaches the front porch of the houseboat Desire. The "houseboy," a springy, fifty-year-old Kashmiri named Chandraka, helps them aboard the floating mansion and escorts them inside.

The houseboat is at least one hundred fifty feet long and thirty feet wide. The cedar interior is ornately decorated with an embarrassment of intricately carved designs, Victorian furnishings and tapestries, crystal chandeliers, and magnificent Kashmiri carpets. The bathrooms have modern fittings and plumbing, and each of the four guests has a private bedroom with thick mattresses and plump pillows.

Charlotte is stunned by the opulence. "It's so surprisingly sumptuous and, and —*Victorian*."

In a thick British accent, Chandraka responds. "When the English came to Kashmir, the Maharaja forbid them to buy land and build houses in his kingdom. Instead of going home, the English—how do you say it?—found a *loophole*. The Maharajah had forbidden them to stay on land, but hadn't said anything about water. And that is how houseboats came to Kashmir. Have you had dinner?"

Chapter 59

The chopper lands by a squat building near the main Srinagar terminal. "We've attracted a lot of interest," Rossi says. Indian police cars swarm toward the helicopter like iron filings to a magnet.

The CIA agents seem surprised, agitated. Gordon pulls out his cell phone and places a call. Gideon can't hear the conversation, but it's clear that agency plans have been revised. As Gordon listens to his new orders, he glances inadvertently at Gideon, betraying the subject of the call.

Over the past few hours, Gideon had devised a clever plan to manipulate the two agents into liquidating Aviram. He had liked the irony of using one adversary to eliminate another. But now he suspects that his cover is blown. Feeling less smug by the second, he considers the escalating threat. Someone at Langley had probably figured out that Gideon was in the chopper and rallied ground support from the Indians.

Herb Rossi looks at Gideon. He hasn't shut down the engine yet. "We can be out of here in ten seconds," he says, just loud enough for Gideon to hear.

Gideon has made up his mind. "Shut it down!"

Free of his seat harness, Gideon lifts himself out and smiles disarmingly at the passengers, who are just now unbuckling their seat belts.

"Gentlemen, welcome to Srinagar," he says, approaching the two.

A ferocious right palm to the tip of Gordon's nose smashes the cartilage into the man's face and brain. Instant death. Before Troy realizes what has happened, Gideon's left hand grips the man's trachea and twists, wrenching it free from his neck.

There was no other choice, really. "Herb, help me out here," he yells.

As police cars surround the chopper and uniformed Indian officers begin to emerge with weapons drawn, Herb and Gideon quickly move the bodies into the pilot and co-pilot seats. Herb is clearly shaken.

"Congratulations," Gideon says. "You have just become a CIA agent. Follow my lead and I'll keep you safe. Otherwise…"

Gideon shows a pistol he had taken from Gordon.

"See if they have any ID. If they do, hand it to me. We don't want anything on their bodies."

Captain Durjaya Gutta, who had earlier protected Charlotte and her companions, nervously points his pistol at the chopper. He is not sure what this incident is all about, only that two CIA agents are on board and the pilot and co-pilot are terrorists wanted by American intelligence—the false story handed down to Gutta via Indian intelligence.

The door of the chopper opens. A dozen Indian weapons immediately point at it like needles finding true north. Two men emerge.

"Hold your fire!" Gideon says in a broad American accent. "CIA!" He holds Gordon's credential as he walks toward one of the vehicles, then puts it back into his pocket before anyone can see the photo. "You spooked 'em with all these cars, dammit. Had to put both of 'em down. Who's in charge here?"

Gutta lowers his pistol and rises from a crouch behind his vehicle. "I am, sir. Captain Gutta." He motions for two of his men to enter the chopper behind the two Americans.

"All right, Captain Gutta. We were promised cooperation here. What are your orders?" Gideon speaks with a commanding confidence.

"To assist in any way possible… and take the two terrorists into custody."

"I think you'll be taking them to the morgue instead. Now listen up. We have information about one more adversary inside the terminal. He's old, but very dangerous. I'll need four men while the others clean up here."

Gutta nods and then gestures to three men. "And I'll go with you," he says to Gideon.

A cell phone chirps. Gideon reaches into a shirt pocket and removes Gordon's cell phone. He grunts, "Uh-huh," masking his voice.

"Hammer?" Allison says, using Gordon's code name.

"Yeah."

"This is Kingdom. What is your status?"

"It's done here."

"Good news." The caller shows no sign of detecting the wrong voice. "Blackstone is on his way to Srinagar. Should be there in about ten hours. So—tell me how it went down."

"Scuffle on the chopper. Had to put 'em down."

"Check. Two more agents are arriving to give assistance. but Operation Goldfinch is now history. We want those bodies and everything on 'em. If the wogs get pissy about it, call me."

"No problem. But listen, explain that to the Captain here—"

"No, wait…"

Smiling, Gideon hands the cell phone to Gutta.

C IA Agents Flay and Schoenecke enter the terminal. Their casual tourist clothes do little to camouflage their agency affiliation. The telltale combination of athletic build, short hair, aviator shades and cocky attitude gives them away. That, and the fact that there are almost no American tourists in Srinagar these days. It's just too dangerous.

Flay, a sandy-haired ex-Marine with a square jaw and fists like large hams, searches out an Indian policeman. "We're looking for Captain Gutta," he says to the tall officer. "It's urgent."

The Indian stares at Flay for a moment before saying, "One moment, please." He picks up a radio and calls Gutta.

C aptain Gutta trails behind Gideon and Herb Rossi on the long march to the terminal. His radio burps static and then a voice says, "Captain Gutta, there are two Americans here for you."

Gideon hears the message. Two CIA agents. Would they know Gordon and Troy? Would they have the photograph of Gideon?

"I am attending to an urgent matter," Gutta responds. "I'll contact you as soon as I'm free."

"Yes sir."

Gideon stops and turns to face Gutta. "Excuse me, Captain, but I overheard your conversation. It's possible that the two bad guys in the chopper have American accomplices here on the ground."

Gutta stares at Gideon, calculating what this means.

"How would we know if these two—?" he asks.

"I've been undercover for years. If these two are accomplices, they'll know me."

281

"How did they know to ask for me?" Gutta says suspiciously.

"It would not be hard to ask for the person in charge. They're probably impersonating CIA agents."

Gutta hesitates at the mention of impersonation, eyes Gideon warily for a moment. "Is it so easy to impersonate an agent?"

"Hey, c'mon Captain, you know me. You just talked to my boss in Langley. Here—" he hands the cell phone back to Gutta, "call her back, dammit. I thought we were on the same team here."

Gutta softens. "All right. If the Americans are bad guys, do you want us to arrest them?"

"At least!" Gideon replies. His meaning is clear.

They enter the terminal through a small customs door that inspects passengers arriving on small aircraft and are immediately accosted by a slim Indian woman in a passport control uniform. The Indians show identification. Gideon and Herb show passports. With his fingertips, Gideon nervously caresses his belt buckle and its hidden dagger as the officious agent compares his photo to his actual appearance. In an era of electronic communications, it's possible that his wanted poster has been received even at this distant outpost.

Gutta barks at the agent, urging him to hurry up. The agent angrily stamps the passport and all six men proceed down a corridor to customs. Carrying no luggage, they stomp through without breaking stride and within seconds emerge into the main terminal, still a churning sea of humanity.

It is not difficult for Gideon to spot the two pale American agents. He guides his Indian escorts to a more secluded area behind a pillar. Glancing sideways, he sees Aviram asleep in a frayed seat just thirty feet away. The battleground is quickly defining itself.

"I saw the Americans," he says to Gutta. "They are very dangerous, so here is our plan. The old man to my left is also a hostile agent, but of another persuasion. He is carrying plans and materials for a terrorist attack on Mumbai."

Gutta studies Aviram. "But he's asleep!" Gutta says skeptically. "What kind of terrorist sleeps on the job?"

"I doubt that he's sleeping. He is Hizb-ul Mujahideen."

Gutta winces at the mention of the largest terrorist organization in Jamma and Kashmir. Aviram's ethnic appearance is so similar to many

Kashmiris—the product of Kashmir's ancient Jewish heritage—that this outrageous lie seems credible.

Gutta continues to study the old man as Gideon unfolds the plan.

"I am going to make contact with the Americans," Gideon explains. "They are weapons dealers who are anxious to abduct the old man, who has invented a new kind of explosive that avoids all known forms of detection. This is what he carries with him. The Americans want him to show them how to make it."

Gutta turns his attention to Gideon. "So the Americans want the old man. Why haven't they made their move?"

"Because they don't know what he looks like. No one does but me. So listen carefully. I am going to let the Americans know I am here. I will then walk over to the old man and he will hand me a package. This will tell them that I have verified his identity. At that point, I will step away and they will attempt to abduct him. You must capture or kill both Americans—*and* the old man. I will make sure that you get full credit for this operation. Now I suggest you inform your men and spread out strategically."

Gutta nods compliantly as Gideon motions to Rossi and they start walking toward the two CIA agents who are standing near a beverage kiosk.

"Hey, good to see you!" Gideon says in a loud voice as he approaches the confused agents. And then, as he puts out his hand to Flay, he quietly adds, "Pretend you know us."

Flay shakes hands with Gideon and Rossi, and so does Schoenecke. "Who the hell are you?" Flay asks.

"Hammer," Gideon lies. "Kingdom told me you were assigned to assist."

This is the big test. If either of these two men know agent Gordon, Gideon will have to implement Plan B, and that could unravel his hastily concocted plan.

"And this is Godfather?" Schoenecke stares grimly into Rossi's eyes as he speaks. Gordon mentally shelves Plan B for the moment.

"So whatever happened to mandatory retirement?" Schoenecke says, a dig at the older man.

Rossi takes a step toward the cocksure agent, but Gideon restrains him. Schoenecke stiffens and snarls.

"I wouldn't make him mad," Gideon says to Schoenecke. "He can whip your sorry ass any day of the week. We haven't got much time here, so—"

"So where's the Sicarii?" Flay interjects.

"Had to take him out. And the pilot. Operation Goldfinch is over."

"So we're out of here, then."

"Not quite. The reason the bastard diverted to Srinagar was to pick up a package from a member of Hizb-ul Mujahideen. The courier is actually their quarterback, here to make a deal. He's a very high value target. It's your job to sack the quarterback. Dead is good, alive is better."

"I haven't heard anything about this," Schoenecke says skeptically.

"Of course not! We just learned about this in the chopper," Gideon replies, leaning close to the broad-faced man. "Even a Sicarii will talk under the right circumstances—like dangling ten thousand feet up in the air."

"And what about you two?" Flay asks.

"We'll be running interference. The police here are in league with Hizb-ul Mujahideen. They'd like nothing more than to get their hands on some CIA agents."

"Jesus!" Flay says. "We were told the police would be supporting *us*. We just asked for the Captain."

"Then they already know you're CIA. And they know Godfather and me. So we'll just try to head 'em off at the pass. Whatever you do, don't let the police take you in or you'll never be seen again."

"What happens to you two?"

"We've gotta move now," Gideon says, dismissing the question, "before the police figure out how to get all four of us. I've spotted a guy who might be the quarterback. If he thinks I'm the Sicarii, after he hands off, sack him."

"What's in the package?" Schoenecke asks.

"Pre-payment for services."

"Christ, those guys'll work for anybody these days."

Gideon ushers Rossi away from the agents. He sees that the police have scattered. Flay and Schoenecke hold back, then casually follow Gideon and Rossi, watching them approach an elderly gentleman who seems to be dozing in a seat. The old man's right hand firmly clutches a small satchel.

Gideon whispers instructions to Rossi, who nods his understanding.

Gideon walks up to the old man and bends over him.

"I've been waiting for a long time," Aviram says without opening his eyes. "I have the disguise. Are you going to kill me now?"

Gideon says nothing.

Aviram opens his eyes. They are sad. Bloodshot. The light has gone out of them. "Weiss sent me here to be sacrificed."

"He knew about the tracking device?"

"Weiss knows everything. Plans everything.

"And the rogue agents?"

"As I said—*everything*. If you don't kill me, he will. Before I return."

"Is he here now? Have you seen him?"

"I don't have to see him. I can smell him. He's here—watching. To make sure. If you don't take me somewhere to kill me, he'll think that I made a deal by betraying him."

Gideon nods slowly. The battlefield has expanded. He places his palm on Aviram's liver-spotted right hand and the old man releases his grip on the satchel.

"Lying to a Sicarii is not permitted," he says. "Now stand up and shake my hand."

Aviram slowly unwinds his bent body and straightens into a standing position. Gideon hands the satchel to Rossi, then puts out his left hand. Aviram shakes it once, twice, and then Gideon embraces him, almost tenderly, patting him on the back. He had plotted to have others put the old man out of his misery, but now—feeling the stubble Avi's cheek and his humid breath and his trembling chest—Gideon changes his mind.

"Goodbye, Avi," Gideon whispers.

And then Aviram feels the cold finger, the dull pain—duller than he had imagined. It penetrates into his chest like an icicle, numbing everything. Not so bad, really. Still he is cradled in Gideon's arms. But his legs are weak now, and Gideon gently helps the old man back into his seat, surreptitiously removing the *sica* from the old man's back.

"Close your eyes now, Avi," Gideon says. "Go to sleep."

Aviram sighs as Gideon and Rossi slowly walk away.

Flay and Schoenecke walk up to the sleeping man.

Flay bends over and says, "Old man, come with us now. Don't put up a fuss or you'll be very sorry."

The man does not move.

Schoenecke touches the man's shoulder. Nothing. He shakes the man. Aviram slumps forward, revealing a small wet wound in his back.

That's when Schoenecke's world collapses.

Suddenly he understands. *The Sicarii!*

And then there is movement.

The police. From all directions. Shouting words he can't understand. Pointing weapons. He must escape! He draws a pistol, and so does Flay. Crouching behind the row of worn seats, with people screaming and scattering in all directions, they begin to fire. And take fire. Two rounds strike Aviram's dead body, making it jump. Five rounds chew through seat backs. Two policemen are struck and drop to the floor, writhing in pain.

The two agents rise and streak for the exit, but three officers are waiting for them. Believing that surrender is not an option, Flay raises his pistol. Three shots slam into his chest, and four into Schoenecke as he attempts to flee. Every security person in the airport has converged on the scene.

David Weiss walks out of the terminal as if nothing has happened. He is surprised that, despite the violence inside and the chaos outside, a taxi is waiting. The rear door opens.

"Get in, David," Gideon says.

It's not exactly a smile that distorts the face of David Weiss as he lowers his head and slides into the taxi's rear seat. More of a sneer, really.

"Quite a scene you staged in there," Weiss says as the taxi moves out.

"Just a little object lesson—that it's unwise to cross a Sicarii. By the way, Aviram told me everything. But let me ask you a question anyway. Your appeal for my cooperation—?"

"Let me point out that you failed to provide the cooperation we sought when you sent our tracking device on a wild goose chase. So in a way, you still owe me. And by the way, I'm more than willing to accept a bill for services related to Aviram."

"What I don't understand is this. All of Kidon is rogue, or are you just operating a small rogue operation within?"

"You seem to be confused. Kidon today is a eunuch compared to the old Kidon. Eviscerated by our new leaders. Our little skunk works is not rogue—it is the *real* Kidon beyond the touch of politicians. We do the work our country has lost the courage to do. We are the true patriots of Zion."

From the window of the taxi, David watches the Bell 214 rise above the terminal and veer toward the mountainous horizon. With all security focused on the mayhem at the terminal, it had been easy for Herb Rossi to reclaim his helicopter. Strict Sicarii protocol, of course, called for anyone who knew the location of its headquarters to be terminated, but Gideon had felt that Rossi could be relied upon. He will find out very soon. If not, he will be easy to find.

"I assume that you will let me go... to balance the books," Weiss says.

"Let you go? Of course. We're working on the arrangements as I speak—to *let you go* into the arms of Hezbollah."

For the first time since they met, David Weiss shows real fear. He is on the Iranian-backed terrorist organization's Top Ten list. They would like nothing more than to tear Weiss apart limb by limb. Weiss is not afraid of death, but he fears the slow torture and humiliation that Hezbollah would joyously inflict.

"Just kill me now, Gideon," Weiss says. "You are not a man who enjoys inflicting pain. You are a professional."

"Then you must do one thing. Call off your Kidon team. Instruct them not to interfere with my mission. Then I will kill you swiftly."

He hands Weiss the phone. Weiss makes a call and gives the order, then gives the phone back. "This will be my pennance for my friend Aviram," he says.

Gideon pushes Weiss's head toward his knees. Weiss can feel the icicle penetrating his lung, the sting of it, and then the spreading numbness that moves through his entire body in a surging, soothing swell. So warm, so peaceful...

"Take me to Dal Lake," Gideon says to the driver, handing him a fistful of Indian rupees. "Then drop my friend off at the nearest cemetery."

As the taxi approaches the southern shore of Dal Lake, near Hotel Khatarnakh, Gideon can make out the landed Bell 214, rotors still winding down. Rossi has come through. The CIA weapons onboard will come in handy.

He is at Ground Zero at last.

Chapter 60

The early morning light streaks through the dirty rear window of the taxi as it takes a right turn from Boulevard Road onto Hazratbal heading north. Despite the comfort of the houseboat and the watercolor beauty of the setting, Charlotte did not sleep well last night, and she imagines the others didn't either. All night her mind crackled with the anticipation of standing in the tomb of Jesus. Of being so close to saving her mother.

```
...locate the savior.
```

Her mother's message had been clear enough. But what will Charlotte do when she gets to Roza Bal? How will she obtain evidence to prove that Jesus is interred there? And even if it could be proven, what then?

```
When you have the proof, reply to this message.
```

This tomb has been known for many years, even if it had never been taken seriously by academics or religious scholars. Would the bones of Jesus still be there, or had they been plundered already by her adversaries? Even more frightening, is it possible that Roza Bal is an elaborate trap, and she is leading her family into it?

```
...be careful. There are many who will kill to
obtain what you seek.
```

Her gut tightens as she contemplates the unknown. But her attention suddenly shifts to a mob clogging the road ahead—protesters tentatively held at bay by fifty or sixty Indian soldiers. Some protesters hoist weapons defiantly into the air. How many, she wonders, also carry explosives?

"Do you want me to continue, miss?" the driver says with a tone that makes his own lack of enthusiasm clear. Instead, Charlotte motions him on. They have come too far to turn back now.

As the taxi approaches the vocal mob, a soldier stops the car. Charlotte rolls down her window and flashes her CCN credential.

"We cannot guarantee your safety if you enter the Old City," the soldier warns. "You should turn back and request an armed escort."

Charlotte looks down the road. She sees sandbagged bunkers with machine guns. Smoke rising into the air from a score of fires. Small bands of insurgents chanting themselves into a frenzy.

"Thank you, but no," Charlotte replies.

The soldier shrugs and waves the taxi on. There are hundreds of protesters—Kashmiris, Pakistanis, even a handful of Buddhist monks. They yell at each other. They taunt the uniformed soldiers.

Shots are fired. A chorus of screams echoes through the streets and people scatter, but it is unclear what has happened, or where. No bodies are visible.

"We should go back, miss," the nervous driver complains.

"How much farther?" Charlotte asks.

"Perhaps a mile."

"Keep going then."

Charlotte glances at Curt, who is shooting video through the open taxi window. Ever the photojournalist. She and Curt have been in similar circumstances before—in Africa, Kosovo, Iraq—but never with her son and father.

To hell with her father. Somehow he is the cause of her mother's disappearance, and probably Miriam's present difficulty as well. He deserves whatever he gets.

But Greg...

The unfolding scene, the treacherous gauntlet ahead, the view of Curt shooting through the window—it all brings back that terrifying day in Iraq when she and Curt were abducted by terrorists. Charlotte can taste the acid rising in her throat. Fear, perhaps. No, more like dread. Like tempting fate.

Hazatbal Road turns right, but the taxi stays left on Ganderbal. After nearly a mile, a narrow road veers off slightly to the right. The mob seems to prefer the main Ganderbal thoroughfare, drawn as to a parade. Only a few stray protesters roam this street, which is now separated from the main road by a Muslim cemetery.

"Mazar-e-Shouhda," the driver explains, giving the name of the place. "It is where martyrs for Islam rest. I hope the cemetery is not full—there will be more martyrs today. We are almost there."

The taxi drives another quarter mile. A minaret appears on the right, and the taxi stops. The driver looks across the street to his left and Charlotte follows his gaze. An unassuming rectangular white building with a green roof stares back at her. A green sign with white hand-painted lettering reads:

ZIARATH HAZRATI YOUZA ASOUPH

AND

SYED NASIR-U-DIN

Youza Asouph. *Yuz Asaf.*

Jesus.

"Let's go," Charlotte says, handing the driver enough rupees to reward him for the dangerous drive. The foursome emerges from the taxi, which immediately roars away.

"So this is it?" Curt says, raising the camera to his eye.

"It could be a shrine I guess," Charlotte says. "But who is this *Syed Nasir-u-Din* who's getting second billing?"

Thompson answers. "A fifth-century Muslim who looked after the tomb. He was also the descendant of a famous Imam. When he died, they buried him next to Yuz Asaf, or so the story goes. After a while, the locals began to think of him as a saint. He eventually became more revered than the mythic Yuz Asaf. Ask anyone here, and they probably can't tell you who Yuz Asaf was."

"There are two sets of remains in there?" Curt says. "So how do we tell the messiah from the crypt keeper?"

Charlotte ignores the questions. Doesn't hear them, actually. Standing in the street outside the tomb of Yuz Asaf, she feels suddenly exposed and vulnerable. Lacking faith, what other credential qualifies her for entrance into this sacred space? She is adrift on a spiritual sea but fails to counsel the stars for direction.

Her arms hang listless as dropped oars. She can only stare at the building. Her feet will not move, though her mother's life may depend on them.

In the distance, the sound of a machine gun stutters. Is Jesus, the Prince of Peace, buried in this land of intolerance and violence? Has his message been forgotten, just as the memory of Yuz Asaf has been replaced in the public's heart by the sweeper of his tomb?

Curt urges the group forward. "Let's not stand in the middle of the street, okay?"

Curt is shooting everything in sight. He is obsessed with surfaces—how things appear in the lens, not what they mean. He worries about how light strikes a face, not how a face can radiate light.

Charlotte turns toward him, envious of his detachment and objectivity. She used to be like that. It's what made her tops in her field. But now that something big is at stake, she has grown tentative. This is no time for reflection, she tells herself. It's time to locate the savior.

She motions to the others and marches to the south side of the shrine, finding an entrance chamber with a green wooden door. A pair of sneakers has been carefully set outside the door.

"Be reverent," Thompson says. "Someone is inside."

Charlotte opens the door and steps into the room followed by the others. Inside, a young Pakistani of about twenty is seated cross-legged on the floor with an open Qur'an on his lap. He looks up at Charlotte and the others as they quietly enter. He rises immediately and walks toward the door, apparently upset that his devotions have been interrupted.

"Alláhu Akhbar," the man says perfunctorily.

Charlotte nods but can't bring herself to repeat the Islamic expression as expected. She wonders if this Muslim has any idea that he has been paying respects to a Jew.

Charlotte enters. The spartan chamber is dim except for streaks of golden sunlight slanting through the eastern windows. The only decoration is a large Kashmiri carpet hanging on the far wall. In the center is a large green wooden box like a small room inside the larger chamber. White-trimmed glass windows surround it allowing a view inside.

Across the street, the young man who greeted Charlotte stares grimly at the shrine and makes a phone call. The time of waiting is over.

Inside the shrine, Charlotte peers through one of the smudged windows on the green box and sees a sarcophagus draped with a red cloth.

"My God, there it is!" Charlotte exclaims. Her heart begins to pound.

"I'm not so sure," Thompson says. "I've seen old photographs. Originally, intricate wooden fretwork surrounded the sarcophagus, which was quite deteriorated. Not like this. And the *colors!* Originally the shrine was blue and white—*Hebrew* colors. Now the blue has been replaced with the green of Islam. I'm sure the sarcophagus is an imitation."

"So we're too late?" Curt asks.

A new voice interrupts, deep and resonant. "By a few hundred years."

"Dr. Bhatt," Charlotte says, turning to see the Kashmiri carpet merchant standing in the doorway. "We were all hoping you were okay!"

"You brought to my humble store quite an adventure."

"Come to pay your respects?" Curt asks.

"Every day that I am in Srinagar, yes," Bhatt responds as he steps toward the group. "For me it is a kind of home. For almost two thousand years my family has been entrusted to care for this shrine."

Charlotte is astonished. "You're the custodian of the tomb of Jesus?"

"No more. Muslim radicals removed us from our hereditary role and appointed a local committee to renovate and look after the shrine. They didn't like the possibility that such a long-time object of veneration might be a Jew. They looted just about everything of historic value, including the original sarcophagus and its remains."

"So this one *is* a fake," Thompson says.

"It always has been," Bhatt replies.

The tumultuousness of this statement dashes Charlotte's hope of locating the savior. Suddenly despondent and angry, she stares at Dr. Bhatt as if he is personally to blame for centuries of deceit.

"Even before the body of Syed Nasir-u-Din was placed in the tomb," Bhatt continues, "the bones of Jesus had been removed. Below this floor is the original crypt. The building you are in was built over it. In that crypt, my family guarded the remains of Jesus for hundreds of years, laying the length of his sarcophagus East to West in the Hebrew tradition, not North to South as we Muslims align our dead. But then the crypt was filled in."

Charlotte is suddenly hopeful. "And the remains of Jesus—are they still down there, buried in the crypt?"

"I'm afraid not. But we rescued him, and hid him well." Dr. Bhatt grows agitated, glancing nervously at the windows.

"Just wait—wait a minute," Charlotte says. "You said that you moved the remains before anyone could take them. If that's true, then the bad guys don't have them yet."

"But they may think that they do," Bhatt says. "We substituted someone else for Jesus. There are many old bones in Kashmir. Who would know?"

Charlotte has lost track of Greg. She finds him inside the inner chamber. In the north-east corner of it, near the sarcophagus, he kneels by a stone slab. Charlotte enters the small room and looks down at the stone.

"The feet of Jesus," Greg says.

Carved into the slab are two footprints side by side. The soles of the bare feet clearly show healed-over wounds.

"Crucifixion wounds," Greg adds. And then he points out a faintly inscribed cross. Taking a deep breath, he stands and looks around the small window-lined inner chamber that surrounds him, scowling. "Like being in a big cage," he says.

"What—?"

Suddenly, Dr.Bhatt yells, "It's a trap. We have to get out of here."

The boy rushes out of the chamber, quickly followed by Charlotte. Thompson needs no encouragement to evacuate. He leads the small troupe.

As they scurry toward the door, Dr. Bhatt says, "If anything happens to me, Greg, the carpet reveals the location—"

He cannot finish.

As Thompson reaches to open the door, it swings open, striking him in the face. Seven men in ski masks barge in with automatic weapons. The leader barks orders in some foreign tongue. A second man grabs Charlotte and forces her to kneel. A third man roughly hauls Greg over to his mother. They have been culled from the herd.

Curt instinctively lunges for the third man, trying to protect the boy, but a fourth man raises his AK-47. In less than a second, ten rounds tear through Curt's body. It flies backward in a bloody tumble. Bullets shatter the glass windows of the inner chamber and shards fly everywhere.

Charlotte watches in horror. Greg flinches at the flurry of explosions from the automatic weapon. Thompson utters a prayer. Dr. Bhatt merely lowers his head, knowing that this violent act has sealed his fate. Once begun, an act of bloodlust is unstoppable.

The masked leader yells Pakistani curses at the fourth man, slaps him on the side of the head, obviously upset that the noise may have attracted attention. All of the terrorists begin to yell at each other until the leader steps forward and forces Thompson and Dr. Bhatt to their knees. He stomps to a position behind Thompson, whose entire body shudders in terror. He produces a long knife. Grabs a handful of hair. Lifts Thompson's chin, exposing his neck. Looks upward and excitedly recites what could be a prayer—an explanation to Allah, perhaps, of the need to execute this heretic.

Charlotte is screaming for the man to stop. She screams until a fist to the side of her head sends her reeling to the floor.

The man finishes his fervent prayer. His hand is shaking, the knife trembling. He moves the blade to Thompson's throat.

And then Greg speaks.

He repeats the leader's prayer word-for-word. From memory.

This stays the sweep of the blade. The leader, confused and frozen in place, stares incredulously at the boy.

Greg slowly walks toward the leader. No one stops him. They only stare at him as if a holy child has appeared among them.

The prayer is finished and Greg calmly says, "Do you speak English?"

"Somewhat," the leader says nervously.

"Is there no chance for repentance?"

The leader lowers the blade and cocks his head. What is this talk of repentance from this strange child who shows no fear?

"You want me to give this heretic a chance to repent?" The leader's English has a British tinge.

"No, you do not understand me."

Greg stands so close that the leader could slice off the boy's head with one sweep of the blade. Greg can hear his grandfather panting, can smell the foul breath of the leader.

"It is *you* who is offered repentance," Greg says.

The leader is speechless.

Still as a statue, he stares at Greg. And then his head explodes.

The blood spurts onto Greg and Thompson, onto Dr. Bhatt. Greg falls to the floor, believing the chunk of skull that struck him was a bullet.

Shouts, gunfire, screams of pain. Shadows and stomping. Prayers and curses. All at once.

Hands on Greg's fallen body.

"Boy, are you all right?"

Greg sits up. He is in a pool of Pakistani gore. Glancing around, he can see Thompson seated, leaning against a brown-haired American in a

Kevlar vest. Alongside Thompson lies Dr. Bhatt, the source of a Nile of blood. He is dead.

Panicky, Greg stands and whirls, finds Charlotte alive, massaging her jaw. He rushes over to her. Charlotte shakes the fuzziness out of her brain and wraps her arms around her son, sobbing in relief, crying with bewilderment.

"Charlotte and Greg Ansari?"

The two of them look up at a tall American in a business suit.

"Sorry about the mess, Are you okay?" the man asks.

Charlotte and Greg both nod, though they're not really sure.

"My name is William Wyatt. I'm director of the Central Intelligence Agency. I need you to come with me right now."

They stand up. Charlotte is wobbly, but then she sees her father on the floor. He is spattered by blood and bits of human tissue. She rushes over and throws her arms around him, for a moment forgetting her grudge.

An agent walks up to director Wyatt and says, "We have two agents killed, sir. Three of us are unharmed, plus yourself."

"Curt's dead," Thompson whispers to Charlotte. "And Dr. Bhatt."

"I know. And you're hurt!"

"No—someone else's blood, I'm pretty sure."

"What happened?"

"The CIA saved us. But I'm not sure we're better off."

"Charlotte!" Wyatt shouts at her. "We are leaving now! All of us."

Thompson looks up at his daughter. "I think that we've just jumped from the frying pan—"

Two agents help Thompson to his feet. They rudely begin to usher Charlotte and her father out the door.

The boy looks up at Wyatt and says, "Is there no chance for repentance?"

"I'm not looking for them to repent," Wyatt says, grinning at the boy's odd statement.

"No—*you*." Greg says.

Wyatt stares at the boy, failing to understand.

And then he hears muffled grunts and a faint scream. He and the agent beside him turn to see Gideon standing in the doorway pointing a pistol at them.

"I spared the two outside. They saved Charlotte and Greg," Gideon says.

The agent next to Wyatt tries to pull a pistol from his belt and takes a bullet in the head. Wyatt watches him collapse onto the floor.

"Unnecessary," Gideon says. "As for you—my supervisor doesn't want me to kill any more of our clients, so please don't be stupid."

Gideon walks over to Wyatt and binds the man's hands with a plastic tie. Charlotte and Thompson come back into the room.

"So here's the deal," Gideon tells Wyatt. "If you promise to call off your spooks and let me do my job, I won't kill you. Fail to make that promise, and it's out of my hands. Frankly, I'm hoping that you tell me to fuck off, because then I can settle things right here."

"All right," Wyatt says. "It's a deal."

"Scouts honor?"

"You have my word, dammit!"

"Naturally, I know you're lying to save your skin. But that's all right, because once we know you haven't kept your word, it'll be open season on director Wyatt. Of course, if I'm wrong, then someday maybe we can be partners again."

Gideon strikes Wyatt with the butt of the pistol. Hard. Wyatt crumples.

A new voice interrupts. "Impressive! Now please drop your weapon."

Gideon drops his gun and turns slowly around. Standing in the doorway, Weiss' Indian contractor Layak points a mean-looking pistol at Gideon, then waves the barrel downward, signaling the Sicarii to kneel. Layak has entered quietly, stepping in front of Charlotte as if the woman is no threat, but keeping Thompson and Greg in front of him. He steps over a body, moving closer to Gideon while keeping a safe distance.

Gideon stares at the man's eyes and sees fear. "I'm kneeling in front of you," he says, "but you are the frightened one."

"I've heard stories about you Sicarii. So tell me, can you really dodge a bullet? Or kill a man with a piece of paper?"

"Paper cuts can be fatal," Gideon says, seeing Charlotte slowly bend to retrieve a 9mm Glock from a downed CIA agent. "Maybe we can negotiate something here. What do you want?"

"I'm a contractor, like you," Layak says. "My reputation is on the line, like yours. I was hired to find what Charlotte is searching for, and I'm delighted that you led me to it. It's in the sarcophagus, I assume."

"You know, we contractors should stick together. You want it? Help yourself. No need to kill anywhere here."

"Except you," Layak says. "Since the untimely death of Mr. Weiss, I'm sure there's a bounty on your head. Dead or alive."

"I vote for *alive*!" Gideon says.

Charlotte stands with her feet apart, arms extended, the pistol steadily pointed at Layak's back. A shooter's practiced stance. Clearly, she has done this before. She glances at the gore spread throughout the room, at Curt's body soaked in his own fluids, at her blood-spattered son cradled by her trembling father. She looks back at Layak.

"Sorry," Layak says, taking aim at Gideon. "It's just business."

"Drop your gun now or take a bullet in the back!" Charlotte says.

Layak is startled at first, but then smiles. *It's only the woman!* If she's going to be this way, he'll have to take her out.

In a blur, he wheels. Aims with deadly accuracy at Charlotte's body. But before his finger can pull the trigger, a bullet explodes into his chest. Another into his hip. He flies backward. Charlotte steps toward the flailing man and fires again. Then three more times. He lands on the floor. She steps over to his lifeless body. Looms over it. Points the gun and fires again.

"Goddam terrorists!" she says.

Gideon gets to his feet. "Israeli contractor, actually. Where'd you learn to shoot like that?"

Charlotte's arms go limp, the gun dangling at her side. "Why is everyone surprised? You travel to dangerous places, you learn to take care of yourself."

She marches over to Greg and puts a hand on his shoulder. He looks up at her face and sees not the soft look of a mother, but the hard, determined expression of a warrior. He has never seen this look before and wonders where his mother went.

Charlotte turns to her father. "Curt's dead," she says. "We'll never find the bones of Jesus now. We'll never save Mom."

Her whole body sags under the weight of failure. The exhilaration of revenge has evaporated. Turning to Gideon, she says, "And I thought you were protecting *us*. Hah!" This final grunt is drenched with disdain.

She slowly walks over to Curt's body, kneeling down beside him. The camera is still in his hand, pointing toward the door, red light gleaming.

It is still switched on.

Greg walks across the room and stares up at the large Kashmiri carpet hanging on the wall.

"I recommend you leave now," Gideon instructs. "With all the noise in here… Take Wyatt's car—here's the keys." He throws them to Thompson.

Charlotte grabs the camera and then begins to gather up weapons. She turns to her father, who is motionless. "Dad, search everyone for ammunition! I'll get the guns."

Dazed, Thompson looks up at Charlotte and then begins the search.

Gideon watches Charlotte, who has snapped into some kind of command mode. She is a flurry of activity.

He leaves the room to find a more distant vantage point. It's his job to protect, not assist.

Greg reaches for the carpet, grabs its fringed bottom and tugs gently. Nothing. Loops on the back of the carpet hang from an eight foot silk-wrapped rod, which is supported by metal brackets bolted to the wall. Holding the fringed bottom again, Greg shakes the carpet like he is snapping the dirt from it. A wave rolls up the surface and pops the rod out of its iron embrace. The carpet falls and the rod falls onto the floor. Greg quickly rolls the carpet around it.

"We can go now," he says. "We have what we came for."

Chapter 61

Charlotte and her family sit sullenly amid the plunder as the shikara glides calmly toward their houseboat. None of the oarsmen questions the bloodied appearance of the three Americans or their motives for carrying a boatload of arms across the placid water. Not even the slightest twitch of anxiety or curiosity. In this country, at this time, there is perhaps nothing unusual about the American's conduct.

Chandraka, the houseboy, greets the boat and alone expresses dismay at their condition—especially at their cargo. "My dear friends," he says, "it has not been a good day?" A classic Kashmiri understatement.

"Depends," Charlotte says. "Here, take these guns."

Chandraka grabs an armful of weapons from Charlotte. The whites of his eyes show all around the irises. "Shall I put them in your room, Ma'am?" He turns his head and holds the guns like an armful of rotting fish.

"Anywhere'll do," she replies, stepping out of the boat and grabbing one end of the carpet roll. The other end is secured by Greg.

Inside the houseboat, Charlotte finds a pile of weapons dumped on the floor. She picks up an old Uzi, inspects it, then finds a clip of ammunition that seems to fit. "I've seen this used in Africa," she says. "Ah, there it goes." She manages to re-arm the weapon. "Dad, you stand guard. Here's the safety. If there's trouble, click it off, point the gun and pull the trigger. A lot of bullets come out all at once. I'll be in the shower."

Thompson holds the Uzi uneasily as he turns toward the doorHe imagines a small army of terrorists pouring down the short stairway from the deck. "Just hurry up," he says.

Greg unrolls the carpet. It is splotched with blood. Compared to the fine hanging carpets in the houseboat, this one looks like the result of a dumpster dive.

"Truly magnificent workmanship," Chandraka says, as if the stains had suddenly vanished. "Pure silk... and very finely woven. In all the world, only Kashmiris can make a carpet like this. But the pattern—it is not a typical Kashmiri design."

"**N**o weapons, no money, no communications," Wyatt says angrily. "I felt naked out there, looking for a friendly among a lot of unfriendlies."

"But he didn't kill you, sir," Allison replies.

"Got one good lump on the head, though. So here I am, with an Indian patrol on Hazratbal. Had to have Singh vouch for me on the phone to convince our compatriots here that I'm who I say I am. Might as well have been killed, for the humiliation. What've you got there?"

"Predator images show they left Roza Bal in your car, sir. Parked it near Dal Lake. We know what houseboat they're on. We could easily take it out."

"The houseboat? Get a grip, Allison. We don't need an international incident. We've made too much noise here already. Send the details to our Srinagar office. We'll launch a nighttime mission, very quiet this time."

"And what about the Sicarii, sir?"

"Now it's personal."

Showered and dressed in their last changes of clothes, Charlotte and her family sit in front of the bloodied carpet that Chandraka has hung on a wall in place of an unsullied carpet.

Charlotte cradles the Uzi like a baby in her arms. Chandraka brings them a platter of vegetables, cheese, bread and goat meat. It is gone in minutes.

Greg is mesmerized by the carpet, his eyes fluttering slightly as the design elements filter into his brain, sifting and sorting themselves into intricate relationships and possible meanings. His face flickers and twitches as new combinations emerge in his consciousness.

"Chandraka pointed out the centerpiece," Thompson explains to Charlotte. "You see, in the center of the design—a lamb. Not a typical Kashmiri carpet motif. And Greg noticed a long vertical object running up each side of the carpet."

"Like a walking stick." Charlotte cocks her head to study the objects more thoroughly. "A shepherd's staff, maybe? Seems to be tiny leaves growing out of the staff."

"The lamb is a clear reference to Jesus, the Great Shepherd. Who's also the sacrificial lamb." Thojmpson's eyes dart over the design. "I think the staff on each side is the rod of Moses and Aaron."

"You mean the rod that turned into a serpent?"

"And the rod that smote the rock and caused it to pour out water. And turned a river into blood. And brought about a plague of locusts. Probably the first magic wand."

"I don't get it," Charlotte admits. "If the carpet is about Jesus, why include the staff of Moses and Aaron? What's the connection?"

Taking this as an invitation for another lecture, Thompson says, "In the Bible, God instructs Moses to make twelve sturdy rods out of wood—that's one rod for each of the twelve tribes of Israel. And then God tells Moses to inscribe on each rod the name of the current head of each tribe. Specifically, he tells Moses to write Aaron's name on the rod of his tribe, the Levites, and then to put all twelve rods into the tabernacle. God then promises to choose one of these tribes by making its rod blossom. The next morning, wouldn't you know, the rod of Aaron, sitting in for the tribe of Levi, was not only budding and blooming, but yielding almonds.

"From that time forward, the priests of Israel have descended from the Levites—the tribe of Levi—with direct descendants of Aaron being the highest ranking. The Bible refers to Aaron's rod as the *rod of God*. And according to tradition, the rod was passed down from Aaron to David and then disappeared from all records. Some believe that Joseph, a descendant of David and the stepfather of Jesus, came into possession of the rod and gave it to his son, who used it for some of his miracles, like healing and raising Lazarus from the dead. Perhaps Jesus brought it with him. If I remember correctly, old records about Roza Bal mention the rod of Jesus being there."

"*Assa-i-Issa,* the stick of Jesus!" Chandraka says. "I know of this relic. It was removed from the Tomb of Yuz Asaf many years ago."

Thompson is intrigued. "Do you know where it went?"

"Of course. It is at Ziarat-i-Baba Zain-ud-din Rishi."

"And what is that?"

"Sorry. It is a Buddhist shrine built over a cave where Yuz Asaf once lived. Assa-i-Issa is preserved there. I have seen it myself."

"So, even if the carpet is a map directing us to this shrine, where do we look when we get there?" Charlotte asks. Suddenly she stands, checks the action of her Glock and strides for the stairway. "I'm going to check outside. They could have a drone flying around watching our every move."

As Greg continues to study the intricate designs of the carpet, the thread of this conversation weaves and warps into his mind. It troubles him. He has been looking for a code in the design, or maybe in the knotting of the…

Of course! It strikes him suddenly, like he was whacked on the head by the stick of Jesus.

"Get it down!" he shouts.

Chandraka, who is much taller than Greg, pushes the hanging rod out of its brackets and lowers the carpet to the floor.

"Did you figure it out, Greg?" Thompson asks expectantly. "Is it those little lozenge shapes around the edge? I've had my eye on them."

Greg ignores his grandfather. Hurriedly, he pulls the silk-enshrouded rod from the hanging loops. "That Buddhist shrine has a counterfeit relic," he proclaims.

Thompson looks confused, then enlightened.

Together, Greg and Thompson tear apart the rod's silk covering like children unwrapping a Christmas present. Inside the shiny packaging is a wooden rod. The rod of Moses and Aaron. The rod of Jesus. It is just over eight feet long and tapers from nearly two inches in diameter to a little more than an inch where the end is capped with a metal ferrule. The wood is hard and dark, brownish-black with a faint greenish patina.

Thompson detects an almost imperceptible inscription on the fat end. "This could be Aaron's name, written here by Moses."

He wheels and shouts for Charlotte, who skips down the stairs excitedly. "Did he crack the code?" she asks.

"Look, Char. It was in the carpet. The rod it was hanging on—it's the rod of Jesus!"

Charlotte does not share his excitement. In fact, she looks disappointed. "Fine, so we'll give it to a museum. But unless this is made out of Christ's thigh bone, how the hell does it help us find his remains? By my count, we're almost out of time, guys. What else have you got?"

Thompson slumps into a chair and shrugs timidly, the balloon of exhilaration suddenly deflated.

Charlotte is frustrated. Angry. Her scorching gaze reaches Greg, unfairly accusing him of failing to decrypt the inscrutable carpet.

"The rod is the key," he says flatly.

"The key?" Charlotte steps closer to her son.

Thompson leans forward and asks, "The key to what?"

"To finding the bones of Jesus. The real ones."

Greg's confidence is contagious. Charlotte and Thompson glance at each other expectantly, waiting for more details.

"We'll need tools," Greg says. "A hammer. A pick-axe would be better."

Charlotte senses a plan coming together. Even with the right tools, they'll still need a way to leave the houseboat undetected in case they're being observed.

"Chandraka," she says, "how well do you know your neighbors?"

"Sir, I have the houseboat under surveillance," Allison says. She is hunched down in front of a large monitor that displays a top-down image of the Desire and four or five houseboats on either side. The image rotates slightly with the movement of the Predator overhead.

"We're in position on the south shore, six of us," Wyatt replies. "In about an hour it'll be dark enough to move in. What's going on?"

It has been years since he worked in the field, and despite his humiliation by Gideon, he likes the surge of adrenalin, the quickening pulse. It makes him feel alive again, to be part of an operation. To have his life on the line. He can appreciate why Charlotte Ansari turned down many offers to anchor her own news show from the safety of CCN's Boston studios and continued instead to be a field correspondent in many of the world's most dangerous locations.

He hates the thought of abducting Charlotte and her son and caging her in some hellish rendition facility in some obscure corner of the globe, essentially obliterating her future. For a vibrant, headstrong woman like that, better that she were killed. Perhaps, if he has the chance, out of professional courtesy...

"This is very odd, sir."

"What's odd?"

"Well, it's almost like a party. People from the other boats—they're moving about, from boat to boat. Carrying things—food, maybe? Some are boarding the target boat, sir… and now one, no two are leaving it. There's maybe fifteen, twenty people milling around."

"Damn! It's a diversion. Can you identify these people? Can you see Charlotte?"

"We're zoomed in all the way sir, but it's hard to tell from our top view."

"Greg! Look for Greg, he's a kid. Shorter."

"A few kids down there, sir."

"I don't think Charlotte's having an open house, Allison, so find her and Greg. Keep searching, they'll be out in the open at some point. Just making it tough for us to pick them out."

"Well, that's interesting."

"What?"

"Everyone is now going back to their houseboats—no, wait! They're all getting into little boats, loading them up with stuff."

Allison continues to provide play-by-play analysis of the Predator images. Minute by minute, director Wyatt grows more frustrated.

"Okay, now the little boats are leaving the houseboats," Allison reports. "They seem to be heading in different directions. Maybe ten all together."

Wyatt watches through binoculars. "I don't have enough men to intercept them all," he says. "We'll have to target some of them and hope for the best."

Wyatt communicates specific instructions via radio to the other five agents. At best, they can seize six of the boats.

The ten shikaras land along a mile-long stretch of the south shore, each of them immediately intercepted by an agent wielding an automatic weapon.

As Wyatt waits for his target to reach shore, Agent 1 checks in: "No targets in this one," he reports.

Wyatt's quarry finally docks. Through his binoculars he can see that the two occupants are Kashmiri. No need to frighten them.

The other four agents check in. No targets found.

"Anything happening on the Desire, Allison?" Wyatt asks.

"Nada. All's quiet, sir. Maybe they were in the other boats. Wait—hold on. I just pulled back and there's two people unlocking the door to your SUV. Getting in. Starting to pull out."

"All right!" Wyatt says.

He orders his agents up to Boulevard Road. As the black SUV pulls out of a hotel parking lot and begins driving west, Wyatt and two agents march into the center of the road. Wyatt holds up his hand. The other agents hoist their automatic weapons threateningly.

The SUV swerves around them, starts to move away.

Wyatt fires, hits the back right tire, and the vehicle veers off the road, sparks flying from the rear wheel. Within seconds, the agents are at the vehicle, weapons pointed at the occupants. Looking inside the open driver's window, Wyatt sees a fifty-year-old Kashmiri man, and next to him an Indian woman.

Wyatt opens the door, plucks the key from the ignition and pulls the man from the vehicle. "Who gave you the key?" he demands.

Chandraka looks at Wyatt and says, "A nice American woman. She gave me money and asked me to fill the car with petrol because the owner would soon be taking it for a long drive. Put the keys on the visor, she said."

Wyatt violently slams the vehicle's door shut.

"Will you be seeing her again?"

"I don't think so. She and two others left in a shikara. She said they have to catch a flight."

I'll bet, Wyatt thinks.

The other agents converge on the SUV. Wyatt gives them a palms up gesture of futility and speaks to Langley. "They slipped through. We're closing up here until we get a line on them."

D usk is settling quickly. Through the zoom lens of the CCN video camera located in the front window of a neighboring houseboat named Chelsea, Charlotte watches six armed Americans climb into three vehicles, one of them Wyatt's SUV. The vehicles speed off, kicking up gravelly plumes and leaving Chandraka and the maid from the Chelsea standing in the road.

With a grin, Chandraka turns his face toward the houseboat and gives Charlotte a dramatic thumbs-up.

In thirty minutes it will be dark. Charlotte, Thompson and Greg will slip into a shikara with their tools and weapons, quietly glide across the dark water, and climb into a waiting taxi that Chandraka is about to wrangle.

And then they will liberate the remains of Jesus Christ.

God willing.

Chapter 62

Chandraka has insisted on coming along. Now that he has experienced the exhilaration of espionage, he is no longer content with the mundane duties of a houseboy.

With a fistful of money taken from the pockets of her defeated adversaries at Roza Bal, Charlotte bribes the taxi driver into undertaking the dangerous journey back to the shrine and the gruesome scene of the crime including Curt's body. Until now, she has not allowed herself to think about Curt's horrible death. Events have forced her to focus on survival and the achievement of her mission. But now, the possibility that she will once again see Curt's body lying in a heap—it's too much. She fights back tears. It will do no good to show weakness now; Thompson and Greg need her to be strong.

Surely, someone would have come to Roza Bal to pay respects and found the carnage, reporting it to someone else. Or the sounds of the battle would have attracted attention. Or Wyatt would have described the incident—his own version, of course—to the Indian authorities. Certainly the shrine will have been cleaned up, the bodies hauled out, the crime scene sealed off.

So, what will become of Curt's body? Will they find his press credential and notify CCN? Perhaps this has already been done; Charlotte has not watched TV for a while.

A new and frightening thought invades her consciousness. Since the slaughter at the shrine almost certainly has been discovered and investigated, returning to Roza Bal carries much greater peril. How many criminals have been caught returning to the scene of the crime?

At a military checkpoint, Charlotte is about to show her CCN credential to gain quick access through the barrier, but suddenly reconsiders. Wyatt certainly would have alerted the Indian military to watch for CCN personnel. Too dangerous.

"Hide your faces!" she instructs Thompson and Greg. "Don't let them see you're Americans. Chandraka, tell them you are taking your family home."

Chandraka nods and does what he is told. The Indian gatekeeper argues with Chandraka about the dangers of entering the Old City, but Chandraka is unyielding. They are allowed to pass.

The southern end of Hazratbal Road just beyond the checkpoint is relatively quiet. A few men with automatic weapons strut about eyeing the taxi suspiciously, but they let the vehicle drive by unmolested. In the distance, Charlotte can hear a gun battle waging. Rapid-fire shots crack and pop, sounding like the Fourth of July fireworks finale on Lake Minnetonka back home. Suddenly, a thunderous explosion rattles the taxi. A red glow emerges from behind flat buildings ahead. Black smoke ascenda into the heavens.

Within minutes, the taxi stops outside Roza Bal.

There is no police cordon here, no yellow crime scene tape surrounding the shrine. No congregation of curious residents. No indication at all that a massacre had occurred that morning inside the unremarkable white structure.

The unceasing battle across town may be the perfect diversion.

Chandraka tells the driver to wait for them, but once all the taxi's occupants have exited, the vehicle speeds away. Chandraka shouts a Kashmiri curse.

Charlotte carries the video camera in her left hand and a snub-nosed shotgun in her right. A 9mm Sig Sauer pistol is jammed into her waistband. Thompson has a pistol too; the larger automatic weapons had been too intimidating for him. He also carries his ever-present leather satchel. Chandraka carries two hammers, a hatchet, and a crow bar, the only tools available on the boat. Greg carries a flashlight and the rod of Jesus.

They approach the shrine's door. Light emerges from the windows. Fearing that someone may be inside, Charlotte halts the others and quietly puts down the camera. Raising the scattergun, she opens the door quickly and steps through, sweeping the room with the barrel of the shotgun as she has seen it done in countless TV police shows.

Two men are seated cross-legged on the floor. Except for them, the room is empty. The bodies have been removed, the broken glass cleared, the gore mopped up. Multiple bloody stains are still visible on the floor and the walls. Startled, the two men look up.

"Sushil? Ashok?" Charlotte is clearly surprised at finding Dr. Bhatt's son and his friend in the shrine.

"**W**hat is it Allison?" director Wyatt replies. He is in a sour mood.
"Sir, I thought it prudent to surveil the shrine this evening. Infrared pictures are lousy, but I just detected four individuals entering the building. These guys are carrying objects of some kind. Could be weapons. I thought you should know."

Wyatt's mood is suddenly sweetened. If this is Charlotte and family, what would they be doing back at Roza Bal? The only thing that would draw them back to this grim location, he suspects, is if…

"**C**harlotte!" Sushil says. He leaps to his feet, followed by Ashok.
"It's all right!" she says to the others, and they enter the shrine behind her. Seeing his Kashmiri friends, Thompson races over and embraces them. Greg watches passively.

"I'm sorry about your father," Thompson says to Sushil, whose eyes are red with grief.

Sushil nods. "We were called this morning. The committee didn't want to clean up the mess, so they called us. For a very long time, our family looked after the shrine and…"

"This morning, your father told us about your family's connection to the shrine," Charlotte says.

Sushil turns to her. "This morning? But—were you here when—?"

"Yes," Thompson replies, "we were here when your father was killed. And Curt."

"It's our fault," Charlotte says.

Sushil looks at her, confused by her remark.

"We came here looking for the remains of Jesus, but it was a trap," Charlotte explains. "If we had not come, your father and Curt would still be alive. I'm so sorry, Sushil."

Charlotte stands there with a pistol in her belt, a shotgun in her right hand, and tears in her eyes.

Ashok takes the weapon from her hand, then takes her hand and soothingly massages the back of it with his thumb. "Charlotte," he says gently, "you seem to be a lightning rod for trouble. What do you know about the remains of Jesus?"

Charlotte withdraws her hand. She needs to maintain the appearance of strength and independence. "Your father told us that the genuine relics were separated from Nasir-whats-his name's bones long ago and hidden away."

"It's true," Sushil says.

"So as family, you must know the location," Thompson suggests.

"Unfortunately, no," Sushil says. "We know that the hiding place was changed from time to time. When I was a small boy, I remember that my father once brought the remains home because he feared that enemies were close to finding them. That was about the time when this shrine underwent major renovations. I remember that he carefully moved the remains from a clay jar and placed them into a metal box."

"You actually saw the bones of Jesus?" Charlotte exclaims.

"Yes, of course. For centuries our family was charged with guarding them. The bones, as you can imagine, are small fragments now, mostly dust. My father sealed them in the box and told me that he would hide them in a new place. I wanted to know where, but he said only the patriarch of the family could know, I suppose for security reasons.

"Over the next few months he had the family make a grand carpet from his own design. He told me that if anything ever happened to him, I should look for the carpet because it concealed the new hiding place. Then he hung the carpet in the shrine so I never had to go looking for it."

"And did you figure out the location?" Charlotte asks.

"Never. I've spent countless hours staring at that carpet, trying to decipher its message, but the location still eludes me. For a time I thought it pointed to a shrine above a cave where the rod of Jesus is displayed, but if it is there, I don't know the exact location. And now the carpet is missing. I'm afraid the hiding place may be lost forever."

Ashok has been studying Chandraka, who is still holding the tools. "Charlotte," he says, "may I ask why your friend has brought hammers to Roza Bal?"

"To find the remains, Ashok," she says. "We think they're here."

Sushil reacts instantly. "Impossible! What would make you think that?"

"Your father told us that the carpet *reveals* the location. So we took the carpet with us this morning. We all saw the symbols of the rod of Jesus and came to the same conclusion you did—that the remains must be somewhere at or near that museum. But then Greg made a startling discovery. Hand it to me, Greg."

Greg hands the rod to his mother, who holds it up.

"May I present the rod of Jesus—the genuine article."

Sushil and Ashok approach the rod reverently but astonished.

"You discovered it where?" Sushil asks.

"It was the rod that the the carpet was hanging from," Thompson responds, "beautifully concealed in a silk wrapping."

"But why does this lead you to believe the remains are here?" Ashok asks.

"Greg made the connection. The carpet was not pointing us to the shrine above the cave. It was telling us that the remains would be found where the rod of Jesus was located. Right here. Your father told us that the carpet *revealed* the location. And it did—when we removed it."

Charlotte marches to the far wall. Bloody spatters surround a clean rectangular space where the carpet once hung.

"The remains must be right here, inside this wall," she says. "Sushil, you said that your father brought home the relic about the same time that renovations were being made. Isn't it possible that he hid the bones of Jesus right here in this shrine?"

The entire assemblage of relic seekers stand before the wall, staring at the blank space, wondering—hoping.

It is eerily quiet.

"The shooting has stopped," Chandraka says. "The battle must be over."

"Our diversion has expired," Charlotte adds. "Quickly, we must open up this wall."

Ashok takes the shotgun and walks outside to stand guard. Thompson hands his pistol to Sushil. "Here, you know how to use it."

Charlotte hands the video camera to Greg. "Shoot everything, son. Don't stop. If we find the relic, this will document the chain of evidence."

Charlotte and Thompson each take a hammer and Sushil grabs the hatchet. They begin breaking up the wall. Using the crow bar, Chandraka pries loose inch-thick chunks of plaster. Inside the wall, as expected, is a hollow chamber. Charlotte plunges her arm through an opening, searching for the metal box.

Nothing.

"More!" she says. And the team begins busting up more of the wall.

"Quiet!" The voice is Ashok's from outside the door. "An army vehicle."

For a long minute, the team stands motionless, weapons drawn.

"All clear, but hurry!" Ashok says.

The hammers shatter the plaster and the hatchet slices through the lath beneath. A gaping hole is opening up. As it opens upward, the hammers suddenly strike something hard, something impenetrable. Prying away the plaster reveals a stone ledge.

"It might be what the metal box is sitting on," Charlotte says. Frantically, she starts to pound away the wall above the ledge, and suddenly she hears the hopeful sound of hammer on metal.

The box! It must be.

The crow bar tears away more of the wall, revealing a small metal box about eighteen inches long and a foot wide. Sushil pulls it out, scratching his fingers in the process, and then sets it on the floor. The box is heavy with a sturdy lock. He lowers it to the floor, crouching for a closer look. Charlotte and Thompson kneel beside him.

"Anyone have a key?" Charlotte asks sarcastically, fingering her hammer.

"I've been waiting years for this," Sushil says, removing a pendant from around his neck. The pendant is decorated with Arabic calligraphy. It opens to reveal a small key.

"Every family member has one," Sushil explains.

He places the key into the lock and turns. The top of the box opens. In the dim light of the tomb of Jesus, Christ's remains become manifest. Small pieces of skull. Fragments of bone. And dust, just as Sushil had described.

Greg continues to shoot everything.

"It is my sacred duty to guard these remains," Sushil says solemnly. "Thank you Charlotte. And Greg. Now I must take them to a new home. They must never fall into the wrong hands. Of all people, you must know the danger."

"But I need this to save my mother."

Sushil places his hand tenderly on Charlotte's. "The loss of my own father is still fresh in my mind. This relic cost me his life. It is very hard, I know, but this is more important than your mother. I will not be the first one, in all the generations of our family, to let even one particle of holy dust escape our guardianship. Certainly you can understand."

"Sushil, please! Just one fragment—"

Sushil abruptly cuts her off with a wide sweep of his hand and pulls the box closer.

Spurned, Charlotte sits back on her heels for moment, then impulsively draws the pistol from her belt, pointing it at Sushil. "No, *you* don't understand. This is my mother's life. We've been through a lot to find this."

Thompson stares at his daughter. "Think about this, Charlotte. Ashok has protected us with his life. If the relic belongs to anyone, it's him."

Charlotte grips the gun with both hands now because her hands are trembling. She glances at Greg, who continues to shoot video. Thompson extends a hand, puts it on top of the pistol and pushes it down. Embarrassed now by her actions, Charlotte does not resist.

"I'm sorry, Sushil," she says, studying her scuffed knees.

Ashok races into the room and Sushil rises to a standing position, instinctively readying his gun. "Quickly, we must leave!" Ashok yells. "Three military vehicles are coming."

Greg is still shooting video.

"You can stop now," Charlotte instructs Greg.

Sushil closes the box, picks it up, and heads for the door ahead of the others. Suddenly, he stops and turns. "I wish I could stay to protect you, but—" He looks down at the box, then turns and sprints from the shrine.

Charlotte and her companions are not far behind. Thompson carries with him the leather satchel and the wooden rod.

Outside the shrine, Ashok intercepts them. "I recommend that you tell the soldiers you are a news correspondent. Probably they will escort you to safety."

"Actually, I think they'll escort us right into the hands of the CIA. We've got to make it back without them."

"Then I will protect you," Ashok says. He pushes the group across the street and into the dark Muslim cemetery where they crouch in a deep shadow.

"Do you know where Sushil will hide the relic?" Charlotte asks him.

"Only he knows. I am just a friend, not family."

"Do you have a cell phone, Ashok?" He does. "Can I use it?"

Ashok hands the phone to Charlotte, who turns to her son. "Greg, do you remember Herb Rossi's number?"

Of course he does. Charlotte punches in the number.

Three military vehicles pull up outside Roza Bal. Soldiers begin to surround the shrine.

Herb answers the call.

"Herb, thank God. It's Charlotte Ansari. I'm in a hurry, so please listen. We're in a bit of a jam in Srinagar. By any chance, are you and your chopper in the neighborhood?" Thompson and the others anxiously look on as Charlotte listens. "Lucky for us!" she says finally. "Let me put someone on who can tell you where to meet us."

Ashok takes the phone. "I'm going to send you to the south end of a cemetery in the Old City. I have GPS on my phone, so we'll call you..." There is a pause, and then he says, "Fine."

Turning to Charlotte, Ashok explains, "Your friend says he knows where we are."

Charlotte touches the small lump in her chest. She knows what the message means. Gideon is with Herb Rossi and is tracking her location.

"He says he's just a mile from here. Let's go."

Her guardian angel.

As the others begin to follow Ashok through the large cemetery, she stops and looks back at Roza Bal, her hopes dashed. Losing the remains of Jesus has doomed her mother. Staring grimly at the desecrated shrine, she sees Wyatt's SUV pull up alongside the military vehicles.

It doesn't take Charlotte long to catch up to her companions.

Allison's voice is shrill. "Six individuals have left the shrine, sir. Five are moving through a large open tract of land to the west..."

"The cemetery," Wyatt replies. "How far are they?"

"They're about a quarter of the way across."

Wyatt turns to the Indian captain who stands alongside him. "They're crossing the cemetery," he says. "Send two vehicles and half your men to the west end. We'll flush them toward you. But don't kill the woman or the boy."

The soldiers, collaborating with the CIA agents, enter the east end of the cemetery with flashlights and readied weapons. Charlotte can hear the faint thwack-thwack-thwack of Herb's chopper.

Thompson stumbles, painfully bruising his leg, but Ashok helps him to his feet. They keep going, running now, hoping to converge on the chopper before the soldiers find them.

"The soldiers are driving to the west end," Chandraka says, pointing toward two military vehicles racing down Hazratbal.

"Trying to cut us off from the other side," Ashok explains.

The sound of the chopper is louder now. Charlotte looks up and can see its lights. It is descending rapidly toward the center of the cemetery.

A rapid series of gunshots stutter. The fugitives flinch. Ashok can see muzzle flashes. The soldiers are getting close.

"They're firing at the helicopter!" Ashok says. "Hurry."

The chopper sets down about twenty yards from the group and the door flies opens. A man jumps out holding an automatic weapon. Charlotte and the others sprint toward the chopper then stop in fear.

The man with the automatic weapon is an Indian soldier!

"Hurry up!" the soldier orders.

Even with the loud whine of the rotor, Charlotte recognizes the voice of Gideon. She motions the others forward.

Ashok pushes Thompson through the open door, and then he and Chandraka help Charlotte. Greg needs no help; he flies through the door like a bird, followed by the surprisingly agile Chandraka.

"Get in!" Gideon yells to Ashok.

"You are the *prith* that Sushil told me about," Ashok says.

"I said get in!" Gideon aims his weapon at the Kashmiri, who quickly climbs into the helicopter.

Gideon slams the door closed and pounds it. The helicopter rises quickly. Shots ring out as the chopper banks sharply over the two military vehicles at the west end of the cemetery.

"I said don't shoot!" The voice comes from the east, and Gideon recognizes it as Director Wyatt's.

The soldiers and agents converge on the landing zone seconds too late. In the darkness, Gideon is easily taken for one of the Indian soldiers. He endures a torrent of cursing by a CIA agent, and then slowly makes his way closer to the director, who motions for everyone to return to the shrine.

"Allison," Wyatt says into his mouthpiece, "they got away." He stands rooted to the spot as if staying right here will somehow change the result. "Did any of them split off?"

"Not that I could see, sir," Allison answers.

Wyatt is now thirty yards behind the rest of the team, except for Gideon. Wyatt notices the man in the soldier uniform and says, "Return to your vehicle, soldier!"

Gideon walks slowly, taking an angle that brings him closer to Wyatt.

"Allison, do everything you can to trace the route of that chopper. I want to know where it's going."

"Already on it, sir, but it's flying very low. Probably off the radar."

"I'm heading in. Let me know when you have something."

Gideon approaches the director.

"I said return to your vehicle!" Wyatt mistakes his adversary for an Indian soldier.

"My vehicle just took off," Gideon says, making no effort to disguise his voice.

Wyatt's heart sinks to his gut. "So we meet again," he says, wondering how many more words he will utter before he dies.

"Apparently, you didn't take me seriously this morning. It seems you're still after Charlotte and her son."

"I have no more choice in the matter than you do."

Gideon is several feet from the director. For a moment, he stands there without a word, without a movement, and his frozen state is terrifying.

"For God's sake, just do it!" Wyatt says. "Get it over with."

"There might be a way to redeem yourself." Gideon speaks very quietly, a near-whisper. "Without betraying your commander-in-chief. If you could confirm a rumor… perhaps we could reach a truce."

"Yes—perhaps we could." Wyatt's voice cracks as he feels the sharp point of a blade in his back.

"I need some information about another client of ours, someone I believe you know. If you have any evidence that this party might be working with other parties to fulfill our exclusive contract with him, that would be a serious breach. Very serious consequences. I could be persuaded to ransom your life for his."

One of the other agents has noticed that Wyatt did not return with them to the shrine. He shouts for the director.

"I'll be right along!" Wyatt shouts back.

And then he says to Gideon: "I have no death wish. Give me a name."

"There will be no second reprieve."

"Just give me the name."

Gideon does.

"He's your client? Unbelievable!" Wyatt seems almost amused. "What a world this is." The painful prick of a dagger in Wyatt's back terminates his digression. "All right, here's what I know. Your client has friends in high places, in the US as well as Israel. I think he's working all sides. I'm certainly getting pressure. Need I say more?"

Gideon cocks his head, considers the information, than wraps his arm around Wyatt's neck and flexes, stopping the flow of blood through both carotid arteries. Within seconds Wyatt drops to the ground unconscious but alive.

Gideon disappears into the night.

Chapter 63

The chopper flies low over Srinagar. After a few minutes, the aircraft begins rising to clear the mountains that ring the city. Exhaustion has sucked the speech out of everyone. No one has said a word since escaping the cemetery.

Choppy air suddenly buffets the helicopter, shaking the passengers and sending a small surge of adrenaline—perhaps the last of it—through their bodies.

Thompson stirs from his stupor. Turning to Charlotte, he says, "Your Guardian Angel bailed us all out this time."

"Except for Curt," she says solemnly.

"I'm so sorry, "Thompson replies sincerely. "I know you loved him."

Charlotte looks at her father sharply. *Did she love Curt?* She feels anger that her father might have known—and that he has betrayed her affection in front of Greg.

"I mean as a colleague, of course." Thompson adds.

The oppression of failure still weighs on Charlotte like a thousand stones, burying her alive. She has lost the crumbling prize. Sacrificed Curt to the god of her arrogance. Run out the ticking clock, almost. And like a prisoner, she is chained to the one person she despises most. Her father.

A faint, thin rattling noise draws her attention to Greg, who is fumbling with the video camera, summoning the ghosts of chaos past. She hears shots and shouting. She knows this scene by heart. Greg watches impassively, as if watching an animal documentary.

Charlotte grabs the camera and scolds her son for watching the bloodshed, as if he hadn't been at the center of it. She sets the purring camera on her lap like a kitten and strokes it, trying to find the OFF button. But the tantalizing images flash in her irises. Mesmerized, not horrified, she watches the replay of this tragic day. She can't turn it off.

The flickering picture in the small viewer trembles and tumbles. Charlotte imagines Curt holding the camera as bullets slam him backward against a wall. The picture steadies, cocked slightly to the left but miraculously pointing toward the mayhem from its position on the floor next to Curt's body.

Charlotte watches William Wyatt and his agents storm the room and slaughter the terrorists. She watches Gideon overtake the agents and knock out director Wyatt. She watches the Kidon agent stealthily enter the chamber and point his gun at Gideon. And she watches herself pick up a pistol and point it at the Israeli's back, holding it in both hands the way she had been taught. She is surprised at how steady her hands look. No tentativeness, no trembling. She watches the Israeli contractor wheel and raise his gun, and then fly backward, his chest exploding. She watches a tiny, flickering Charlotte step forward and fire again at the man. And then again. And again. And again.

And again.

Charlotte's heart is pounding. Bruising her sternum. It makes her wonder if the device inside her is still sending out its beacon, if Gideon is tracking her.

Her hands are sweaty. She finds the FAST FORWARD control and spins up to a change of scene. The camera is pointing at Greg, and she can hear her own words coming from the camera's speaker: "Shoot everything, son. Don't stop. If we find the relic, this will document the chain of evidence."

In the viewer, Greg reaches for the camera and begins to shoot as instructed. Charlotte FAST FORWARDS through the destruction of the wall and the discovery of the box, but returns to normal speed as the box is opened. There it is. She had not imagined it. The bones of Jesus!

So close.

She is startled to see herself draw a pistol and point it threateningly at Sushil. She had forgotten this! My God—she'd been so desperate to succeed. Sushil stands suddenly, leaving the box on the floor. Through the tiny speaker, she can hear Ashok's voice shouting that soldiers are approaching.

But then Charlotte watches something extraordinary. As Sushil and Charlotte turn their attention to Ashok, Thompson reaches into the metal box and takes a fragment of bone. It is done quickly, a magician's sleight-of-hand. So quickly that Charlotte rewinds the sequence and watches it again.

Yes, Thompson has stolen one of the bones of Jesus Christ.

Charlotte switches off the camera and glances at her father, who is studying her carefully. Their eyes meet. For the first time since she was seven years old, she smiles at her father.

And he smiles back.

The hopeful glow of dawn faintly bathes the rubble of outlying New Delhi. How odd that Delhi now seems like a sanctuary to Charlotte, though just a short time ago she and her family had been chased from it by terrifying forces.

The chopper lands on the same spot from which it had taken off. In the dim light, unfinished buildings and the surrounding debris field suggest a battle zone more than a construction site. Numb with fatigue, the helicopter's occupants have not spoken for more than an hour. They stagger from the Bell 214, instinctively ducking as the rotor above their heads winds down. They had left with a few bags, but now only Thompson's ever-present satchel remains.

The small group huddles together as the downdraft ends and Herb Rossi races toward them with the energy of a much younger man.

"I've gotta say, Tommy, you pulled me into something here!" Herb says.

"Sorry, my friend," Thompson replies.

"Sorry? For what? I haven't had this much fun since smuggling—uh, well, since my last big adventure. I thought for a minute there that the tough guy with the gun—you know, the one in the army uniform—was gonna do me in. But he's not such a bad guy. Wouldn't wanna be on the wrong side of him, though, I'll tell you that! Seems to be a pretty good friend of yours."

The group turns toward Charlotte. *Friend?* No one had thought of Gideon that way until now.

"You two made a fine team there at the end," Charlotte says to Herb.

Herb beams. "That guy said I was the best pilot he'd ever worked with." He reaches into a jacket pocket and pulls out a wad of paper money. "Even paid me for my services. Gas money, he said. Now, who the hell hijacks a chopper and then pays the pilot? Wouldn't mind teaming up again, know what I mean? Made more from him than from you, Tommy—not that I mind, you bein' a friend. Made me feel twenty years younger. Money can't buy that!"

Charlotte glances around the construction site. It looks the way she feels—in disarray. Over the past half-hour, she has moved from exhilaration over having obtained a sample of Christ's bones—*perhaps!*—to despair over their next goal, the second relic. The one that could confirm the identity of the bone fragments.

The bones had been a known target. The second relic—well, she didn't even know what it was. Or what it could be. How can you find something when you don't even know what it is? How will you know when you find it?

Exhaustion makes her own bones ache. "Where are we going from here?" she asks Thompson. "Any ideas?"

Greg, Sushil and Chandraka turn to Thompson.

"To my apartment," Thompson says.

"Are you crazy?" Charlotte is suddenly animated. Infuriated. "They know where you live. We'd be sitting ducks there."

"I need a few things. In case you haven't noticed, my satchel is all I have left."

"*Then* where do we go?"

"I have a place," Ashok says. "They will not look for us there."

Herb claps his hands enthusiastically. "And I will drive."

"You've done enough, my friend. You risked your life for us already." Thompson slaps Herb on the shoulder.

"This adventure of yours is not over, Tommy. I expect you'll be needing me again, so I'll just stay close. End of discussion. Now let me get my chariot."

Which, to their chagrin, is a rattly, patched-together pick-up of indeterminate age and brand. It seats three at best, not counting the rusty open bed.

CIA director Wyatt gnashes his teeth as he dials the number. Next to being killed by that damn Sicarii, this is Wyatt's worst case scenario—humiliating himself before the director of India's Intelligence Bureau, Ajay Sanghvi. The portly man will gloat in intelligence circles for months over how his humble organization again rescued a doomed CIA mission. Even worse, he will extract no end of favors from Wyatt.

The phone connects. Upon hearing the hoarse whine of Sanghvi's voice, Wyatt almost hangs up. The voice nauseates him. But the stakes are too high, so he continues, saying, "Ajay, director Wyatt here."

"Ah yes, your girl said you'd be calling. How may I help you again, Mr. Wyatt?"

Help you *again*. A small reminder that the Agency is running a tab. Wyatt clears his throat, buying time to swallow the bile. "I must ask for your support, Ajay. It's very urgent."

"I gave you the use of our police and army in Srinagar. Did they not perform as you expected?"

Damn, this man knows how to irritate Wyatt. "They performed admirably," he says, choking out the words.

"Then I take it your plan was not sufficient?"

Wyatt holds the phone away from his ear. This galling bastard wants Wyatt to admit that he, the director of the greatest intelligence operation in the world, had failed. So be it.

"Affirmative, Ajay." It's a tepid admission, but possibly acceptable.

"I see… and so this help you are seeking is in Srinagar?"

"No, no—in Delhi. We have American citizens who have gone rogue and we need to bring them in. They evaded us in Kashmir, and we believe they returned to New Delhi."

"Why don't you pick them up? You have my permission—they are your citizens."

"The problem is, Ajay, we don't exactly know where they are."

"I see. But I don't know how we can help you."

"I have a plan, Ajay, but it will take some manpower."

"Go on."

Wyatt can hear the gloating smile on the other end of the call. The more Wyatt asks for, the greater the debt—and the American's humiliation.

"A man was murdered here in Srinagar. He was key to our investigation, and we believe he hid these American traitors in a small Kashmiri carpet shop he owned in Delhi."

"I'm aware of that shop. Owned by a Kashmiri named Dr. Bhatt, I believe. As I recall from the report, you launched an unsuccessful raid on Dr. Bhatt's shop without our permission. Is that right? And you found nothing?"

Wyatt clears his throat. "Unfortunately, yes, and I apologize for that. A communications foul-up."

"Mr. Wyatt, I don't mean to speak out of turn here, but it seems to me that after you illegally launched a clandestine mission on our soil, we nevertheless reciprocated by fully supporting your request for armed assistance in Srinagar, a mission that failed, by your own admission, because of faulty planning. And now you want me to find and arrest Americans with no idea of where they may be hiding, except somewhere in a city of about fourteen million people. Am I correct?"

Sanghvi is angling for a personal apology. Wyatt grits his teeth and says, "I am deeply sorry for that raid on the carpet shop, Ajay. I take full responsibility for that. But if you'll listen to me, I don't expect you to do a door-to-door on this thing. We suspect that someone among Bhatt's extended family might be hiding the Americans in Delhi. You know, sons or cousins or something. If you could identify these people—they can't be living too far from that Kashmiri shopping district, I wouldn't think—and then send some of your men to investigate…"

"Yes yes, I see where you are going with this. I'm looking at photographs of the Americans as we speak, wired over from your Langley office. I know this woman—the CCN correspondent. She interviewed me once. A shrewd but honorable lady, as I recall. Promised to send me a tape of the interview, and actually did. I have it here in the office! And she is a traitor, you say?"

"Ajay, I can't go into all the details on this, I'm sure you understand. But I need to get my hands on these Americans as soon as possible."

"Well, it's not out of the question. But before I agree, there is a matter in Pakistan that is causing us some distress, and I believe that you have some resources that could lend some weight to your request."

Chapter 64

Ashok's apartment is strewn with clothes and unwashed dishes, bachelor-style. "It's wonderful," Charlotte lies, and then collapses into a dusty upholstered chair. Ashok begins a frantic routine of ordering the chaos.

Herb claps his hands and then stuffs them into his pockets. "Well, I've seen you all to safety," he says. "Think I'll go home for a change of clothes and to feed the cat, if you don't mind. What say I meet you back here in the morning? A good night's rest is in order."

Greg is standing by a window, looking down at a busy street. "They'll be looking for you there," he says.

"Who's that, son?"

Greg turns. "CIA. They know you. You flew two of their agents from Delhi to Srinagar and they're dead now."

"Damn!" Not a literate reply, but the most honest one that Herb can muster. He steps further into the room. "You really think…?"

Charlotte stops rubbing her red eyes to look up at the old pilot. "Absolutely," she says. "Some way I'll get you out of this, Herb, I promise— but right now Greg is right. They'll hold you responsible for the agents. And you're one of their few direct links to us."

"Then I guess I'll stay."

"What about the cat?" Thompson asks.

"Hell, it's just a stray like me, comes around ever so often for a handout."

"I'm a terrible host," Ashok says. He has already redistributed the apartment mess. "Soon I will make us food. Would you like some tea?"

Everyone nods in agreement, except Greg, who asks, "Do you have Internet access?"

Ashok smiles. Of course he does. This is India! He shows Greg to a back room that contains a tower computer and two monitors. Greg wiggles a mouse and the screens light up. Ashok leaves for the kitchen as Greg launches a browser and navigates to the website of *The Minneapolis Herald*, then searches its archived stories for coverage of the Lake Minnetonka massacre of a few days ago. He finds at least one story published for each day following the "home invasion," as the event is called.

The consensus seems to be that several men broke into the Minnetonka mansion to steal precious artifacts from the private collection of a wealthy corporate CEO. There is no mention of terrorists or Mossad or CIA. The FBI became involved, according to one story, because a couple of the criminals were from the "Middle East," but the FBI spokesman went out of his way to explain that this event undoubtedly was a burglary gone horribly wrong, not an act of terrorism.

In an early story, Greg finds a fascinating detail that is not mentioned in any of the subsequent articles. The reporter wrote that the murdered CEO was found in the room housing his collection "holding in his hands a copy of a book titled The World's Great Wisdom Traditions, which could well serve as the theme of his extensive collection of religious relics and other objects."

He searches Google for the title and finds it in a book store's offering online. The author is Thompson Walker.

Greg does not believe in meaningless coincidences. When delicate threads of synchronicity begin to weave, Greg is compelled to find a pattern. Here the threads all intersect at the same point. His grandmother's coded email message, *find the relic... and then locate the savior*. The rich CEO, collector of religious relics. And in the collector's hands, in the relic room, a copy of a book by Greg's grandfather.

What Greg and Charlotte have done is locate the savior, but they have not accomplished the first directive, to find the relic.

His grandmother and grandfather eerily are linked together, though Grandma Walker has been missing for years. What is the connection?

And Gideon. Certainly Gideon was there at the Minnetonka Mansion. And at Greg's home later, where he scrawled messages to Greg on the foreheads of the terrorists. Perhaps Gideon had left a message as well at the CEO's mansion. A message, yes. The book in the CEO's hands.

It makes no sense for the CEO to have been holding this particular book—his grandfather's—at the time of his murder. The book must have been planted there deliberately. The book must be the key to this pattern. The link between Greg's grandmother, grandfather, and the missing relic.

Other pieces of the puzzle begin to spark, dancing like fireflies in Greg's brain. The Bible pages marked in blood by Gideon, the Guardian Angel. The numbers inscribed on the foreheads of the dead terrorists at Greg's home. The family photos showing the shadowy man with the sharp nose and bushy brows and sinister moustache. A flood of images cascade before him, and smells too—that man's tobacco breath, sweetly musky. It is this remembered fragrance that sweeps Greg backward, past the sparkling fireflies, through damp mists, and into a room filled with pipe smoke, that same musky scent.

Greg is now sitting on bony legs. The legs bounce gently, and Greg realizes that he is a child, maybe three or four years old, sitting on the knees of this big-beaked man with a moustache who is laughing and bouncing him up and down.

Greg turns his head in the dim light—a partly open curtain allows in a shaft of sunlight from the lone window—and sees another man sitting on a sofa, staring sternly at the man with the moustache. The second man is familiar.

Greg stiffens as he recognizes this second man as his grandfather, Thompson Walker. And behind Thompson, another man nearly obscured in shadows—Greg's father, Mihad.

As if feeling the child's body go rigid, the moustached man says, "Had enough then? All right, down you go." And the man kisses Greg on the cheek, his hairy mustache tickling the boy's skin. "I have some questions for you now, my boy…"

And then the curtain is pulled and the room goes dark. Greg sucks in his breath, unsure of what is happening, but he has returned to Ashok's bedroom.

Why had he not remembered this man with the moustache before? Some dim recollection had made the man's image stand out among all the others in the family photographs. But with his eidetic memory, why had he not recalled this encounter until now?

And then, in a sudden rapturous epiphany, all the pieces settle into place, and he sees the dark logic unfolded, everything spread out before him, and it frightens him. He wishes it not to be true. But he sees it too clearly now. He counts backward, and the numbers all tally. He knows the identity of the second relic—so obvious now! Everything makes sense.

But he still doesn't know where the relic is.

"It's the sixth day," Charlotte says. CNN International TV chatter fills the empty space as she considers this more closely. "We had seven days to find the relics. It's hopeless—we don't even know what the second relic is."

"We still have a day," Thompson replies, but his voice lacks conviction.

Suddenly, a photograph of Mike Ansari appears on the TV screen, diverting Charlotte's attention. She leans forward. Why is her husband's photograph on the news?

The news reader, Ben Jacobs, an old friend of Charlotte, explains. "We just received news from Kashmir that an American citizen, Mihad Ansari, was killed in a fall while climbing in the Himalayas. Many of us here at CCN knew Mr. Ansari, who was known as "Mike," because he was the husband of CCN international correspondent Charlotte Ansari, who disappeared earlier this week and has become the subject of a global manhunt because of her alleged involvement in several violent deaths in India. We mourn the death of Mr. Ansari, who was the proprietor of a..."

The news of her husband's death grabs Charlotte by the throat. Suddenly, she can't breathe. She leans back in her chair, struggling for oxygen. Out of the corner of her eye, she sees Greg standing in the doorway staring at the screen.

"Dad?" he says.

Charlotte can't let her son see her in such a panic. She swallows hard, fights back tears, and sits up straighter. "It has to be a mistake, Greg."

"Mountain climbing they said." Greg seems excited, but not shaken. Is the boy not capable of normal human feelings?

"I'm sure it's mistaken identity," Charlotte says. "We left him back home in Minnesota. He's so busy working on the restaurant business..."

"In the Himalayas," Greg says, interrupting. "That's where we were. He was close to us, but he didn't tell us."

"It's a mistake, Greg! That's all..."

Greg turns from the photo of Mihad on the TV screen to his grandfather, who is staring at him with a mournful expression—no, not mournful; compassionate. And expectant! "No—no mistake," Greg says, still looking at Thompson. "He was there on purpose."

Thompson turns to Charlotte, but she doesn't notice.

"I don't know what you mean," Charlotte says.

Greg continues to stare at his grandfather. In his mind, more pieces are falling into order. Thompson turns back to Greg with an expression that seems to beckon the boy to explain, to get the secrets out.

"I know what the second relic is," Greg says, jumping forward several steps in the conversation.

Charlotte shakes her head, trying to keep up. "What?"

"The book of Luke, chapter two verse twenty-one. It says, 'And when eight days were accomplished for the circumcising of the child, his name was called Jesus, which was so named of the angel before he was conceived in the womb.'" He turns to Charlotte. "Your Guardian Angel gave me this verse. Marked it in blood in a Bible for me to find."

Charlotte is dizzy from the news of her husband's death, her son's jarringly dispassionate response, and this sudden unraveling of clues. "Luke, okay—the circumcision of Jesus. But I don't understand—"

And then she does. A young man's circumcision, the ritualistic removal of flesh. Suddenly she stands up. "What became of the foreskin?"

An unmarked green van pulls up in front of Ashok's apartment building. Two men in Indian police uniforms clamber out of the front seats and adjust their uniforms. They glance at each other wordlessly, glance up and down the street, and then purposefully stride toward the main door.

"The Holy Prepuce," Thompson says, also standing up. "For hundreds of years, one of the holiest of relics. Apparently, it was saved by someone who was at the ritual, someone who knew the boy's divine nature and passed it down through the ages. We know this, because it turned up in a church in Calcata, Italy, and became the centerpiece of a citywide celebration of the Feast of the Circumcision on New Year's Day each year. Until the relic was stolen in 1983."

Color has returned to Charlotte's face. "Stolen? Then it is possible that the relic in Jack Curtis's home was this... this *Holy Prepuce*?"

Thompson nods almost imperceptibly. "The Curtis collection. He was buying relics on the black market. That's why he kept his collection so secret."

Greg nods and tells Thompson, "The collector was killed and your book was left in his hands. Was it autographed?"

The question startles Charlotte. Thompson's face turns to ash. The implication is clear. If the book was signed to the CEO by the author, it would not have been a coincidental purchase by Jack Curtis. Which means...

Charlotte's suspicious mind grinds on this fact as she grabs a prepaid cell phone and pushes in a series of numbers. "Yes, the FBI office in Minneapolis. Just connect me, it's urgent."

"This isn't necessary," Thompson says. "Don't jump to conclusions."

"Hello, yes, I'd like to speak to Marcus Elliot. It's about the Jack Curtis murder."

There is a delay. Charlotte explains to her father, "Marcus is the FBI Bureau Chief. He should be able to tell me if the book was signed by you."

Thompson shakes his head. "And what will you learn, Char? He could have bought a signed copy from a bookstore."

A voice rattles in the earpiece.

"Marcus, thank God you're there. This is Charlotte Ansari."

"Charlotte! What in the world—?"

"Look, I know everyone is looking for me. I'm in a pile of shit right now, but I need something from you, Marcus."

"Char, my orders are to apprehend you. How can I—?"

"Marcus, please! I just need one piece of information. My cameraman's been killed, and my family has barely escaped with their lives. I just need one thing from you."

There is a pause, then Marcus says, "What is it?"

"The book that was found in the hands of Jack Curtis, the one written by my father. I need to know if there was any writing in it. An autograph, maybe."

Another pause, longer this time. "Okay, but this is all I can give you."

"Thank you, Marcus."

Thompson can hear the voice in the earpiece. Charlotte closes her eyes, then thanks Marcus and hangs up. She turns to her father.

He sighs. Slumps in his chair.

"The book was signed by you, Dad—under the words 'To my good friends Jack and Luke.'"

"Jack Curtis," Greg says "And St. Luke."

A hard rap on the door startles them. Everyone jumps to their feet. Charlotte looks inquisitively at Ashok, but he shrugs, indicating that he doesn't know who it might be.

"Find out who it is," Charlotte whispers.

Ashok approaches the door and opens it a crack. The door bursts open, sending him reeling backward. Two Indian policemen enter and quickly scan the room. Oddly, their weapons are not drawn.

"You and you, come with us," the taller man says, nodding toward Charlotte and Greg. "And you." He nods at Thompson. "The rest of you may stay here."

A rusty police van grinds to a halt past the apartment building, brakes squealing. Three Indian police clamber out of the vehicle and begin walking toward the door. The Sergeant brushes the two golden stripes on his shoulder as if burnishing them.

His purposeful stride is interrupted by a hand on his arm. One of his Constables silently gestures toward a tall police inspector and a constable who are leading two adults and a young man in the opposite direction. The foursome climbs into an unmarked green van about thirty paces away.

"The Americans!" the constable says. "They've already been apprehended."

"I don't recognize this inspector," the sergeant replies. "Let's follow at a distance."

Chapter 65

In the van, Charlotte sits between her father and son. Thompson holds his leather satchel on his lap and struggles to position the wooden rod between his knees. She looks as if she is being escorted to her own hanging. "After everything we've gone through, for it to end like this!" she says to no one in particular. "How in the world did they find us so quickly?"

Greg taps the transmitter hidden inside his mother. She looks confused. "But only Gideon…"

The taller policeman, seated in the front, turns to face Charlotte. "We are taking you to a safe place," Rahul Pradesh says.

Still confused, Charlotte turns to Greg.

"A second Guardian Ange," her son whispers.

"We learned that the police were launching a search for you in the homes of all of Dr. Bhatt's relatives and acquaintances," Rahul explains. "Gideon sent me to protect you."

"Where is Gideon?"

"On his way to the United States to clean up another matter of great importance."

Rahul Pradesh and his associate escort the three Americans from the van into a squat industrial building on the southern edge of Delhi. They wander down a dark, shabby corridor, pass through creaking double-doors, then enter by electronic keypad into a large apartment that is clean and freshly painted. There are no windows, but the room is well lit. Two men with bruised faces are seated on a sagging sofa.

"May I present Luigi Bugiardini and Adriano Moretti," Rahul says with a flourish of his right hand. "Two of the top agents in Vatican Intelligence."

The two men rise and glide gracefully to greet Charlotte and her family.

"Very pleased to meet you," Luigi says, taking Charlotte's hand gently. "We've heard so much about you."

Adriano, the older man, stands back. "Have you found it yet?" he asks.

Again, Charlotte is confused. She asks Rahul, "Why are they here?"

"They came for Antonio Fortunati. It seems that the prefect of the Secret Archives stole some of the Vatican's property. They came to get it back and return Antonio to Vatican justice."

Wth accusative tone, Cgarlotte says, "Yes, we saw the documents Antonio gave to my father, the documents that the Vatican stole from a Gompa in the Himalayas. We returned them to their rightful owners."

"But what happened to my friend, Antonio?" Thompson says, stepping forward. "He was abducted by terrorists from my apartment."

Rahul stares at Thompson for a moment, then walks across the room and opens a door. He looks inside and nods. A moment later, a weak, wobbling Antonio Fortunati staggers out of the bedroom. His face is badly bruised and swollen. His left leg seems unable to support him, explaining the cane.

"Antonio!" Thompson rushes forward to embrace his old friend. He squeezes too hard and the prelate winces.

"I thought they had killed you," Thompson says.

"They tried. Very slowly," Antonio says. "But your man Rahul arrived before they could complete their task."

"They were looking for the relic?" Thompson asks.

"Isn't everyone these days? They tortured me, but the pain was nothing compared to the pain in my heart for what I had done to my church."

"How many times have we talked about this, Antonio? You did the right thing."

"What right thing?" Charlotte interrupts. "And what relic?"

"The same relic that the Vatican had stolen twenty-five years ago. The same relic that these gentlemen—" Antonio points at Luigi and Adriano— "came to fetch from me. But they arrived too late. Rahul had already saved me." His tone turns spiteful. And the two of them could not overtake Rahul by himself. The Vatican should be recruiting a better quality of agent. I will never know if they would have killed me or taken me back to the Vatican after reclaiming the relic."

Charlotte steps closer to Antonio, can smell the suffering that still clings to him. "You say the Vatican stole this relic twenty-five years ago?"

"Yes, in a manner of speaking."

"You mean the Holy Prepuce."

"Of course!"

"But the Vatican owns the church and all its property. How could they steal what they already own?"

"The question isn't *how*, but *why*. And the answer is that this whole business of parading the Savior's foreskin around a city—the entire business of relic worship, really—had become an embarrassment for a church that was beginning to modernize. This constant vulgar association of Jesus with his genitalia had to end. And so they hired someone to steal the reliquary from the church in Calcata."

"Grandfather," Greg says, interrupting the conversation.

Thompson turns toward Greg as if he had been called, but then realizes that the word had been spoken as the answer to a question.

Or an accusation.

Thompson sees that all eyes are now focused on him. He sighs deeply. "All right, it's true," he says, putting his arm on Antonio's shoulder. "My friend Antonio asked me to do it. I had known the Calcata priest for many years, and ever since..."

"Ever since," Antonio repeats, "we have lived with feelings of guilt for what we did. There was a personal motive as well. I desperately wanted the holiest of all relics in my possession, even if it were to be secreted away in the Archives. Can you imagine, to have the actual presence of Christ within your reach every day? Unfortunately, the ecstasy I imagined became a plague of shame. Every day, the reliquary reminded me of my selfishness. I was planning to return the relic to Thompson so he could experience his own release of guilt by returning it to Calcata. It was when the terrorists abducted me that I figured out the relic could endanger the entire church."

Charlotte's mind is reeling. She paces a few steps, her investigative instincts kicking in. She is trying to piece together the disparate crumbs of information she has learned in the past hour.

"My father asked you to return it to him?" she asks Antonio.

"No. It was my idea, but I knew he would agree."

Greg boldly approaches the prelate. "You do not have the Holy Prepuce," he states flatly, his eyes darting past the old man's eyes as if searching for something just out of grasp. "The reliquary is real, but the remains inside are not."

Thompson steps backward, finds a wooden chair and sits down. Antonio stares into Greg's eyes, and finally the boy's dark eyes stare back. "What is it you are saying, my son?" Antonio asks. "That your Grandfather deceived me?"

Antonio's eyes turn to Thompson, who refuses to make eye contact.

"Ask *him*," Greg says. "He sold the remains to Jack Curtis."

Antonio marches over to Thompson and bends down, his face near his friend's. "Who is this Jack Curtis, Tommy? And is this true?"

Thompson fidgets. Antonio can see tears forming in the old man's eyes.

"I'm so sorry, Antonio," Thompson says hoarsely. "I've made many mistakes in my life."

"All these years we are friends—and you lie to me? The relic was a fraud?"

"How do you think I support myself, Antonio?" Thompson seems to gather some courage. He stands up and continues speaking. "From time to time, yes, I have bought and sold religious relics. In my line of work, I come by them quite frequently. There is an active black market for such objects, as you well know. So when you asked me to relieve the church in Calcata of a relic the Vatican believed to the genuine Holy Prepuce, I knew the monumental value of such a thing."

"Tommy—" Antonio's eyes are flooded with tears of disappointment.

"Listen to me, Antonio. Once I possessed the relic, I was gravely tempted to sell it to Jack Curtis. I had sold him five other relics. He had a seemingly inexhaustible supply of money, and an obsession with Christian relics. Quite a reputation in the black market! My plan was to sell him the real thing and substitute a forgery to the Vatican."

"No—not to the *Vatican*. You planned to give the counterfeit to *me*, Tommy. To your old friend!"

"Yes, it's true. But I couldn't do it, Antonio. I made a forgery, yes, but I sold it to Jack Curtis, the fool. He relied on the seller—*me!*— for authentication. Imagine that!"

Antonio reaches out and takes Tommy's hand. In a whisper, he says, "Is this the truth, Tommy? You gave me the genuine relic?"

"I swear on my wife's life, Antonio, it is true. And you know that nothing is more sacred to me than Miriam."

Rahul interrupts. "So the Reliquary is—where?" He addresses the question to Antonio.

The old man shakes his head while rubbing the back of a bruised hand. "I hope it's still where I hid it."

For God's sake, tell us!" Charlotte shouts.

Antonio gives her a penetrating stare. "For God's sake, indeed."

"Antonio, please, I beg you—"

"I was brutally tortured to obtain that information, my dear, and I did not reveal the hiding place. Why should I reveal it to you?"

"My mother's life depends on me finding it."

Antonio turns to Thompson. "Is this true, Tommy?"

Thompson hesitates, and then nods.

Antonio stares at his feet, thinking hard. He looks up at Greg, who looks back with expressionless eyes. He turns again to Thompson and says, "You've told me a great deal about your Grandson, Tommy. Is this the test you were looking for?"

Thompson closes his eyes and nods.

Antonio stands and walks over to Greg, placing a trembling hand on the boy's shoulder. "Then it's your job, my son, to find the hiding place and save your grandmother. I'm sorry."

"What *test*?" Charlotte asks. "What kind of test are you talking about?"

Antonio and Greg are staring into each other's eyes, oblivious to everything else. Antonio whispers into the boy's ear, "It is here in Delhi, hidden in a place of universal peace. With a pure heart and bare feet, enter the lotus flower that blooms forever. Repeat the number of unity a hundred times plus seven and you shall find your heart's desire."

Greg's piercing, expressionless eyes suddenly dart sideways, a subtle hint of desperation and self-doubt. The old man's riddle means nothing to him. He is devoid of interpretations.

The old man just smiles back.

Rahul steps forward and motions for everyone to be silent. He turns toward the door and readies his pistol, though no one else can detect any noise from outside. Again, he motions, this time for Charlotte and Greg to retreat into the side room. Antonio and Thompson, grabbing his satchel and the wooden rod, nervously follow, closing the door behind them.

Sitting on a bed with rumpled linens, Charlotte holds tightly onto Greg. The sudden hush heightens her tension.

What kind of danger is Rahul sensing? The possibilities reel through her mind.

And then, an immense crash. A volley of gunshots, then another. Shouting and loud screams. Bullets ripping through the bedroom door. Charlotte and Greg dive for the floor. More shooting and screaming.

And then quiet. Except for footsteps crunching on broken glass. The door knob turning. The door squeaking open.

Charlotte covers Greg with her body. Can feel the heat of his fear. *My God, the boy has emotions*! The thought makes her cry.

She looks up to see Rahul looming above them.

"You must leave now," he says. "Take the van. Others will come."

The tall Indian Sicarii drops to his knees and Charlotte can see blood oozing from his stomach and his leg, bubbling up in his mouth.

"Hurry now!" he says. "I'm sorry I failed you."

With a terrible grimace and soft moan, he sinks to the floor. Charlotte crawls over to him to explain that he had not failed them—he had kept them alive. But it is too late.

"Dad!" she shouts. But he is nowhere to be seen. She stands and walks to the other side of the bed. Thompson is lying on the floor, his head against the wall. He looks up at her, his eyes weary. "I'm all right," he says. But Charlotte can see blood on his left arm. She stoops, pushes up his blood-soaked arm, checks him over, and declares that his forearm was grazed by a bullet.

"Greg," she hollers, "find me a tourniquet for Grandpa!"

She turns to find Greg standing right behind her.

"Antonio is dead," the boy tells her.

"What?"

"He's dead. Shot in the chest and the head."

She didn't need the clinical details. Tearing a piece of cloth from Thompson's shirt, she fashions a tourniquet and tightens it above the old man's wound.

"You heard the man, let's get out of here."

Frantically searching through Rahul's pockets, she finds the van keys, grabs the satchel, and leads her father and son into the blood-spattered front room. Thompson uses the wooden rod to steady himself. The bodies of Luigi and Adriano, the two Vatican agents, and Rahul's associate lie scattered among a half-dozen Indian police. The three Americans have to step over the bodies to reach the hallway door, and Thompson trips over Luigi, falling hard onto another body. Using the wooden rod, he tries to lever himself to his feet.

"Greg, you get Grandpa," Charlotte says. "I'll get some guns."

Greg helps his grandfather up. Charlotte scoops up three pistols. Finally they reach the corridor.

"This way!" Charlotte says, turning left. They race to the exit and find the green van. As Charlotte drives out of the small parking area, Indian police cars are already surrounding the building. Charlotte pulls over, imagining that a moving vehicle will attract more attention than a parked one.

Slouching in the driver's seat, she motions for Greg and Thompson to put their heads down. A black sedan with diplomatic plates slips through the police cars and pulls up to the building's door. A tall, suited man springs out. Even from this distance Charlotte recognizes him; she knows all the top US administrative officials by face and by name. This man is CIA director William Wyatt.

When Charlotte is certain that all of the police attention is now on the building itself, she slowly drives away into the Delhi streets.

Chapter 66

In the seat behind Charlotte, Thompson winces with pain. Charlotte shoots him an unsympathetic look. "Serves you right," she says angrily. "How many ethical and moral breaches does this make, Thompson?" She can't use the word *Dad* right now. "Let's see, knock up a parishioner, drive away your wife, use your notoriety to sell black market relics..."

"None of this is helping save Miriam," Thompson replies.

Charlotte ignores the comment. She is starting to tremble, an aftershock of the violence she has survived. Diverting herself, she glances at the Garmin GPS affixed to the windshield.

"Greg, find out where the hell we are."

"Where are we going?" Greg asks, tapping the Garmin's touch screen.

"How the hell should I fuckin' know?" she shouts angrily. The trembling is worse now, and she's sweating.

"It's not his fault," Thompson says. "And you might watch your language around the boy."

"Oh, that's great, coming from such a moral authority."

"Look, just calm down. Antonio gave clues to Greg. He knew that—"

Thompson can't go on. The mention of his deceased friend sharpens his loss. He fights back tears, gasps silently, and looks out the window. Charlotte watches her father in the rear view mirror. She knows the old man has lost his best friend. The thought reminds her of Curt. And of her husband, Mike. She is really alone now, except for Greg. Mostly alone even *with* Greg. But someone has to be strong here.

She grips the steering wheel and resolves to regain her composure. Her *mother*—that's what she should focus on now. Saving her mother.

"We're going north on, uh, Ma Anandmayee Marg." Greg struggles to say the name of the street.

Charlotte looks at Greg, then at the GPS. It means nothing to her. Greg was right. They need to figure out a destination.

"What Antonio told you," Charlotte says to Greg, "did it make any sense at all?"

"A place of universal peace. A Lotus flower that blooms forever."

"Gibberish. And now he's dead. Think, Greg, *think*! What could it mean?"

"The number of unity, repeat it one hundred times plus seven."

"*Think*, Greg!"

"Badgering the boy won't help," Thompson says.

Charlotte takes this as a taunt. "Why don't you just shut your goddam mouth, all right? Shit, we're coming up to a 'T' here. Greg, right or left?"

"Where do we want to go?"

"Just tell me right or left! Dammit, I can't make all the decisions here! *Right or left?*" She starts to sob. She can't drive and fight back her grief and control her fear and plan their next move all at the same time. It's just too damn much.

"Left," Greg says. "On Outer Ring Road."

And then he does something that calms her down, something that he has never done, at least not since he was very young. Greg reaches over and touches his mother's arm. It is like a laying on of hands, a healing. The warmth of his touch sends waves of tranquility throughout Charlotte's body. A small gasp escapes her lips, the kind of whispery breath you hear when morphine finally deadens the pain. The touch is a drug; she can't get enough of it. For years, she has thirsted for human touch, for real human contact, and Greg's touch is like a long cool drink after years of salt.

But then, the calming hand is gone, and its fingers are tapping the GPS again. No problem. She is thinking clearly again. Now she wonders if the touch had actually happened or if she had imagined it.

"A place of universal peace," Thompson is saying, trying to figure its meaning.

Greg is looking out the passenger window. He sees scrubby, dusty trees, a few low buildings in serious disrepair, and in the distance the gleaming white edifice of the Baha'i Temple, which rises like a single beautiful flower on the horizon. He turns to his mother, then back to the glistening Temple, which is sliding slowly past them in the distance.

…enter the lotus flower that blooms forever.

He recalls Antonio's words. Looks back at the Bahá'í Temple. And then he recognizes it. Adrenalin surges through his body. The Temple is an architectural impression of the unfolding petals of a lotus flower. The late afternoon sun dazzles the petals, making them glisten and shine, even in the smoggy Delhi air. This lotus flower, frozen in time, will *bloom forever*.

Greg manipulates the GPS screen. "Take the next right!" he shouts.

"What is it, Greg?" Thompson asks, and then looks out his right-hand window to see the immense lotus flower looming on the horizon.

"Of course!" Thompson says. "The Lotus Temple, built by the Bahá'í Faith, the religion of universal peace."

Hidden in a place of universal peace. Antonio's words.

"Is the relic here, at this Temple?" Charlotte asks.

"It fits the clues so far," Thompson says. The excitement has dampened the pain in his forearm. "Six years ago, when Antonio briefly visited me here, I took him to the Lotus Temple. It's one of the biggest tourist destinations in the world—just behind St. Peter's Basilica. We spent the better part of the day there. Antonio didn't want to leave. He told me later that he experienced such peace and joy at the Temple that he regained some of the faith in God that he had been losing. It makes sense that he would visit the Temple again and maybe think to hide the relic there."

Charlotte veers sharply right, heading down a road that points directly at the Temple.

Thompson cradles his injured arm in his other hand as he follows Charlotte and Greg from the parking area to a wide stairway that leads to an underground visitor's center.

Turning to the left, they gaze down a long, straight pathway toward the Bahá'í Temple, which rises from the green horizon like a glimmering white lotus blossom. The perfect symmetry of the Temple and the grounds is breathtaking. As the three start walking toward the Temple, Charlotte is overtaken by a feeling of exhilaration, as if she has finally arrived at the end of her journey.

The line of visitors and pilgrims is long and everyone is hushed, reverent, dazzled by this oasis of beauty hidden within the dust and decay of New Delhi. Surrounding Charlotte and her family are representatives of many different faiths—Hindus and Buddhists, to be expected in India, but also Christians and Jews and the occasional Muslim. They make a rich ,flowing river of color—thousands of Indian saris, American blue jeans, Buddhist robes, turbans and hats of every hue. Many are stunned that there is no charge to visit the Temple and no begging for donations. The Temple, Charlotte overhears from two visitors immediately behind, is the Bahá'í mother temple of the continent, a gift from the Bahá'í worldwide community to India, and is open to people of all faiths.

Over the past week, Charlotte has endured intolerable strife because of religious differences and obsessions. This jewel-like monument to the common foundation of the world's major religions seems like a perfectly suitable place to end the small religious wars that have been swirling around her.

She studies the many uplifted lotus petals of the Temple and the lotus leaves that jut out from the core like canopies. Impetuously, she turns to the visitors behind her and says, "There seem to be many entrances to the Temple."

"Oh yes, nine in all. And nine reflecting pools surrounding it."

"Why nine?"

"Nine is the number of unity—the highest number that can be reached before beginning the series of single-digit numbers again."

These words enter Greg's consciousness and connect with Antonio's whispered clue: *Repeat the number of unity a hundred times plus seven…*

But where? And for what purpose?

The line of visitors moves down the long path, each step bringing the Temple nearer, revealing more of its details. The carefully manicured lawns and perfectly groomed trees and flowers comfort Charlotte. Her eyes travel down the many walkways, each with beautiful curved balustrades, bridges and stairs. Here, in this sacred place, she breathes in the fresh fragrances of living things instead of the stench of smog and decay that defines Delhi. She is anxious to complete her quest, but at the same time longing to just stand here, surrounded by unexpected beauty, serenely watching the golden afternoon light burnish the lotus petals of the Temple.

At last they approach a long structure built into the ground with windows at knee height. Ahead of Charlotte, people are taking off their shoes and handing them through the windows in exchange for a claim ticket. Shoes are not allowed in the Temple. As Greg removes his shoes, he recalls Antonio's words: *With a pure heart and bare feet, enter the lotus flower that blooms forever.*

He hands over his shoes. The bricks of the walkway are warm.

Finally, they approach the Temple itself. Greg begins a slow circumambulation, and the others follow him. He counts the entrances—yes, there are nine—and the reflecting pools—nine of these as well. The number of unity. He counts twenty-seven marble-clad lotus petals in all—nine times three.

Though not prone to emotion, Greg feels a shiver of delight as he enters the interior dome of the Temple. The inner leaves enclose the interior in a canopy made of crisscrossing ribs and shells, and these layers seem to disappear as they rise. As Greg looks up at the ceiling, he feels as though he is being lifted upward toward the sky. He has never before thought about God, but here, in this magical marble sphere, he could almost believe...

A touch.

His mother's hand on his shoulder.

He must move on. There is work to do. A relic to be found. But leaving this space is like abandoning oxygen.

Another touch. Reluctantly, he follows Charlotte and Thompson out of the sacred silence of the Temple and onto the monumental stairs. The golden sunlight bounces off the calm waters of the reflecting pools. The low murmur of visitors surrounds him.

Charlotte whispers, "What next, Greg?"

He doesn't know. He's sure that somewhere on this plot of land is the object of their quest. All the clues point to these grounds. But *what next?*

The solace of the Temple gives way to the agitation of Greg's brain as it starts to grind again on the puzzle.

Hidden in a place of universal peace. Check. This clue fits the grounds of the Lotus Temple. *With a pure heart and bare feet, enter the lotus flower that blooms forever.* The Lotus Temple—done that! *Repeat the number of unity a hundred times plus seven and you shall find your heart's desire.*

"Nine hundred and seven," Greg says. Charlotte looks at him oddly.

Evoking the number does not magically produce the relic. But what, then, is the significance of the number? Antonio seems to specify a sequence—enter the Temple, and then somehow use the number to...

He can't solve the riddle. It is the final solution, but he is out of clues. He desperately wants to return to the solace of the Temple, a place where time stops and tranquility permeates one's being. He whirls and marches back into the interior dome. He stands there, hoping to be taken into the sky, relieved of his perplexity. He notices how cool the marble floor is on the soles of his feet. So soothing. Calming.

And then he understands.

It comes to him in a white flash.

He walks out of the Temple, past his mother and grandfather. He finds the pathway to the visitor's center. Charlotte and Thompson follow speechlessly.

Greg approaches the shoe station, waits for a group of visitors to retrieve their footware. When it is time, a smiling Indian volunteer looks up at him through the window reaching for his ticket.

"I lost my ticket," Greg says. "Number 907." Lying does not come easily to Greg. He looks as uneasy as he speaks.

The Indian takes Greg's discomfort as embarrassment. "I see," he says. "Could you describe your shoes for me?"

Greg has no idea what kind of shoes Antonio was wearing. "They're with a small package," he says boldly.

Greg and Thompson look on curiously as the Indian lowers his head, searches through some shelves, and then looks up.

"Yes, here they are!" he says proudly. "And the package."

The Indian hands over a pair of sandals—clearly Antonio had brought with him a pair of sandals to leave with the relic—and then, beaming, shows a small woven bag to Greg. "Have a good day," he says.

Charlotte's heart begins to pound as she sees Greg take the bag. It must be the relic! She and Thompson hand over their claim tickets and nervously slip on their shoes.

"My God," she says to Thompson, "we may have found it!"

"In which case, I am more frightened than ever," Thompson replies.

Chapter 67

Charlotte pulls the van out of the parking area and takes a right onto Outer Ring Road. "Open it!" Charlotte commands, unable to control her emotions. Greg opens the small woven bag and removes a small glass jar. The lid is twisted on so tightly that he can't loosen it, but the jar is made of clear glass and Greg peers at the contents.

"I'm sure it's sealed in a vacuum to preserve the contents," Thompson says. "Don't try to open it. What do you see in there?"

"Some small flakes of something, some dust. Is this it?"

"You wouldn't imagine a large mass of material now, would you? After 2,000 years, human tissue would probably have turned to…"

"There's only one way to know for sure," Charlotte says. "Have it analyzed. But we have another mystery. Mother never told us how to get in touch with her, or what to do with the relics when we found them."

Then we must trust that she will contact us before time expires," Thompson replies. "Right now we have to think of a place to hide."

"It's too late!" Charlotte exclaims. She is looking into the rearview mirror. Thompson turns around and sees an Indian police car coming up rapidly from behind, its lights flashing. In its slipstream is a black sedan. Thompson takes the glass jar from Greg and stuffs it into his leather bag.

Before Charlotte can think, the police car forces her off the road. With guns drawn, two police officers leap from their car and approach the van. Instinctively, Charlotte and the others raise their hands.

"Charlotte Ansari?"

Charlotte nods.

"Please step out of the vehicle."

The other officer escorts Thompson and Greg out of the opposite side of the van.

"What's wrong?" Charlotte asks. "Was I speeding or something?" She knows that speeding is not a guns-drawn offense, but she is improvising, trying to think of a way out of this jam.

"We've been asked to take you in for questioning?"

"Who would want to question me?"

The black sedan pulls up behind the van. A tall American steps out followed by an Indian in a business suit. They approach Charlotte.

"I'll take over from here," the American says, dismissing the police officer. "Charlotte, you're very difficult to keep track of."

"I know what you want," Charlotte says to William Wyatt. "But we don't have it."

"Well, a thorough search will determine that. I suspect that you didn't stop here at the Lotus Temple for worship, am I right? Of course I am. Before we escort you to one of our fine rendition facilities, let me be the first to thank you for doing the hard part."

"How did you find us here?" Charlotte asks.

"One of Delhi's fine police officers saw you drive away in a van. You're not invisible, you know. But you are complicit in multiple crimes involving the deaths of American, Mossad, and Vatican intelligence agents, the prelate of the Vatican's Secret Archives—who was innocently vacationing here, I might add—and assorted other mayhem. It could take years to sort this out, and I imagine you'd be incarcerated the whole time, so really it's in your best interest to simply disappear."

"What about my father and son?"

"Same problem, I'm afraid."

"It's hard to imagine you are my government."

"Your government? Not anymore. You're a woman without a country."

"I just wish my camera was running right now, you sonofabitch." Charlotte says this, but her mind is hoping that her Guardian Angel will come to rescue her, as he always has before. Her hopes fall flat, however, when she remembers that Gideon is on another mission and Rahul is dead.

"Put her in our car," Wyatt says to the Indian officer. "And the others too."

Charlotte is escorted to the sedan. The suited Indian stands outside.

"Hello, Ajay," Charlotte says to the director of Indian Intelligence. "About that follow-up interview—I think it won't be happening."

"Sorry, Charlotte," Ajay says. "This makes me very sad, but it's politics."

"It always is."

Ajay suddenly turns his eyes toward the van, and then upward into the clouds. Charlotte follows his gaze. She hears the whap-whap-whap of a helicopter before she sees the craft zooming down toward the van. The two police officers and Wyatt merely stare at the chopper as it lands in a small field nearby.

Charlotte smiles when she sees Herb Rossi step from the helicopter, though she can't imagine how he could remedy this situation. Herb opens the other door and a woman emerges. The woman walks confidently towards the van, leaving Herb to guard the helicopter.

The two Indian officers raise their pistols as the woman approaches, but Wyatt motions to lower them.

Charlotte watches the woman stride right up to director Wyatt. The helicopter rotor is still rhythmically beating the air, ready for an escape, but the noise prevents Charlotte from hearing the conversation between Wyatt and the woman. Oddly, Wyatt hunches his shoulders and lowers his head as she speaks.

Finally, Wyatt motions for Ajay to bring Charlotte over to them. The woman looks eerily familiar, but Charlotte can't quite recall…

"My dear Charlotte," the woman says. "Director Wyatt has just learned that the matter he has been obsessed with is done. You are free to go."

"I don't understand," Charlotte says.

The woman ignores Charlotte's confusion and turns to Wyatt. "You may leave now, knowing that we always honor our word. Pleasant dreams."

Wyatt instructs the police officers to abandon the mission and drive away. With a look of ferocious resignation, he grabs Ajay by the arm and heads back for the black sedan, slamming the car door after he climbs in.

"Really, you need to explain what—"

The woman turns to Charlotte. "It's so good to see you again after so many years."

Charlotte is shaken. So many years? She studies the face more closely. "Mother?"

"My name is Eve now," the woman says. "Your father will explain."

"Mother!" Charlotte's mind seems to crack open. Emotions pour out of her. She rushes to her mother and throws her arms around the woman. Eve gently holds her daughter."

Finally, Charlotte backs away. "Your name is Miriam Walker," she says.

"I haven't been Miriam for many years."

"You said you were in mortal danger. That's why we—why we came here and found the relics!"

"I am always in mortal danger, Charlotte. And you accomplished your mission brilliantly, though not the mission you thought you were working on."

"I'm very confused, as you might imagine. How did you find us?"

Eve taps on Charlotte's transmitter. When we learned that Indian police were converging on our safe house, we decided to mobilize."

"What did you say to Wyatt to get him to back off?"

"Gideon knows where director Wyatt lives. And to prove that no one is safe from us, a man who is very important to the president of the United States is about to be executed for unpardonable crimes. Wyatt will make sure you're cleared of any possible charges. Oh, and I had one other small item of persuasion in case my gentle persona carried insufficient force."

Eve gestures toward the helicopter. Charlotte turns to see six heavily armed Sicarii agents standing next to Herb Rossi.

"Your pilot came highly recommended by Gideon. But I must go now."

"What? But what about the relics?"

"They're yours. Do with them whatever you want."

Eve turns to go. Charlotte grabs her. "Wait... I have so many questions—"

"I'm sure you do. And your father can answer them."

Eve steps closer to Greg. "You know why I'm really here, don't you?"

Greg nods.

"I'm so glad. So happy to meet you at last, my grandson." Eve gives Greg a huge motherly hug. Greg lets her, but does not show any particular emotion.

"Are you ready, then?" Eve asks Greg.

Greg turns to Charlotte. For just a moment, he looks indecisive, and this moment will live in Charlotte's memory for a very long time. But then Greg nods and turns toward his grandmother. Eve smiles, then approaches Thompson. He whispers something into her ear. She looks at the wooden rod he is leaning on. He gives it to her and she smiles.

She strokes the old man's face with her palm and kisses him lovingly. "One day, very soon," she says.

Eve and Greg start walking to the helicopter. Frantically, Charlotte starts after them. She can't fathom why Greg is walking toward the chopper. Thompson grabs her, restrains her. "Let him go, Charlotte. It's not your choice."

"Where is he going?"

"With Miriam. With *Eve*."

Charlotte looks at her father with tremendous grief and consternation. By the time she turns away, the helicopter is lifting off.

Charlotte has never felt so alone.

Chapter 68

Charlotte drives without seeing the road. Her thoughts are on Greg and her mother, and on all the unanswered questions. Thompson shows her a fistful of money. "To get you home. It's from Eve."

"You were part of it all along, weren't you?"

He chews his lower lip and then nods guiltily. "In a way."

"I'm such a fool. For caring about mother."

"Your mother is an extraordinary woman," Thompson says. "And so are you. But you never knew the real story."

"I know that you drove mother out of the house. I was listening!"

"You *believed* I drove her out, and you never forgave me for it. The truth is, your mother left us. It was time. We argued that night because I couldn't bear to lose her—that's what you overheard."

"Then why didn't you stop her?"

Thompson looks out the window. The grimy scenery floats by like the passing of years. "Charlotte, your mother was a Woman of the Lineage. She was supposed to become the leader of the Great White Brotherhood, which we know as the Sicarii," he says softly.

He has never before ordered his memories and put them into words, so he proceeds slowly. "As a headstrong young woman, however, she rebelled against her Order. She didn't like the idea of having her life designed by tradition, or having responsibilities heaped on her that she didn't choose. Apparently no one suspected her deep antagonism and so she was allowed considerable freedom. Eventually, she escaped and found her way to America, to Minneapolis, a pretty good place to hide out. We met while I was going through a rough patch. She had come to my parish, and I found her one afternoon in the back pew of the church, despondent and out of money. I'm sure that I fell in love with her immediately. Oh Charlotte, if you would have seen that shining face, so vulnerable and… and so beautiful. Since that day, I've never loved anyone else, except you and Greg.

"But the Sicarii are very good at finding people. Before long, they tracked down Miriam and threatened to bring her home. She was pregnant

349

with you at the time. Because she was the bloodline, she had some negotiating leverage. She bargained to stay with us until you were seven years old, and then she would voluntarily return to the Brotherhood to take her rightful position. In exchange, the Sicarii would let you live your life in America with me. And with complete ignorance of the Sicarii organization."

Charlotte's head is dizzy with these revelations. "So the night I heard you and mom arguing…"

"I was very angry with her. I said some things I have regretted all my life, things I'm sure you overheard. Over the seven years of her bargain, she studied the Sicarii beliefs, with help from some of the Brothers. To you, they were just friends of the family. But it turns out that you had a much larger role to play than I could have imagined. The Brothers honored their pledge to leave you at home, but as the only daughter of Eve, the bloodline of the Woman of Lineage, it was necessary for you to conceive a child who might become the male heir to leadership."

"Greg!" The name escapes from Charlotte's lips.

"According to Sicarii beliefs, a Woman of Lineage rules until a male candidate is conceived of two direct descendants of the ancient Jewish bloodline. Mihad was a Persian Jew, a direct descendant like you."

Evoking the name of Mihad, Charlotte's husband, summons ghosts that instantly haunt Charlotte. Images swirl in her mind. The dashing young Mihad. The night in the car that ended in oblivion and pregnancy. The loveless marriage.

"I was raped, wasn't I?"

Thompson nods sadly and rubs his eyes to hide tears.

"To conceive an heir to the bloodline?" Charlotte asks.

"They felt it was the only sure way to avoid missing the opportunity."

"The *opportunity*? I'm talking rape here. What kind of opportunity are you talking about?"

"Try to think the way they do, Char. Nothing is more important to them then the appearance of a new Divine Light, a male child divinely delivered—*born*, that is—under specific circumstances. Parentage fulfills only one of these. If a candidate does not fulfill them all, he cannot be the Divine Light. That is why Mihad could never be the Divine Light. His birth did not meet the requirements."

"And Greg—"

"Greg's birth met the requirements, but that is not enough, either. Certain mental and intellectual conditions must also be present."

"You're talking in riddles."

Thompson sighs deeply. "I've dreamed for years of having this conversation with you, and now I'm at a loss for words. How ironic."

"Just tell me what's going on."

"I'll try. The truth is that Greg is three-quarters Jewish—one quarter from you, and one-half from Mihad, a full-blooded Jew. Maybe you're aware that Ashkenazi Jews have the highest measured IQ of any ethnic group."

"I had no idea."

"It's true, but they also have the highest incidence of Asperger's Syndrome. For the Brotherhood, a candidate must possess abnormally high intelligence and certain other abilities that are sometimes found in Asperger's kids. The Brothers believe that such candidates are not suffering from autism but possess a unique mental and spiritual gift. The only way to determine if someone has this gift, which is manifest in every Divine Light, is to conduct a very difficult test."

Charlotte shakes her head incredulously. "Are you saying that this whole adventure was a test to find out if Greg was a Divine Light?"

"Let me finish. For the Brothers, this was a test, yes. But for all the other forces involved, it was a battle for possession of the relics. That was no joke. Good people died."

"So you want me to believe that this whole relic thing came up at just the right time to be used as a test for Greg?"

"If not the relics, something else would have provided the opportunity. For years, the Brothers planned for this. They had a transmitter implanted in you so that when the test was unfolding they would always be able to locate you. Gideon was assigned to be Greg's bodyguard. The Brotherhood had no intention of losing a true Divine Light.

Charlotte chokes back a cynical laugh. "And all along I thought Gideon was *my* Guardian Angel."

"You and I were along for the ride. It's always been about Greg."

"So now that they have Greg—"

"—the Guardian Angel has been reassigned."

Charlotte nervously looks into her rearview mirror. The thought of having absolutely no protection makes her feel incredibly vulnerable. She wonders how much of her courage during the past week was due to her sense of being protected.

"So, I imagine former, uh, 'candidates' have also been tested like this," Charlotte suggests.

Thompson nods. "Almost every other candidate for the past two thousand years has been tested through difficult situations. There is no other way. Your mother spun this particular test into motion with her melodramatic emails. Gideon left clues for Greg. Eve suggested that you draw me into the adventure, as you call it, so I could be present to personally assess Greg's performance. I told your mother that he was one cool customer under pressure and had an astounding ability to unravel mysteries. Just after she entered our little drama from the helicopter, I told her how Greg had solved Antonio's puzzle and located the last relic."

"This story is just too incredible, Dad."

"Even after the events of the past week?"

"You're saying that for my entire life, all the people close to me were agents of some kind. That even my own parents have been manipulating me."

Thompson nods. "It pains me to admit it. But many others were involved too. You never formally met Mihad's father, but he visited Minneapolis often. I think he was checking up on his grandson. He always refused to meet you in person—I think he felt guilty about approving the rape—but he was nearby on many occasions. Greg identified pictures of Mihad's father in some family photographs. Several times, when Greg was very young, he played with Greg—but never revealed who he was."

Charlotte recalls the mysterious sharp-nosed man in the photographs. "Why did you go along with this ugly charade?"

"In the beginning, I cooperated with the Brothers because it was the only way I could maintain some contact with your mother. They would give me tidbits of news now and then, even pass along an occasional note from Miriam. All to keep me cooperating, I'm sure, but I didn't care. Mainly, though, I hoped to reconcile with your mother some day. Love can really mess you up. When she asked me to observe Greg's test from the inside, I initially refused. But then she told me that her time as leader of the

Brotherhood was coming to an end, and if Greg proved to be the Divine Light, she would be able to retire. She suggested that we might be able to reunite. All I needed was hope, Charlotte. Hope that Miriam and I could finally be together. Can't you understand? Haven't you ever loved someone that much?"

"Sounds like horse trading to me." Charlotte's tone is bitter. Her father's true confessions are not winning her over. "You bartered Greg for Mother. I lose a son, you gain a wife. Oh, and I also lose a mother. The mother I loved all of these years was clearly a work of fiction." Frustrated and angry, Charlotte suddenly pounds the steering wheel. "Damn! I'm such a fool."

"Don't be angry, Char."

"You don't think I have a right to be angry? My husband and his family plotted to rape me, my own father played me for a fool, my son has been taken away from me—God knows if I'll ever see him again—and I just learned that my mother is the supreme leader of a cult of assassins. Yeah, I think I have a perfectly goddam good right to be angry." She starts to cry. Tears flood her face. "And now I'm all alone!"

Thompson looks at his daughter. He wants desperately to reach out to her but he knows better.

"You've still got me," he says timidly.

She steps on the brakes, veers to the side of the road. With a hard look she says, "Give me the relics!" The tears have been obliterated by rage.

Thompson reaches into his leather bag and removes the box of bones and the jar of tissue.

Charlotte grabs them and says, "Now get out!"

Thompson looks at her. Did she really ask him to get out of the car?

"Now!"

He opens the door and steps outside. She floors the gas pedal and the car lunges forward, slamming the door shut. Thompson stares into the dusty rooster tail as Charlotte speeds away.

Chapter 69

Gideon drives from the hotel to his destination in Raleigh, North Carolina. The humidity slicks his skin and the A/C temporarily fogs the windshield in his rented Ford Fusion. It's early, but already the rush hour has clogged Glenwood Avenue on the way into the city.

This mission is serious business. It's not often that a Sicarii is authorized to terminate a client. It hasn't been done in over fifty years. Such an action requires a unanimous vote of the entire council. But the rules are painfully clear. Any violation of the terms of agreement is subject to corrective action. In this case, Gideon's evidence of client malfeasance was incontrovertible and the council quickly, though reluctantly, authorized this "final action"—*reluctantly* because such action also means that no final payment will be made. And also because this particular client was considered to be well-aligned with the principles of the Sicarii.

The client arrives at a large complex and pulls into the parking ramp. He usually arrives at work early so he can teleconference at a reasonable hour with associates in Europe. Gideon parks the Fusion, inspects the curved and deadly sica hidden in his belt, and checks himself in the rearview mirror. His disguise is minimal—Buddy Holly glasses, a small paunch-pad under his shirt, fake pork chop sideburns. Now it's just a matter of waiting. The client's reserved parking space is just fifty feet away.

Gideon has been brought up to date on news from Delhi. Now there is just one last bit of business to complete. He settles into the front seat and switches on the local PBS news station. In his business, you can never be too informed about world events.

Patiently, he waits and listens to the news. Five minutes go by, then six. And then a female news reader delivers a message Gideon has been waiting for: "We have just learned that Charlotte Ansari, the senior international correspondent for CCN who has been missing and suspected of complicity in several murders in India, has now been found and exonerated. Ansari's fans will be pleased to learn that she is alive and well. Full details of why she was missing and what she was doing have not yet been released, but a government spokesperson said that Ansari was involved in deep investigative reporting that led to the break-up of a major terrorist cell in New Delhi. She is reported to be on her way back to the United States."

Gideon smiles and turns off the radio. He knows that he is part of the bargain that has allowed Charlotte to return home a free woman. And he is certain that this news will not be celebrated by his client.

Another five minutes go by during which a dozen vehicles pull into the parking ramp. At last, an Escalade SUV slips past Gideon's automobile and turns into the client's reserved parking space.

Time for action.

Gideon slowly gets out of his car and saunters toward the Escalade. The client's windows are rolled down; obviously he prefers fresh air to A/C, even on a hot and humid day like this.

The client is having a heated cell phone conversation. He is so passionately involved that he does not notice Gideon standing behind the vehicle. Gideon slowly moves alongside the SUV, listening to the conversation.

"Yes, Mr. President, I understand, but still this is totally unacceptable. Do you know how this thing got so botched up?"

Gideon steps even closer to the passenger door.

"Yeah, I'm sure you'll find out. But right now I'm looking at a major setback here. I don't know if I can keep up the flow of donations like we both know is needed, that's my problem, and yours too. People will be starting to question whether we have a partnership or not. Who will believe that American intelligence could blow something this important? I fear a real crisis of confidence."

Gideon abruptly opens the door, slips into the Escalade and sits down in the passenger seat. He does not look at the client, merely stares straight ahead at a sign that reads RESERVED FOR PASTOR CRATE.

Startled, Pastor John Crate turns to Gideon. Even though he does not recognize the Sicarii agent, he is suddenly very afraid.

"Mr. President, I have to go now," Crate says into his phone. "Can we continue this conversation later? Good, thank you."

Crate switches off the cell phone.

"Please raise the windows," Gideon says softly.

Crate complies.

"And turn on the damn A/C."

Crate switches on the air conditioning.

"So tell me, pastor, how is business at Millennial Broadcasting Network?"

Crate tries to act calm, but he's a lousy actor. "If you mean God's work, business is just fine as usual."

"Actually, I was referring to a certain business arrangement between you and the Brotherhood."

"Oh. I see." Crate, the master of oratory, is at a loss for words.

Looking straight ahead, Gideon says, "I was reviewing the terms and conditions of this agreement, and discovered that you are not in compliance."

"How do you mean?" Crate is getting even more nervous. His right leg is bouncing up and down. Despite the cool air blowing on him, his forehead is slick with sweat.

Gideon still has not looked at Pastor Crate. "The agreement clearly states that we have exclusive rights to fulfill the contract. And yet we've learned that you hired or coerced other entities to perform the same services. Obviously, this made our job much more difficult and resulted in the needless deaths of many people including several of my associates. Good friends, I might add."

"And you know this how?

"It might surprise you that even in our business, adversaries sometimes share information."

For the first time, Gideon turns to look Crate directly in the eye.

The pastor turns away. "You can't possibly think that I would entrust a mission of this importance to one contractor!" He is trying out his booming evangelist voice on Gideon. Clearly, it will take more than *the voice* to intimidate a Sicarii.

Gideon merely smiles. "Actually, that *is* what we think. And as you may recall, there is a serious penalty for a violation of that clause. Do you remember what that penalty is, pastor?"

Crate turns to Gideon, his eyes fluttering and lips twitching. Certainly he remembers. He just never thought he would be found out.

"I am a personal friend of the president of the United States. Did you know that?"

"Of course. You were just talking to him. Are you wanting to use one of your lifelines now? I wouldn't count on the president, or the CIA director either, for that matter. Maybe your wife." Gideon hands Crate a cell phone. "Maybe you'd like to call right now. Hope you can reach her."

Crate nervously shifts his considerable carcass. "You didn't do anything to my wife…?"

"She's fine. I looked in on her this morning—pretty woman, for her age."

"Look, we can work something out here. The Network has an almost inexhaustible supply of funds. How much do you need?"

"Hmmm. I just heard you tell your good friend, the president of the United States, that funds were going to be a problem in the future. I'm not really sure I can trust you, John. The truth is, no matter how much money you have, you don't have enough. But we're not unreasonable. You now have sixty seconds to present your defense, and then I'll pass judgment and execute the sentence."

The word *execute* sends a shiver through Crate's body.

Crate is used to articulating his thoughts, but panic is interfering. He starts to speak, sputters a few words, then tries again. "Okay, look, here's the truth. When I say 'God's work,' I mean it, really mean it. We are on a timeline to build the new Temple in Jerusalem. We are raising money day and night, because once the Temple is built, Jesus will come again. It's up to us, you see? We are the agents of Christ. We hired you people, the Sicarii, because your beliefs are so close to ours. You were once Jews, but you saw the light and accepted the Gospel and have promoted the Cause of God. I knew the terms of our agreement, that's true, but can't you see that in this case we could not take any chances? We needed to get the relics into our hands no matter what. If they fell into the wrong hands, and were found to be, heaven forbid, authentic and true, our funds would dry up overnight and the Return of Christ could be delayed indefinitely. So yes, I violated the contract, but only for God's sake. If you kill me, you are killing the chief agent of Christ's Second Coming. Do you want that on your conscience?"

Crate has orated himself into a self-righteous fit of vainglory.

Gideon emotionlessly stares at Crate for a few seconds. This silent space seems to deflate the great Pastor Crate.

357

"My God," Gideon finally says. "Do you honestly believe that you control the actions of Jesus Christ?"

Crate flinches at this verbal slap in the face.

"Let me tell you the truth," Gideon continues. "If the relics were truly the bones and tissue of Christ, you wouldn't trust the government with them. You know the government. You would fear leaks, or maybe future administrations that might be less sympathetic to Christian values. So you set up the CIA and the Brotherhood to duke it out, hoping the relics would be destroyed in the process. Or that the losing party would find a way to destroy them.

"I believe it's also true that even though you preach the resurrection of Jesus, you really don't give a damn. Probably don't really believe it yourself. But it plays well to the masses, doesn't it? Has for a couple thousand years. So why do you really want to get your hands on the relics? To protect your base. Your financial contributors. You've gotten rich off this scam! Oh, and if you had the relics, you could also use them to blackmail the Vatican, a much bigger and wealthier organization than Millennial Broadcasting Network. I wonder how much you could get from the Pope?"

"This is preposterous!" Crate's denial lacks conviction. "I am a dedicated man of God. I would never use Christ's relics for personal gain."

"But you sell Blessing Water to donors with the promise of financial gain if they send money to you. And it's true, isn't it, that Blessing Water is just tap water with a label slapped on the bottles?"

"Your facts are all wrong..."

"It doesn't matter, really. The punishment for your offense is execution. Sentence imposed. Time for..."

"Please! Please, no. I'll do anything!" Crate is babbling now. He has wet his pants and the stench of urine fills Gideon's nostrils.

Gideon removes the sica from his belt buckle. He grabs Crate by the back of the neck and forces his face into the steering wheel. The man is trembling uncontrollably.

Gideon whispers, "This won't hurt, I promise."

He plunges the short blade into a specific spot in Crate's back. Crate emits a hiss, then a gasp. He looks up, wondering if the knife has really gone in.

"That's all there is," Gideon says. "Go and meet Jesus now." He removes Crate's wallet from his breast pocket, takes the credit cards and money, and throws the remains onto the floorboard, mimicking a robbery.

Slowly, Pastor Crate lowers his head, closes his eyes and grows very still. Anyone passing by might think he is praying.

* * *

Greg stands in the very spot that his father last stood, not knowing this but knowing it nevertheless. He is the eye within the hollow socket of this gaping stone balcony. He searches the vast mountainscape—the veined rocks and crumbling slopes and dark crevices—for the shattered bones of a man who is already a distant memory. The cold Himalayan wind erases the past. The strangest thing now is not what is going to happen, but Greg's astonished, confounded knowledge that it will.

A shawl of pale light warms him beneath his seraphic white robe. And then the silence of this vast empire of white peaks is replaced by a rhythmic chant like a rumble deep in the mountain's throat. Greg turns from the high metropolis of clouds to the company of angels facing him— forty Brothers in White, their robes fluttering like slow sparks in the swirling breeze. He does not have to count to know there are forty. On this holy evening, there will be forty Brothers. Forty candles. Forty of everything, just as Gideon had inscribed on the foreheads of the terrorists to illuminate Greg with the One Great Truth of his destiny. The purpose behind it all.

This is a birthday party he will never forget.

At thirteen, when most Jewish boys celebrate their Bar Mitzvah, their coming of age, Greg is entering the holiest celebration of all, the ordination of the Divine Light of the Sicarii. It is no coincidence that his birthday falls on the day following the successful completion of the tests; this was according to a plan conceived nearly thirteen years ago.

A warm hand takes his arm and guides him toward the Brothers. The hand belongs to the sharp-nosed man from Greg's family photos, though the face has eroded with the passing of time like the surrounding mountains.

This is Greg's grandfather, Assim. Mihad's father. The kindly old gentleman with the aromatic pipe and the bouncing knee.

Assim whispers to Greg, "I'm so happy to see you here, my boy."

Greg nods, but he knows that in a few minutes he will no longer be a boy, but a man.

As Greg approaches the Brothers, they separate to provide a corridor for his safe passage. It is Moses parting the white sea.

The chanting of the Brothers fills him up. It vibrates inside him, throbbing and pulsating, loosening his deeply rooted emotional constraints and opening up new channels of feeling. It is an awakening of the spirit, an intensifying of emotions to equal his heightened intellect. The chanting opens him up and wrings him out. This is more than a coming of age. It is a second birth. A birth of human feeling. Suddenly he misses his mother.

Assim guides him to a great stone stairway that winds around the outside of a large chamber. Greg does not have to count the stairs; he knows there are forty. Slowly, he climbs to a large slab of stone that juts from the wall, a platform that contains a replica of the Ark of the Covenant, or what Greg assumes to be a replica. It is a gold-plated box just under five feet long. Two cherubs sit securely on the lid. The angels are facing each other, their wings merging into an arch, the Throne of God. Long carrying poles are threaded through gold rings on each side.

Greg steps onto the stone platform, mesmerized by the glimmering Ark. A soft hand takes his and a thumb tenderly strokes the back of his hand. He turns to see the Woman of Lineage: Eve, Miriam, Grandmother. Eve's proud face is flushed with excitement. She releases Greg's hand and places a necklace with many jewels around his neck. He does not need to count the gemstones; he knows there are forty.

It is the mystic number. The number of the Shekinah, the Divine Light. The Glory of God. The light that appeared at the birth of Moses and forty years later as the Burning Bush. The light that appeared at the dedication of Solomon's Temple, and at the birth of Jesus as the Star of Bethlehem in the year 7 BCE. The Divine Light that appears only at intervals of forty years. The Divine Light that is always present at the birth of a spiritual king. The Divine Light that is the namesake of the title to be bestowed upon Greg this very day.

This newest Divine Light was born thirteen years ago in 1994, a year that coincides precisely with the forty year cycle of the Divine Shekinah.

If no Divine Light candidate—no direct male descendant of the pure bloodlines—had been born in 1994, no candidate could be born until 2034, and there could be no Divine Light to take charge of the organization until thirteen years after that. Already, the Brotherhood had suffered the supreme disappointments of 1954, and before that 1914. No Brother still alive has personally known a Divine Light.

To miss the Shekinah year of 1994 was unthinkable, so the Brotherhood had contrived an elaborate plan to achieve success. And it had worked. Not only was a male heir born in that holy year, but now this heir had passed the most rigorous tests.

Eve grasps Greg by the shoulders and turns him to face the beaming faces of the Brothers below. The chanting stops. Ancestral silence fills the chamber.

"Brothers in White," she says, her mellifluous voice echoing in the great hall, "I present to you the Shekinah Legacy!"

The Brothers erupt in cheers and applause. The explosion of joy almost lifts Greg off his feet.

After a long period of celebration, Eve holds out her arms to calm the Brothers. "We have a new Divine Light, the first in more than a century. But this new Light did more than pass our tests. He surpassed our expectations."

Eve steps toward the golden Ark. "As you all know, the Ark of the Covenant once housed our ancestors' most cherished objects. The tablets on which God inscribed the ten commandments. A gold jar containing manna, the sustenance that God provided to our people on their forty-year trek through the wilderness. We had thought these precious items lost forever. But the last of the holy objects once contained in the Ark—the rod of Moses and Aaron, which was saved and passed down to Jesus, but then was lost—is now found!"

The awestruck crowd emits a whispery gasp, like wind in the trees.

Eve reaches to the wall behind her and brings forth the rod discovered by Greg in Kashmir and given to her by Thompson. She hands it reverently to Greg and then slowly opens the Ark.

"At no time in the past century has the Ark been opened—until now. Our new Divine Light, who found this cherished object while on his quest for other holy relics, will have the honor of placing the rod into the Ark. How ironic that while the rest of the world was obsessed with finding the bones and tissues of Jesus, the holiest relic of all—this simple rod that connects the Divine Lights from Moses to Jesus, and now to Greg—was ignored by all. Now it is home. May it rest here eternally, guarded by the Brothers in White who watched over the Tomb of Jesus."

Greg trembles. He is not used to feeling emotion; he fears that he may drop the rod. Cautiously he places it into the long-empty Ark and Eve closes the lid.

Suddenly he is drawn as if by gravity into the wide embrace of his grandmother. He feels her humid breath on his neck and nestles into the soft folds of her bosom, hungry for his grandmother's love.

And he cries.

Chapter 70

Home is intolerably empty, and the many "welcome back" messages from CCN staff over the past two weeks have failed to cheer her. By generously clearing her of any suspicion of wrongdoing, director Wyatt had offered an olive branch to her. Actually, to the Brotherhood.

She runs her fingers over a small raised bump on her skin, the incision site through which the transmitter had been removed by her doctor. She is glad that she is no longer a blip on Sicarii monitors, no more a participant in their dangerous reality show. Still, she feels oddly vulnerable now that communication to her Guardian Angel has been severed. But what difference does it make, really? The Brothers have no more interest in her, and Gideon has probably been reassigned several times already. Even if she were still broadcasting her position, who would care? Nobody would be watching.

"Take two weeks off," Bud had told her. "Hell, take a month. You deserve it, with what you've been through in Iraq and Minneapolis and India…"

Two weeks. After a tsunami of TV interviews—in which she reluctantly spun fictions about her role, and Curt's, in the breakup of a terrorism ring, only loosely based on the truth—Charlotte had retired to her home in Minneapolis. Now she knows that coming here was a mistake. Every empty space in the house reminds her of Greg and Mihad, and every memory is painful. She can't bear to think about Greg now, and what he is doing, how he is being groomed for a high position in the family business.

"Where is Greg?" her neighbors had inquired. "How is he doing?"

She had crafted more lies. After years of truth telling, she quickly had become a master in fabricating falsehoods. "He's with his grandmother," she had said more than once. "After the events of the past couple of weeks, being home was too difficult for him. He'll be going to an international school over there." These stements were not so far from the truth, she figures.

Several times, CCN and other stations have played a tribute piece about Curt. How could Charlotte have worked with this wonderful man— loved him, even—and known so little about him? On her first tearful viewing of the tribute, she was stunned to learn that Curt's wife, Barbara, had died in an Australian car accident two years ago. Hadn't Curt told Charlotte that Barbara had recently left him? My God, he had told no one about his loss. When Charlotte called CCN about this, she learned that the organization didn't know about it either. Only when the producer tried to contact Barbara to arrange a statement did he find out about her death.

Charlotte thinks back to her almost-affair with Curt, the feelings that he had stirred inside her, his intense need to protect her and experience love again. He was never being unfaithful, as Charlotte was. He was alone and struggling and reaching out to her. He was an honorable man.

Charlotte has never loved Curt more than she does now.

The news channels have also been filled with the murder of a popular but controversial evangelical leader, Pastor John Crate, the founder of the giant Millennial Broadcasting Network. They had obsessively played and replayed security camera footage of a pudgy man with thick glasses and bushy sideburns entering Crate's parked car and exiting a few minutes later. Law enforcement had declared it a robbery-murder, and it had remained a local police matter despite the broad publicity.

Even so, conspiracy theorists had magnified the crime into something much more interesting. Rumors of an adulterous affair had cast suspicion on the husband of the mysterious mistress. Crate's position on Israel had earned him many enemies, some crime bloggers noted with alarming detail. One theorist reported that, according to an "anonymous source inside the current administration," Crate's well-known relationship with the president recently had soured, so it was possible that the government had "taken him out." Now that such unsubstantiated rumor and innuendo was in circulation, the cable channels felt free to report on it, lending it more credence.

Charlotte is clever enough to put together the pieces of this puzzle. Charlotte knows that her husband had become a follower of Pastor Crate. He had faithfully watched the corny TV shows, even had corresponded personally with Crate. She had occasionally overheard telephone conversations between the two, and while Crate and his organization seemed creepy to her, she had lacked motivation to question Mahid about his involvement. Frankly, she didn't care. The murderer with the pot gut didn't look familiar to her, but she is convinced it was Gideon or some other

Sicarii agent. Clearly, Mahid's death, Crate's murder and the family business are all interconnected.

And that's all she really wants to know.

She can't stay in the house any longer. It makes sense to move into her apartment in Boston, maybe sell the Minnetonka home. She makes a mental note to call a real estate agent, arrange for a flight, catch up on her journal entries, stop the self-pity, and go back to work as soon as possible.

That should keep her busy!

As she wanders into the kitchen to make a cup of sweet Indian tea, the doorbell rings. The sound startles her; self-imposed isolation has not helped her unwind.

She opens the door. A FedEx driver hands her a package and asks her to provide an electronic signature, which she does. As the driver returns to his van, Charlotte looks down at the return address.

Her heart jumps and starts to beat uncontrollably. She races into the living room, slamming the door behind her.

She had almost forgotten! The day after she landed back in the United States she had packaged up the two relics and sent them to the Paleo-Genetics Laboratory in Thunder Bay, Ontario.

Charlotte tears open the package. A cover letter accompanies a bound report. Trembling, she sets the report on a coffee table, holds up the letter, and begins to read.

```
Dear Ms. Ansari:

It was good to hear from you again! We
appreciated the accurate portrayal of our
services in the Viking Bones story that you did
three years ago. Accompanying this letter is
a report of our scientific findings of the two
samples that you sent to us.

As you know, Paleo-Genetics Laboratory is the
premiere DNA testing facility for ancient and/or
degraded biological samples of bone, teeth, hair,
```

mummified tissue, insect and plant material, and biological specimens on textiles. We have deep experience and advanced technologies to deal with the presence of inhibitors and highly degraded and fragmented DNA.

The two marked samples that you provided were characterized by a significant amount of degradation consistent with the age of the specimens, both of which originated approximately 2,000 years ago according to our evaluation. Fortunately, you provided an adequate amount of material for us to test. To obtain the information that you requested about these samples, we decided to run an expanded battery of tests, including analysis of mitochondrial DNA, nuclear DNA, and Y-Chromosome DNA. These tests allow us to determine sex, ethnicity, and kinship of the sample donors.

The accompanying report provides the details of our extensive testing and states our scientific conclusions. If you have any questions or need additional clarification, please contact me. Also accompanying this letter is our invoice, made out to you personally as requested.

Best Regards,

Horace Grandview
Executive Director
Paleo-Genetics Laboratory

Charlotte sets down the letter and stares at the wire-bound report. She can't make her hands move. She is frozen in place. People have died for these results. Was it worth it?

Her entire body quakes with anticipation. On her coffee table is a ticking bomb. Or perhaps a dud. All she has to do is pick up the report and read the executive summary. Thirty seconds, tops, and she will know the truth.

Slowly, she reaches for the report, lifts it up, and clutches it to her chest as if it were a holy relic instead of a photocopied document. She holds it out and studies the cover:

Scientific Analysis of Two Ancient DNA Samples

This is it.

Chapter 71

From Charlotte Ansari's Notebook

It has taken me a month to complete this notebook and this is the last entry. When I began this task, I thought it would only take a couple of days. Reliving the events, though, was much harder than I had imagined. And even as I finish, I don't know that you will ever read these words. Perhaps I have written this as much for myself as for you.

I can't begin to describe how difficult it is for me to imagine you as the leader of a Brotherhood of assassins. Even after writing this brief history, and seeing all of the preceding events with the eyes of current knowledge, it is hard to understand how this came to be.

I have received nine letters from your grandfather since I abandoned him on the side of the road in New Delhi. I haven't opened them, though I have kept them. For what reason I can't fathom. Every day I check the mailbox for a letter from you and hopefully weed through my emails for the same reason. But nothing. I hope that you haven't forgotten me. That you will not forget me. That one day, under some circumstances, we will be reunited.

The day I began this notebook was the day that I received the DNA results on the two relics. That report is now in a very safe and secret place. When the report arrived, I was almost too afraid to read it, to be the only person alive who would know with certainty the human source of the two relics. At last, though, I decided that I would not stay ignorant out of fear. And so I opened the cover and read through the table of contents, which gave no clue to the outcome of the tests. I remember turning to the Executive Summary. I stared at the title at the top of the page for a few seconds. All I had to do was glance downward and my eyes surely would spot a telltale word, a meaningful phrase. In a second or two, all my perplexity, all the mystery and intrigue that legions of zealots had obsessed over, would be resolved.

But I can tell you with some pride that I never looked down. In a rush of illumination I suddenly awoke to the reality and the foolishness of the relics. If religion is based on belief in bones, if it is willing to brutalize and kill to protect its traditions, if it seeks to treat men of faith as competitors, and truth as something exclusive to one club, and material things as having any significance to spiritual reality except as metaphors, then we would be better without religion.

And so I decided that, in the end, the facts about the relics did not matter much. At least to me. If the bones were from Jesus, then his resurrection was a spiritual one. Maybe a resurrection of the spirit of his followers. Without that resurrection, we would have no Christianity. For me, that is quite enough. I don't need a dead man coming back to life to understand his message.

If you ever read this, my son, you may be astonished to read such words from your world-weary mother, who never gave a thought to religion except as a young girl. Yet here I am, after all of the horror we went through, pondering such things. After all, I've had plenty of time to think. You might be even more surprised to learn that I have become something of a religious person. (Perhaps the word "spiritual" is more apt.) The one moment in all of our adventures that I felt truly at peace was at the Lotus Temple in Delhi, the holy place that celebrates the truth at the root of all our religions. So why should I be interested in the petty differences?

I never read the DNA report, though I remained intensely curious—the way one is curious about the outcome of a whodunit, even though the ending has no bearing at all on one's life. I decided, however, that not peeking at the results was my own personal test of conviction. (Actually, I think I was afraid that learning the truth might change me. You know, fan the flames of latent prejudice, or drive me out of my newly-found bubble of peace by filling me with doubts or suspicions. Let me tell you, I'm not anxious to leave that bubble right now!)

I conquered my inherent curiosity by plunging myself into the writing of this notebook. These written words, I found, are my connection to you. I've convinced myself that when I write them, somehow you receive them. I would prefer a two-way conversation, but for right now, one way will do.

I am sustained mainly by the memory of your touch, though you may not even remember it. The way you reached out to me one day in the car. I felt your love flow to me in that fleeting touch, and it was thrilling. That's what I am holding onto these days. The memory of it has become almost tangible. That is my holy relic. And none other matters to me.

Next in
Sons of Zadok (Book 2)

Years later, in a place no map named honestly, a young man stood on a stone balcony above the Himalayas and looked down into a world that no longer belonged to him.

The air was thin and cold. Prayer flags snapped in the wind below the fortress walls, and somewhere deep in the mountain, bells sounded once, then fell silent.

He had grown taller. Harder. The boy who had once been protected by others had become a leader, someone others now watched for guidance.

Below him, hidden chambers glowed with coded light. Men and women moved through corridors cut into ancient rock, quiet as ritual, precise as memory. They did not call this place a monastery, though it had once been one. They did not call it a fortress, though it could survive a siege. They called it home only when they were alone.

The young man rested both hands on the cold stone rail and listened to the wind moving over the peaks.

Behind him, a woman's voice said, "They're ready to brief you now."

He did not turn at once. He already knew who it was.

Miriam.

Not dead. Not vanished. Not what the world believed.

He had learned that names could lie. Histories could lie. Families could lie. But blood had a way of remembering.

When he finally turned, she stood in the doorway in gray silk and shadow, composed as ever, her eyes unreadable.

"There's been movement," she said. "Your mother is asking questions again."

At that, the young man's face changed almost imperceptibly. Not fear. Not anger. Something colder. More difficult.

"And Gideon?" he asked.

"Still alive."

A flicker crossed his expression and was gone.

Miriam stepped farther into the room. "The old struggle isn't over," she said. "It has only changed shape."

He looked at her for a long moment, then past her, toward the dark interior of the mountain where old texts, old weapons, and older loyalties waited.

Below them, the clouds were beginning to close over the valleys.

"The relics were only the beginning," Miriam said.

The young man said nothing. Below them, the clouds closed over the valleys like a gate.

Somewhere far away, Charlotte Ansari was still living as if the worst had already happened.

It had not.

https://www.calumeteditions.com/books/sons-of-zadok/

About the Author

Gary Lindberg has spent his entire adult life as a screenwriter, movie director and producer, author of fiction and nonfiction, and book publisher. He is the author of four Amazon #1 bestselling novels, three books about the unknown history of Elvis Presley, and other fiction and nonfiction titles. He cowrote and co-produced the Paramount motion picture *That Was Then, This Is Now* starring Morgan Freeman and Emilio Estevez. He has won over one hundred national and international awards including two Grand Awards from the New York International Film and TV Festival. Currently, he resides in the Minneapolis area.